THE LATE B
FRANKIE GREEN

Laura Kemp

About *The Late Blossoming of Frankie Green*

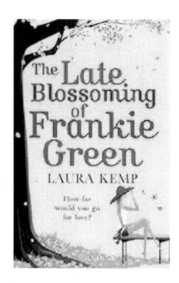

Frankie Green's happy ever after is put on hold when her childhood sweetheart husband complains things are boring in bed.

When he asks for some space, she sets out to win him back by getting herself a sex education.

Little does she know that her hilarious, tender and embarrassing journey of enlightenment is going to change everything...

A story full of humour, heartache and happiness, of friendship, coming of age and overcoming insecurity.

For the friends who are family

One night in May...

Frankie

Frankie shivered as she waited for Jason to unveil his surprise.

'Keep your eyes closed,' he said, rustling about with something as his movements shook the king-size bed.

With a smile on her face, she couldn't believe that after fourteen years together he still made her all tingly. In fact, tonight was the tingliest she'd ever felt, she decided, as a wand of fairy dust sprinkled excitement on her toes, which raced all the way up her bare body. Except for the bits covered up by her new matching white M&S underwear.

It was their first wedding anniversary and they were in the same posh hotel room where they'd started life as Mr and Mrs Green.

Soon they'd be making love in their familiar way, his body on hers was all she desired. The girls teased her for having only slept with one person but she was so relieved she hadn't had to kiss any frogs like they had – and still had to. But his muscular weight was the measure of their love; it was solid and secure and, secretly, she wanted to feel possessed by her man. Just as she had done at lunch when he led the way to their table overlooking Cardiff Bay's glorious waterfront. Their hideaway was only ten minutes from their house in the city but she saw no need, and had no desire, to go anywhere else.

'This way, Mrs Green,' he'd said, guiding her to her seat with his lovely old-school manners. She had a glass of pink fizz, her favourite, while he had a bottle of some fancy lager, one he hadn't tried before, then he'd tried to persuade her to try some chorizo. But she stuck to her trusted bangers and mash followed by banoffee pie – the exact meal they'd had for their wedding breakfast.

The only fly in the ointment had been when she'd brought up starting a family next year. A cloud had crossed his usually cheerful face. He didn't think he felt ready, he'd said, taking her hand and squeezing it affectionately. 'I just want to enjoy us for a bit longer, there's so much fun to be had. It was a big enough deal to get married, wasn't it?' he'd said, smiling his irresistible smile.

She'd felt bitterly disappointed, not because she felt broody. After all, they did have masses to finish in the house and she honestly had nothing to worry about because she had years before her biological clock started ringing. But because that's what couples did, wasn't it? Domestic bliss equalled the patter of tiny feet. She was tired of her hairdressing clients asking when she was going to have a baby. On the plus side, Frankie was flattered he still prized her company and didn't want to share her after all this time.

They'd met in the first week of college: he was her first and only boyfriend and she loved it that way. She was forever his Tinkerbell, the pet name he had given her from day one, owing to her long blonde hair, blue eyes and her figure that back then was a perfect hourglass, but was now a tad plumper thanks to her love handles. He was the only one for her. He was perfect, with his boyish good looks and easy-going nature. He was positive, kind, generous and…

'Almost ready, Tink,' he said, from his pillow. She beamed, hearing the thrill of anticipation in his voice. What was he going to produce? A piece of jewellery, maybe, or some lingerie? Whatever it was, she would adore it because he knew her taste was simple but elegant.

There was the muffled sound of fabric then a click. It was all too much for Frankie so she peeped through her eyelashes. And then she wished she hadn't. In the place of the box from Tiffany's she'd been hoping for was a fluffy black handcuff attaching one of her blindfolded husband's wrists to the bed railings. He'd used her scarf, her best flowery one in fact, to tie round his head to hide his eyes. Inside her head she screamed 'Oh my God' but she was so horrified, the words wouldn't come out. Instead, her eyes nearly popped out of her skull.

'Frankie? Are you there?' Jason said. 'Say something! What do you think?' he asked, as if he was showing her a new T-shirt.

'You… look like a hostage,' she said, aghast at how the blindfold made his crew cut and stubble seem like he'd been taken captive. Wincing, she knew this wasn't what he'd intended. It was a good job he couldn't see her face, which was contorted with shock and disgust. Kinky sex had never appealed to her – whenever she came across it in magazines, she'd flick past to find the romantic questionnaire instead. Mum had given her a copy of *Fifty Shades of Grey* and while Frankie had soaked up the love story, she was bewildered by all the equipment.

Jason's laughter turned her stomach now. 'Come on!' he said, 'I'm your slave, do whatever you want to me.'

She ran through her options like a shopping list: lock herself in the loo? Say she had a headache? Or have a go? But what was she supposed to do to him, specifically? Cover him in whipped cream and call him Margaret?

'The only thing I think I'm capable of, Jason, is tickling you,' she said, wincing at her cluelessness as her fingers wiggled. 'I'm sorry. I'm just confused, this is so out of the blue.' She pulled his mask up onto his forehead so he looked like a camp Rambo; she needed eye contact. That way they could be honest, which was how they'd always operated. But while his big brown eyes usually shone with warmth, now they were hurt.

'I was just trying to liven things up,' he said, staring down. Then, after a pause, he added, 'Because…'

'Because?' she asked, warily. What was going on?

'I dunno, things are a bit, you know, predictable in bed, that's all.'

'Oh,' Frankie said, touching her face as if his words had slapped her cheek. She smarted from both the shock of his confession and the naive shame that she hadn't realized he'd been unsatisfied when she thought they were a flawless fit. 'You never mentioned it…'

'No,' he said, meeting her gaze with embarrassment, then looking away again.

A chill snaked its way around her heart as she waited for him to elaborate. But he remained quiet, pensive.

'We're okay, aren't we?' she asked nervously, searching his troubled face for a smile. Because they did it twice a week, which was 'very good' according to the experts. And Jason always seemed content afterwards. 'Oh, God, is it because I've put on a bit of weight over the last year? It's just because I'm so happy, that's all.'

'No, don't be silly, you're perfect,' he said, reaching for her hand then placing it down softly on the duvet as if it was porcelain. 'Maybe that's the problem. You're too perfect.'

3

'What? I don't understand,' she said, wishing – no, praying that he would leap up, yell 'joke!' and they'd have a laugh then clean their teeth together, like they did every night. But he was silent. It was a very bad sign. There was no denial, no 'everything is fine'. This was even more worrying than the sight of him trussed up. 'Jase?' she asked, her heart running up her throat with fear as the bed tilted and she lost her balance.

'I love you, you know that, don't you?' he said.

'Yes,' she replied in a tiny voice, with her heart now in her mouth, terrified of what was about to happen. This was how people started talking when there was a heartbreaking and life-changing 'but'. When bad things happened and they became defining 'before' and 'after' moments. Like the time Mum told them she was leaving. She pushed the memory of her parents' split out of her mind; she was anxious enough already and didn't need to think of that too. This wasn't supposed to be happening to her. 'What is it?' she said, panicking. 'Because whatever it is, we can put it right. We're in love. We're together forever, like you always said, remember?'

But, oh, Frankie's fear mounted as he failed to answer her. It was a pathetic sight as Jason sighed heavily, unlocked the handcuff and threw his mask to the floor. He turned his back to her, sitting on the edge of the bed, bent his head and rubbed his eyes with the heel of his palms. Then he spoke. 'Don't you ever wonder what else is out there, Frankie? Don't you wonder if we got together too young and we missed out on stuff? Like, we needed a change but we thought the wedding was the next step instead of being brave enough to live a little, then settle down. Don't you ever wonder that?'

Inside, she screamed, "No, never" – but her voice let her down. She wanted him to stop – how much more could she take? – but she could see by his drooping posture that he wasn't finished.

'Ever since we got married, I've felt sort of numb. Lost. As if everything's a grey blur. I even went to see a doctor, thinking I had something wrong with me. But there wasn't. I knew then I wasn't happy. And it's not fair on you to carry on. Because I can't. Not like this. I'm so, so sorry.'

His words were clearly well-rehearsed which was the most hurtful thing of all. He'd obviously been waiting to tell her. This wasn't some spur of the moment thing; he meant it.

Panicking, she stalled for time. 'The doctors? Why didn't you tell me? We tell each other everything.' He just shook his head. 'We can sort it out,' she pleaded, desperate now. 'We know each other inside out.' Jason's shoulders began to shrug as he broke down.

She reached out to him, trying to steady him yet he remained aloof. 'Please, Jason, tell me you're not giving up on us?'

'I can't... It isn't.'

Frankie hugged herself, feeling pain at the charade of their marriage, at how differently they saw their futures. 'Oh, God, no,' she whimpered as the tears came. This time, he turned around and embraced her and they hung onto each other, seeking a comfort that was impossible to find.

'I wish I didn't feel like this,' he offered. 'I never wanted to hurt you. I love you so much, Tink.'

She moved back from him, her breathing quickening. 'You're talking as though that's it. It can't be, you can't just announce all of this as though it's your thing. It's *our* thing.'

'I just feel overwhelmed,' he said, 'like my whole life is planned out. It's not that I want to travel the world or anything, I just feel hemmed in. I need some time... Some time out.'

'So go on holiday, do a climbing course, learn to fly, maybe that's all you need,' she said, madly trying to convince herself that was the answer. 'If it's the baby thing, we can wait for a few years,' she said over-brightly, as if it was the most reasonable offer going.

'I don't feel as if I'll ever be capable of being responsible enough for fatherhood. I need to sort my head out. Away from...'

'Me,' she whispered, 'Away from me.' She felt nauseous at his retreat. 'How have we gone from being happily married half an hour ago to this? How did I not see this coming?' she wailed.

Even as she said this she began to make a mental list of all the times he'd worked late to avoid coming home, the appointments he'd made up to get out of choosing new kitchen tiles, and the excuses he'd come up with to prevent any plans taking shape. Frankie had translated all of them as signs he was preparing to feather their nest as their marriage headed towards its next phase of parenthood. She'd thought all those extra hours at his dad's scaffolding business and refusing to go on holiday this year had been about him preparing for the future. But it had been his escape. From her. She wept as she registered that everything she thought was true had been pulled from under her and was now out of reach.

Her vision swimming with tears, she felt the terror build. 'So what now then? Because you seem to have it all worked out.'

'I think I should move out, give us both some space. So we can work things out. If we can.'

It was all too much to take in.

'Is there someone else?' she asked, eager to lay the blame elsewhere, convincing herself if it was just a quick fling with another woman then it could be overcome. Failing that, she could find a reason to hate him.

'No, of course not, it's not about anyone else, it's about me. And you.'

'If it's the sex thing, I can change, I can,' she said, knowing but not caring that it was a desperate and hollow plea.

'I'm so sorry, Frankie,' he said, suddenly looking exhausted.

It was over. She could see he'd made up his mind. Frankie felt herself tumbling off the edge, grabbing empty fistfuls of air. Freefalling, she was losing everything she'd ever wanted. The love of her life, her best friend, her soulmate, her future, their past. Terror took its place. She was going to be alone, without him. She didn't want to let go, she wanted to hold on, but he was out of reach. If only she could handcuff herself to him now.

Two Months Later, a Tuesday Night in July...

Frankie

A plump pink blob which curled slightly at one end appeared beneath Frankie's nose and she wanted to cry. How was she expected to put that in her mouth?

She looked at Letitia, who was nodding encouragingly at her.

'Go on, babes, try it,' she said. 'It's a bit rubbery, it is, but I guarantee, the "pulpo" is totally lush.'

Frankie gulped and turned to Em, who was prodding it with her fork.

'Cephalopoda mollusc. Among the most intelligent and behaviourally diverse of all invertebrates. The scientific Latin name of octopus derives from ancient Greek, which translates as "eight-foot".'

'That doesn't help, to be honest, Em,' Frankie said, holding her throat. 'Can't I just start with the patatas bravas or those ham croquette things, because this is my first time trying tapas and, you know, I need to work up to it.'

Over the table packed with exotic dishes, Letty pouted her Spanish genes; she was all crimson lips, with flashing eyes. She finished off by tossing her señorita mane of black curls with a bare shoulder, peeping out of a stunning, and, by the looks of it, expensive black pencil dress. Then she broke the spell with a brazen cackle which revealed her closer Valleys girl roots, which were all heart and gob.

This had been Letty's idea to get Frankie back out there and broaden her horizons. She'd resisted her invites for weeks, preferring to stay in with the girls because she'd wanted to hide from the world. And, privately, she'd thought, on the off chance, that she'd be there if Jason appeared at the door of their marital home, where she remained after he moved out. But then she'd run out of excuses – and Jason hadn't come back. Reluctantly, she had realized her friends only wanted to help. Even so, she still felt the fear, staring down some tentacles.

The restaurant was smack bang in the city centre, fifteen minutes away for all three of them, albeit from different directions. Frankie was from across the river in the busy and cheerful suburb of Canton where she was born and bred, Letty was living it up in the boho-chic area of Pontcanna while Em called the shiny redeveloped docklands of Cardiff Bay home.

To Frankie, Viva Tapas was all exotic and low-lit, with clattering pans and hisses of steam where the chefs worked in an open-plan kitchen-diner. The stainless steel set-up was very dramatic, but she could never live with something so stark and clinical; the wooden units of her kitchen made her two-up two-down in a quiet cul-de-sac homely and safe. Well, they had before Jason had gone. The heavy wafts of sherry and garlic were atmospheric, but she found it a bit overpowering. It was boiling in here too, not helped by the raging heatwave which had wilted her top-knot on her walk into town.

She pulled up her top, regretting the adventurous neckline which made her now feel exposed. Thank goodness for her comfy pants and bra, which held her in nicely. Scratchy undies might look nice but they weren't soft enough, which was was why she had stuck to the same style for the last ten years. When you'd found a formula that worked, you stuck with it.

But in here it felt a bit dangerous. This was the problem with going along with Letty's daring ideas. Not that she meant any harm; she was incredibly loyal, just a bit overwhelming at times. At least Em was here, the sensible buffer to Letty's boisterousness. Frankie pitched in somewhere in the middle – it had always been like this.

They'd met in their first week at secondary school when Em and Letty moved into Frankie's neck of the woods. Floyd and Em had arrived from London for their dad's work while Letty's mum had left the Rhondda for a new start after Letty's dad had gone out to buy some milk and never come back. Frankie, who had been split up from her primary school mates, didn't know anyone in her class. So the three of them had bonded immediately when they discovered they all had distinctive names.

She was Francesca because her mum thought it was classy, while her dad liked it for being the female form of his favourite singer, Frank Sinatra. Em was Emerald Good-Fellow, thanks to her hippy parents, who were in their crystals phase when she was born, and among the first to double-barrel their surnames for equality reasons. Then there was Letitia Cox, christened after her Spanish granny but called Titty – amongst other things – by the boys. Poor love. How they'd wished they'd fitted in like all the other Rebeccas, Samanthas and Rachels. From that beginning, the threesome had loved one another fiercely. And Frankie had no idea how she would've coped if she hadn't had them over the last two months post-Jason.

There had been the initial deep depression at finding herself alone for the first time in her life. That meant a few days moping in her pyjamas at Dad's, where he'd let her talk and howl, all the while trying to get her to eat. She'd been so low she'd even accepted an invite to stay over at Mum's, which she had spent her childhood trying to avoid: her mum tried to help but couldn't quite keep it up. After five minutes of being allowed to analyse the breakdown of her marriage, she'd been told to 'shush now' because Corrie was on.

There were sudden bouts of crying when flashbacks of happier times hit her at the checkout or the wheel of the car, and one infamous night when Em held her hair back as she was crouched over the loo after too much to drink indoors.

Then anger struck, when she'd bagged up his belongings and cleared the cupboards of his cereal and mugs. A brief stint of numbness too, when she'd cut hair on autopilot, deflecting sympathy with a wave of her scissors. Now, she was living with it; the 'acceptance' phase, the magazines called it, which meant her grief was less raw. Yet she still held onto the belief that she could win Jason back. He just needed time, she was convinced of it. One day they'd look back and see it as a blip. They still spoke or texted every day or so. Did he ring out of guilt? Partly, she suspected, but they loved each other. And he always picked up, no matter what time she called him or what insult she'd slung at him in the last call. He was also still her husband – in dark moments she wondered for how much longer – and fundamentally a kind man too. Even though he was sleeping on his brother's sofa, he still paid half the mortgage. It kept the hope alive. Only this afternoon she'd replayed her dream of him coming back to her, saying he'd made a mistake and 'could they start again?' Where and how they would begin, she still didn't know. But she would make it work, it was all she wanted.

After much soul-searching, she realized she *had* had her head in the sand; that was undeniable, otherwise she would've seen the break-up coming. Frankie couldn't be someone she wasn't. And she'd never want to be. Yet she conceded, at the age of thirty, she needed to loosen up and live a little. That Jason hadn't been talking entire rubbish and maybe she should've tried to make things more interesting. Which was why she'd agreed to taste something with eight arms – or were they legs?

'Look, babes, I understand, you're a bit scared,' Letitia said, warmly. 'But you need to come out of your shell.'

'I like my shell,' Em said, staring matter-of-factly through green eyes. She nodded to confirm it, making her poker-straight red bob swing until it fell quickly back into precise place.

'This is about Frankie, remember, not you,' Letty said, wagging a red-nailed finger at their friend.

Frankie didn't want this to be about her at all, so she changed the subject and asked how they both were.

'Busy. Tired. Annoyed with Floyd,' Em said, referring to her big brother to whom she had offered her spare room for the night, after his landlord had sold his flat. That had been six months ago. 'He's lovely but he's noisy and messy and he still acts like he's fourteen.'

Frankie nodded sympathetically, knowing how larger than life, six-foot-enormous Floyd could be. She could imagine Em accusing him of making her neat flat look untidy just because of the way his limbs sprawled when he sat down. And he'd fill the place with his personality too.

'The other day,' Em continued, 'for no reason whatsoever, he tucked two mangoes in his vest and announced he was "a lady". He's thirty-four, for goodness sake.'

Letty stifled a laugh which Em ignored, looking downcast. 'Work is mental too.'

Ah, that was the real reason for her peaky pallor. It meant so much to her. Of the three of them, she was the career woman. If they'd been in *Sex And The City*, Letty would've been Samantha because she was sex-mad and she worked at a glitzy public relations company, Em was Miranda the lawyer (minus the girlfriend), and she was sensible Charlotte. With no fourth gang member, Frankie had considered christening her sleek black psychic black cat Carrie courtesy of her white paws, which she imagined to be Jimmy Choos. Until *she* turned out to be a *he*. So it was Leonardo di Catprio instead after her favourite actor.

'It's this weather,' Em said, now animated. 'Did you know, a rise of just four degrees from twenty to twenty-four Celsius means sales of burgers increases by forty-two per cent? Make that ten degrees, as is forecast this weekend, and you're looking at three hundred per cent more barbecue meat and fifty per cent more coleslaw. It's not just getting the supplies, which everyone is fighting over, it's finding the space too.'

'Well, I never knew that!' Frankie said, in awe of her friend's important role. Frankie's idea of an emergency was her hairdryer breaking down. Which actually wouldn't ever happen because she was capable enough to have a spare. Two, actually.

'And it's all to be done in this heat. It's making me feel ill.' Em was too pale to enjoy anything beyond spring and autumn.

'What about Simon? Have you seen him lately?' Frankie said gingerly; it was always a gamble asking about Em's private life. But she wanted her to know she was interested and ready to listen, to show she wanted to pay back her friends' support and relationship talk wasn't taboo. After all, he was the only bloke Em had mentioned in forever.

'No,' Em said in a clipped voice. 'No Simon Brown news.' She always referred to him using his full name, it was one of her quirks and it was charmingly old-fashioned.

Then she went silent. But she was fidgeting with her hair, double-checking the top button of her white crisp shirt was done up, and the slightest flush of pink came to her cheeks. Frankie ached for her – it could only mean she was still besotted. Yet she didn't dare point it out – she'd been the one who'd 'had it all' but look how much of a fantasy that had been.

Frankie waited until Letty had finished ordering more wine – and flirting with the waiter – then turned the spotlight on her. She always had something, or more accurately someone, happening in her life. 'What about you and that Aussie, the personal trainer? Or have you moved on?'

'Come to your senses more like,' Em tutted, referring to the awful fact he was in a relationship and had a young kid.

Frankie prayed she'd stop there. Both her and Em had made known their disapproval, there was no need to drag it up again. Letty shifted in her seat for a second. Frankie knew she felt terrible about it. But did she feel terrible enough to have called it off?

Letty, who spoke like a bottle of shaken up Coca-Cola, launched in. 'It's just sex. And yes, I know I said it wouldn't happen again but I'm only killing time before I meet someone. There's nothing in it. Just keeping the motor running.'

Em arched a cynical eyebrow.

'Honest to God, I mean it!' Letty said, defensively, but with vulnerable eyes. 'Why does no one take me seriously?'

'We do, we do,' Frankie said, knowing that this was Letty's greatest insecurity. In work and in love, Letty yearned to be seen as more than a pair of boobs – admittedly, she did have great ones. But she'd been treated badly by blokes and had never had the break to become an account executive at the public relations company where she was secretary, so it was a raw nerve.

'Give me some credit, I'm hardly going to fall for a man called Lance Boddy, am I? A man who named his gym The Boddy Shop! I mean, how naff is that?' she said, laughing, throwing her hands in the air like a flamenco dancer. The trouble was, Letty had form. 'I could fall into a bucket of naked men who had 'boyfriend material' stamped on their heads and I'd still come up sucking my own thumb,' Letty had said the last time she'd been dumped, that time, by a model. She just didn't like run-of-the-mill guys. But why did that mean they treated her so badly when she was so fabulous? It was all very unfair.

'Twenty-first-century fitness is about being lean and smart. But he makes it sound like he's a rescue centre for old bangers!'

Just like that, Letty covered up what she considered to be a show of weakness with humour. It was how she dealt with things. Underneath, Frankie knew that Letty was just like her and Em, wanting her own special someone.

Then two pairs of eyes flicked towards Frankie. It was her turn. 'Right, well, I'm not bad, you know. Jase came round to collect some stuff the other day, that was awful. But lovely too, just to see him,' she said, feeling her chin wobble. She paused. It was no use, she couldn't keep it in. 'I still want him back, I still love him,' she admitted, crumbling, feeling a relief at letting it out. 'Like, I miss him every day, so badly. The bed is too big without him. I feel like I'm rattling around the house. My heart jumps every time I get a text or the phone calls. I see shadows of him everywhere.'

Letty got up to give her a *cwtch*, the Welsh word she used for a cuddle.

Em went into problem-solving mode, as ever. 'You need a project,' she said. This was classic Em – hand her a situation and she would try to fix it. 'Something to keep you busy. Distracted. You can't waste your time wondering what will be because it might never happen. Get on with things, that's the only way. Talking of which, I'm starving. I'm going to start.'

Bless Em, but she could be so blunt and it only made Frankie feel worse. Letty clocked her despair. 'There's nothing wrong with keeping the faith,' she said kindly. Thank goodness for Letty's soft side. 'But I also agree with Em,' she added, making Frankie groan.

'Distraction is good at a time like this. And I know just the thing – going on the rebound can work wonders.'

'I didn't mean that sort of distraction,' Em said, stopping to frown, before she carried on loading her plate. 'I meant exercise or an evening class or something. Not the kind you do with your PT.'

'But it could make Jason see sense, you know, make him jealous, and if it doesn't then at least Frankie is getting some practice after what he said,' Letty added.

'I am here, you know,' Frankie coughed, feeling a sting from the mention of Jason's boring-in-bed comment. It had been a serious blow to her confidence.

'Oh, I'm so sorry, babes,' Letty said, with genuine concern, 'We didn't mean to make you feel bad… Now, are you going to try some of this octopus?'

'In a sec,' Frankie said, hesitating.

'Well, let me just take a shot of it first. I'll put it on Instagram, I will,' Letty said. 'Bit of a crop and a filter... and there... boom. It's on my feed.'

Frankie didn't get why people shared photos of avocados and sunsets but she guessed in Letty's circumstances it helped her to see the positives when she was struggling to find any. Then, no more time-wasting, it was over to Frankie.

She took a breath to prepare for her Bushtucker Trial. Unfortunately, Ant and Dec were nowhere to be seen to save her.

As Frankie raised her fork, Em launched in with one of her 'interesting facts'. 'Did you know reproduction is a cause of death in octopuses and males can only live a few months after mating?'

That was it. With her stomach churning, Frankie's hand dropped to the table with a clunk. Playing it safe seemed far more tempting right now than living a little.

Wednesday

Em

The next one-hundred-and-twenty seconds are going to determine the rest of my life, Em thought.

As she sat on the toilet seat behind a locked door during her morning tea-break, she could hear echoes of footsteps marching past the ladies'. It was usually her clip-clopping purposefully on her way to human resources, the canteen or the manager's office. Instead, due to an act utterly out of character, she could soon be waddling her way down the corridor. And then, worse, barefoot and stranded at home.

Once more, it took her breath away when she thought about that night. After hiding her feelings for five weeks, six days, twenty one hours and twelve minutes, she'd finally been able to let her head clock off and her heart start the night shift. His shy smile, his delicious lips, his considerate question: if she was really sure? The fact he didn't laugh when her name badge poked into his chest. How they melted into bed yet she felt as if she was flying a slow-motion loop-the-loop.

She didn't believe in magic but that was the word that kept coming to her as she recalled Simon Brown's touch. Looking back, it had all seemed so inevitable and – now she could admit it – it had felt like that in the build-up too. Yet hadn't she always said fate was nonsense and that free will and hard work got you through life?

It had been the most frustrating and bewildering thing that had ever happened to her, she thought, as the digital numbers on her watch counted upwards. She and Simon Brown had instantly clicked, something that very rarely happened to her. She knew she was geeky – her brother Floyd had nicked all the touchy-feely genes and she'd been left with a better understanding of details and numbers than of people. That's why she'd been so surprised by their friendship. Simon Brown had come from his small store in Bristol, where he was assistant manager, to her mammoth one for a six-week secondment shadowing her. It meant they were together every day, including breaks, when he would ask questions and listen to her answers. They occasionally touched, her guiding him with an arm to look at something in the warehouse or him reaching out to ask for an explanation about stock control. Each time she felt an electricity race through her, as if she was being rebooted. But she told herself 'stop right there' when she began to yearn for more. It was unprofessional. And he wouldn't see her as anything more than a colleague, she was sure of it.

Yet he was different – men in his position were usually cocky know-it-alls, round here they said blokes like that 'thought they were chocolate'. But Simon Brown respected her. At his leaving do, he said as much in his speech.

Then as easily as he took off his tie and rolled it neatly to fit into his pocket on the walk across the industrial park to TGI Friday's, he'd told her he'd really enjoyed working with her – in fact, what he meant was he'd *really* enjoyed it and… After that it all fell into place, as if it was the most natural thing in the world. They found a booth and spoke all night, oblivious to the party people leaving as soon as they'd realized there would be no raucous piss-up. She'd asked if he wanted a nightcap at hers – a Scottish whisky from her Highlands hike last year, which turned out to be his favourite Scotch. Sexual encounters had been few and far between for Em – she wouldn't sleep with just anyone. Not that she was given the option. There had only been two others before Simon Brown: one from school, the other someone at university. But sleeping with him had been a revelation, a wonderful one, because it was sex on a different level. Physical had met mental.

Then, the morning after, came the excuses. Again, remembering it as she perched on a white plastic toilet seat, Em felt her heart respond to the hurt – the pain of having fallen for someone who didn't feel the same. And her insides lurched when she considered how things were supposed to be. She'd decided long ago she would get married, have two children, a boy and a girl, with eighteen months between them, unless she was lucky enough to have twins. But when Simon Brown walked away, he took her hope with him. She'd clicked and dragged the file marked 'life plan' into the trash can.

Seeking calm, she looked at the floor tiles between her polished court shoes; the sight of straight lines and right angles usually soothed her. But not today. She was so desperate not to be pregnant in this situation that she apologized to any god who might be up there for being an atheist. If he or she could possibly help her out, she'd definitely reconsider religion.

Returning to her default strategy, she rationalized her situation. Statistically, she was very unlikely to be expecting. She'd Googled it last night and a study on unprotected sex suggested the chances of it leading to pregnancy between a young couple on any random day was five per cent. And having taken the morning after pill, the probability was reduced to almost nothing. Her aching boobs were not a definitive sign because she always had that at her time of the month.

On the other hand, she was late. Very late. And just like her mind, her body ran like clockwork. Unfortunately, there were no figures available to support Em's belief that things like this didn't happen to people like her. But she simply wasn't the type. That's why she'd put off doing a test. That night had turned out to be her first and last one-night stand – quite unintentionally because she hadn't expected it to be a one-off – she was simply too averse to risk-taking.

For heaven's sake, I'm deputy store manager, she thought. Started as a Saturday check-out girl, joined for good on a graduate scheme and hand-picked for the future manager programme. The boss was due to announce his retirement any day and she was sure to take over.

But she knew this line of thought was hopeless. Since when did a sperm and egg check with their owners that conception was convenient? She stared at the test in her hand, willing it at first to hurry up, then wishing she had forever. This just can't happen, it can't… Oh shit, it just has, she thought, as the word 'pregnant' appeared on the stick. There was no ambiguity. She'd spent more on the digital variety rather than the two-lined version because it presented the facts in unarguable plain English.

Em felt the colour drain from her face as the tears threatened. She looked up, blinking hard, trying to force the emotion back. Logic, where are you? she begged, clearing her throat in a bid to regain control. So she started with the facts.

I am thirty-one and single, she began. I have a good job, a pension and my own flat. I've never had a meaningful relationship – the closest I've come is with this man who didn't want to be with me. It took until Simon Brown to find someone I really liked, therefore it is unlikely I will meet anyone suitable again soon. The kind of man who likes quirky American box sets, trekking in the hills and making culinary wonders with leftovers from the staff shop. The kind of man who doesn't care about looks or tiny breasts or freckles. The kind of man who is not just more mature in years – say, thirty-seven, like him – but in experience and approach.

Face it, Em, she told herself, he made it clear that he was sorry, so so sorry, but they could never be together. He has moved back to his store, an hour away, and he has commitments. You know what you have to do.

Em stood and felt her shoulders pull back, assuming her management pose. She opened the cubicle door, threw the test in the bin, washed her hands then brushed down her suit. She noted with satisfaction how her work face reappeared, revealing nothing of her turmoil.

With a deep breath, she went out into the corridor and made her way down the stairs and through the thick plastic curtains which marked the divide between staff only and the shop floor. Head up, she thought, as she swept into the public arena, scanning the shelves for gaps and checking the gondola ends were brimming with this week's special offers.

Right, she thought to herself, recalling the first thing on her mental to-do list, I need to have a chat with Gary the produce manager about some very unsatisfactory wonky carrots.

That Night

Letitia

Letitia stared at her reflection in her vintage dressing table mirror. Warmed by the soft lamp lighting, her happy face of flicked eyeliner, full lashes, flawless olive complexion and red lips looked back. But from the dusky pink velvet stool where she was sitting, all Letty saw was a clown. For underneath, she was as distressed as the wood of her flaming vanity unit.

Only now, when she was alone, with her front door closed, could she remove the bubbly mask she presented to the world. In private, she had as much bounce as damp popcorn.

Sighing, she squelched her expensive cleanser onto a circle of cotton wool and began to wipe her forehead, eyes, cheeks and chin.

Her mobile buzzed and she glanced at it, seeing Mam's name on the screen. She couldn't face her weekly update from Spain. Sick of the weather, Mam had moved there ten years ago with her second husband Phil and Letty's half-brother Luke. He was nine years younger than Letty so Mam had decided when he was eleven that he was young enough to adapt to a new life. Letty was invited but Wales was home. Even though Granny had left Spain as a child during the civil war, there was still family out there to help Mam and they lived a cracking life running a restaurant in Almeria. Letty just didn't want to hear about it now. Or put on a brave face.

Mam was unaware that Letty was up to her false eyelashes in debt; they thought she was minted because she dressed tidy. That was the problem, she spent her way to happiness when life brought her down.

Letty didn't want Mam to think that her daughter, whom she'd brought up alone, was a waste of space. Dad, wherever he was, was responsible for so much of this mess; hardly around when he was with Mam, then not turning up for access and slack on the maintenance. The only memories she had of him were bad, always chopsing on with excuses, he was: just waiting for a cheque to clear or not much work on at the minute.

Her face now nude, she couldn't lie to herself anymore: she was exactly the same as him. Full of shit. Why else would she be hanging out with Lance? When all she wanted was to find The One.

She lobbed the pad, filthy from the day, into the bin. But she still felt dirty at the thought of what she was: a mistress to a man with a girlfriend and a baby. How could she justify it as passing the time?

But it wasn't as if she was getting a kick out of it. She'd been miserable. Lonely. Weak.

She'd joined Lance's gym in her neighbourhood to better herself, that was the irony. She was done with casual flings, which she'd begin with an open heart only to discover she was regarded as a 'good time' and nothing more, Letty thought exercise would be the investment she needed to turn things round. She didn't actually fancy him at first – he was a walking cliché of sunny blond hair, Pacific ocean blue eyes, diving board cheekbones, plump lips and a golden, muscular body. Girls mobbed him and, to be honest, she expected him to be a tool: most good-looking men were.

But over three months of personal tuition, she got to know him. He was modest but ambitious, hard-working but easy-going. And he was making her feel good. Fan-bloody-tastic, actually. He was like a life coach, praising her at every sit-up. The more defined her body became, the more she earned his respect for her mental strength. They clicked too: the sessions were a laugh. They shared bits and pieces of their lives way past closing time. His relationship was rocky: feeling neglected by him working such long hours when he built up his gym, his partner had been unfaithful. They'd thought a baby would fix things. It had only been a sticking plaster. On her part, she wanted someone to love her the way she wanted to love someone. Like him.

She should've just cancelled her membership. But one night at the end of hot yoga, when he'd been taut and topless, he'd pushed down on her hips to make her stretch even deeper. The heat between her thighs had overflowed into her soul. She'd wanted to drown in it, submerge herself. In him. Ever since, for two months, they'd been stealing moments together. Anywhere and everywhere. Today, after work, in an art deco lift in a boutique hotel where she'd dragged the metal gates closed and untied her silk wrap dress so it tumbled to the floor to reveal she was naked bar a pair of midnight-blue couture French knickers and killer high-end heels. The memory of that pleasure made her flush all over again. But it was the afterwards that had left its mark. Because he didn't cut and run like the others had. He never ever did. She was always the one leaving him. It made her feel in control – that what she was doing was temporary. She could give him up any time she liked. It was just sex: nothing more than the physical thrill of racing pulses of anticipation, heavy eyelids of lust and abandonment. With Lance, it was a very good substitute for the love she craved.

He'd ask to stay over at hers but she consistently refused. It proved she wasn't taking it seriously. And appeased the hideous guilt of having sex with a man who was a father, and taken. She didn't want to let him into her cocoon either: her rented ground-floor flat, in the trendy area of Pontcanna with its bars, cafes and indie shops, was where she could repair her soul.

The trouble was though, Lance talked as if she was the one who'd bail out; as if he was the victim. Reality became suspended when he'd imply he had no intention of calling it off. Every time she saw him, she braced herself for the 'I think we need to cool it' cold feet conversation. It never came. Instead he appeared to hang on her every word, laugh at her jokes and flatter her at every opportunity, talking about the future.

But that would mean walking out on his girlfriend, his son – it was obscene. So she kept him at bay, she had to. He would only dump her as the others had done. Always unavailable, whether there was another woman or a career at a critical point.

Why, at the age of thirty, was she putting herself through this yet again? she asked herself, applying moisturiser with her fingertips.

Because he treated her nicely, asked about her day, opened doors for her. No man had ever done that and meant it. Not even her dad. His approval had been missing her whole life, that's why she was such a sucker for it now.

Like today in the car, Lance had been really chuffed for her when she told him the PR company had won a massive contract: okay, she was only a personal assistant but she'd done her bit, schmoozing the clients over lunch. Her boss had even thanked her personally and Letty hoped it meant he might finally fork out for the day-release course she wanted to do to get an industry qualification. Lance praised her people skills and bigged up her potential. But Letty was so lacking in confidence she believed Ross only let her wine and dine people because she was a bit of office totty. How she wanted to get in on the actual public relations bit, to have her own accounts and apply all the stuff she'd picked up in the ten years she'd been in the business. Bright young things with degrees had always pipped her at the post when she'd gone for jobs. She'd joined this company a year ago when the grapevine hinted at expansion and opportunities later down the line. But so far, no good.

A sad smile came to her as she remembered how Lance had called her a drongo for being so negative. She'd dismissed him then. Work was work, it paid for her clothes, that was all she'd admit to. Again, there had been the denial of what she craved inside: recognition for who she was not what she looked like.

Letty got up, wandered about her room, picked up her book, threw it on the floor then flopped on to her four-poster bed. The next man who sleeps here will be the real bloody deal, she told herself.

If only Lance wasn't with someone else: because she knew she could love him. Whatever she'd said about his crappy name for his gym. He wasn't a bimbo, far from it. An all-rounder both physically and academically, he'd been selected for Olympic swimming trials before an injury cut short that dream. So he'd used his head instead to become a sports physio, which took him round Oz and to the UK via Dubai. A weekend in Wales when he'd lived in London stirred something inside him. He made a promise to himself that one day he'd return for its broad beautiful beaches and relaxed pace of life when he was done with 'raging'. Six years ago, at the age of thirty-four, he did, to set up his gym, bringing with him, Helen, the Aussie girlfriend he'd met in Earls Court. Next year, he'd open another gym in Cardiff Bay and then after that, who knew?

But while he was with the mother of his child, the only thing the L-word would stand for on Letty's part would be 'loser'.

She never wanted to know about his other life, she didn't want to make his girlfriend and baby real. Sometimes though it was unavoidable. Like today when his girlfriend had texted as

Lance drove Letty home.

Sat outside her place, Letty had challenged him to answer it, as if she was testing the depths of his duplicitousness. Which was stupid – how could you have degrees of being a lying unfaithful bastard? Would she really walk if he sent her a text back in her company? But he'd refused to even read it.

'I don't want to give you the old boohoo,' he'd said. 'My girlfriend doesn't understand me, all that bull.'

Letty had pushed him then, she didn't know why at the time, but she could see the reason now: she was further in than she'd thought.

He'd given in. But not in the way she'd imagined. Instead of whining about Helen, he'd taken her hand and kissed it. 'There's something I need to say. And don't do your block…'

Her heart raced again now as she lay flat out like a starfish on the bed.

'This isn't just about sex for me, okay?' he'd said. 'I've told you Helen and I are pretty much living separate lives. It's been like this for months and months. I'm there for Eddy. Nothing more. This… you… that's what keeps me going. I think I might be…'

Her head going bananas, unable to handle what he had been about to say, she'd jumped out of the car and ran inside.

Still now she hated herself for the tiniest of thrills she'd felt when he'd said life with her was better.

She was only human, she thought. But she wasn't a home-wrecker. Was she?

The Next Day...

Frankie

'What you want to do, love, is to move on, that's what you want to do,' Phyllis said, patting her new hairdo.

Not that same piece of advice again, Frankie thought, as her client took off her pink gown, folded it just so and went to put the kettle on. Along with 'it'll pass' and 'don't be so hard on yourself', 'move on' was as useful as cold straighteners.

And as much as she loved this gorgeous 77-year-old widow, what did she know about modern love?

If only Frankie could move on from Jason. She'd dreamed last night they'd been on honeymoon in Greece and awoke crushed to find a stubbly kiss on her nose was in fact Leonardo the cat's rough tongue. Going downstairs this morning, she'd seen the chip in the hall wall which Jason had bashed as he'd carried in his beloved new high-definition telly. He'd refused to take it when he left because, he'd said, 'you'll miss your reality stuff'. Making breakfast, she'd found an old Cheerio, his favourite cereal, at the bottom of the cupboard. Traces of him were everywhere: he'd been living there seven years.

She had had to reset her brain to remind herself it was actually her house. It had been since she was twenty-one when Dad impressed upon her the need to buy young: prices in Cardiff were only going to rocket. She'd cried when she moved out of Dad's terrace – after her good-for-nothing Mum had run off with a car salesman who lived in la-di-da Penarth Marina when Frankie was ten.

She had been the woman of the house. She'd begged to stay with Dad, because she didn't want him to be alone. And so with no brothers or sisters, she was Dad's partner in crime but he'd told her to get on the property ladder which she accepted begrudgingly.

They were still thick as thieves: he was only round the corner so she still popped in to see him far too often. 'What if I had a bird here?' he'd tut from his battered chair where he was reading the paper, his feet kept warm by Judy, his slobbery old black Labrador, when she'd walk in unannounced. He never said it, but Frankie believed he'd never recovered from Mum's betrayal. If only she could fix him up with someone – he only ever went out for a pint of Brains with his mate Gareth. But she was in no position to match-make.

Thank God for her job: it'd been her saviour. Using her hands unlocked her creativity; the metronomic movement of her scissors and the tug of her brush during a blow-dry kept her mindful, in the here and now, rather than moping about the past or despairing over her future. She loved the way her clients felt good about themselves when she'd finished. She wished it was that easy for her. And being mobile, she'd been able to stuff as many appointments as she could day and night to fill Jason's gap. One day she wanted to open a salon of her own but, for now, she liked the driving. Particularly coming up here into the Valleys, she thought, looking out of Phyllis' second-floor boxy sheltered flat window where rows of old miners' houses clung to the hillsides beneath sweeping, blowy skies. Laughter, tragedy, legend and love ran through the Rhondda like seams of coal; emotion and drama were in every sandstone brick of every rugby club and pub, corner shop and launderette.

'Time for you to take a pew,' Phyllis said in her lovely lilt from her tiny kitchenette. 'I've a Victoria sponge for you, made it special, I did.'

'Oh, bless,' Frankie said, watching her carry in a tray of her best china, which tinkled as her hands shook. Pride of place was a beautiful cake so tall and dusty with icing sugar it rivalled any wintry Welsh mountain.

'That looks amazing. I would've loved to have seen your wedding cakes, back in the day.'

'Yes, they were a sight to behold,' Phyll said, her eyes staring at the memory. 'People from the next Valley would come to admire them. I was known as Phyll The Cake. That's how it was then, you'd be named after your job. It helped too if there were lots of people with the same name. My David was Dai The Fish, he was a fishmonger, see, so he didn't get mixed up with Dai the undertaker because he was Dai The Death. Talking of which, you're a bag of bones, you need fattening up.'

Using an ancient silver cake slice, Phyll cut Frankie a giant piece. It was true, she had lost weight, thanks to what Letty called The Dumped Diet, which made eating a chore. Victoria sponge was different though. Phyll examined her over their steaming cups of tea – Welsh Brew, of course – with sparkling blue eyes.

'Delish,' Frankie said, 'better than any Mary Berry sponge, I bet.'

'Never mind that. How are you?' Phyll said, jabbing the air with a sprightly finger.

'Oh, you know...' Not that an old lady would understand the emptiness or meaninglessness.

'As a matter of fact, I do.'

Frankie stopped mid-chew and looked up to see Phyll's face crinkled up in amusement.

'Married fifty years to my Dai. Then he was gone. My family didn't want me living by myself. Made me move in here, they did. I thought, that's it, that's your lot, girl, but never underestimate life.'

'What do you mean?'

'This wash and set, it's to make me look nice for Norman across the corridor. We're courting. He's taking me to the pictures tonight. You've done a good job, I think he'll mistake me for that Scarlett Johandsome.'

Pensioners dating? Frankie was agog. 'What's he like then?'

'Very polite. Ever so funny but not crude, mind. He's got a lovely head of hair and treats me like a lady – what more could a girl ask for?' Phyll said.

'Quite a catch then,' Frankie laughed, marvelling at the way women always wanted the same thing, no matter how old they were.

'Oh, I should say so.'

'What are you going to see?'

'He says I can choose, so either that one with George Clooney or the Judi Dench one. Afternoon showing because of the seniors' discount.'

Phyll was silent for a few seconds but Frankie knew she wasn't finished.

'Life goes on, you know. Dai was the love of my life. Always will be. But you have to get on with things.'

'But how?' Frankie asked, feeling beaten and hopeless that even this pensioner had a better love life than her. 'Because I still want him back.'

'Live your life, and if it's meant to be, he'll come knocking.' Then she said the most curious thing: 'But you might find if he does, that things have changed.'

In the traffic jams on the way home, Frankie sat in her old red Mini mulling over Phyll's words and it was still taking up headspace as she let herself in. In the early days of separation, getting up and about, showered even, had seemed an impossible challenge. Yet now, she could do it. Maybe they were all right, Phyll, Em and Letty, maybe she was capable of moving forward. Maybe she could come up with a plan to win back Jason.

After a tea of spaghetti hoops on toast and a large glass of wine, she couldn't help herself: she needed to check Jason's Facebook. As his page came up, her heart cracked all over again at his profile picture: he was grinning in the sunshine on his stag do in Magaluf. Hers was of their wedding day.

Then her stomach turned choppy when she saw his latest post. A photo from a surfing course. He was amongst a gang of people in wetsuits pulling 'wild and crazy' faces on a stunning beach. Behind the group were huge waves and their boards had been stabbed into the sand as if they were showing off their kill. I know that place, Frankie gasped, it was Oxwich, a gorgeous spot they had visited many times as a couple to walk Dad's dog and share chips as the sun set. How could he!

With adrenalin flowing, she zoomed in – and she was floored by a stab of jealousy. He had his arm round a blonde girl, one of those gorgeous sporty types. Admittedly he was doing the same to a bloke the other side of him, but that wasn't the point! He looked happy, deliriously so. It was obvious he had discovered a new lease of life. And he looked so incredibly hot. Brown from the sun, his teeth looked even whiter and his wet suit, oh my Lord… It was peeled down to his waist, exposing his ripped chest. Frankie began to imagine him with that girl, doing it in the sand dunes on a surfboard. Doing all sorts of things. Not that she knew exactly what because as he'd said SHE WAS BORING IN BED.

Jason was having fun and loving it. He was clearly not wondering about her. Hell-bent on trying to forget all the awful boring sex he'd been having with me, she thought.

Once the at-it-like-rabbits phase had ended, she and Jason had settled into a twice a week routine on a Friday night and

Sunday morning, which she hadn't thought was bad after so many years together. There'd been no need to experiment – love was all they needed. At least she had thought it was.

But now, terrifyingly, she understood what he'd meant: sex with her had become regimented, middle-aged. She knocked back another glass, then another, her mind racing for words to describe what sex should've been but wasn't. Exciting. Erotic. Adventurous. Thrilling. Tears began to prick her eyes as the cat appeared on the armchair of the sofa. He always popped up when something was on Frankie's mind, so much so she swore she had a mystic pet. 'Oh, what am I going to do, Leonardo?' she said, before realizing asking an animal for direction was verging on mad cat lady territory.

She needed to talk to someone who understood. Letty. She'd know what to do. Frankie picked up her phone, and with one eye screwed up because she couldn't focus both, scrolled down her contacts. She dissolved as soon as she heard Letty's voice.

'Oh, babes, maybe Jase just needs time,' Letty said.

'I just feel so helpless.'

'I know. What you've got to do is take control.'

'But how? Because I don't want to go on the pull. I've no confidence. I don't think I could sleep with anyone ever again.'

'You will, trust me.'

'If only someone could teach me what to do. I'm good at learning. I always liked—'

'Jesus, Frankie! That's it!' Letty sounded excited.

'What?'

'Get a teacher! Someone to show you the ropes. You'll feel empowered and when Jason comes back with his tail between his legs, you can show him what he's been missing.'

Frankie's head was swimming now. Doing a course in hairdressing was one thing but in sex?

'I don't think so. It's just too… weird. And I'm tired.'

'Fine. But sleep on it. And do me a favour, because you've been drinking, you'll forget this in the morning. So, go and get a glass of water, two paracetamol and then before you go up, write it down on your Cath Kidston chalkboard.'

'Write what?' Frankie wasn't following her here.

'The sex education of Frankie Green, of course.'

'Of course,' Frankie replied with sarcasm. 'Aged thirty-and-three-quarters. Like Adrian bloody Mole.'

A sex education was entirely ridiculous. And there was no way Frankie would ever contemplate it.

Saturday

Em

I really should've just bought the coleslaw, Em thought, feeling a wave of nausea at the smell of mustard, onions, mayo and lemon juice as she started on her contribution to the barbecue. Frankie was hosting one this afternoon as part of her 'getting on with things' project, which pleased Em. Not many people took her up on her advice.

But if she didn't make the coleslaw herself, because she always made everything from scratch, people might ask questions. She wasn't ready to announce her condition let alone her decision.

Em took a moment to steady herself by looking at the horizon out to sea from her apartment kitchen window. Four days she had known and her distress hadn't subsided. Discombobulated, that was how she felt, going about her business at work. She knew people were wondering what was up – she was hardly an airhead – so she had to try twice as hard to concentrate. The odd moment when she would forget, the memory that she was carrying another being would storm in and she would need to take a minute in whatever aisle she was in. Stick her head into the freezer compartment, busy herself with the shelf labels. Deliver herself a good talking to that she was not to panic, she could deal with the consequences. The problem was the hormones, which had altered her ability to think clearly. Like last night, when she'd worked out exactly how pregnant she was. Although she was quite certain of her decision, she had wanted to know all of the facts. An innocent 'ten weeks pregnant' search on Google had sucked her in deeper and deeper, click after click. She swung from horror and fear to wonder and amazement as she learned not only was she a walking test tube of chemicals but the foetus – the size of a prune – already had tastebuds, knees and elbows. Bile rose in her throat; a flood of human chorionic gonadotropin was working away to develop the placenta and that caused sickness.

A long groan, the sound of scratching and a loud yawn came, which told her Floyd was stirring. He never bothered to shut his door, so she was used to his morning soundtrack. But while she needed ten minutes to come to, he would be raring to go as soon as he'd flushed the loo. And true to form, he bounded into the kitchen.

'Afternoon,' she said, pulling herself together with an instinctive bit of sibling sarcasm.

'You sound like Mum, Emerald,' he said, sticking the coffee machine on and clattering around, opening cupboards and drawers before slamming them shut as he searched for mugs and breakfast.

'Very funny,' she said, 'except Mum would've woken you up hours ago to do sun salutation yoga at dawn. Instead, I've been slaving away making beef burgers and marinating prawns for Frankie's barbie.'

'Excellent. I'll be making a cocktail and providing the tunes.' Floyd held his arms aloft, taking in an imaginary round of applause.

Em couldn't help but giggle at the sight of him. Six foot four, his crazy sticky-up bed hair added even more inches to his height, and with that big beard, bare chest and baggy boxers, he looked like a castaway.

'I know. Gorgeous, aren't I?' he said, trying to flatten down brown tufts with one hand and adjusting his black-rimmed glasses with the other. People never guessed they were related on first sight. Like Dad, Floyd was a boyish, brown-eyed brunette, whereas Em had inherited Mum's green eyes and mousey hair, which they both dyed – albeit very different shades of red: Mum's was hennaed, Em's was chestnut. But Em and Floyd shared straight noses, expressive eyebrows, a willowy and lean physique, and the second the sun came out, their complexions blossomed with freckles. That though was where the similarities ended because Floyd was like a spaniel to her self-sufficient Siamese. Not that they fought like cat and dog; they got on and always had done.

But that's not to say Em was entirely happy sharing her home with him. It was extremely gratifying that she'd bought her own place thanks to hard work. She could clear her head up in this smart fourth-floor two-bed apartment, which felt like her own ivory tower. The spotless white kitchen overlooked the

Bristol Channel and, on a good day, all the way to Somerset, while the bedroom vista took in the immediate bustle of the upmarket docks, the distant skyscrapers of the city centre and the rising hills beyond. It was hard to enjoy the views when Floyd was bashing around, but she had a soft spot for him, he was fun and good company – most of the time. He'd had a run of bad luck; first his cow of a girlfriend Sasha had left him, then his landlord had decided to sell up, leaving him homeless. Even so, she needed to know what his plans were because that was the way she was. And she wanted to imagine that one day her radiators wouldn't be covered by his enormous T-shirts. 'Any flats coming up?' she asked.

'Trying to get rid of me?' he said, pulling a pretend hurt face as he plopped two sugars into his cup.

'No! You said you wanted your own place, that's all,' she said, returning to her food prep.

'I do but there's nothing coming up in my price bracket. Cheap as chips equals scummy, and professional pad means out of my league. Just like it is with women,' he said, laughing at his own joke.

'But you're always pulling!' she said. 'How can you complain about that? Speaking of which, I didn't hear you come in last night. Anything to report?' Em revelled in his roller-coaster love life because it was so different to hers, which resembled a big dipper, having not heard from Simon Brown since *that* night. Floyd fell for someone every week yet they never lasted. She rarely met any of them because it never got to that point where he would introduce them to the gang.

'Well, now you come to mention it,' he said with an enigmatic lift of his right eyebrow.

'Ooh, what? Who is she?' Em said, dropping her knife and twirling around.

'So, you know that bird I've been after, the one at work?'

'Which one?' she said because Floyd was spoilt for choice for alpha females at the legal firm where he was the in-house counsellor. To them, this hippy offshoot represented something free and unfettered compared with their structured lives.

'That lawyer, the one who looks like Nicole Scherzinger. We went for drinks,' he said, taking a slurp of his coffee.

'Sounds promising,' Em said, trying to keep it low-key. He looked happy still playing the field but she wanted to see him settled because he'd be a great dad and husband.

But Floyd shook his head. 'That's where you're wrong,' he said, 'I thought I was open-minded sex-wise – don't make that face – but she's twisted.'

'I'm not sure I want to hear this, after all.'

'Don't be such a prude! The second we got back to hers, she jumped on me—'

'My ears!' she said, holding the sides of her head.

'And she produced a…' and he stopped to mouth the word 'strap-on dildo' before resuming. 'So I scarpered. I mean, fair enough, but not on a first date,' he said, shrugging.

'Never!' Em gasped.

'Yep. So, wahey,' he said, doing jazz hands, 'I'm back on the market.'

'You really are unbelievable – don't you ever just want to be by yourself for a bit?' Em sighed in judgement. She was a staunch believer in being alone if you couldn't have the one you wanted. It had made her resourceful and independent. 'Don't you think it's a bit pathetic that you seem to need someone?'

'Cor, you're touchy today. You all right?' he said, eating cereal straight from the box. 'Not that you'd ever tell me, of course. I mean, I'm only a qualified professional who earns a living listening to people.'

'I'm fine,' Em said, returning to the coleslaw, she didn't need anyone's help, thank you very much.

Later...

Frankie

Ten minutes before the barbecue was about to start and Frankie's Mum appeared with a bowl of coronation chicken.

'Hiya, love!' she said, handing over the tepid dish which turned Frankie's already churning stomach to curd. Mum marched into the kitchen and began rearranging the nibbles to make room, pride of place, of course, for her contribution.

This was just typical of her mother, Frankie thought. Poor timing not to mention turning up uninvited. But then Frankie only had herself to blame – she should never have told her she was having a party. She was nervous enough as it was, hosting a do for the first time minus Jason.

Thank God Dad had already been and gone, setting up trestle tables borrowed from his painter and decorator friend Gareth in the garden. Frankie always died inside when her parents came face to face. They were very good at pretending to be friends but she worried Dad felt his loneliness even more keenly when he had to make small talk with his successor, a Lego-haired car salesman who loved Jeremy Clarkson and Top Gear.

'Colin's just parking up,' Mum said, flicking her brassy and dated weathergirl hair. She'd tried to persuade her to update it – it was a terrible advert for Frankie's hairdressing skills – but Mum knew best. As she'd always done. 'Any drinks going? How are you? Excited? Gorgeous weather for it. I'm sure lots of people will turn up, don't worry, they always do if there's free booze!'

'Thanks for the support, Mum.' Frankie pointed to the gin on the side. 'I'll have one too,' she said, needing a confidence boost. Not only had her mothers just identified Frankie's key worry that no one would come, she had managed to point out that her guests wouldn't be there for her scintillating company but whatever they could get.

Luckily, her mum had been proved entirely wrong and by

midnight, Frankie was in a camping chair, drunk on Floyd's Banging BBQ cocktail and her devoted friends' company. Yes, it had been a success, way beyond her limited expectations when she'd simply hoped not to trip over her maxi dress or cry into her hot dog.

Sadly though, it was time to start thinking about calling it a night, she thought, taking a moment to admire Letty's arrangement of candles and fairy lights.

The summery soundtrack was long gone: a chill-out playlist on low accompanied the murmur of voices of a handful of people outside on bean bags and cushions. Em had gone hours ago with a headache, poor thing. Letty was still there, slapping her bum and asking if anyone wanted a lap dance. She was doing well, Frankie thought, considering how upset she had been earlier, wishing she was in a normal relationship and could bring her man with her. Frankie hoped she'd come to her senses soon and get herself out of that no-win situation. But she would never lecture her friend. Then there was Leonardo, up on the fence on his haunches, sniffing the air as part of his night-time inspection.

Frankie considered getting out of her seat and clearing up. Yet she was made of cement and mesmerized by the glow of the barbecue which was now burning bits of wood. Shift your bum, she told herself. For two seconds she was upright but a bat flying low made her dizzy and she landed with a thump on her backside.

'All right, Frankie?' came a deep, melodious voice.

Her eyes searched the semi-darkness and she found Floyd holding two kebab sticks and a bag of marshmallows. 'I need to go to bed,' she said, smiling at his friendly face, 'that's all.'

'Me too,' he said, settling down on the decking at her feet. 'I miss my bed.'

'It's not far!' she laughed.

'I meant my own bed. It's in mum and dad's garage, I'm in Em's spare room, yeah, and the mattress is too soft for me.'

'How is the flat hunting going?'

'Crap,' he said, 'I just can't seem to find anywhere. I feel stuck. Like I can't move on.'

Frankie nodded and stifled a yawn. It wasn't that she didn't want to talk, it was just she was so tired. 'I better get tidying,' she said, pushing herself up by the armrests. She had to start dropping hints to tell the stragglers it was over.

'I know what you're going through,' he said, which made her briefly stop. Then she waved away the temptation to have yet another conversation about her relationship. She'd spent the night not talking about it, as in trapping anyone who'd listen to the woes of wanting her husband back.

'Right. Do you want me to call you a cab?' She looked up at him, making it obvious it was closing time. But he completely ignored her question.

'It is completely shit loving someone when they're having time out. I've had this for a year now and I know we weren't married, like you, and that's far worse, but I just wanted you to know I know how it is. A bit of solidarity.'

Wow, breaking news – she never knew he was nursing a broken heart. In fact, he acted the total opposite. 'But I thought you were young, free and single?' she said.

'I am. Sort of. Remember Sasha?' he said, stretching his arms out to toast the treats.

'Who can forget her?' Frankie said, recalling the stunning six-foot photographer who could've been modelling on the other side of the camera.

'Total love of my life,' he said, blowing out a flaming marshmallow. 'Best two years ever. Then, you know, when I proposed she said she wasn't ready and she wanted to "find herself" travelling. She told me to ask her again to marry me when she came back but she'd understand if I didn't wait for her. I've tried not to. But there's no one like her, and never will be.'

'Oh, Floyd,' she said, 'I just assumed it was water under the bridge. You hide it well.'

'I can't keep going on about it, can I?' he said, turning to Frankie with a shrug. 'Em has no idea, she was pretty cut up too when she went because they were like sisters.'

Frankie felt really sorry for him – in all likelihood, Sasha was gone, not just as in miles away. But couldn't the same be said for Jason? Floyd deserved sympathy, not some scathing wake-up call. 'Hey, I'm the same with Jason. It still feels wrong. People might think we settled down too young and they do the whole 'there's so much out there' lecture but when you meet the right person, you just know.'

'Yep,' he said, sighing, then missing his mouth so the

marshmallow stained his beard and one of his silly hi-top trainers a gooey white. 'What a pair of losers we are.'

'But you're a very nice loser,' she said, laughing easily at his funny ways and from too much alcohol.

'And so are you, Frankie,' he said, pulling her in for a cuddle. Out of nowhere, his touch gave her a shiver. It had been so long since she'd had any contact with a bloke. But there was no denying they had a special relationship, seeing as she was one of his sister's closest friends. And once upon a time, before Jason, she had fancied him in a best friend's big brother kind of way. They'd come close to a snog once, at Debbie Yates' fifteenth in the village hall, but Em had caught them and stuck her fingers down her throat to show her disapproval. She wondered if he remembered. Probably not, he'd had so many such moments. But if you'd had as few as her then you didn't forget.

'I just want him back,' she said, pulling away, and peering up at the stars. 'You know, he's still in contact. We speak regularly and I know he still cares about me. It's as if he needs to get something out of his system.'

'Well, that's pretty normal,' Floyd said. 'Even though it hurts, I can see why Sasha wanted to get out of here too. I'd done all that in my gap year. And it must be the same for Jase.'

Maybe it was the drink or maybe it was because Floyd was such a good listener, but before she knew what she was doing, Frankie was pouring her heart out. For ages.

'What you need is some fun,' he concluded after a while, 'to take your mind off things.'

'I'm not very good at fun,' she said, the words catching in her throat as Leonardo wound round her legs, seeking a stroke.

'Oh, come on,' he said, picking up the cat and tickling him under the chin. Frankie was amazed the cat had allowed him to touch him – Jason had to only walk in the room and Leonardo would hiss at him. 'This party has been brilliant and... well... um...'

'See? And tonight's not exactly been what you'd call "banging", has it? I'm just so dull. I'm trying to fight it but I have to face it. I'm of no interest to anyone.'

Floyd's eyebrows shot up. Leonardo shot off. He'd seen a moth by a candle. Unless it was an excuse because he'd sensed what was coming.

'What?' she asked, defensively, genuinely wondering how he could assert otherwise.

'If you're so dull,' he said, with a smile on his lips, 'why have you written "The sex education of Frankie Green" on your wall?'

She gasped – she'd forgotten to rub it off. Everyone must have seen it, going in and out for drinks from the fridge. 'I think I'm going to die,' she said, covering her face with her hands. Then she did her best to explain and quickly. It was all just a silly joke.

'Yeah, course. It is a pretty left-field self-improvement plan. And why would you need sex ed? You're married – not a virgin.'

Frankie grimaced then.

'Oh, bollocks. Don't tell me you're a virgin. Please don't tell me you're a virgin. Though it's absolutely fine, I cast no judgement.'

'I might as well be,' Frankie said, staring into the fire. She was beyond caring because nothing could ever be as embarrassing as the knowledge that people had read her sign on the chalkboard.

'What? Don't you do it on a trapeze three times a night like everyone else?' Floyd said with a straight face.

Frankie sighed. His kindness was a small consolation when it was now public knowledge she was crap in bed. Losing Jason was bad enough, but now she felt exposed. She began talking then, not to Floyd but into the darkness, about her broken self-esteem, her fear of change and her angst if she ever dared to try sex again. Soothed by her out-pouring, she finished with a shrug and told Floyd, 'So that's that.'

'Oh, come on, don't be sad,' he said, lightly punching her arm. 'You won't always feel like this, time is a great healer. And sex is subjective, you know, there's no industry Kitemark or qualification to say whether you're good or bad. Although, obviously, I do have a PhD in Loving, so I'm told,' he said, mocking himself. 'Relationship sex can suffer if there are other things going on too, it isn't a separate entity, it's an indicator of loads of things. And like anything else in life, you aren't born forever useless – you can learn.'

'Do you think?' Frankie asked, looking up into his eyes, desperate to believe she wasn't destined to be miserable without

Jason for the rest of her days.

'Yes, of course! Maybe you do need a teacher. God, that'd be a great job!' Floyd said, snickering at his own joke and launching into a stand-up routine. 'Imagine that, applying for it. "Dear madam, I wish to apply for the position of lots of positions"…' he said, clearly enjoying himself.

'Yes, thank you.'

'… "I am very experienced, with many happy clients who can provide references—"'

'Floyd—' she said, feeling fed up now.

'"Testimonials include 'what a whopper!' and 'very hands on'. I am very giving, offer complete confidentiality and a nice hug after—"'

'Seriously, Floyd,' her voice warned, and she held up her hands to show she meant it.

'I am serious, Frankie,' he said, suddenly composed.

'Sorry?' she said, her palms frozen in mid-air.

'Well, why not? I'm a man of the world. Not Russell Brand or anything, but I know a bit and I'm, cough, careful.'

'Come again?'

'Steady on, Frankie, we haven't even got to first base yet,' he said, pretending to look appalled.

Frankie couldn't help it – she began laughing at the situation. He was actually offering to teach her! 'You are hilarious!' she said, slapping her thigh, thinking how stupid, how really, really stupid, this all was! He was a friend! A single friend. A trustworthy one. In the same boat as her, still in love with an ex, hoping they'd come back. A friend she got on really well with. And still sort of fancied. Her heart began galloping as it dawned on her that, actually, he was the most suitable candidate in the world, and what if he did help her? What if he taught her how to be an amazing lover and she could seduce Jason and… It was craziness. But she was desperate. She took a breath – and another large gulp of wine, and then the plunge.

'Okay, Floyd, I'm going to call your bluff, you're on,' she challenged, peering out of the corner of her eyes waiting for his face to fall and the panic to register, at which point she would of course back off. But Floyd's face didn't fall, in fact he just scratched his beard then asked about the pay. She burst out laughing. 'I can offer biscuits, and double-biscuits on bank holidays, if that's okay?' she said, relieved to be able to join in with the goofiness.

'Custard creams?' he asked, putting his hand out to shake on the deal.

She looked at him, still not at all sure if this was just a game. Then she put her hand in his and shook, gaining confidence.

'Does this mean I'm hired, Lord Sugar?' he asked.

'Er, I suppose you are!' she said, tentatively, for the first time daring to believe this was actually going to happen. And why not, she thought to herself, bolstered by whatever Floyd had put in his 'top secret' cocktail. Her heart soared at the prospect of having the chance to find out just why she'd lost Jason, because if she could work that out then she could try to correct it. And therein lay her happiness. But there were so many practical issues to sort out.

'We'd have to have some rules,' she said primly.

'Yep,' he said, now serious. 'Like Em never finding out or she'd kill us both and make one of her fancy hotpots out of our remains. Probably a sausage tagine, in my case.'

A thought struck her then – what if he was only doing it out of pity? She started to bluster, telling him he could change his mind, right now if he wanted to. 'I just don't know what you'll be getting out of it, really. It's not as though I'm any good, is it?'

'What I'll be getting out of it?' he asked incredulously. 'A young lady asks a saddo bloke to teach her how to do it. Does he a) bite her hand off, b) agree out of altruism or c) accept because he needs to get his ex out of his head? All three of the above, thank you very much.'

'Right. Okay then,' she said, heartened. 'This is all so very bizarre. I think I'm in shock!'

Floyd held his glass in the air to make a toast. 'Bottoms up?' he said.

Dear God, she thought, I hope he isn't expecting that.

The Next Day

Em

Em was crouched over the loo, willing herself to vomit quietly. So much for morning sickness, she thought; it was mid-afternoon.

She flushed once more, then realized that was the fourth time, and Floyd would have to be an idiot not to think something was going on.

'Have you blocked the loo, you stinker?' came his voice at the bathroom door.

'Go away!' she said through gritted teeth. She was reminded of their childhood when this sort of exchange would spark off a lecture from Mum about using fewer sheets to save the environment. He wouldn't get a telling off, he never did, because Mum believed in freedom of expression.

She unlocked the door and swung it open to see Floyd's grinning face – complete with one of her plastic pegs on his nose. 'Bugger off!' she said, pushing him out the way.

'Steady!' he said, following her. Then he took in her white face. 'Shit, Em, you look awful.'

'Why thank you, Prince Charming.' She didn't want him poking his nose in when she was yet to get her head around this situation.

'Are you all right?' he said, leaning in with concern.

'Oh, I think I'm just hungover. Or it could've been a dodgy burger at the barbecue,' she lied.

'That's weird because I'm okay. Hang on,' he said, as Em saw the cogs turning, 'you didn't drink yesterday, you drove my car back. What's going on?'

'Nothing,' she said, reaching for the TV controls to find something that'd grab his attention. But she was out of luck – there was no sport, no *Top of the Pops 2* to laugh at, and not a single documentary. She picked a channel at random and hoped for the best when the adverts had finished.

'You've been acting weird lately. You know,' he said,

assuming his favourite pose of crossed legs and steepled fingers. Then in his 'work voice' he said: 'My door is always open if you're having any issues.'

Em's poker face focused on the telly and she muttered: 'I'm fine.'

But then the music started for *One Born Every Minute* and she began to fluster. This was not the moment to see newborn babies – but if she reacted he'd notice. So she sat very still and considered what to do.

Floyd picked up his guitar which was upright against the wall beside the settee and began to pluck at a few strings. This was a good sign, she thought, he could sit for hours playing music – she could eat a cushion and he wouldn't notice. She plotted her exit. It had to be quick, before she witnessed a birth. Because the sight of medical staff would remind her she had yet to make an appointment with the doctor to make what she had decided official. Should she offer a cup of tea? No, she didn't want to pull him out of his reverie. She was just about to get up when 'waaaaah!', a baby announced its arrival into the world.

From nowhere, tears came to Em's eyes, her breathing began to shudder and her shoulders started to shake. Two seconds later, as the tiny little thing took in gulps of air and fought the light with fists, a wail came from her mouth.

'What the shit, Em?' Floyd said, dropping his guitar. He moved in to comfort her, then pulled back, obviously wondering if he was to blame and he was about to get a dead arm. 'Have I done something? Because if I have I'm sorry. The blocked loo thing, I didn't mean it,' he said, his eyes wide.

Still crying hard, Em shook her head to show that that wasn't it. She couldn't speak and neither did she want to. She needed to keep this secret to herself; he was a flipping counsellor and trained to crack her.

Knowing now he wasn't about to get it in the neck, Floyd put an arm around her, stroking her hair with his free hand. Immediately, everything changed. She felt disarmed, but not in a bad way. Safe, that's how she felt, and just as protected and loved as the day he'd picked her up when she'd fallen over during playtime at school and knocked out a milk tooth. That was the best thing about brothers and sisters – you could be deadly enemies one minute, but should there be a threat, you'd morph into one, united. His hug was a basic gesture but one that proved her worth, she realized. It was enough to halt her distress, to make her see he was her ally and she was going to need him. If she sobbed at a stupid TV programme with no warning, then how was she going to cope for the rest of her life? She had to make sure she had some support. 'Floyd, I need to tell you…'

'Shhhh, there, there,' he said, still in soothing mode. 'Let it go, let it all go.'

'I'm…'

'Let it all out,' he said.

'I'm trying to!' she said, raising the volume. 'Will you just stop interrupting?'

'Oh, sorry! Go on.'

While she wanted to escape his bear hug because now her nose had cleared she could smell his unshowered body, she decided to stay put. Em didn't want to see his reaction. She knew him so well, and whatever reserve he showed his clients, when it came to her, he was prone to over-excitement even at the smallest revelation. He might be thirty-four but in her mind he was only ever a few seconds away from shouting 'Mu-um!'.

'So, Floyd. I'm in a situation,' she began, feeling him nod. 'And I'd appreciate it if you didn't tell Mum or Dad. Or anyone.'

'Yup, roger that,' he said, earnestly.

'Right,' she said, suddenly stuck for words when public speaking had never been an issue before. 'The thing is, Floyd… you're going to be… an uncle.'

'Oh, that's lovely!' he said, squeezing her. 'Who's having a baby? And why are you upset about it?'

For someone educated up to the eyeballs, Floyd was a total thicko at times. 'What do you mean who's having a baby?' she said.

'Well, one of our friends. Or a cousin or… You know, people get called "uncle" all the time, even if they're not related. Like Uncle Barnaby, Dad's friend. He was a legend, he was. He brought us sweets behind Mum's back. Lemon sherbets, if I remember rightly. Oh,' he said as if the penny had dropped, 'you're not worrying about your fertility, are you? Is this why you're sad? Seriously, you're a whippersnapper, you have all the time in the world.'

'Floyd Good-Fellow, you are insane. Let me spell this out: the word "uncle" derives from the Latin avuncular meaning "little grandfather" and is a family relationship between a person and his or her parent's brother.'

'I know!' he said, offended. 'I'm not stupid.'

'You're doing a very good impression of it. Listen to me, Floyd, I'm pregnant. Me. No one else. Me.' It was the first time she'd said it to anyone: the prospect of speaking it aloud had weighed heavily upon her but thanks to Floyd's exasperating idiocy, it had come out easily.

Floyd scrambled to his feet. 'You?' he said, his eyeballs popping.

'Yes, me,' she sighed.

'But how?' he said, his arms wide.

'A sperm fertilized one of my eggs. It's called reproduction.'

'I know that! I meant, I didn't even know you were seeing someone.'

'I'm not.'

'What the actual fuck? What are you going to do?' he yelled, showing zero of his professional cool.

'I've told you,' she said, strangely calm in the wake of his discomposure, which only made her more certain of her resolve. 'You're going to be an uncle. I've decided I'm keeping the baby.'

Three Days Later

Frankie

He'd meant it, she still couldn't quite get over it. Even now, the day after Floyd had texted suggesting a 'meeting' to 'finalize the arrangement'. He was due here any minute and she was in a state, having changed her outfit three times already. Standing in her dressing gown, the dilemma was this: too much flesh on show and she'd feel a fraud, too little and she might as well be going to a funeral.

She was painfully aware of the irony of the situation: he was going to end up seeing her naked, so why was she bothering getting stressed about what to wear? Because the experience she did have had been ground to dust by Jason's departure. Unable to fall back on that, she was starting from scratch. She didn't have dating experience to help her out. She didn't know the code of signals and glances which paved the way to bed. She was going in at the deep end.

And there'd be no 'will-we-won't-we-have-sex' build-up, which made it really confusing. Did she need to bother making an effort at all and cut to the chase by greeting him with nothing on? Or should she get into her best underwear just in case he intended on marking her with score cards? There was also the matter of the teacher-pupil relationship; should this be reflected in her clothes?

She could hardly put on a school uniform. She shuddered at the thought of the tacky role-play she knew Letty had got up to over the years. Nothing, nothing, would persuade her to wear a naughty schoolgirl outfit and if Floyd suggested it, then that'd be the end of it, she vowed. That thought persuaded her to go for what she suspected she'd wear all along – skinny jeans and a baggy tunic top. It was the closest she'd get to looking like it was no big deal. Leonardo, who'd been observing her panic like a watchman from the windowsill, signalled his approval by jumping across to the bed to curl up nose to tail.

As she reached for her trousers on the floor, she caught sight of her bum in the mirror. It was then she acknowledged her biggest fear, the thing that underpinned all of her anxiety: being nude with another man. She'd never been naked with anyone but Jason. He'd only slept with one girl before her – Tanya Weeks. So his experience had been limited. But for all she knew, he could be out there right now doing it, finally realizing that Frankie's body wasn't normal. What if she was actually really hairy or had odd-shaped nipples and she didn't know it? And what if she was a freak 'down there' compared to other women? She stopped to examine herself: the plump bottom-heavy size fourteen body had become slimmer. Still a pear, but she was a size tennish pear and her boobs were perkier now they'd got a bit smaller. It wasn't too horrific a sight, surely? Then there was the matter of Floyd's 'thing'; she was going to see only the second one of her life in the flesh. She had to face up to it, so she forced herself to say the word 'penis' out loud and ended up gagging on it, which certainly didn't bode well.

It wasn't too late to pull out, she thought. What on earth was she doing getting herself into this? And what if after all this she wasn't into him enough to be physically able to perform? Sure, they had a banter going and he was handsome in a wholesome kind of way. But no one other than Jason had ever given her the thrills. There wasn't time to text Floyd because he'd be on his way, but if she let him in she could say 'thanks, I've changed my mind', and return to the safety of what she knew. Not this terrifying cliff edge on which she was teetering – she felt the fight or flight sensation running through her veins. Sweat formed at the backs of her knees and her palms were clammy. This was total insanity. This was—

Sugar! There was the doorbell. Leonardo scarpered under the bed. This was a terrible mistake. Frozen, she wondered if she should pretend she was out. But then her famous banger of a Mini was in the drive and the downstairs windows were open. He would only try to ring and he'd know she was refusing to pick up. Defeated, she slowly trod down the stairs, seeing his tall, dark outline through the frosted glass. She paused on the bottom step. This was horrific – why hadn't she realized it was going to be like this?

He knocked again, then he bent down and she saw the letter box flip open. Please, God, let him slip a note through saying he's had a change of heart. Instead, a pair of brown eyes creased with a smile peered through and met hers.

'Aren't you going to let me in?' Floyd said, amused. 'Or are you out?'

'Yes, I'm not here,' she said, blushing.

'Oh that's a shame because I've got a takeaway and I was going to share it, but I'll just have to sit on the step and stick my snout in like a pig. Unless you can pass a fork through the letter box?'

Frankie squeaked as some of the tension inside her escaped like air from a balloon. She had no other choice but to answer the door.

'Hi,' was all she could manage when she opened up because her mouth had dried up.

'Shall we do it now then? On the stairs?'

'WHAT?'

'Joke. It was a joke, Frankie. Calm down. Let's just eat.'

Floyd led the way into the kitchen and started rattling around for plates and cutlery. 'Sit down,' he told her, while he laid the table, switched on the radio, then complained she was far too young to be listening to Radio 2 and switched it to 6 Music. 'Good day?' he asked warmly, uncovering plastic cartons of fragrant Thai rice, noodles and vegetables, and unscrewing a bottle of wine. He seemed to be completely at home here, busying himself with the food and looking up every now and then with 'go on, I'm listening' eyes.

How could he be so normal, she thought, when I'm having a meltdown? 'It was okay. Did some hair. You?'

'Dreadful,' he said, plonking himself down on the seat next to her. That was another thing, she thought, he didn't seem to have any personal-space issues. Surely if you were about to embark on an intimate journey with someone, you'd at least have the decency to be a little distant at first? 'A lawyer broke down on me, the bus was disgustingly sweaty and now I'm being forced to converse with a statue.'

'I don't think I can go through with…'

'Fine. Have a drink, eat something,' he said, with his mouth full, waving his fork at the feast.

It was as if he'd waved a magic wand instead because she began to defrost with her first bite. And after half-an-hour of his company, she had relaxed a little.

'I'm so sorry about earlier,' she said, clearing the plates.

'This is just really alien to me.'

'Oh, I do this all the time… not!' he said, smiling. 'This is why I'm here tonight, nutjob, to work it all out.'

He was right – neither of them had done this before and she needed to trust him or there was no point continuing.

'But if you want to back out…?'

Frankie had been waiting for this – she knew there'd come a moment when she had to commit herself either way. She needed to move on, like Jason was clearly doing, and she needed to prepare herself should he come back. It was like having to take some nasty-tasting medicine. Well, actually it might be a really tasty spoonful. It might just be a bit humiliating and cringey in the build-up to swallowing it. But she had to do it regardless. 'Not at all,' she said, clearly.

'Me too. But the first thing we should be clear on is that we can stop this at any time if either of us wants to,' he said. 'We'll need a safety phrase too – for example, I dunno, say Custard Creams – should anything happen mid-clinch that we're not happy with.'

'Like what?' she asked horrified, being reminded of Jason's handcuffs. 'Because I'm not doing anything kinky. If you're a pervert, you better tell me now.'

Floyd cracked up laughing and then regained his poise. 'I'm not. It's just, sometimes people say stop in the heat of the moment and they don't mean it. It's like acting.'

Frankie didn't think she'd ever done that with Jason, but she nodded anyway.

'You want to add anything?' he asked.

'Neither of us should be involved with anyone else. It'd be too complicated, grubby, if anyone else was involved.'

'Totally,' he nodded, kindly, unaware he resembled a child with noodles down his front.

'And could we make sure we always have a cuddle?' she said. 'Because I don't want it to feel dirty, and we're mates so…'

'Fine. Now,' he said, rubbing his hands, 'you got a list then of what you want to do?'

Oh lordy, this was the gift that kept on giving her a red face. 'Well, I've had a few thoughts,' she said, rifling in her pocket for a piece of paper she'd scribbled on last night. The task had taken hours; she'd had to get over her embarrassment first, which led to a crisis of confidence. If she baulked at confessing sexy

48

thoughts to herself, how was she going to cope in front of Floyd? Then, once she'd got over that with a stiff reprimand and a biscuit dunked in tea, she had encountered the hopelessness of her naivety. Her to-do list was all so basic – it was as if she needed L plates. The only way to get over it, she decided innocently, was to do a search of 'female fantasy' and 'best positions' online. But she was completely unprepared for the never-ending pop-ups which seemed to appear faster than she could delete them. In a daze, she had to mute her laptop in case one of her neighbours heard either the moaning or the language. And now, eek, she was expected to put her inner most insecurities and desires into words.

'Ready, Frankie?' Floyd said encouragingly as Leonardo slunk in to see what was happening.

'Do you want to read them or shall I say them out loud?'

'Fire away,' he said, 'I'm all ears.'

Meanwhile...

Em

The sun-bleached streets passed in a blur as Em gazed out of the window on her bus ride home.

As usual, her feet were killing her, having spent all day marching around the store. But it was this tiredness, this fatigue, she was unused to.

A bump in the road made the bus jerk, and before she knew it, her hand shot to her stomach. She shut her eyes and wondered how she'd become such a slave to instinct. It betrayed what she had always prided herself on – her ability to box up emotion and apply common sense.

The jolt made her want to get off. It was only when the number forty-two had pulled away that she realized she'd been on the completely wrong bus and she had ended up the other side of town. What was up with her? And to compound matters, she was bursting for the loo. She'd have to go to Letty's place which was just round the corner.

Usually Em would have sauntered through the gentrified delights of Letty's neighbourhood of Pontcanna, where the streets were lined with bistros, delis and gift shops. But thanks to her brimming bladder, she broke into a trot, like a demented chicken.

Please, God, be in, she thought, finding Flat One on the list of buzzers. 'Desperate,' she said by way of hello as Letty invited her into the shared hallway of the grand old building. Em rushed into the ground-floor flat and found the loo, from where she shouted: 'You've got damp in here, you need to get the landlord to do something about it.'

'Well, thank you, Kirstie Allsopp,' Letty said, stirring something that smelled good as Em reappeared into the kitchen. 'Have you thought about opening a charm school?'

Em hung her head, feeling ashamed. 'I'm so sorry, I just worry, and thank you for letting me use your loo. You've got a lovely place,' she said, much more stylish than Em's, which was strictly Ikea flatpack.

Letty had turned the blank canvas of magnolia walls, scuffed wooden floorboards and cobwebbed high ceilings into a chic show home, the kind you'd see in an interiors magazine. Sumptuous throws, candles, rugs and lamps dotted the lounge-diner, which had a vast grey L-shaped sofa and a gorgeous dark blue feature wall. Her bedroom resembled a boudoir with its four-poster bed, and she'd turned the box room into a bijou walk-in wardrobe. While she could do nothing about the shabby kitchen, she'd perked it up by painting the wooden cabinets a high-gloss white, and she'd created an extra 'room' in what was once an overgrown yard with gravel, pots and a table and chairs. But Em wasn't envious, she basked in her friend's special touch, which covered everything she touched in glitter. Letty, now out of her work stuff and in tight green joggers and a vest, even managed to make dressing down look good.

'That's okay, babes,' Letty said, she never stayed cross for long. 'Want some dinner? Pasta's ready.'

'Yes, please. I'm starving.' In fact, when wasn't she? Her appetite had always been healthy but now it was Olympian. Porridge with blueberries and honey on toast for breakfast, oat cakes for elevenses, jacket potato with everything at lunch and then the nosedive into doughnuts on her afternoon break followed by a big dinner. Then cheese and biscuits before bed. With pickled onions, big craving handfuls of them, which before this baby, she had never liked.

'Good, plenty here,' she said, jumping from the hob to the fridge, 'Will be two minutes. Hey, would you do me a favour, by the way?'

'Of course. What is it?'

'I've got this idea that I want to talk to my boss about,' Letty said, her eyes firing with enthusiasm. 'A social media thing for the company. I need your eyes on it. Would you have a look for me?'

'I'd be honoured. I love a presentation.' And Em dearly wanted Letty to be recognized as someone who had brains not just breasts.

'Fab! Cheers, babes. I'll email it to you. Right, this is just about ready,' Letty said, dishing up.

Em shovelled in a big twisted forkful of creamy spaghetti. 'It's gorgeous. What is it?'

'A little something I learned from an ex,' Letty replied, winking. 'He was a shit but at least I picked this up! It's carbonara with blue cheese added right at the end with the egg.'

Em's mouth seized up, recalling the advice she'd read about foods to avoid in pregnancy. Soft cheese was fine as long as it had been cooked through. But it didn't taste hot. And the egg was still virtually just cracked.

'Bit of wine in it too, just to make it… What's the matter?' Letty looked at her, confused.

Em gulped and lay down her fork. 'I'm just not all that hungry,' she said quietly.

Letty nodded slowly with hurt in her eyes, then carried on eating in silence.

It was no good, Em realized. Not shouting about her private life was one thing but offending her friend was unacceptable. Letty didn't deserve this. She launched into it – there was no other way.

'I'm having a baby. It's Simon Brown's.' She didn't dare stop. 'I haven't told him yet. I feel a complete fool, not least because of the lectures I've given you in the past about being careful. But there we are. So, now you know,' she said, awaiting a quite justifiable performance of dramatics by Letty. Who surprised her actually with an outpouring of sympathy.

'Oh, you poor love,' she said, getting up to give her a *cwtch*.

'Feel free to tell me off,' Em said into her hair.

Letty pulled away, gripped her by the shoulders and spoke firmly. She would never do that, she said, everyone's human and there for the grace of God went she. 'What's important is that you're okay. Are you feeling okay?'

'Well, no. And yes,' she said, explaining how she felt constipated, sick, knackered and weepy. But weirdly, she'd never had a single doubt about what she was going to do. 'I've always wanted kids. Always. They're just so… straightforward. I also realize I'm thirty-one, I have a dreadful romantic track record and I'm an oddball.'

Letty leapt in to protest. But Em was adamant.

'I'm not like you or Frankie or anyone. This might be my only chance to have a baby. By the time I meet someone, I might be menopausal. And I've worked it all out: I can afford to take nine months off and if Mum and Dad can't help then I can dip into my savings. Go on, you can tell me I'm mad.'

52

'Well, it'll be hard, really bloody hard. But it looks like you've thought it through. And I don't know anyone as capable as you. So I think you should go for it. Just as long as you're certain.'

'I am. And once Floyd had got over the shock – mostly that I'd had sex at all – he said he'd be hands-on, changing nappies and stuff.'

'Me too. Auntie Letty will do whatever she can to help. Although I've never held one or anything. But, whatever! I'm in awe of you, I am.'

But Em didn't feel awesome – she felt as if she was floundering. Her life plan had been her crutch; her way of exerting control over uncertainties. But now it had red pen all over it. And there was the question of telling Simon Brown. If she did at all. It was the next question on Letty's lips.

'I know he has a right to know,' Em said, 'but there are circumstances.'

'What do you mean?'

'We're not together, so it doesn't matter.'

'Imagine if he finds out – and he will, guaranteed. You never know, this might be the trigger that makes him declare his love. You don't have to tell me how much you like him. I can see it on your face.'

Cringing at her feelings being laid bare, Em said: 'That's just it. He won't come running.'

'How do you know?'

She wanted to scream BECAUSE I JUST DO and stop this conversation right now. Within a matter of days, her life had been turned upside down; she was already sick of confessing things, because it went against who she was. Yet, much to her dismay, in that time she had seen how being pregnant was affecting her. The knowledge that she was up against unscheduled sobbing which could strike at any moment, made her face up to the fact she was vulnerable. No longer the self-sufficient island she'd always been. The pain of admitting out loud why Simon Brown couldn't be involved wasn't just because it was hurtful and a bruise to her ego – it was also because it was out of her jurisdiction. But if she wanted back-up, and she would need it, seeing as she was going it alone, she had to spill.

'Because,' she began, flinching as she took herself back into the pain, '…he's got a child already, a six-year-old. He's divorced and penniless. They were only going out a few months when she fell pregnant. She was terrified and considered anything other than marriage an abandonment.'

Em remembered how she had woken up the morning after the night before, expecting her head to bang from the whisky. But the only thing thumping out of control when she had turned to see Simon Brown facing her, sleeping beside her, had been her heart. Right now, as she sat with Letty, she could still taste the exhilaration of finding it hadn't been a dream.

There, in the half-light of her bedroom, she had watched him, admiring his steady even breathing and the perfect curve of his shoulder, the stillness of his eyelids and the rise and fall of his symmetrical lips; he had looked composed and peaceful. As if he had meant to be there. She'd had to go to the loo, so she'd sneaked out with her dressing gown not wanting to disturb him. Then she had begun to make coffee; she had wanted to take him a cup back into bed where she imagined they could've held onto the moment – and planned their next. But he had stirred while she was in the kitchen and walked in, wearing his unbuttoned shirt and black boxers.

'Hey,' he'd said, his smile matching the spring sunshine which was flooding the room, and he'd taken a seat at her breakfast bar. It had been the most natural thing in the world and she had known, she still did, that both of them felt no self-consciousness.

'American pancakes?' she'd asked. He'd opened his mouth to speak and together they'd both said 'with bacon and syrup'. She had basked in the reflection of her own happiness as they'd eaten. He had washed up, stacking plates and cutlery in the optimum drying position on the drainer, then he'd made more coffee. It had been too good to be true. And of course it had been. Because when the conversation turned to the rest of the day, when she had asked if he fancied going to a farmers' market, she had seen his face become tense. He had had to be somewhere. Em had felt the air cool as he had sighed and explained his circumstances with haunted, defeated eyes.

'He didn't want to be responsible for anything happening to her and the baby so he went with it. He didn't say he was "pinned down", he's far too decent to say that, but that's how it looks to me,' Em said. 'They both tried, he said, for the baby's sake, but they were unhappy. Eventually, they faced up to it that it had never been right. He let her stay in their house, which was his, because he didn't want the baby to suffer.'

Dipping his head towards the counter in her flat, Simon Brown had said he had accepted it, he took responsibility for it and he'd worked through it well enough to cope with the separation from his daughter, but he'd stopped right there. He had felt unable to move on from it. He had brightened when he'd talked of work; it had saved him, he'd said, and she had made him believe he could love again. But he'd said he was too frightened.

'He's been living with his mum ever since. So you can imagine how he'd receive my news,' Em said.

'But you can't not tell him.'

'He told me he'd never want any more children because he'd messed it up with his first. And if he did have another in a relationship then he'd feel so guilty that he wasn't able to offer both kids the same upbringing. So it was best not to get involved.' Em had spoken his reasoning word-for-word – it wasn't hard to remember because it had scorched her heart.

'Then the apologies came. For taking advantage, for not being upfront, and I had to stop him – I couldn't let him know how broken I felt. I told him it was okay. Plenty of people, plenty of friends, have sex once then get past it. It doesn't have to be any different for us. As far as he knows, I shrugged it off and waved a casual goodbye. He never saw me crying.'

Letty held up her hands, acknowledging the difficult odds. 'But, Em, love can conquer all. Surely?'

Em sniffed. 'Can it? The worse thing is he said if he was ever going to get together with someone it'd be me.'

'There, you see?' Letty said, desperate for a silver lining.

'No. He was softening the blow. He doesn't love me. That's all there is to it.'

Back at Frankie's...

Frankie

Frankie cleared her throat as the list shook in her trembling hands.

'So, I've called it, um, "Frankie Green's Sex Education" and then in brackets I've put "How Not To Be Boring In Bed",' she said more boldly than she felt, trying to put off the evil moment.

Floyd nodded encouragingly. 'Yes, good. I'm getting a sense of ownership from that. And it's always handy to make a note of your name should you forget it.'

'Shush!' she said. 'I won't do this if you're going to take the piss.'

'All right, all right,' he said, holding his hands up by way of apology, 'I'm sorry. Carry on.'

Frankie stared back at the sheet of paper to collect herself. Just treat it like an adult education class, she told herself. Some people learn a language, others do pottery – I'm signing up for lessons in love-making, that's all. 'As I was saying,' she said, 'I've made a list of ten things I need to do... that we need to do, um, would you mind closing your eyes or not looking at me because this is embarrassing.'

'Sure, no problem, in fact, why don't I sit under the table and you can pretend I'm not here?'

'Yes, good idea,' Frankie said, delighted.

'I was joking,' he said before sighing, heaving himself up and squeezing under the table, tucking in legs and arms like a spider playing hide-and-seek.

'Ready?' she asked as the sound of him shuffling about finally stopped.

'Fire away! By the way, you know this is quite ridiculous because we are going to have to touch one another at some point?' came a voice from below.

'Look, I just need a run-up, that's all,' she explained. 'Right, so here I go. Number one, I've called it Not The Missionary, and by that I mean I need some direction in positions other than lying flat on my back.'

His hand appeared out from beneath the table to ask a question.

'Yes?'

'Sorry. Can I just check something? Do you mean you've only ever done it like that? I'm not judging, I just need to clarify it so I know my starting point.'

Frankie was crestfallen. Even though she'd anticipated she'd feel like a freak and he was right to ask, it still stung. 'Well, that's the only position I am properly familiar with,' she said, utterly grateful she didn't have to look Floyd in the eye. It hadn't been such a bad idea to get him to sit under the table, see? 'We got together young. We tried a few things at the beginning, but then after ten years, you sort of fall into a pattern…'

'That's fine, not a problem,' Floyd said. 'Proceed.'

'Okay. Um, number two, that's the… er… sixty-nine,' she said quietly.

'What?' he said.

'The sixty-nine,' she repeated slightly louder.

'The sixty-nine?' he boomed. She flinched, worrying about her neighbours.

'Yes,' she said, 'thank you for making me feel even more mortified, Floyd.' She heard a snigger and was tempted to boot him when he produced both hands from below in an act of surrender. 'I, um, chose this because I found it very hard to co-ordinate everything while things were going on downstairs. Legs and lips and hands and tongues and… well, I just got all tangled up the time we tried it.'

'The time you tried it? As in once?'

'You're making me feel like a fridge, Floyd.'

'Sorry. Again. I'm just making sure, that's all. The soixante-neuf is like learning to drive.'

She felt a pang of gratitude. Which dissolved quickly as he made references to 'floppy gearsticks' and 'erect handbrakes'.

It was time to move on. But as she drew breath she realized it was like leaping out of the frying pan and into the fire. 'Number three, spanking. I've never done this. I can't really see how hitting someone or being hit would be pleasurable.'

'Righty-ho,' he said, 'it is a niche area. It's all about the spur of the moment, that one.'

'Number four, something risky. Somewhere where we might get caught. Although even thinking about that makes me scared.'

'Right.'

'Number five, dressing up. But not as a naughty nurse or schoolgirl because that makes me want to throw up. Something else, I'm not sure what exactly.'

'We'll find something,' he said, all businesslike.

Amazingly, Frankie was beginning to feel empowered getting this off her chest and she was almost enjoying herself. 'Number six, erotica. I don't mean watching porn, because I've accidentally clicked on some sites and I don't think I'll ever eat cucumber again. But perhaps lap-dancing?'

'Lap is not erotica. It's a bunch of office lads smirking over their stiffies. Leave it with me. Next?'

'Number seven, it's talking... dirty.'

'As in, "I can't believe how filthy the car is"?'

'Shut up! Number eight, um, orgasms because it didn't really happen... at all... and it was clearly my fault and I was obviously not doing it right.'

'Well, I happen to think the opposite – it's the man's job to make sure of it. And really, this shouldn't be a category by itself because hopefully we can approach it as we go.'

Frankie was stunned – it had never occurred to her that it was a joint concern. She'd thought it was her problem, not that she'd minded because it was all about that connection with Jason. But if there was a possibility every time, well, that would be nice.

'Number nine, sex toys. And I don't even want to talk about this, it's so frightening.'

'Oh, there's nothing to worry about. Vibrators, love eggs, you name it, I've done it. Although no strap-ons, right?'

'Strap-whats?'

'Forget it.' Then she heard him rubbing his hands as he said: 'So what's number ten? Is it something spectacular? Swinging from the chandeliers?'

'Not quite,' she said, pausing, because this was the one she was most scared of. That's why she'd left it until the end. 'It's the bondage thing,' she said softly. 'That was what Jason wanted to do the night he left. He had black handcuffs, and even now the thought of them makes me want to be sick. They were just so...

tacky. But it feels like I need to do it to get over it, and there must be other ways, if you know what I mean. Oh, God. Why did I not just agree to it? Then we'd still be together.'

'Hey,' Floyd said, 'don't go off on one. And that isn't true anyway,' he reminded her gently. 'Small steps,' he said. 'And whatever happens, we'll always stick to the lesson plan, always. No add-ons, no deviations – it will give us boundaries and it will keep things professional. We don't want either of us feeling things have got out of hand.' And then his hand was on her knee.

His warm touch did something to her body. There was a strength, a security even, flowing from him to her. Her worry seemed to drain away, and for the first time, she felt as though this arrangement was entirely possible. Maybe it was because she'd known him for so long – they already had an intimacy, a foundation on which to build.

Suddenly the pressure of his fingers changed. It was a subtle shift, setting off the hairs on the back of her neck, going from safe to… what was it? Sexy?

Her breathing changed, it felt shallow from the nerves of anticipation but deep with something physical, a sensation she hadn't felt in a long time. She shut her eyes and she was floating, swirling and rolling, as if she was underwater.

'AAARGH!'

'WHAT IS IT?' she shouted, jumping up, dancing around like she was on hot coals.

'I've got cramp in my leg, bloody bollocking cocking cramp, aaargh.'

He scrambled out from under the table and began hopping then clutching his limb, while Frankie flapped her hands with adrenalin.

Finally, he stopped moaning. 'Well, that was good timing,' he said, sheepishly, ruffling his hair, then coughing and fidgeting with his T-shirt. 'Sorry about that… I better, you know… shift it. If that's okay?'

'Yep, fine,' Frankie said, still in a daze. 'Hair. Tomorrow. Work, I mean, so, yes, I'll see you… soon, then.'

'Righty-ho,' he said, walking to the front door, followed by a suspicious Leonardo.

Frankie's heart began palpitating. She needed to process what had just happened and there was still the goodbye to come.

Would he go to kiss her or offer a hug? She sincerely hoped not now, the moment had passed, and if he did, she would most certainly die.

Instead, he crossed the threshold, turned back around and put out his hand. Frankie was so relieved at the inappropriately appropriate offering that she shook it like a rattle.

'Laters,' he said, offering an entirely unnecessary salute. 'I'll be in… er… touch.'

Good God! That prospect did nothing to settle her! Frankie shut the door and gave Leonardo a full-on wide-mouthed silent scream.

Thursday

Letty

'Right, everyone, ten press-ups, ten squats and ten burpees – NOW!'

Letitia automatically dropped to the floor and gave it her all. Usually she was pretty easy-going, but when it came to The Body Shop circuits class, she was hideously competitive. Not only did she want to show the men she was as good as them, but she wanted to thrash the other women. Particularly that skinny blonde in a pink Nike bra and tiny matching shorts at the front who was flirting so obviously with Lance. This was the problem with paying for a PT – you thought of them as yours, when in fact you were just one of a number. So when you got together for group sessions, you ended up fighting for his attention.

Letty pretended she was better than that and played it cool by hovering at the back. But who was she kidding? She'd spent half an hour beforehand shaving armpits and legs and doing her make-up and hair – not just for this but for later when Lance was her property. And she'd deliberately worn her halter-neck black crop top and trendy patterned leggings to show she meant business. She didn't want to look like a simpering fan when she was actually his lover. There was no need to try to catch his eye because she'd already hooked him. She pitied the blonde for being so transparent.

'Okay, good effort. Find a station and you've got forty-five seconds on each then move round clockwise. Go hard, guys, or go home!'

Letty picked the skipping ropes and began to jump in time to the high-energy music.

'Mind if I join you?' said the blonde.

Oh, Betty Swollocks, she thought, not her. Letty wanted to say 'go away, leave me alone, this isn't a social, it's serious exercise', but instead she nodded then focused on her reflection in the mirror so she got the message. But she didn't.

'Lance is so good, isn't he?' she purred, her voice completely unaffected by the physical effort.

Letty gave her a 'yeah' and carried on, watching her face begin to glow. This bloody foundation is supposed to be sweat-proof, she fumed, and I can feel a perspiration moustache forming.

'He's just so inspiring,' she continued, 'if it wasn't for him, I'd never have been able to do that triathlon at the weekend. He's just so giving.'

Giving? You can say that again, Letty thought, and then she began to wonder how giving he'd been with the blonde. This was worth pursuing, she realized, because if he was two-timing her, then she'd walk, no question. It might be a case of double standards seeing as he was married, but still.

'How long have you been with him?' Letty panted.

'Six months. His deep-thigh massage is out of this world.'

Letty felt a rage rising at the thought of him touching someone else. It wasn't as if she'd had to square the circle of him sleeping with his partner because he'd said they were in separate rooms and why would he lie to her – it wasn't something he was proud of. And she knew physical contact was part of his job. He'd told her that. To him, people's bodies were like the engine of a car. But his hands kneading the blonde's legs, well, how could he be professional in the face of perfection?

A whistle blew and the pair of them moved to the mats for sit-ups.

'How often do you see him?' Letty asked, keeping her eyes straight ahead to show she was not bothered.

'Three times a week, we have such a laugh. Have you just started with him?' she said, bobbing up and down effortlessly.

Letty seethed at the suggestion; her body didn't look like it had had six months of one-to-one instruction. She had the start of a six-pack, thank you very much!

'Same as you, but I've had a few injuries,' she lied, then she couldn't help herself. 'Lance says my hamstrings are the tightest he's ever felt – and that includes the southern hemisphere. I think I'm a special case. He's very attentive.' She added an imaginary 'so back off, bitch'.

The whistle went again and – shit – the next was a partnering up abs exercise in which you took it in turns to lie on your back, held on to the other person's ankles and raised your legs. Letty had no desire to stare up at the competition's privates.

'So sorry, I'll have to move on. My hammies aren't up to this.'

Thank God, she thought, moving on to the plank. But as she got down onto her front, she caught Lance walking over to the blonde – and oh no, he was only offering to be her partner. Peering from beneath her arm, she saw they had an easy way with one another. The intimacy as they touched and they way their bodies were positioned like something out of the Kama Sutra. He was laughing while she was in the full flow of a story. If they hadn't gone to bed then it was only a matter of time, judging by their blatant attraction. She had unwittingly thrown them together and she had no one to blame but herself.

Letty concentrated on her forearms which were wobbling from the strain of supporting her weight. What had she been thinking? If he was sleeping with her when he had a girlfriend and baby at home, what would be stopping him from lining up his next bird right in front of her? There was no point trying to moralize because he clearly didn't have any morals. And if you play with fire, you're going to get burnt, she thought, those were the rules. At the moment, she was slightly singed, nothing more than that, and she could escape without any long-lasting scars. She'd miss him but she'd put it down to experience and move on. She scrabbled around her head for the self-help mantras she kept on permanent stand-by and cited them to herself as the strain made her legs shake. *It was just sex, there was no relationship, the hurt is superficial. It was just sex, there was no relationship, the hurt is superficial.*

Two toots of the whistle, the first short and the second long, indicated it was time for a drinks break. She had to go. Now. Slip out and that would be that.

Letty picked up her towel and strolled casually to the water fountain, which was right next to the door to the changing rooms. She filled a plastic cup, downed it and then quickly disappeared.

Normally, she'd hang about until everyone was gone so she could be alone with Lance. But she wasted no time in opening her locker, grabbing her bag and heading for the exit. She was back to square one. Again. Destined to return home to nothing more than a pile of 'Sorry, we missed you' postcards, which were the product of late-night online drunk-clicking.

Just then, she felt a hand on her arm. Turning round, he was there, his eyes full of concern.

'You okay?' he asked, glancing behind him then giving her a kiss on the lips, which melted on her mouth. 'Where are you off to? I thought we were going back to yours?'

She wanted to erupt, but blowing her top would show she was jealous and she was better than that. Yet shrugging him off with a breezy 'let's just be friends' betrayed how she felt, and she knew she'd end up being eaten up by a bitter resentment. Instead, she chose honesty. To a point. 'I just don't want to get hurt, Lance,' she said, trying to back off. She needed to put some distance between them because being this close to him made her dizzy.

He held onto her, his eyes searching hers for an explanation. 'Have I done something wrong? You know how I feel about you. I—'

The door swung open, Letty leapt away from Lance as the blonde appeared. The timing was actually perfect or she would've been drawn in, unable to leave. It made her see things in a different light. Was this just infatuation on her part? And perhaps the girls had been right that he was only after one thing. That he'd played her all along. If he really loved her then he'd sort out his own mess first. It wasn't an ultimatum: it was for her survival.

'Come back to me when you've sorted things out. At home.'

Lance went to speak but the blonde was calling his name.

Letty couldn't bear to watch him leave her so she walked out of the gym and out of his life.

Monday Morning

Em

Em's phone buzzed on her way up to the meeting.
She squirmed when she read Letty's message:

> Have you thought any more about telling Simon? X

Only constantly, Em sighed, switching off her phone to make sure she wouldn't be side-tracked. Today she had banned herself from thinking about him because she needed to be sharp.

The manager's PA, Sly, had tipped her off that Mr Roberts was going to announce his retirement in the boardroom and had invited a select few to hear it first. She wanted the job – and she knew she deserved it. She'd run the place when he'd had his heart bypass operation, and done it very well too.

The certainty she felt about her career made her reflect then on the unpredictability she was inviting into her life with this baby. But now was not the time to dwell on it. She left her baggage at the door as she strode in. The first to arrive, as usual; time-keeping was one of her life tenets. Even when she was a check-out girl, she was the only one not rushing in late with a hangover on a Saturday morning.

The room was windowless and one of the fluorescent strip lights was flickering. That was bound to be a distraction, so she'd make sure she sat with her back to it. It was a tiny thing but details like this gave her an edge.

A booming voice called her name. 'Emerald!'

It was Mr Roberts. Old-school, greying and like a headmaster, there were no chummy chats with him. He liked boundaries and respect. That's why he was on his way out. The rumour was he'd jumped before he got pushed because he didn't match the modern management style. He was a bit of a dinosaur – not quite triassic as he was still returning good results. But he was certainly one of the last of his breed. Whilst she liked his forthright ways, she knew he was compromised by his distrust of technology and delegation. She went over and shook hands. 'Mr Roberts,' she said, waiting for him to speak because she'd learned he thought more of a person who could contain themselves rather than blather on to fill a silence.

He took out his comb and brushed his thinning hair back over his bald bit. 'The trolley boys have asked for sun cream,' he said, 'wouldn't have happened twenty years ago. That's health and safety for you.'

We have a duty to protect our staff, Em thought, but she'd never say that to him. Instead, she said: 'Well, I hope you've given them own brand rather than the expensive stuff.'

He laughed. She'd pitched it perfectly. 'Always thinking of the business, Emerald, you'll go far!'

That, she thought, is the plan.

A waft of perfume signalled Sly's arrival.

'Em, my darling, how are you?' she asked, peering over her half-crescent glasses, which sat between immaculate silver styled short hair and a sleek M&S trouser suit.

'Great, thanks. Any coffee coming? I'm gasping.'

'Chef is sending some from the cafe. Along with some biscuits,' she said, winking at Em as she busied away on the tablet she carried everywhere.

What Mr Roberts lacked in warmth, Sly made up for in spades, letting her chosen ones know she held them in high regard. And it was Sly who'd told her at the Christmas do that the boss would be recommending Em for his post when the time came. There'd be a shortlist, obviously, that's the way they had to do things, but she wasn't to worry.

'So, who else is coming to the meeting then?' Em asked, fishing for a heads-up.

'You'll see,' Sly said, welcoming Sally from the cafe who wheeled in a trolley of refreshments.

Whoever it was, Em wasn't worried – she knew this industry like the back of her hand. No one could come close to her.

Apart from Simon Brown... who walked in at that very moment.

A kaleidoscope of butterflies fluttered inside her as she saw his fresh face and boyish, twinkling eyes. Stop it, she told herself – there is nothing exciting or handsome about his looks. He is completely unremarkable to look at with his inquisitive chestnut brown eyes and short nondescript brown hair. But that made things worse! That meant he was perfect!

What on earth was he doing here anyway?

'So glad you could make it, Simon!' Mr Roberts said. 'You're a bit of a late entry to all of this – we're going through interesting times.'

Oh my word, Em realized, finally. She felt betrayed as it all clicked into place. He's in the running for the job after I trained him up. I never took him for a snake, Em thought.

She might be the best here in this branch and she might be more senior than Simon Brown but he was clearly a rising star. And she'd helped him on his way! The floor began to shake as the reality set in: he's here to steal my job. The man who makes my heart soar is swooping in to ruin everything, even more than he already has.

Smile, woman, she ordered herself, just as he noticed her.

'Em!' he said, beaming. 'Great to see you!'

Her inner Richter Scale went off the graph in the earthquake of emotion she felt. Disgust at his duplicitousness, revulsion at his cheek and, most terrible of all, complete enchantment at being in his company. She could only nod back or she feared she'd crumble all over the carpet.

Fortunately, just then Mr Roberts pulled a chair from under the table, indicating he was ready to start. Three more people, assorted deputies and heads, had entered the room but Em hadn't even seen them arrive, she was too distracted by his presence and the fact he was the competition. She took a gulp of coffee and waited just a moment to see where Simon Brown was going to sit and then picked the chair furthest away from him. The words 'I'm carrying your baby and you don't even know it' circled in her mind as she tried to fix her gaze on the manager.

'As you are all aware… retiring… awaiting confirmation of my leaving date… interview process will begin' was all she could take in as nausea crept up on her. How cruel nature was to inflict nervous sickness on top of morning sickness! Ginger biscuits, that's what she needed, her eyes scanning the plate to see if there were any. She reached out, grabbed two and began nibbling. But it was too late. Em could feel her palms going clammy as wooziness took hold. Now of all times, when she needed to be composed.

Out of the corner of her eyes, the light was flickering. She had to get out, she was going to be sick. So she stood up, apologizing to Mr Roberts as she supported herself with her hands on the table, explaining she felt unwell. Em heard voices, 'are you OK?' and 'she's awfully pale', then she felt her legs go. She collapsed on the floor and everything went black.

Something cold was soothing her banging forehead when she came to. There was a smell of damp paper towel mixed in with a familiar calming scent. Oh no, it was all coming back to her – it was Simon Brown's aftershave. She opened her eyes and two faces were peering at her. Sly and Simon Brown, who'd laid his suit jacket under her head. Their faces seemed to have the most enormous features, as though she was seeing them in the back of a spoon. She had dreamed of being close to him again – why did it have to be when she was splayed out and helpless?

'The ambulance is on its way,' Sly said, mopping her brow, 'you fainted, got quite a bang to the head on the table as you went down. There's a bit of blood but you're okay, darling, we're here.'

'I'll go with her,' Simon Brown said to Sly as Em announced she was fine, tried to get up and got as far as lifting her neck before a bolt of pain shot through her temples. Brilliant, this is truly brilliant, she thought to herself, feeling completely humiliated.

'No running off now, an ambulance is coming,' Sly said.

'Is that really necessary?' Em groaned.

'Health and safety, health and safety,' Simon Brown said, smiling, which made her tummy flip all over again.

Honestly, she thought, disgusted at her body's betrayal by reacting like that when she was in no fit state.

'I'm going to be sick,' she said, which saw Sly fly off for a metal bin and return just in time. This just can't get any worse, Em thought, as she wiped her mouth on the wet paper towel.

Two pairs of boots appeared by her head as Simon Brown and Sly moved back to allow the paramedics some space.

'My name's Lucy,' two feet declared. 'Can you tell me yours?'

'Emera— Em. I'm fine, I just felt dizzy.'

'Well, you've had a bump to the head and it'd be best all round if you come with us so we can get you checked out.'

'Really. There's no need. I just need a lie down.' In a dark room. After a cold shower. Miles away from Simon Brown.

'You were unconscious, you feel sleepy and you've vomited. We're on our way back to the hospital so we'll take you,' Lucy insisted as her cohort nodded and helped her up.

There was no point protesting, Em knew, and so she stepped forward but her legs wobbled. Before she could complain, Simon Brown bent down and picked her up, one arm cradling her head and the other under her knees. As he walked towards the door, he looked down at her and said: 'Sorry, Whitney. Kevin Costner wasn't available so you'll have to do with me instead.'

Lying there floppy, on the edge of unconsciousness, with her face against his chest, she realized all those times when she'd begged a higher being to answer her wish that he'd turn up and carry her off to bed, that she should've specified 'not a hospital trolley'.

Later

Letitia

'So, what are you having?' Ross 'The Boss' Gittings said as they waited at the bar. He was smaller than Letty but she'd never really noticed: he was one of those charismatic types who seemed larger than life. Or at least his 5 foot 5 inches.

'Vodka slimline tonic, please,' Letty said, knowing a large glass of wine on an empty stomach would turn her into a howling drunk within five minutes which was not the image she wanted to project. 'Shall I get a table?'

'There's one at the back,' he said, pointing with his phone. 'It's nice and private.' Great, she thought, all the better for not being disturbed, so I can dazzle him with my idea. This diversion was exactly what she needed after the inevitable split with Lance last night.

He hadn't contacted her last night nor today. It was clearly over – it was a good job she hadn't fallen for him properly, she kept telling herself when tears forced her into the ladies'. But she wanted to prove herself in her job if she couldn't do it in her love life. That was the trigger she needed to ask Ross for five minutes after work. He'd promised her 'all the time in the world after work', provided, he'd insisted, he'd get the drinks in.

Letty was thrilled – she was finally being treated like one of the boys: the suits disappeared after hours all the time to talk deals and contracts over a pint. Now it was her turn! And she looked the part in a very tailored cream suit jacket and pencil skirt teamed with a sheer black armless pussy-bow shirt and patent spikes.

They'd gone over the road from their swanky city centre office to The Vine, a wine bar where Ross held fundraisers for a children's hospice. He was so well-connected, he'd have the place heaving with at least one celeb guest such as a footballer or rugby player, which guaranteed coverage in the local press. And Letty had plans to increase his exposure – as well as her own talents. To be able to achieve at work would help her get over Lance and find some much-needed self-worth.

'So, how's things?' he asked as he got to the table with their drinks. He smiled as he undid the top button of his crisp white shirt and loosened his expensive purple tie.

'Great, thanks,' she said, answering his cheers with a clink of her glass. 'Christ, this is strong!' she said, holding her throat as the vodka burned her tonsils.

'You said a double, didn't you?' he grinned, blue eyes winking as he took a long swig of his lager.

'I so didn't! I need my head straight!'

'Boring!' he said, running his hands over his bronzed head, which he shaved to hide the fact he was balding. 'Work's over.'

'Well, it isn't for me,' she said, laughing. 'That's what I wanted to talk to you about.'

'Oh, go on then,' he said with a fake huff. 'I was hoping you wanted a drink because of my rapier wit and good looks. Confess your undying love, that sort of thing!'

Inside, Letty chalked up his comment as inappropriate – he'd never have said that to a male employee. Then again, maybe it was just a bad attempt at a joke. He was late forties, divorced and spent all of his time in the company of blokes: perhaps this was just the way it was.

'I think we, you, us, as in Gittings PR, needs a social media presence. As in Facebook, Twitter, Instagram, that kind of thing.' Ross raised his eyebrows, indicating she could continue. 'I'd like to volunteer to do it. I'm on top of my work, and I'm not saying I need more to do but I'd really like the chance to show what I'm made of. Develop this myself, push our brand, make us look up-to-date with hashtags and campaigns and... I'll show you now.'

She pulled her work tablet out of her bag and began to scroll through the presentation – tweaked only slightly by Em, to Letty's joy – which indicated how interaction with customers online made a business look human. There was a list with examples of successful corporate accounts and it also gave an opportunity to show the company's moral compass with its charitable work.

'Do you know what,' Ross said, 'that is a very interesting idea. I'm impressed. Email it to me and to Nick and we'll have a look.'

Nick was his deputy: a new arrival from a rival agency who

appeared to be a decent guy.

'Done!' she said, forwarding the presentation on her phone with a tap of her fingers. She really was buzzing at how well he'd received her idea: this feeling was dynamite when it came to her confidence. So she went on. 'You know, I'd really like the chance to do more… if there are any openings coming up, say, if you were looking for a new account executive? Not that I'm unhappy with what I do. I'm just really keen to get on.'

That, and earn some more money. Because she was on her last credit card – she owed around £3,000 which sent her into a panic every time she thought of it.

'I'll bear it in mind,' he said.

'Great! And perhaps you could revisit my application for the course that I want to do? It really would benefit the company,' she said, draining her drink. 'Oops, that went down quickly!'

'Yes, I've heard that about you,' Ross said, deadpan. 'Fancy a go?'

Letty stopped, that was two inappropriate comments now. 'What?' she asked, feeling her excitement drain away and replaced by anger as he showed how low she was in his regard.

Quick as a flash, he was holding up his hands and apologizing. 'Sorry! It was just a joke!'

But she wasn't laughing. Letty considered whether it was worth telling him he had made her feel uncomfortable. If he'd been a random slimebollock in the pub, she'd have given him what for. So what was the difference? He was her boss, that's what, with power over her. Yet if she made it clear now then he would see she meant business: that she wanted to progress, that she wasn't a walkover. And Christ, after Lance, she felt nothing but.

Terrified but needing to show she had a backbone after all, Letty went for it. 'Ross, I'm all for a bit of banter but not that, all right?'

'I don't know what you mean,' he said, his eyes darting around the bar.

'The innuendo. It's not on. Let's keep it professional.'

He blew out his cheeks and rubbed an eye: classic signs of discomfort after being rumbled. And she was relieved too because she couldn't do without her job. She was paid well above her level, was included in bonuses and she got six weeks' holiday.

Feeling pleased as punch for speaking out, Letty stuck out a firm hand to show she was prepared to put it behind them.

For a moment, he sized her up, looking from her hand to her face. Then he shook her palm and she couldn't believe she'd done it!

She hid her smile, instead channelling her best Dragons' Den Deborah Meaden impression, nodding with gravity before gathering her mac and bag and getting out of there before she did a victory wiggle on the pavement.

All the way home, she imagined she was Beyoncé, doing it for all the ladies who'd been taken for fools. By the time she got home, she was the star of a blockbuster and head of her own multi-national empire. Well, she could dream.

The reality was that she'd managed to wrestle back her professionalism from Ross.

Now this was a change for good, she thought, kicking off her heels into the hall. What a difference twenty-four-hours made: last night she'd snotted mascara all over her pillow because she was a victim. But now, she was on top. He could obviously see that she had inner steel: forget Beyoncé, she was actually Madonna in a metal bra.

It was the most empowering thing she'd ever done. Letitia Cox was no pushover!

If it had been that easy to sort him out, then she could take control elsewhere too. Get Ross to sign off the PR qualification, sort out her finances and never fall for a waster ever again.

Letty wanted to celebrate. She picked up her phone and wondered who to call first.

But neither Em nor Frankie picked up. This was the downside of being single, not having someone special to share things with.

Hey-ho. She'd just have to have a party herself with some vino.

She wasn't going to let anything spoil the start of her new life.

The Next Day...

Em

What if this was a sign? Em wondered as the orderly showed her to the waiting room. That fainting yesterday and spending the night in the University Hospital of Wales was a warning of trouble ahead. She self-consciously pulled her suit jacket tighter over her draughty gown as she pondered it: what if she wasn't doing the right thing having the baby?

Then again, it could all be out of her hands, she thought, finding a seat beneath a torn magazine. The nurse had said on her evening rounds that while there had been no bleeding, only a scan in the morning would show if the baby was unharmed. Getting to this point had been the most horrific wait: she'd hardly slept, her mind going over everything.

She had come to at 9pm last night, wondering a) why there were lots of people in her bedroom and b) why she was attached to a drip. When she realized she was in a ward, she saw a mental slideshow of Alice in Wonderland snapshots of her collapse: being carried through the supermarket, talking to Simon Brown in the ambulance about her first dog Einstein, having a light shined in her eyes and then a blankness.

It turned out she'd suffered concussion plus dehydration, brought on by hormones which could induce fainting. She'd apparently managed to tell the doctor she was pregnant just before she passed out. The lady in the bed next to her had said her 'lovely friend' – Simon Brown – had sat with her all evening. He'd left a card for her, some kind of humorous thing which she didn't get. Already having committed the words to her memory, she read through them again in her mind.

To Emerald (I never knew that was your proper name!), it said in his neat and contained handwriting, *I stayed as long as I could before they chucked me out. I hope you're feeling better. Work asked me to tell you to take as long as you need. Make sure you do – I'll send you a box set to watch. You told me not to contact anyone, in fact you were quite adamant about it, so I didn't.*

Hey, great news about the baby, by the way! Your fella's a lucky chap. Lovely to see you, although sorry was in these circumstances. Catch you later, Kevin Costner x

There in that card had been everything she liked about him – he was considerate, gentle, thorough, discreet, amusing and concise. But what would he think of her now? That she'd wasted no time meeting someone else, that he meant nothing to her. It was such a mess – he knew about the baby but, really, he knew nothing at all.

Em blew out of her cheeks, full of despair at being signed off for a week when she needed to be on top form at work. Would this wreck her chances of promotion? She knew it shouldn't but not everyone was as objective as they should be. And if she was going to be a single parent then being fit for the job, keeping her income going, was vital. Not that either mattered to her at this moment, she realized, because all she cared about now was finding out about the baby. If her fears were confirmed, the fears which had eaten away at her in the longest, darkest hours of the night, then she wouldn't even get the chance to be a mother. Tears welled up again – she had never cried as much in her whole life than in the last twelve hours.

'Emerald Good-Fellow, please,' said a woman in green scrubs whose outfit complemented the grotesque pea-coloured walls.

'You by yourself, love?' she said, guiding her into a room and shutting the door.

Em nodded. She'd had no battery left on her phone to call anyone last night. But it didn't matter – Mum and Dad were away at some festival in Eastern Europe, Floyd was at his company's London HQ, the girls would only fuss. And the father, well the less said about him the better. Other people would only complicate things.

'Well, you're with me. I'm Bethan. The sonographer. Take off your jacket, hop up on the bed, lift your top and brace yourself because the gel is cold.'

How could there be life in there? Em wondered as the gel plopped out icily onto her belly. To the naked eye, there was no way of telling she was pregnant. Women like me, she thought, we are a whole secret army, hiding a secret, the biggest there could be, before we become visibly expectant. Yet to each of us, our secret is our everything: how could people not see it in the glow of our eyes and in the ridges of our fingertips? But there was also a wonder, a physical squeeze, of having that knowledge to yourself before it it became public property. And it could all be taken away from her, Em thought, with dread in the dimly-lit room.

Within seconds, the gel was rolled warm by a probe, piece of ultrasonic equipment which looked like a microphone.

She shut her eyes and waited, fearing the crackling would go on and on.

'It takes a while to get ready, don't worry,' the sonographer said. 'And the lights aren't broken, we just need it darker than normal so we can see the monitor more clearly.'

Her words were meant to be reassuring but until Em knew everything was okay then nothing could calm her nerves. Suddenly, out of nowhere came a very loud and very fast repetitive thud. The sound seemed to wrap itself around her, fill her ears and her heart. The baby! It was alive.

Bethan caught her open-mouthed gaze and smiled. 'If you look at the screen then you'll see baby any second…'

Em turned her head towards the monitor.

'…now! There! Safe as houses. And that's a lovely strong pulse.'

A tiny thing was bouncing around on the screen. Even though it was a grainy image, Em could make out a skull and some little blobs for arms and legs. How was this even possible? That there was a person jigging about inside of her yet she couldn't feel a thing.

'I'd say eleven weeks, eleven plus one actually… and, I'm just double-double-checking everything, but baby is absolutely fine. So… congratulations!'

Em was so overwhelmed she began spouting from her Googling. 'At eleven weeks, it measures four centimetres long. The bones of the face are formed now. The eyelids are closed, and won't open for a few months yet. The earbuds look more like ears as they grow,' she said, as tears rolled down her cheeks. 'It is no longer an embryo but a foetus,' she said, mopping her belly with a tissue and getting off the bed. 'The major organs are formed and its tail has gone.'

'Wow, you have been reading up!' the sonographer said. 'Baby must have been very much wanted.'

'Actually, it wasn't,' she said, floating with happiness knowing now she wanted this baby more than anything, that she'd bring Frankie up to speed and make a start on feathering her nest, 'but it is now.'

Thursday Night: Lesson One

Frankie

'Frankie? Where are you?' Floyd said out of the darkness.

There was a patting which she presumed was him searching for her on the bed with his hands.

'I'm just making sure no light can get in,' she said, scanning the room for the slightest chink. For about the millionth time in her rigorous preparation, which she wasn't about to mention. It wasn't just for her own benefit – she didn't want Leonardo to creep in and see anything either.

'But it's like the dark side of the moon in here!' he said. She could hear the humour in his voice, but this was important.

'I'm just making sure. The last thing I want is for the blanket on the rail to drop off.'

'Good point. Then there would only be a pair of thick curtains plus a pulled-down blind to protect you from daylight. This might be a good time to tell me if you're a vampire.'

He was right. She was being a bit obsessive. But she couldn't help it. The darkness was a cover for her inexperience; if she couldn't make him out, then he wouldn't notice her face of fear or her pathetic boobs or her whatsit, which by now she was convinced was abnormal. 'I don't want you to see me, that's all.'

She heard a deep sigh from the direction of the mattress, which she approached millimetre by millimetre so she didn't trip up. What a great start that would be if she fell face-first on his thing.

'Don't roll your eyes at me!' she said. 'Are you rolling your eyes at me?'

'Jesus Christ, are you wearing night-vision goggles or something? This reminds me of the Blair Witch Project.'

If she wasn't in this situation, she would have laughed at that, she thought. But she was and it was so not funny. Far from it, the complete opposite in fact. It had been from his arrival. A warm-up cuppa, as he'd put it, didn't calm her down at all. He seemed to be taking it all in his stride, which was lucky, because if he hadn't said they should drink it upstairs 'to get in the mood' then they'd still be chatting in the kitchen. Feeling around for the duvet, she finally found it and sat on the edge, at the opposite end to Floyd. 'I'm on the bed now,' she announced, staring blindly into the black.

'Excellent. That's a good start. What with both of us being on the bed.'

'I'd really appreciate it if you were a bit more understanding.'

'Sorry. I'm just trying to put you at ease.'

'Oh, I see. Right. Okay.'

'So, how do you want to do this then? Because we can just go at your speed or I can start things or whatever…'

This was the bit she'd been dreading. The seconds before they actually touched. It was the most excruciating, bum-clenching, toe-curlingly awkward moment of her entire life. Her heart was going like the clappers and she had sat on her hands to stop them trembling. 'Um, I dunno. Oh God. Well, I've got three positions in my head and I don't know whether to tell you what they are or to just get on with it.'

'It's up to you.'

Frankie gulped. 'Right, well, I'll just do them then.'

'Okeydokes.'

There was a silence. She could hear his breathing and then the muted sound of the duvet rustling.

'Can I just ask a question, Floyd?'

'Sure!'

'When shall we take our clothes off?'

She heard air shoot out of his nostrils in three bursts.

'Are you laughing at me?'

'Yes,' he said, 'totally. I thought we could take our clothes off after we've had sex.'

Thank God he couldn't see her blush. This was utterly mortifying. She cleared her throat and tried to pull herself together. 'Okay, okay, I know I'm being ridiculous,' she said, taking a deep breath, 'I'm sorry. Right, I'm, er, coming over now.'

Frankie edged towards him, reciting in her head the order of her moves: on top, turn around then on all fours. Sit, twist, bend. That's all she had to remember. Her fingers slowly slid across the cover as she sought him out. She was getting closer, she could sense him, so she began to grope the air. She came into contact with something wet and immediately recoiled.

'Ow!' he said. 'You've just poked me in the eye!'

'Oh, shingles, sorry, are you okay?' she whispered. 'Oh God, this isn't going very well.' She stood up and fumbled blindly over to the wall and switched on the light. Leonardo was sat absolutely still like an Old Bailey judge on her dressing table – oh no, he'd witnessed the whole shambles.

'Argh!' Floyd shouted, covering his eyes. 'You could've warned me you were so ugly.'

Frankie had had enough. 'Look, the point of this is that you teach me. There doesn't seem to be much of that going on. All you do is crack jokes.'

Floyd pulled an offended face then turned his mouth down as he scratched his beard. 'Do you know something? You're absolutely right. I'm not being very instructive, am I?'

He thought for a minute while Frankie crossed her arms, waiting for him to take charge. And then an idea came to him. He leapt up, pointed both forefingers at her and announced: 'By jove, I've got it!'

'Finally!' she said, irritably tapping her right foot. Because she was approaching the point of throwing in the towel.

'So the plan is this: you are freaking out about this, maybe we don't have to actually have the sex? How about we perform these positions with our clothes on – just think of it as a game of Twister.'

Frankie couldn't believe the relief that overcame her at this apparent solution. She beamed and nodded frantically: what a brilliant approach! It was entirely educational and she didn't have to strip off.

'Perfect!' she said, clapping her hands.

'Oh. Right. No offence taken,' Floyd said, looking disappointed.

Meanwhile...

Letty

What a bonkers week it's been, Letty thought, as she left work and made a beeline for some therapy of the retail kind. Click-clacking her way through town to Cardiff's mammoth St David's shopping centre, she needed a hit to help her get to grips with it.

For, everything she'd known about her friends and herself had been turned on its head in a matter of days.

Take Em, who was the queen of self-control and hard work. Now she was not only up the duff, but on bed-rest.

Then there was Frankie: the only woman in the world who could make the Virgin Mary blush had got herself a sex teacher.

And as for Letty, well, she'd gone from being a mistress to a sister doing it for herself. All of it, it was so unlikely. Things were changing and she swung from feeling empowered to uncertain.

Nothing more had been said by Ross at work about his behaviour: he was acting as normal, yet he still hadn't signed off her day-release course. And Lance, well, what a surprise, he'd dropped her like he apparently dropped his flies. She knew because she'd checked every possible social media channel he was on – from his Facebook page to his Instagram work-out shots – and their ever-so-chummy updates showed he was alive and well. He was deliberately not contacting her.

She needed a fix of happiness: only shoes could do that.

And she knew exactly which ones – a pair of sandals on sale at Vivienne Westwood.

As she entered the resplendent store, beneath its regal golden sign, Letty felt majestic by association. She went straight to a punky assistant, in bondage trousers of course, and asked to try on her heart's desire.

A minute later and she was on the catwalk of the polished wooden floor, parading up and down, feeling completely kick-arse. The size fives were sublime: from the front, four brass-tone buckles on black calf leather fastening straps exposed just enough skin and toe. From behind, the flash of the signature orb on each twelve-centimetre heel.

Versatile, they were businesslike by day but gave a hint of dominatrix by night. It was as if these shoes had been made for her. Timeless. A work of flaming art. The mark of a new start.

And when they did all of that, they were a snip at £275, reduced from £550. She needed them: if she was going to progress in work and love then she had to project the person she was going to be. Strong, self-assured and confident.

Handing over her credit card, the one which hadn't maxed out, she fought the urge to pay her respects with a curtsey to the overhanging pink neon sign which spelled out Vivienne Westwood's name.

The buzz of the buy and its life-changing meaning lasted all the way home on the number twenty-five bus, right up to her doorstep. Her excited fingers fumbled with the keys, which fell from her hand. She leant down to retrieve them; she was going to get changed, go for a run and then have a healthy tea.

At least she was until she saw two black swooshy trainers walk up behind her.

And then all of her intentions and projections dropped like a stage curtain because it was Lance. The person she had no feelings for whatsoever. In opposite land. Suddenly, the ache she'd anaesthetized returned harder and deeper than before: telling yourself you were doing the right thing was like two paracetamol every four hours. It only masked how much she missed him.

Letty got up and looked around, her heart reaching towards him, trying to claw back her happy.

'I've done it,' he said, simply. 'We can be together.'

She tried to take it in: he was smiling and he had a holdall with him.

'Thought I could stay over, if that's okay?'

She felt her gob drop and her bottom lip quiver and she was only bloody speechless. She hadn't actually believed he'd do it. He wasn't serious about her. That's how she'd dealt with losing him. Except he bloody well was. Now it was all topsy-turvy because apparently he was handing to her what she'd always wanted.

'Letty?' he said, his face becoming anxious. 'Say something?

Please?'

A huge guffaw, out of shock and disbelief, came from inside her. 'You better come in then,' she said, still reeling, opening the front door, through the hall, then her door, not daring to look in case he wasn't following her.

But he was there and they both had wet eyes and then their mouths were on each other and they kissed their way to her bedroom, where the dam holding back her emotions broke.

Dreamlike, they were making love, as far from sex as possible.

Afterwards, spooning naked, feeling his breath on her neck, hearing him say he'd never been happier. That Helen had agreed it wasn't working. How he loved Letty. And she finally confessed she felt the same.

In the twilight, she savoured the truth that they could remain together when they'd have parted before. But she held on tight, not wanting to take any chances, not wanting to break the spell.

Finally, it had happened, she thought, only just allowing herself to conceive it. She'd found him: her Mr Too Bloody Right.

Back At Frankie's...

Frankie

Why hadn't they thought of this before? It's genius! Frankie mused as she tightened her ponytail and adjusted the waistband of her jeans to prepare for her first practical. She was excited rather than nervous; the same feeling she'd felt at the start of college when she sat in the lecture room with a new pen and pad, poised to take down everything the tutor said. That's how she had to think of this, that's all it was! But just in case, she'd shooed out Leonardo and shut the door.

Floyd cleared his throat to announce he was ready to begin. 'Welcome students, er, student, to the School of Sex Education,' he said in a deep posh voice.

She beamed to show she was paying attention.

'Your time here is for your benefit,' he said gravely, 'so no pricking about, you at the back!'

She looked over her shoulder and tutted at an imaginary pupil – she was enjoying this game!

'In this classroom you will learn a set of skills which will equip you to go out into the world... and win back your man.'

Frankie applauded and waited for his words of wisdom.

'Now, let us begin!' he boomed. Then he inhaled deeply and roared his exhale before huffing on his specs and giving them a wipe on his T-shirt. Popping them back on, he said: 'So, assume we've done the foreplay bit, snog snog, grope grope, etcetera, what's the first position on your list?'

'Me on top, sat up,' Frankie said, relishing the lack of pressure.

'Okay, a nice easy one to start with,' he said, lying down on his back on the bed. 'You need to kneel with your legs either side of me and sit on my... er, here,' he said as she manoeuvred herself square on his groin.

This is absolutely fine! Frankie remarked to herself, getting comfy with a wiggle. She could feel the buttons of his fly and a warmth from his body and maybe there was a tiny bulge but she put it down to excitement.

'This feels like we're about to play mercy!' she said, having a great time, pleased as punch she was with Floyd who was so cool and funny. 'You know, we hold hands and you try to throw me off and I try to get your arms back by your head!'

'Yes!' he hooted, before adding sternly, 'If we were seven years old, that is.'

Oh, she thought, her bubble burst.

'But full marks for enthusiasm,' he said, seeing her face and trying to cushion the blow. 'And we'll cover the adult version of mercy later on in the course,' he said, which made her worry. That's not what she'd meant at all.

Sit up and think of England, she told herself trying to find her previous state of mind.

'Now before we continue, remember this is about you being in control – not the man – you. So think about tempo and touch. You can go as fast or as slow as you like, and you're in charge of where you want the man to put his hands.'

'Right.'

So she reached for his hands, which were warm and relaxed, and put them on her hips, looking up to check this was okay by him.

'Yes, good. So start off by rocking your hips backwards and forwards,' he said.

Shy now she actually had to move, she began to gently to-and-fro. 'Is this right?' she asked.

'Good rhythm, yes, but push deeper and I'll move with you so it's authentic… now don't forget while you're doing that, you can touch the man's chest, perhaps position his hands to your upstairs kneecaps—'

'My what?' she said, stopping dead.

'Sorry, technical term for boobs, you'll pick up the jargon as we go along. Don't stop,' he said.

'Okay, I'll try the… upstairs kneecaps bit.'

She placed his hands a few inches from her body and he outstretched his fingers to resemble two spiders before doing a comedy breast squeeze.

'I don't actually do this action when I'm having a fondle, just so you know,' he clarified.

'No, of course,' she said, accidentally knocking into his palms as she rocked.

'Sorry,' they said in unison, both looking elsewhere in embarrassment.

'Now if you want to get the man gagging for it, you could decelerate. Yep, like that. Really push down on him, go-od, put your weight on his arms so that your boobs are in his face but he can't touch. Excellent, well done, and I like it when the woman lifts her chin so she looks like she's really getting lost in it. It's quite voyeuristic. Oh, yes, you're doing very well,' he said, closing his eyes, 'very well indeed.'

This is brilliant, Frankie thought. She had a sweat on now too – this was quite a work-out! And, quite unexpectedly, she had started to feel a bit oo-er too. Back and forth, back and forth, she was really getting into the swing of it! She hadn't done this with Jason because she'd been too worried that naked, her boobs would look droopy from this angle.

'Right, I think you've mastered that. What's next?' Floyd said out of the blue. Frankie eagerly swivelled herself around so she was sitting on Floyd facing his feet. 'Hmm, you could do that a bit more seductively. Think Sharon Stone, lift a leg over slowly then let the chap have a good eyeful of your doo-daa as you turn.'

'Good point,' Frankie said over her shoulder, committing it to memory and thinking what a good teacher he was. 'And could I lean forwards, hold onto his thighs like this?'

'Yes, excellent,' he said, holding on to her hips.

Her confidence soared then, helped by no awkward eye contact. 'And how about if I lift my arms and put my hands in my hair and arch my back like this? Does that work?'

'Ye-es,' said Floyd, his voice sounding different, more hoarse. 'Eeee-xcellent.'

She felt a lump in his jeans, probably from his pants bunching, she thought. 'Right, shall we do the next one?' she said to his wriggling toes, which were covered by what could only be Secret Santa socks because they declared 'I'm Too Sexy For My Socks'.

'Uhhh,' he replied.

'Floyd?'

'What? Yes. Good. Sorry. Go for it,' he said in a strange voice. Perhaps she was hurting him? Oh no, she thought, perhaps she was too heavy. He wasn't muscly like Jason was, he was leaner and longer. So she pushed herself off and got on all fours with her backside in his face.

'I'm ready,' she said.

'Actually, I think we've covered enough for today,' Floyd said quickly.

'But we were meant to do three positions,' Frankie said, confused. 'We've only done two.'

'Yes but thinking about it, the third one, doggy...er...style, is completely pointless for you as the man has to do the work so you wouldn't learn anything. Nothing. Nada. Zilch,' he said, with growing authority. Then he coughed. 'As it happens, two positions were plenty. Well done, lovely to see you, keep in touch.'

Frankie hung her head then, mortified that she had made such a fool of herself. She was obviously rubbish. That's what he meant, that's why he wanted to stop. She got back onto her haunches then turned around, hugging her knees at the farthest end of the bed. It was all so disappointing, she seemed to be doing okay and then something changed.

She sneaked a peek at him and saw him fussing around with his trousers. He looked up then through steamed-up specs and briefly caught her eye before squeezing his nose with his thumb and forefinger.

'I'm sorry,' she said, studying her nails, wondering specifically what she'd done to halt the proceedings. 'Was I... did I hurt you?' she asked, cautiously flicking her eyes to his face and back to her hand again.

'Not quite,' Floyd said, looking sheepish, his groin squirming.

Frankie should've known – he was trying to tell her she really was beyond hope. 'It's all right, you can say it. You've changed your mind, you don't want to do this anymore,' she said.

'What? No! If it was a game of football, I'd say it started well, lost its shape in the middle, then we salvaged a point at the end. You can't argue with that for the first game of the season.'

But it didn't feel like that to Frankie. 'I'm probably being really thick but I don't really understand.'

Floyd took a breath, held it then groaned. His body sank and he held out his palms. 'Look, it's nothing you did. Well, actually, it was everything you did. It's me, not you.'

'Right...' she said, shaking her head because he was

contradicting himself – she was even more puzzled.

He sighed and then used both forefingers to point at his nether regions.

'I'm sorry, you're going to have to spell it out because I...' she said, as it dawned on her. That big lump in his trousers, it wasn't from his pants at all! And she'd been the cause of it! Which meant she wasn't as crap as she'd thought. A smile came to her lips, which she then tried to hide because she didn't want him to think she was laughing at him.

'Yes, yes, go on, mock me. I got a boner. A stonker. A stiffy,' he said, blushing, 'I am but a weak man. Have a good old LOL at my expense.'

Frankie composed herself hurriedly and thought of something sad like Leonardo in that plastic white collar he'd had to wear after he was done.

'What can I say, Frankie?' he said, shrugging. 'It was purely biological. Just a physiological reaction arising from stimulation which leads to the relaxing of the corpora cavernosa and their arteries which bring blood into them to dilate and the veins leading out expanding. In layman's terms, literally a rush of blood into the wotsit.'

'Yes, of course,' she agreed, nodding vigorously, chastising herself for even thinking there was anything more to it. 'Equivalent to, say, a shiver when it's cold.'

'Exactly. Except it's quite painful because it's taking ages to go down. I've been thinking "dead puppies" for the last minute or so. Anyway, I suppose it's one of the perils of the job,' he said frowning. Then he rubbed his hands together and announced the lesson was over. Next week, he said, the sixty-nine might be a bit trickier. 'You could do it on a banana while sitting on the washing machine while it's spinning but that's a bit *It's A Knockout*. We might have to consider actually doing it. In the flesh.' He looked right at her, his eyes unreadable.

'Can't we wear swimming costumes?' Frankie said, desperate for a solution because the thought of topping and tailing gave her a serious case of the willies. Which was just what she didn't want.

He laughed. 'It's a thought,' he said, scratching his beard. 'A stupid one, I'm afraid. I just can't see a way round it.'

'But you could get some Speedos?' she pleaded, distressed by the thought of being starkers. After all, the reason it had worked today had been because they'd been clothed.

'There are reasons why I can't wear them. Personal reasons. I won't go into it, but let's just say I had a bad experience in them once.'

Frankie waved her arms – she didn't want to know. She got up from the bed and asked if he wanted tea and biscuits. 'We can talk Em's baby, which is the unlikeliest but most deeply touching thing I think I've ever heard.'

'You know, you could be right,' he said, beaming, with his hands still over his crotch.

As she left the room, she looked back to see him jabbing his finger at his bulge.

'You've let me down,' he said to his crotch, 'but worse, you've let yourself down.'

Saturday Morning

Em

'Afternoon!' Floyd said, winking at Em as she yawned her way into the kitchen.

'You sound like Mum,' she said, almost zombie-walking to the coffee maker then sitting down and helping herself to Floyd's breakfast at the table where he was tapping away on his laptop. She was still feeling worn out from her collapse, which annoyed her, having never taken a day off sick in her life.

'Except Mum would've made roasted flaxseed toast with wild bee shit honey,' he said, pretending to slap her hand. 'Not jam on white value-brand bread.'

'You do know this is the first time I've ever slept in later than you in the twenty-seven point three weeks you've been living here?' she said. 'And I have got a good excuse.'

'Indeed, woman with child, you have,' he said, 'and how are you feeling? Still yakking up every five minutes?'

She gave him a withering look.

He immediately backtracked. 'Shit, yes, sorry, I forgot. Far too soon for jokes. I'm a complete bellend. Hey, by the way, I've been reading up on babies and apparently they can hear through the womb, so I thought I could play some guitar to it, you know, so it gets to know me. I can be his pretend dad if this Simon isn't, you know, around.' He was trying to make it up to her after his crass jokes. The sweetheart.

Since the hospital, it was like a switch had been flicked in Em. To think now she was embracing this unfamiliar turmoil in her life. It would've been so easy to walk into a clinic and then walk out, problem solved. Nobody would've known. Yet the scan had tapped into something even stronger inside; that of maternal instinct. And while she could blame someone or something else for this change in her life, ultimately she realized no one else – bar Simon Brown – was responsible; it had been of her own doing. If he wasn't to be involved she simply had to do her best. Just as she had with work.

The only spoiler was that she was going to have to kick Floyd out because there'd be no room for him. She started thinking of ways to broach the matter. But Floyd hadn't finished.

'You're awesome, you know. Like, obviously this isn't what you've planned but you're going with it, as if you're at peace with it. I could do with some of that, to tell you the truth.'

'How so?' Em said, taking in Floyd's drooped shoulders as he returned to his computer.

'Sasha,' he said, putting his arms up in front of him and crossing them to defend himself from her inevitable fury. 'I know, I know, you don't like her but.'

'Like her?' Em screeched. 'I saw her as a sister! And then look how she treated us! You, I mean.'

'I still love her, Em. I can't just switch off my feelings for her like that,' he said, clicking his fingers. 'I'm not a robot. Like you.'

Actually, she wanted to say, some robots these days can express emotions through non-verbal cues such as posture and gestures. But that was probably what he wanted her to do – divert her, throw her off the scent. She went back to the subject of Sasha.

'But she said no when you proposed to her!'

'She needed to find herself. I'm cool with that. If you love someone, set them free. She's worth it – beautiful, engaging, ethereal...' he said, with his head in his hands, staring into space.

'For someone who is an expert in reading human beings, you really are stupid.'

'She'll come back. Why else would she keep in touch? She misses me, it says here, see,' he said, pointing to his computer, 'and look, she's sent a picture of my name written in the sand on Krabi beach an island in—'

'Thailand. Not strictly an island. Part of the mainland but only accessible by boat. And home to dropouts who can't handle real life.'

'I see you haven't forgiven her,' Floyd said.

'Forgiven her?' Em squeaked, feeling a surge of protection for her brother. The memory of that summer evening this time last year was still fresh in her mind. He'd told everyone he was going to get down on one knee. He'd spent hours dressing up the balcony at his former flat, which overlooked the river, with fairy lights and candles. He'd cooked a five-course meal, he had champagne on ice and rather than prejudge the kind of ring she'd want, he'd bought her a flashy camera. It was so thoughtful the way he'd gone to all their favourite places and taken pictures of them with it, so she could scroll through. The last one was a beach in Wales they'd visited and he'd written 'will you marry me?' in the sand. Trust her then to keep him dangling with her own scrawl on a crappy Thai beach. 'No, I haven't forgiven her. And what is she doing in Thailand? I thought she was going to rescue street orphans in Bolivia?'

Flakey, that's what she was. And disloyal, considering how close they'd been, her and Sasha. She was a perfect match for Floyd – and for me, Em thought. She shared many of her interests, such as world cinema and baking; things they'd do together without Floyd. Sasha had encouraged her to be herself – love your inner geek, she always said. It helped too that she was so beautiful to look at, although Em didn't feel intimidated by her almond-shaped green eyes, her long swishy blonde hair, never-ending tanned legs and graceful posture. Quite the opposite, actually; in Sasha's sunny company, Em felt vicariously special, honoured even to catch her rays. Which was why her departure had hurt her too.

'We all loved her and look what she did to us.'

'You make it sound as though you're the one with the broken heart, Em. If I can deal with it, then you can,' Floyd said.

'Oh, Floyd, it's just that you're sitting around waiting for her to come back and even if she does, well, she'll ruin your life again at some point. You need to find someone else.'

'I have been trying! I did a runner from that strap-on bird if you remember?'

'Someone decent. Normal. These women you go out with, they're just so off-the-scale. High-maintenance. Or maybe you should just give it all up for a while. Throw yourself into some kind of volunteering or something?'

'Funny you should say that,' he said, which Em warmly welcomed – she loved people walking the walk rather than talking the talk.

'Oh, brilliant,' she said, patting his shoulder. 'What sort of thing? Helping the needy? Skill-sharing? Working with deprived youngsters?'

'Something like that,' he said, his lips dancing.

Em gave him a lovely big smile. At last, he'd come to his senses!

Meanwhile...

Frankie

On her way to see Dad, Frankie made her mind up.

Losing sleep over it was bad enough. But things got worse when a confidence-building exercise suggested by Letty had backfired – she'd tried to practise on a bottle of ketchup on the bathroom floor but an over-enthusiastic squeeze led to a spurt of sauce into her mouth. She had gagged and spat and screamed in a meltdown worthy of an Oscar. If she reacted like that when she was nowhere near an unmentionable, then how would she cope with a real one? Especially when he would be attending to her downstairs and she'd be worrying about her scent and not breaking wind. It was clear she couldn't go through with the sixty-nine – or anything else which required actual sex. They hadn't even kissed and she was expected to put his thing in her mouth. No, she thought – lucky enough to see a space in Dad's road, which was always full of football fans' cars on Saturdays, it was that close to Cardiff City Stadium – it was out of the question. She was going to text Floyd later to thank him for his help but she was calling it a day. He was bound to be grateful, considering she wasn't what you'd term 'a natural'.

Collecting herself before she got out, she reflected on this morning's job, doing wedding hair in the bride's room at a country manor house near Cowbridge. Usually, she loved these appointments because it gave her exclusive access into the inner sanctum of womanhood. Sipping on a glass of fizz, she would get the flutters from the magic: elders fussing with their hats and corsages; the jittery bride cocooned by her giggling bridesmaids; and the constant knock-knock on the door from deliveries of flowers, sandwiches and gifts. So much planning went into so few hours, it felt like you were asking the impossible for it all to come together at the same time. But of course, it generally did – and even if it didn't, the majority wouldn't know the doves you'd wanted to be released for the photos had been replaced by white homing pigeons. At least, they hadn't at her own wedding; that's what she would tell brides-to-be, both to put minds at rest and to relive the happiest twenty-four hours of her life.

But today, she'd created boho down-dos and elegant up-dos with the heaviest of hearts because of those now-tainted memories. The joy of her bridesmaids, Letty and Em, helping her get ready now felt delusional. Her bouffant dress which she knew wasn't trendy but had been what she'd always wanted felt foolish. Dad bursting with pride when he was finally allowed into his own lounge to see 'his princess' felt pitiful. And as for Jason's brimming eyes when he said his vows... now she wondered if they'd been filled with angst.

And look how it had left her. With the hare-brained way she was trying to win him back. She now knew it was off-kilter, warped even. There had to be a better way without so much humiliation.

Thank God for Dad. He'd give her a sausage sandwich and a pint of tea to make it all okay.

'Hello, love,' he said, opening the immaculate front door of his terrace in Canton with a pencil behind his ear. 'This is a nice surprise. Coffee? Tea? Or fairy juice?'

He meant squash – that's what he'd called it when she was small and obsessed with pixies and sprites and it instantly put her at ease.

'Tea,' she said, dumping her bag in the chintzy 80s wallpapered hall, which dated from before Mum's departure. The poor man was surely hanging on to the past. 'And I need some comfort food.'

'Oh, why's that then? Funny enough, I've got my Saturday sizzlers on. In the grill though, apparently healthier. Bloody killjoys that people are. But there you go. S'cuse the dusty clothes, I've been measuring up. Thinking of doing some renovations. Possibly.'

Into the kitchen they went and she slumped onto her elbows as he buttered four slices of own-brand white bread.

'I just feel so hopeless. Helpless. I miss Jason so much, Dad.' She didn't need to say any more because she knew he understood about losing the love of your life.

'That's natural, love. Oh, shavings!'

He opened the back door which led to the garden to let in some air because he'd burned the bangers. A plate landed

95

before her and after a squirt of ketchup she tucked in.

'Did you feel like this when Mum left?'

'Of course,' he shrugged as he patted the brown sauce. She noticed he'd given himself the charred bits, the sweetie. 'Change is unsettling. But you get used to your new circumstances, eventually. This'll be good for you. You won't see it now, love. But you will.'

'Yep, I guess,' she said, not feeling it but thinking if Dad could get through it then she could too. She'd always wondered how Mum could've deserted him: he was the loveliest, gentlest man on the planet. He'd been the one who'd been 'mum', her mother being unable to show her love beyond a quick peck at bedtime. But with Dad, he was as warm as a faithful dog. He still was, in spite of being rejected.

Her phone buzzed with two messages, they must've been sent when she was out of range earlier.

'Mum,' she said, rolling her eyes at Dad. 'Oh god, you'll never guess. She's asking on behalf of Aunty Sandra if she can have the wedding present money back! She's a bit short, apparently.'

'Oh, Sandra!' Dad said, tutting. 'Your mother's sister was always tight.'

'What I can't get over is that they've obviously spoken and agreed my marriage is over. It's just so undermining.'

But then Mum never quite got social niceties or nuances or normal things. Like, when Frankie was a kid when she had to go to her marina show home every other weekend, she wasn't allowed to touch anything; 'fun' was being dragged round antique shops, and she was expected to eat curry.

'Then, get this, she wants me to go round and do her an ombre. I despair, I really do.'

'Well, she wants to see you, love, that's just her way.' Hmm, Dad was too charitable. Mum only ever got in touch when she wanted something. She had never called her just to say 'hi' or to tell her she loved her. It was the same when she would ring the house after she'd gone. Brief, contained conversations about school, and then the pause before she hung up, as if she had wanted to say something meaningful but could never bring herself to say it.

Frankie huffed then went on to the next message.

'It's Jason! He's sorry for not texting earlier, work's been mad busy. Everyone wants scaffolding up for their summer renovations.'

As much as she wanted to be wary of him, she lapped up his excuse. It was true that this time of year was full-on. And still, even when he'd been putting up scaffolding, it was clear she had been on his mind.

'And oh God, he wants to come round to see me. Is that good or bad? Like, is he going to hand me divorce papers or is he going to ask to come back?'

Quickly, she ran through her options. If he was going to end it properly she had to make sure she looked so gorgeous he'd rethink. But if it was about the possibility of getting back together, then she'd have to keep going with her sex education so that when he came back to her, she'd never be boring in bed ever again.

Dad, though, was calm in the face of panic.

'The one thing I know, love,' he said, 'it's pointless prejudging anyone or anything. I'm afraid you're going to have to wait and see.'

Then he collected their plates, plopped them into the beige plastic washing up bowl, ran the taps and began to whistle as he looked out onto the concrete side-return of next door's house.

Oh. It wasn't quite the reaction she'd hoped to have from him. It made her feel a bit flat. But then, he would be cautious, seeing as he'd never opened his heart up to anyone again.

Monday

Em

Em felt fantastic. She was so excited about being back, she'd practically run to work.

Even better, she was first in of the managerial staff. It meant she could thank her colleagues for their concern over her health but wave it away as old news, seeing as she'd been in since 6 a.m.

Besides, she wasn't ill – just pregnant. The nausea had suddenly gone and her energy levels were back to normal, which she put to good use making sure the store was clean, safe and stocked for 7 a.m. when the doors opened.

Getting everything ready for curtains up always seemed an impossible task. Night-shift shelf-stackers were flagging, cardboard boxes littered the floor and there was a rush on to unload three 40-foot trailers of groceries, which amounted to between 80-90 pallets. But somehow, it got done – just as the *Great British Bake-Off* contestants managed to deliver a final tweak when the timer went off, the butchers, bakers and fishmongers would have their wares laid out as the first customer entered the shop. After that, she'd given a talk to the new recruits who were being till-trained about the supermarket ethos called Helping Hands. Help those who looked like they needed it, but never badger those who didn't.

Now, she was sat at her desk, scaling the wall of emails which had built up in her absence. Four hundred and ninety-seven in eight days, most of which were corporate announcements, queries and union notices, plus a few messages about the baby.

HR had sent through a wad of documents about maternity leave, which she flagged and filed to read tonight. She had decided to tell the HR manager about the baby earlier than she was compelled to by law. The rules said you didn't have to say anything until fifteen weeks before your due date but Em wanted to be up front – and it wouldn't be long until she would be literally up front too. It meant they could plan her cover – and it would help her chances of promotion if she could demonstrate that she thought strategically.

Sly poked her face round the door. 'Darling, managerial meeting in ten minutes, just to remind you,' she said. 'And no bloody fainting this time.'

Em laughed and nodded. She couldn't wait to get stuck in. 'Anything I've missed?' she asked, wanting a heads-up just in case.

'Mr R has just this second notified head office of his decision to take early retirement,' Sly said, winking. 'You better dust off your CV because HR will want to get this sorted ASAP, what with Christmas starting in September here.'

Em did a quick analysis: however much they'd appreciate her heads-up of her pregnancy, she didn't want to be busting at the seams at her interview. The sooner the better meant she could make her case without a bump as a physical barrier because people made assumptions about appearances. Her waist had thickened, yes, and her boobs had grown a cup size already, but she hoped she'd be one of those women who didn't show too early. And she was due in February, so she would be there for the build-up to Christmas and through the season, which was the busiest time of year.

'Perfect, thank you,' Em said, giving her a thumbs up. 'I'll be there in five.'

She sat back and put her hands behind her head, determined to beat Simon Brown to that promotion not with underhand tactics but graft and good ideas. Maybe, just maybe, she could almost have it all. The job, the baby, the house. Not the man, obviously, but three out of four wasn't bad. During her time off, she'd squared the circle in her head; she would be doing it herself. It wasn't ideal, far from it, but lots of people managed it, so why couldn't she? What with Floyd flapping around her by insisting she didn't lift anything 'in her condition' and Frankie and Letty talking babygros and cots, Em was entirely grateful to know she wouldn't be going into it alone. Yes, she'd have to be mum *and* dad, but Floyd would be around, as well as her two best friends.

She checked her watch, seven minutes to go, she had time to do a bit more deleting, so she refreshed her email. Simon Brown's name appeared at the top. Her eyes widened and her heart leapt at the sight – then she felt afraid. What did he want? The subject line made her gulp: it said 'stuff', which could mean anything. She desperately wanted it to be work-related because personal things would only make her think again and she'd done enough of that. Glancing at the clock on the wall, she wondered if she should save it until after the meeting. But what if it was to do with Mr Roberts' announcement? News travelled fast and she needed to be in the know if Simon Brown had any inside knowledge that he was sharing. She had to read it.

> Hi Em, how are you? I'm good, busy here at the branch but I'm doing all the bits and pieces you taught me!

Get on with it, she thought, what do you want?

> I'm not sure if this is the right forum to discuss this but I didn't want to put you on the spot in a phone call.

He knew her so well, she thought, which made her feel warm – then flushed because it just emphasized how right they would've been together.

What was coming? What was he going to say? Oh, don't even think of asking me for interview tips, she thought.

> I might be way off here, and I sincerely apologize if I'm wrong, but I've done some calculations and I'm wondering if we need to talk.

Em shut her eyes. She didn't want to read on. She'd dotted the i's and crossed the t's and put everything away very neatly into a box. But when she read his next sentence, the box flew open.

> Is the baby mine?

Em reeled, stood up, sat back down again and re-read his note. She sat there, biting her lip, realizing she was an idiot, thinking she could iron out life's creases. She was going to have to tell him the truth.

She rubbed her eyes and sighed, feeling dread at the prospect of all the mess. He would support her, of course he would, Simon Brown was the most responsible human being she'd ever met. But to hear him tell her he'd be there for the baby but not her was going to be like slow torture. They'd be connected forever through this child and she would have to watch him make a life for himself with someone else, and it was going to hurt her every time she handed the baby over. There'd be split Christmases and birthdays and awkward parents' evenings, and what if he got married and their child was a bridesmaid or a page boy? It was unbearable and— Shit. It was a minute past eleven, she realized, leaping up from her chair and running down the corridor. She was late. She was never late. And she wondered if this was how it was going to be from now on, chasing the pack, on the back foot and forever behind?

Tuesday Night

Frankie

Once again, Frankie was standing in a pile of clothes, trying to work out what to wear.

In the days leading up to tonight and Jason's visit, she'd spent hours poring over her situation with Letty, who had impressed upon her the need for dignity, whether it was a dumping situation or not.

'Play it cool, let him do the talking, and do not cry. Not until he's gone,' she'd said, 'because running mascara is a bit of a bunny-boiler look and that's not cool.'

The bottom line was this: Frankie needed to blow Jason's socks off.

The first layer was easy; her pink lacy Wonderbra and matching pants gave her something to hold onto, a sort of brace to keep her upright. There was also the fact he was a boobs man. But did she go for tight top and mini shorts? No, too obvious and too much like her mother. One of her summer dresses? That was the 'old' her – and she wanted to present an up-to-date version of herself which said she was all new and improved. So she found her cerise polka dot playsuit which she normally wore on the beach, but what the hell, her legs and shoulders were tanned from the weather, and it showed off her new slimline body. A bit of lip gloss, a fluff of her pre-curled hair and she actually looked pretty good. When she stroked him, Leonardo gave her a purr of approval – it was as close as she'd get to a thumbs up.

Downstairs, she set up a few props to show she hadn't spent the entire day obsessing about Jason's visit. The plates stacked in the drainer showed she wasn't the fuss-pot who'd insisted they had to be immediately dried and put away, and the pile of long-haul holiday brochures she'd picked up at lunchtime screamed a more adventurous spirit.

It was all designed to tell Jason she was no longer that girl who arranged the cushions every night before bed. She was more spontaneous, more self-assured and less bothered by playing house. Which, actually, when she'd finished and surveyed her work, was a tiny bit true: she was less Kate Middleton since they'd last come face to face. The door went and she blew out of her cheeks to calm herself – this was it.

Frankie told herself to act blasé – Letty's orders. But, oh my, that was easier said than done when she saw him. All the familiar traits were there – the same beautiful big brown eyes, the deliciously dark pinprick mole above his even deep red lips and the slow flutter of his thick eyelashes every time he blinked, which she knew so well. But they seemed sweeter and more intense. His hair had grown and was streaked from the sun. Her mind then wandered to the girl on the beach – was his fresh look a result of her? No, she soothed herself, he was always like this in the summer. Working outdoors gave him faint crinkles around his eyes and bulging arms which stood out so keenly against his white T-shirt. He was beautiful, completely and utterly breathtakingly handsome.

'Hi,' he said, smiling shyly, not moving from the doorstep, 'it's great to see you, Tink.' She felt sixteen again, wanting to cross her eyes and make a fainting joke to Letty and Em, just as she had when she told them he'd asked her out. Her senses were going wild but she had to sit on them.

'Hi,' she said, breezily.

Then boom. 'You look amazing,' he said, 'really amazing. Wow.'

Frankie's body tingled all over from her scalp to her toes. There was no doubt about it. The connection with him was still there, she was certain he could feel it too.

He moved towards her and kissed her on the cheek, just missing her mouth. She had to give it to him, it was entirely appropriate. Intimate but not overly so – an austere peck by her ear would've been too stiff. A snog, well, she couldn't even go there or she'd have a hot flush.

She wanted time to stop, so she could breathe him in and save his touch for when he was gone. But remembering Letty's advice, she pulled away so he could follow her in. 'I've made some lemonade,' she said, walking to the kitchen, desperate for a cold drink to reduce her soaring temperature.

The ice cubes jiggled as they fell into two glasses, new ones she'd bought because all the others had been from their wedding list.

'Do you want to sit in the garden?' she asked, leading the way, wanting to show some initiative. She was grateful for sunglasses too so she could hide her eyes, which were drinking him in.

'How you doing then?' he said, settling down onto the other beanbag she'd 'casually' thrown outside before he arrived.

'Great, loads of work on, lots happening,' she said, churning out a line she'd prepared earlier. 'You?' she asked, as aloofly as she could.

'Same here, mad busy. I'll be glad when autumn comes and work slows down. Although I can't complain really. Business is booming.'

'How are things at your brother's?' she said, stirring her drink with her straw to make herself look not bothered. Inside though she was, thinking of him sleeping on the couch in the minging student area of Cathays where his brother lived.

'Jimmy's Jimmy, you know what he's like. Works hard, plays hard, doesn't clear up much. In fact, at all. I didn't know this, but Mum comes to clean at his, and the cheeky bastard doesn't even pay her. So I'm getting her a day at the races, a ladies' day thing, to say thanks.'

'That's sweet but bet she loves it, having her two boys together,' she said, making sure she kept it about him.

'Course she does! She can keep an eye on us,' he said, pausing, then, 'She says hi, she misses you.'

What was Frankie to make of this? Was it a kick in the shin or, dare she believe it, a reminder she was still considered family?

'I keep meaning to ring her but I'm so busy,' she said, which was partly true. She stuffed more clients into her day now because there was no one to go home to. And the sound of her mother-in-law's voice would make her go over how much she was missing being part of the family.

'She'd love that. She really would. In fact,' he said, with another pause, 'that's why I'm here. It's her 60th next week, and I don't know how you feel about it, but we're having a surprise party at the house if you're free?'

Blimey O'Reilly! This was *so* not what she'd expected! She raised her eyebrows because she couldn't trust herself not to let out a whoop.

'There's about forty coming. We've a DJ, a hog roast and we're putting a marquee up the night before, when she's away with Aunty Liza for a girly thing. I don't know if you feel funny about it, what with us, you know, and it'll mean questions and stuff but…' he said, his voice trailing off, awaiting some kind of sign about how she felt.

Never mind the questions, she thought, this was a brilliant opportunity to find out how he was doing without her. His mother would get tipsy and spill the beans. He definitely didn't have a new woman on the go – if he had she would be going not her. Oh my God, it was all too much! Still, she kept a straight face and ignored his probing. 'I think it's okay but I'll check my diary and let you know,' she said, already planning a shopping trip to get herself a new outfit.

'Nice one,' he said, before asking if she needed anything doing because he had his tools in the back.

'No, I'm on top of it all,' she said, smugly.

'You're doing really well,' he said. 'I thought you might be…'

'A mess?' she said, knowing now was the time to show a smidgeon of vulnerability. 'Things are better than they were, definitely, and I'm finding my way, but there are still some days when I'm a bit down.'

'Me too,' he said. 'It's weird being on your own after years of what we had, some days I think I've made a mistake…'

Bloody bingo, Frankie thought, memorizing his words to relay to the girls later. He wasn't saying he wanted her back, but there was obviously a seed. She knew she needed to be very careful, so she stayed silent.

'I don't expect any sympathy from you, just so you know. I just wanted to tell you how things are. With me.'

She could feel her spine straightening as she took in his words. But she had to keep her cards close to her chest.

As instructed by Letty to cut things short, she looked at her watch.

'Sorry, you've got things to do,' he said, standing up. She offered him a smile which said 'sorry, yes' but of course, there was nothing on the horizon – apart from bouncing on the sofa with glee once he'd gone.

Right on cue, Leonardo walked in with his ears flat against his head. Frankie called him over and as he meowed in her face, she told him: 'You're not going to believe this, Leonardo, but I have just played an absolute blinder.' Then she grabbed her phone to text Letty that she was a total genius – and to message Floyd to arrange lesson number two. She wanted to perfect the sixty-nine for when Jason pleaded with her to take him back.

Thursday, Lesson Two

Frankie

'What we are about to do is sample one of the most erotic experiences on the sexual smorgasmbord,' Floyd said, taking off his trousers and joining Frankie in bed with a bounce.

Erotic? she thought, pulling the duvet up to her chin, what on earth is erotic about putting your mouth anywhere near the bits and pieces which use the loo?

'You don't look convinced,' he said, examining her in the twilight of her bedroom.

'There's no eye contact,' she said, 'you're closer to someone's feet than their head. It's hardly romantic.'

'Ah, but the sixty-nine is about trust, which I would say is the most important element of romance.'

Frankie stole a glance at Floyd; he had the sweetest look of sincerity on his face. She couldn't equate his expression with the situation: for her, it was as if she was about to sit an exam. On his face.

'You could even say it's more intimate than sex. It has a seedy image problem, that's all. But when you do it, it's the total opposite of that. It's intense, you're feeding off the other person while they're feeding on you. It's emotional.'

Frankie hummed her disagreement in spite of the warmth and safety of his voice. He loved a gag but there was not a trace of humour; he seemed entirely comfortable and genuine.

'Why don't you tell me about the time you did it? What happened?' Floyd said, turning on his side to look at her.

'Promise you won't laugh?' she said, still clutching the covers.

'I do the jokes, not you. It'll help, perhaps I can work out what it is that's holding you back.'

So she clamped her eyes shut and relived the afternoon on her single bed at Dad's six months into her and Jason's relationship when a fumble had become oral. She'd felt awkward from the off, bewildered by what was expected, embarrassed when he was down there, and clumsy when she'd had a go. She'd ended up detaching herself from her lower half and pretended to come quickly so she could devote herself to his needs. After that, when she found herself in the position again, she'd manouevre herself out of it, suggesting she only wanted to please him.

'Why did you remove yourself from the situation? Is it because you think it's dirty?' he said gently, willing her to open up with his kind eyes.

'Not at all, we were both meticulous about cleanliness. He was always showering because of all of the dust and sweat from scaffolding. He smelled lovely. I was just frightened, I suppose.'

'Of what?'

'I don't know. To enjoy it? But I couldn't, not when I had Dad's tea to make.'

'Would you say you had a childhood?'

'Not really,' she admitted. 'But what's that got to do with me squirming over the sixty-nine?'

'I wonder if it's because you didn't feel letting go was compatible with your self-image as having had to grow up a bit too quickly?'

Frankie heard bells ringing in the distance but she turned the volume to mute. This wasn't a sex lesson – it was interrogation! Thinking about the past wasn't going to get her anywhere. And why was he being so serious? Where were his one-liners about 'le soixante-neuf' – the least she'd expected was a quip about wearing onions and a beret. 'Look, I appreciate this analysis but can we move on? Like doing what we're supposed to be doing.'

'Fair enough,' Floyd said evenly. 'It's completely up to you. If you want direction, here goes. To avoid a mechanical sixty-nine, you need to relax, take it slow, listen to your body and mine, think of it like making a circle and our job is to keep it whole.'

'Right, good,' she said, keenly, because she was glad he'd dropped the psychiatrist act. Then it hit her: they were going to have to touch each other. Nerves sprinted up her spine at the looming prospect of having prolonged skin to skin contact: her bottom half had to be bare but she could at least take comfort in keeping her top half covered. The confidence she'd had from last week's session shrivelled. It had been a soft introduction, she realized, one that now seemed silly. Even so she had to do this if she was going to execute her plan to get Jason back. If she didn't at least try, then she could forget even having a stab at saving her marriage. It was time to be brave.

'Cool. Any questions?'

'Yes,' she said with forced boldness, cringing at what she was about to ask. 'What do I do when your tongue is down there?'

'Just feel it. So, shall we give it a go?' he said softly.

She gulped and gave the smallest of nods. 'Can I keep my T-shirt on though?'

At the Same Time...

Em

Early, as ever, Em took a walk on the Cardiff Bay Barrage to kill time. She had a spare fifteen-and-three-quarter minutes which she knew would give her the chance to complete a loop of the blowy strip of land which separated the waterfront from the sea.

Starting at the cafe kiosk, she'd go past the play area up to the locks and back again, all beneath a vast blue sky. By then, Simon Brown would be there and she would have to break it to him. But now, she would seize the dying seconds of his fading ignorance.

After hours breathing in air con under artificial lighting at work, she felt her chest expand with the scent of salt and the sound of seagulls as the evening sun scorched the path. Day to day, this was her special place, the stand-in for the hills and sweeping landscape she ran to when she was on annual leave. It stretched in a straight line for more than a mile – the linear design soothed her. And it had a purpose: to prevent the city flooding. What wasn't to like about it? Em could think here, which was why she suggested it to Simon Brown as a rendezvous point. Her home made her feel too vulnerable: it would be a reminder of his one and only visit there. The barrage was only ten minutes away, and she considered it the back garden she didn't have. The kiosk also did a mean hot chocolate, not one of those fancy artisan fair-trade ones, just a simple blob of squirty cream on top, which she equated with the normal childhood she had always craved. There had been no Cadbury's at their house, only bitter rainforest cocoa powder, from whichever South American country Mum was currently championing.

The thought that always came to her here was that when she was a mum, this would be their playground. There would be a wholesome father teaching the kids how to ride their bikes while she supervised the outdoor gym area, followed by lunch boxes of cheese sandwiches and crisps at the picnic tables.

Fat chance of that now, she thought as a dog galloped past, its tongue hanging out in ecstasy. But who needed a man anyway?

Squinting her eyes, she saw a jogger up ahead and moved to the right of the path to make way. She was comforted by there being another person on their own like her. Very much like her. Her mouth went dry when she realized it was Simon Brown. Of course it would be him. The reflex of joy she always felt from seeing him was now tarnished by the thought he would be in her life forever now, not out of choice but compulsion. He hadn't seen her yet so she stopped to wait for him to recognize her. He was on the attractive side of sweaty, she thought. And he was wearing exactly the same outfit as her; trainers, beige walking trousers, minus the zip-off legs, and a base layer T-shirt. It was lucky she didn't believe in fate, she told herself, wiping her palms on her shorts.

'Em!' he said, sliding to a halt in a puff of gravel.

'Hi. I was just—'

'Doing a loop because you were early,' he stated.

'Yep. You too, eh.'

He nodded slowly. 'Do you want to get a hot chocolate or…'

'Let's walk for a bit,' she said, because then she didn't have to look him in the eye.

'Shall we head back? I'm parked up there and it's on your way too,' he said but he swayed back and forth to show he didn't mind.

'How far have you run?' she asked, spinning around and setting off.

'Five point eight kilometres.'

'Three point six miles,' they said in unison.

Once, this chorus of geekery would've made Em laugh but now it filled her with sadness. They were in tune and they thought the same way. How was it they weren't together? Em wondered. And how terrible it was going to be because she'd always be reminded of it for the rest of her days.

'There's a bench up there,' she said, making her way to it and sitting down where she kept her eyes straight ahead, watching the birds and boats in the freshwater lake.

'So,' he said, settling down beside her. 'How are you?'

She was sick of the preamble: she wanted to get it over with. Then they could work out what happened next. 'It's yours,' she said, watching a bird gliding on a thermal way up high. She listened for his reaction. But there was no sharp intake of breath or gasp. Not even an extended silence for him to digest the news.

'I know,' he said. His voice didn't quiver – it remained normal, light and soft. Em turned to him then to make sure he'd heard her properly. His eyes were honest and true and she knew he had. 'When I worked out the dates... it was quite interesting actually because I used a pregnancy calculator predictor which I found online. You just put in the date of conception and...'

He was rambling and they both knew it.

'I'm due February the—'

'Fourteenth. Or so I believe.' How suited they were, she thought again, feeling the tragedy anew.

'Given the situation we're in, it could be viewed as wryly amusing,' Em said, with zero amusement and omitting Floyd's suggestion of naming the baby Valentine or 'Valentino if it's a dude'.

'You've decided to keep it,' Simon said, evenly. This was the problem with someone as rational as him – there was no reading between the lines and no way of knowing what he really thought.

'Yes. I'm sorry I didn't explain straight away. I was-'

'Shocked. I understand.' The way he had finished her sentence added more pain. 'I wouldn't have pressured you, either way. It was your decision to make.'

He was a gentleman. A frustratingly nice gentleman, Em thought, wishing for once for a show of... something resembling emotion. But she'd been through this with him already, and in her head countless times. He had already turned her down once and he would only do it again. A baby would not bring them together in the way she wanted. It would be a battle to remain friends, she suspected, because of her feelings. The optimum she could hope for was a relationship without strain; a civil, friendly exchange which put the baby first. Romantic notions would only bring more anguish. But how could they get there? This was what she had to work out.

'I'll do my bit, obviously, like I do with—' he added, not even bringing himself to name his daughter.

'I know,' she said, resigned to the fact he would be a father but not her partner. Even though she knew happy endings only happened in fairy tales, it didn't stop her feeling disappointed.

She'd had enough: she didn't want to discuss this anymore. 'We can talk again when we need to make some practical arrangements,' she concluded. 'And what with your experience, feel free to, you know, make suggestions.'

'Well, I'd like to come to the next scan. If that is okay with you?'

'Of course. You're the father,' she said. She expected nothing less from this man who spoke of duty rather than desire.

'Are you taking folic acid?' he said.

She rolled her eyes at him. 'And the rest – no alcohol, soft cheese or caffeine.'

For the first time he laughed. 'Obviously. It's going to be a textbook baby!'

Em shrugged. She severely doubted it – there was nothing textbook about this situation.

She chose to read his flippant comment as an acute misjudgement. It was unfair of her as she knew he was only trying to be nice. Even so, if he could be so trite, maybe he wasn't her soulmate after all. That was how she was going to have to think of him to stop herself loving him. I mean, he'd shown another, harder, ruthless side to himself by being prepared to snatch the store manager's job from her. This would be the approach she needed to survive.

A family came into view: the mother was pushing a pram while the father had a laughing toddler on his shoulders. Em had to get away because she couldn't stand the sight of what she had hoped for.

Standing up, she convinced herself it was clear Simon Brown was intending to treat this baby as he had done with his first; play his part when required and fulfil his responsibilities. Nothing more.

'Do you need anything?' he asked, innocently.

A list popped up in her head: she needed him to love her, to tell her he had been wrong about not being able to commit to her and to be by her side so they did this together. This is not helping, Em, she said sternly to herself. Opening up to him had only caused trouble.

'Nothing, thank you,' she said in a clipped voice. 'I'll email you when I see the midwife next.'

Simon Brown nodded and went to say something. 'Take care,' he said, smiling his lopsided little smile which had always made her heart swell and her stomach contract. Now all she felt was devastation.

Quickly, she walked off and managed to contain her tears until she was out of earshot and the sound of her crying would be swallowed by the wind.

Back at Frankie's

Frankie

Frankie could feel Floyd's hot breath on her inner thigh.

Rigid and fearful, she felt herself retreat, imagining she was on the dentist's chair. 'I'd actually prefer to be having a filling right now', she thought, as she focused away from his boxers and on his left calf which was resting beside her head. She began a game of dot-to-dot in the galaxy of his freckles hoping to find an exit sign somewhere near his ankle.

'I can hear you thinking,' Floyd whispered into her crotch. 'Stop thinking. Remember what I said, this is about making a circle, that's all there is to it.' Ignoring him, she realized they hadn't even kissed and yet here he was about to start smooching her twinkle. For her kissing was the closest she got to heaven. Face to face, mouth to mouth, the sweep of eye lashes, taking in someone else's breath – now that was erotic. This, on the other hand, felt impersonal, anonymous. She could be here with anyone. And then it clicked, if she pretended Jason was down there, well, her tummy responded with a backflip.

'Okay, I'm going to take my knickers off now,' she said, shuffling them down her legs.

'Excellent,' Floyd murmured. 'Me too.'

Once they'd done that, she shifted her body so her eyes – squeezed tight shut until the evil moment – were level with Floyd's privates. Jason's privates, she corrected herself.

'I'm ready,' she said.

'Me too,' came a voice from below.

Dear God, he's not wrong, Frankie thought, opening her eyes, at the sight of his generously-sized thing. No wonder he couldn't wear Speedos!

'Do you want to… commence proceedings?'

She hummed a hesitant 'yes', then blew out of her cheeks.

'Go with the flow, we can stop at any time, just relax.'

Her heart pounding, she inched her way towards him. He smelled lovely, thankfully, of clean laundry, and he had a sweet dark mole like a beauty spot to the right beneath his belly button. She closed her eyes, thinking of her husband, and pressed her lips against his stomach. Smooth and clean, his skin was warm and, when she imagined it to be the love of her life, inviting. Closer now, she moved her mouth towards him: and then she was there, on him, and she heard a murmur, which reassured her. He rocked against her lightly to help her set a rhythm and then she braced herself for the feel of his beard against her – it was going to feel like a Brillo pad, she just knew it.

What's the point of this, she thought, I'll never come, I'm a freak, go on give it your all, it won't make any differ... oh God, oh God, oh God, OH GOD.

When his touch came, all there was was softness. She was swirling, first through the sea, deep underwater, then flying, soaring as colours exploded on the back of her eyelids. It was as if she was hypnotized, no longer nervous, no longer scared, he had flicked a switch and all she could feel was a rich, heavy, luxurious pleasure. But, shit, her mind flashed back to her and Jason doing exactly this position in her childhood bedroom. How she'd tried to go with it but had ended up staring at her abandoned boot-cut jeans on the floor and the stack of Charles Worthington hair products on her bedside table. To take her mind off what they were doing.

Distracted, she realized she'd pulled away from Floyd. The memory had stopped her from getting lost in the moment. She fumbled and groped and felt a panic rise at losing the plot. Here was all the evidence she needed to know she was out of her depth. The semi-darkness was disorienting and yet out of it came his hands, grounding her, pulling her back to anchor.

'I'm here,' he said, 'you've just resurfaced, that's all, you're doing really well. You can do this.'

How could he be so sure? She was at a cross-roads: retreat from her fear or believe in herself the way Floyd did. His hand was on her thigh and it felt solid, secure. She felt a well of determination then. She recalled the softness she'd felt before her mind had led her to the past. And so with a deep breath, she sank back down and took him again in her mouth as they began to rock. Slowly, slowly, she found her groove. Yes, yes, she could do this!

'That's it,' he said as she managed to combine the feeling

and the doing until she was arching her back and pushing against him. She was in ecstasy as waves of what she'd never expected or dreamed was possible began to cover her entire body and—

'CUUU-STARD CREAMS!' Floyd wailed, jerking back and groaning.

But Frankie wasn't quick enough coming to, and she cried in shock when a shot of warm liquid hit her left eye.

'Fuck, sorry, I tried to warn you,' Floyd said, searching the bed for something to wipe up the mess. 'I wasn't going to come, I'd promised myself I wouldn't, there is absolutely no need for me to get any gratification out of this because it's a lesson and it's about you and—'

'Never mind that. It stings!' Frankie said, leaping up to run to the bathroom to splash water over herself. Looking up, she examined her screwed-up reddened eye in the mirror – and she saw she had a grin on her face. It was so inappropriate but she felt the thrill of having almost got it right.

Then Floyd's flustered and concerned reflection appeared beside her.

'Are you okay? Does it hurt? Oh God, don't cry,' he said, going to put his arm around her as her shoulders heaved up and down.

'I'm not crying, you idiot,' she said, gasping for air, 'I'm laughing! This is ludicrous! How long is my eye going to be half-shut like this because I'm seeing your sister tomorrow and how am I going to explain it?'

'I'll Google it,' he said, reversing, which only made her howl because he resembled a dalek with his willy at half-mast.

She grabbed a cold flannel to press against her eye and pursued him back across the hall. Leonardo was sitting at the top of the stairs, with what looked like an actual smile.

'It's fine,' she said, recovering her breath as she landed on the bed beside him, 'don't worry, please.' She took his phone off him and threw it onto the duvet.

'I'm supposed to be the teacher here,' he said, shaking his head, looking appalled at himself.

'You are! You've given me hope, already.'

'Do you really think so?' Floyd said, perking up.

'Yes! I really think so,' Frankie said and then in a small voice: 'I think I was about to, you know...' She mouthed the

117

word 'orgasm'. 'My first one from... anyone... doing... that. You were right, it is like driving, trying to do two things at once.'

Incredibly, she felt she'd achieved something here tonight: nothing major, not yet, but she had taken a step forward towards self-satisfaction for the first time.

'Oh, well done you!' he said, punching the air. 'I hope you can retain this confidence and apply it next time.'

'Thanks!' Frankie said, feeling the glow from a good report. 'Cuppa? Or do you need to shoot?'

'I'll shoot,' he said, buckling himself up. 'For the, er, second time tonight.'

He gave her a hug, patting her on the back in praise.

Then he pulled away and looked a bit sheepish. 'Erm, there is just one thing...'

Frankie flinched as she pulled on her joggers. She knew it, there had to be something. He was going to bring her down. Just be gentle with me, she prayed.

'In the throes,' he said, looking awkward, 'you called me, er, Jason.' Her hand covered her mouth in shock. 'I don't mind,' he said, moving towards the door, 'and no offence, but I always thought he was a bit of a wanker.'

Saturday

Letty

As the water pounded into the bath, Letty shut her eyes and inhaled the seductive scent of oranges and lavender through the steam.

It made her think of Spain: how many times had Mam tried to get her to move out there when Letty moaned down the line? 'You'd love it, chica,' she'd say. 'There's always a job for you in the restaurant, you can find yourself a nice señora!' But she'd always had ambitions to be better than a waitress. She couldn't speak the language either: Mam had spoken to her in Granny's tongue but as a teenager Letty had never bothered. She'd been far more into boys and make-up. When she'd visit for a fortnight, glimpses of their life – old men arguing over dominoes, narrow alleyways and cats eating scraps of fish – did make her wonder if she was meant to be somewhere else. But something always pulled her back.

Her friends, mostly. She couldn't imagine life without Frankie and Em around the corner. And then there was her quest for self-improvement – to make a career of her own. Now she had Lance to keep her here too. Just as she was about to get in the water, an urgent knock came at the door. She grabbed the fluffiest of white towels and went to the communal hall to peek through the spyhole.

It was Lance! In fact, more specifically, it was his disappearing back, where was he going?

She opened the door and saw boxes, piles of them, plus an exercise bike and bulging gym bags.

Then he emerged from behind the raised boot of his car with more.

'Are you doing a car boot sale? Because in this country we do them on Sundays. In a field,' she said.

He flashed a happy smile at her – how could he still be so handsome when his chin was clamped down on a wobbly stack of possessions which threatened to spill from his arms?

She followed him into the flat where he dumped his load. 'What's going on?' she said. 'We weren't meant to be seeing each other tonight, were we?'

He pulled her towards him and began to kiss her neck and shoulders. 'I know we only brought this up the other day,' he said, cradling the small of her back so he could see her face, 'but I just couldn't wait any more.'

She understood him then – he was moving in! To her dismay; he had said he would wait a bit before he left Helen and Eddy. The spare room at his would be his base because he had wanted to make sure his son slowly got used to his parents being separated. Letty had gone along with it but she had been very disappointed. Delighted now, she asked why the change of heart.

'The atmosphere there, it was affecting Eddy,' he said, dropping his head. 'We tried to be civil but we ended up arguing and he was seeing it all. We decided I should go. That it'd be for the best.'

Letty hugged the living daylights out of him. He'd never meant to hurt anyone, neither had she.

At least now they could show they were serious about one another and not involved in some sordid little temporary tryst. But, oh, Letty wished he'd told her he was coming: she'd wanted to make the place special for him. Clear some room in her bulging wardrobe, have fresh sheets waiting.

Yet what did it matter? He was here!

This was the commitment she'd always wanted, even if it had come out of an affair. They could right their wrongs by doing this.

'It's for the best. I know you feel terrible but this is for keeps. Forever. Come on, come with me, I've just run a bath,' she said, leading him by the hand.

This marked the end of their guilt: this was their clean break.

Meanwhile...

Frankie

'Sur-priiise!'

The night sky exploded with camera flashes and confetti stars as Jason's mum arrived at her black tie birthday party.

In shock, Sheila was flapping her hands, switching between laughter and screams as she took in all the familiar faces around her. The DJ, who was positioned beneath a sail canopy hung between two fairy-lit trees, started playing 'Happy Birthday To You' and the crowd swept her petite frame onto the chequered black and white dance floor laid out on the lawn.

In amongst them, Frankie could almost touch the joy. Having spent an hour waiting for Sheila, the guests' excitement had spilled over, helped along by free-flowing fizz served by waiters. Dressing up was all part of it too as sequinned gowns and shiny shoes twinkled in the disco lights.

She'd been nervous about tonight because she thought she would feel like a figure from the past. Three times, she had almost asked the cabbie to turn round on the journey from hers into the leafy suburb of Lisvane. But everyone had made a real fuss of her, and Jase, who looked very handsome in a tux, hadn't left her side. Bob, his bear of a dad, was not one for emotions but when she walked in, his bushy eyebrows did the talking, threatening to fly off his balding head in delight. He had hugged her hard as if she was his long-lost daughter. Jimmy, Jason's brother, had been his usual silly self, telling her she looked 'hot' before introducing his latest girlfriend.

Nobody else though mentioned their marriage, thank goodness; instead, they said how lovely, how really lovely, it was to see her, which made her think Jason might have been told he was mad for asking for a separation. Their warmth made her feel a part of it, in fact, it felt as though she'd never been away from all of this. They were on her side and she drew strength from it to throw herself into the party.

A hand squeezed her wrist and she turned around to see

Sheila beaming and her hazel eyes sparkling beneath her spiky brunette pixie haircut.

'This is so wonderful! I didn't have a clue! Oh, I'm so glad you're here, I've missed you, darling,' she said, kissing her cheek. As ever, she smelled of Chanel No 5, which Frankie found reassuring compared to her mum's cloying perfume, and she looked so elegant in a cream laced cocktail dress.

Before Frankie could answer, Sheila was dragged away by one of her friends. All Frankie could do was wave and shout 'see you later!'.

'Told you she'd be pleased to see you,' Jase said, offering her a fresh flute of champagne.

'She looks so happy,' Frankie said, before giggling as the bubbles kissed her nose. She moved into the shadows of the garden and he followed. 'It's a beautiful night,' she said, taking off her knitted black bolero to reveal naked shoulders and the sweetheart neckline of her pale gold fitted floor-length dress. She'd had to leave without asking Leonardo's opinion because, for some reason, he'd disappeared.

Jase stared at her and she recognized the look in his eyes: it still showed that she meant something to him. Had they been alone, and indeed a couple, they would've started to kiss.

'I've been such a fool,' he said, shaking his head, 'I've…'

Her heart leaped at his words: how she wanted to hear what he was about to say. She shivered as he reached to move a stray lock of her hair which had fallen onto her collarbone. But he couldn't say it here. She wished they were alone, away from here so they could talk properly. He stopped then as if reading her thoughts, and she cursed herself for being too sensible.

Jason pulled at the collar of his shirt. 'It's hot in this,' he smiled, changing the subject, which made her feel as if she'd lost her chance. Regret tumbled inside her tummy, and she felt her face drop.

'It was Dad's idea for us to dress like snooker players.'

'He's really gone to town,' she said, hating the return to small talk.

'She's worth it. And Dad's just sold the scaffolding company and made a mint so…'

'Oh, good for him.' Perhaps it was time to mingle. To get away from him, because it was so very hard chit-chatting politely to her husband.

'Yep and the new owner of the business wants me to be the boss. I've accepted the job.' He rubbed his hands and beamed.

Frankie was pleased for him because he was a grafter. But she couldn't deny the surge of bitterness inside of her – that he had everything going for him now.

And it managed to slip out.

'You better get used to a suit then,' she said, tightly., knowing he hated the pomp of a shirt and tie.

'I know, it's going to be weird being in an office and not on site. But I needed the change of scene. I think that might've been half the problem, you know...'

Thank goodness she hadn't walked off to circulate – this was what he had been trying to say!

Frankie could've punched the air. It was a sign he'd been thinking about them and analysing what had led to his crisis. Seriously, Floyd had it all wrong when he called Jase a wanker – it was probably one of his jokes, she decided. Or he was jealous of him for some reason; Jason was very good-looking after all and he wasn't a show-off and he had a serious side to him and... Just then, the first bars of 'Build Me Up Buttercup' began. It was one of Jason's favourites – he wasn't a music snob like Floyd.

'You dancing?' he asked.

'You asking?'

He laughed and pulled her onto the dance floor where they stayed song after song, twirling and whirling, breathless with laughter and singing along.

It was only when the tempo dropped that alarm bells began to ring in Frankie's head. Letty had told her not to do a slowie with him – she had to 'deprive him of her oxygen' was how Letty had put it. Frankie tried to ignore the words but they turned into capitals in her head when Percy Sledge started belting out 'When A Man Loves A Woman'. It was the song they'd picked for their first dance as a married couple. Her head raced, wondering if he'd asked for it? Or if it was fate. Couples began melting into one and Jason was moving towards her. It would be so easy to do this now, she thought. But the intimacy here wouldn't be on her terms; if she got the chance to feel his body against hers once more, it had to be in her bed and she hadn't finished her course yet. If she went too early, then it could backfire and her confidence was still shaky. Even if she was ready, she couldn't face sneaking off upstairs into his childhood bedroom. She couldn't go back to those days, no matter how equipped she would be.

'I've got to go,' she shouted into his ear, feeling the physical connection between them and fighting her heart to press herself against him, her husband. She needed to get out of here.

'Stay!' he said, their cheeks touching. He was wearing aftershave, she realized, which threw her. Usually he smelled citrusy from his shower gel and deodorant but tonight he had put on something special, something new. It must be for her, she thought, he had wanted to make an impression. She felt herself hover and if he had pulled her in right then she wouldn't have put up a fight. So she moved before he had the chance and kissed him, picked up her bolero and bag from one of the tables and dashed through the house to the front door. She could flag a cab down as she went.

'Frankie!' came his voice behind her as she walked down the drive. 'It's only quarter to eleven!'

'I've got a bridal fair first thing,' she lied, stopping briefly to face him when she reached the pavement. 'Say bye to your mum and dad for me.'

'Let me get you a taxi,' he said, running up towards her. 'Or I'll walk you back.'

'No, it's fine, go back in, it's your mum's party!' The idea of him coming to their marital home was too terrifying: if she was on shaky ground here, it would be worse there. She had to be strict – she couldn't put herself in such a precarious position, not until she'd finished her course.

'You look stunning tonight, Tink,' he said, undoing his dicky bow and unbuttoning his collar. Oh God, he looked even more handsome, Frankie thought, and he had a light layer of sweat on his temples which glistened in the moonlight. His hair was longer, no doubt because she wasn't around to cut it, and she could see the slightest wave forming. It would only be a few weeks and his baby curls would unfurl and he would have exactly the same style as when she first set eyes on him. She was paralysed, knowing she should go but mesmerized by him and their shared history.

'I need to tell you something,' he said, 'so we can try to sort this out… you see, I'm missing you. Badly.'

Her ears filled with the thud of her heart as he wiped a tear from his cheek. Was this the moment when he asked her back?

Was this when everything she wanted became true?

'I've slept with someone else,' he said, his voice cracking.

Oh, no. No, no, NO. This wasn't what was supposed to happen. What about all the attention he'd shown her tonight and the unmistakeable bond between them? She felt a nausea rise and the urge for fight or flight.

'What do you mean? With who? When?'

'No one you know. The other week. I wanted to be honest, not being straight is what got us here in the first place and...'

The cheek of him giving her a lecture on bloody morals. And what a fool she'd been, to think he'd meant it when he said he'd missed and mourned her. His tears were out of guilt, nothing more! She put her hands over her ears – she didn't want to hear any more. The image of that surfer chick appeared before her. She couldn't say anything because she didn't want to show she'd been snooping about on Facebook. She had to go. Now.

Adrenalin racing, Frankie kicked off her heels and picked them up in one hand and with the other, she took the hem of her gown.

'I had to tell you in case you found out from someone else,' he said urgently as he realized she was preparing to go.

He was a bastard. Floyd was right, she thought, beginning to run, her bare feet smacking the tarmac. Images from the night flashed before her then became blurred as tears fell. He had charmed her out of guilt and to soften the inevitable blow when he made his confession. And his plea for her to stay was merely a way of putting off the moment.

'It didn't mean anything. I promise,' he shouted as she turned the corner.

Tuesday Afternoon

Em

This week, Em said to herself, your baby is the size of half a banana. Or what's left of this Danish pastry, she thought, examining her late-afternoon snack beneath the stark strip lighting in her office. Really, she should be treating her body better than a rubbish bin, but she wanted – no, she needed – sugar. It hadn't gone unnoticed by the older women on the checkouts, who predicted she was having a girl. Apparently, they said, if you craved savouries, it meant you were having a boy. She was dreading it when her bump became public property and she would be subjected to the analysis of how she was carrying: neat for a boy, spread all around for a girl. People were already asking her what flavour she wanted! As if she had a say in the matter, she would think. All she cared about was that her baby was healthy.

That was the annoying thing about being pregnant, Em thought, everyone felt they had the right to comment based on old wives' tales. Leave it to medical science, she had wanted to scream at Paula on checkout number seven.

But she was being unfair. Not that she would admit this to anyone, but the magic of procreation had begun to creep up on her. It wasn't just a biological process which combined the genetic material of two organisms! How her body knew what to do, to divert all the nutrients to nourish her baby, was miraculous.

Here we are, in week fourteen, Em thought, and baby already has its own fingerprints. It's learning to use its facial muscles too through squinting and grimacing. Like mother, like baby, she thought, reflecting on today's meetings. The morning ones had been fine but after lunch, her head had been fuzzy. Was this the famous baby brain that Paula had warned of when she bought her Danish pastry?

As much as Em wanted to poo-poo this damaging and hysterical notion that pregnant women couldn't think straight, she had found herself scrabbling for words and drifting off in the midst of sentences. What if this happens at the interview? Perhaps that's what distracted her, she tried to convince herself as she finished her cake in one large gulp. She had only learned of the date of her interview – in a fortnight's time – at lunchtime. The format was a presentation before a panel in the morning, followed by an observation in-store by an area manager in the afternoon. Sly had let it slip that Simon Brown was to be interviewed on the exact same day but in reverse. It was a clear sign that they were considered the strongest candidates; it gave the decision-makers the chance to compare them like-for-like.

How was she going to be able to keep herself together? And by then, she would be two weeks more pregnant and even more scatty. She had clearly lost her ability to compartmentalize her mind: in truth, her thoughts hadn't been on the interview during the meeting – she'd been thinking about going shopping for maternity bras because her pancake boobs had turned into cupcakes.

Em felt as though she'd lost her edge and a thought sidled up to her: what if she withdrew from the interview? What if she counted her blessings? She could remain deputy manager on a decent wage with no surprises. It was going to be hard enough being a single mum without the added stress of going on maternity, then returning to a job she'd barely got her teeth into. Pride was all well and good but her number one priority had to be her child. If Simon Brown became manager and it was too difficult working for him, she could always apply elsewhere or get a transfer.

Just then an email arrived from him, with the subject entitled 'Work In Progress – suggestions?'.

Em felt a surge of anger that he thought he could ask for her advice. I'm not bloody helping him, she thought. Was this how it was going to be from now on? Would she always feel cross towards him and be unable to bear how oblivious he was to her feelings?

Scanning down the message, her chest began to quickly rise and fall as she absorbed his words.

> Dear Em, How are you doing? It was good to see you the other day. I've been thinking a lot about the baby and I really want to play my

> part. Obviously, it's entirely up to you how we do things but I have an idea. Do you know anything about co-parenting? It's when parents are equally responsible for a child, splitting financial, emotional and practical care right down the middle.

Well, that makes sense, she thought, although their working hours would dictate who had the baby. Until she got to the next bit: he was floating something so ridiculous that she smacked the desk with her palm.

> I could move in for the first few months, because the early days can be tough. I can take paternity leave as soon as the baby is born. I'd go in the spare room, obviously!

She was so astounded, Em found herself mouthing the word 'obviously' into space with a grimace.

> I'd be around to cook, wash, change nappies, help with feeds, depending on what you decide. It's not just for you, I wouldn't want to miss out on those precious moments which I had with my daughter.

And, just to clarify, he would pay rent. Nice, Em thought, tasting something bitter in her mouth. He was going to too much trouble to emphasize they were 'co-bloody-parents' and it hurt. How dare he send this jolly little note on the day they found out they were going head-to-head at work? Damn right it was going to be difficult in the first few weeks of being a mum, so why would she want him there to see her at her very worst? How could they live together and share the most magical moment of her life when she was in love with him? She would manage by herself, even if she wasn't sure right this minute that she could. And she'd fight every inch of the way for the job.

Thursday Night

Letty

'Why are you in your "personal trainer" vest? I'm not paying for this, you do realize!' Letty said as they limbered up in the hallway for a run.

'It's just advertising, beaut,' Lance said, shrugging, 'If anyone asks, just say we're on a PT session. It's good for people to see the magic I've worked on you!'

'Cheek!' But she lapped up his compliment because she was as contoured as a Kardashian's cheekbones.

Lance made her dizzy with a kiss on the mouth. Then he set his GPS watch and gave them a 3-2-1 countdown.

'Go!' Letty said as she shot off out of the door and into the warm evening. She squealed at the sound of his feet catching up and they settled into an easy jog as they crossed the road to follow the river path through the acres of Llandaff Fields.

Letty had to work hard to stop herself inhaling a cloud of midges, such was the size of the indecent grin on her face. Life with Lance was wonderful – he'd only been here a few days but she knew this was it. Just as they ran in sync, everything else they did shared a rhythm.

Their bodies were knitted together in sleep and their wake-up calls were slow, intense acts of love made in that blissful place between dreams and consciousness. Breakfast had used to be a solitary rush but now it was filled with sunshine as they sat eating muesli and drinking healthy smoothies. He would run her into work, meet her for lunch then be waiting at home with something cooking and a glass of red so she could unwind and tell him about her day. It was bum-clenchingly smug – in the past, if anyone was describing this set-up to her she would've cringed and pretended to poke two fingers down her throat. Yet now it was happening to her she understood how love made the mundane magical: a cup of coffee on her dressing table waiting for her when she got out of the shower was proof he was here in her life at every level. There'd been no changes at work and she still owed thousands, but Letty was too caught up in her personal life to worry about that at the moment. All in good time.

There was something she was a bit apprehensive about though: playing stepmum. She hadn't realized Lance's son would be staying over every other weekend, possibly a night in the week too. When it came to children, they were as foreign to her as a savings account. But Lance was sure she'd love Eddy when she got to know him. How could she not? His father was amazing! The way he spoke about Eddy, he was so proud. And she had thought Eddy looked dead cute in the photos he'd shown her. Most of all she was excited to see him 'being dad' – the thought of it made her feel all squishy.

Then again, he made her feel squishy most of the time.

Anywhere and everywhere, she found herself bringing him up in conversation, 'Lance thinks such-and-such about that' or 'Well, Lance and I, we did this, that, the other'. It was mortifying how dull she had become – but it was the most exciting thing that had ever happened to her. And it was about time she introduced him to the girls. They'd been surprised at how swiftly things had gone, with Lance moving in, but fair play to them, they took it as a sign that it was love. And luckily for Letty, Frankie's sex education was proving more sensational, more attention-grabbing: Em was more agitated by that than Letty's descent into domestic bliss. Frankie had refused point blank to say who he was: only that he was a friend who was helping her out. How funny that it was Frankie who was making the headlines and not her!

'Hey, Lance,' she said, when her breathing had settled down enough to talk, 'I want you to meet Em and Frankie, now you've made an honest woman of me.'

'Sounds great,' Lance said, easily, 'I'd love to. We can all go for a slap-up meal, eh, what do you reckon? A classy place, nice wine, fancy menu…'

'Are you mad?'

'What are you on about? It'll knock their socks off!'

'I don't want them impressed or amazed – save that for my mam.'

'Now I'm confused.'

Letty pulled up to make her point. 'These are my best friends, Lance, I want them to see you as you are, the person I fell for, a decent bloke, not some flashy bastard. They're the most important people in my whole life!'

But Lance was having a blond moment – he didn't seem to get it judging by the way he was scratching his chin.

'Don't you have anyone in your life whose opinion matters?' she tried again.

'You?' he said, hopefully.

She sighed with exasperation.

'I think this is Sheila stuff, if I'm honest,' he said.

It was time to change tack. 'So who helps you out when the shit hits the fan? Who's there for you when you most need someone? For support?'

Lance shrugged. 'Me, I guess. I just get on with it. Keep going.'

Letty crossed her arms and ground her foot into the floor carpeted with dead twigs and leaves, unsatisfied with his answer. 'But the people you left behind in Australia, your family, your mates, don't you miss them?'

'I left a long time ago, people move on. There's nothing there for me. I'll never go back, Letty. Why would I? I've got you and Eddy here,' he said.

She couldn't believe he could be so matter-of-fact. Things were so simple to him. Her life had been full of twists, turns and dead ends. But maybe he was showing her it didn't have to be like that from now on. To learn to trust herself, that she would find a way. Perhaps all she had to do was 'go straight to go'.

'So what were you thinking then, about the girls?' Lance asked.

'Something cosy. Next week. What night suits you?' she said, setting off again towards the sun set.

'Letty, I can't do nights, you know that, my schedule is chocka,' he said.

'But we're out now, doing this, you'll have some evenings won't you?' she said in hope.

'I cleared my diary this week to spend time with you, to settle in. From next week, it's back to the hard yakka, I'm afraid. The bulk of my work is done at night-time, it's just the nature of the beast.'

Letty was silent, she felt winded because she wanted to spend every available minute with him. The crunch of their feet hitting gravel made her think of a clock ticking, as if she was listening to a countdown of the honeymoon period.

'Come on, Letty, it's not that bad,' he said, elbowing her as they ran. 'We can do lunch. What's a few evenings when we've got the rest of our lives?'

He was right, she realized. This relationship wasn't going to be conducted along the same lines as those preceding it, when insecurity and fear made her erratic and paranoid. No, her and Lance were for the long haul.

A surge of happiness and positivity filled her. So she picked up the pace, knowing he wouldn't leave her side.

'Race you home!' she shouted into the breeze.

Meanwhile... Lesson Three

Frankie

'Well, he-llo there, sexy!' Floyd said as Frankie opened the door in stained joggers and a baggy T-shirt. She'd been doing some gardening and hadn't bothered to get changed: it was a sign of the deep malaise she'd felt ever since she'd found out Jason had been unfaithful.

'Ready for spanky bot-bots?

She sniffed, turned her back on him and walked off into the lounge where she collapsed on the sofa.

'I'm not in the mood. I should've cancelled. I've been caught up in a few things. Forgot you were coming actually.'

'Oh, shit, what's up?' Floyd said at the doorway. 'Or... I can go if you want?'

Frankie let out a long sigh. She felt like a saggy balloon letting out its last breath. 'You're here now. You may as well have a cuppa,' she said, bracing herself for one of his 'hilarious' quips.

'I'll do it,' he said, going into the kitchen, from where he shouted. 'Who said, 'I'd rather have a cup of tea than sex?"'

She rolled her eyes at Leonardo, who had just pounced on her lap for some attention. Floyd was so predictable. 'I don't know,' she answered in a monotone voice, the one people used when presented with a bad gag, 'who said, "I'd rather have a cup of tea than sex?"'

'It's not a joke. I was thinking aloud. It was Boy George.'

A minute later she had a mug in her hand.

'He had a point,' he said, slurping his.

'What?'

'Tea. It's reassuring, dependable, healing. Relationships, well, some of them, can be quite the opposite.'

Hmm, he had a point, she conceded. Because seeing Jason at the weekend had been devastating and damaging, and her fury and disbelief hadn't lifted. She stared off into space. 'You know I'm beginning to think I've been wasting my time.'

'About what?' Floyd said, shuffling into crossed legs on the carpet. 'Chuck us a cushion, would you?'

'That I could get Jason back. I found out on Saturday that's he's slept with someone else.'

Her words brought her to and she studied his face, waiting for him to console her. Instead, he just nodded. Maybe he had misheard her, so she tried again this time more forcefully. 'He's had sex with someone who isn't me. My husband.'

'Yep,' he said, impassively, as if they were discussing the weather.

'Floyd!' she almost shouted. 'I'm heartbroken, I feel like the rug has been pulled from under my feet all over again, what hope I had has gone. I knew I should've cancelled. I should've asked Letty over instead. At least I would've got some sympathy.'

'Sympathy? Why do you want sympathy?'

Frankie's back straightened in outrage and Leo scarpered. 'Because he's been unfaithful. What don't you understand about this?'

'Sympathy is overrated,' he said, maddening her even more.

'Now look—' she began.

'And didn't you think he was bound to have a go with someone else? To see if the grass was greener? That's what this has all been about, him thinking there's something better out there. He won't find it because it doesn't exist, but he hasn't worked that out yet.'

'Floyd!' she shrieked. 'You're supposed to be helping me!'

'Not to mention that you've been getting personal with me. Can I have that cushion?'

It was hardly the same! It was completely bloody different! She ripped one off the sofa and flung it at him so it bounced off his head. Leonardo cantered out of the room in fear.

Floyd laughed, presumably at her feeble throw.

Incensed – in fact, bloody tamping, as Letty would say – she tried harder to hurt him. 'I bet Sasha's sleeping around,' she spat, slinging her accusation as if it was fact.

'You reckon?' he said, neutrally.

'Didn't you think she was bound to have a "go" – or "goes" – with someone else?' she said, mimicking his words.

A vein stuck out on the left side of his temple. She'd pierced his skin and she hoped it hurt.

'Now hang on a minute,' he said, 'this is about you not me. And don't start on Sasha, you have no idea what she's like.'

'Oh, come on, Floyd, you think I'm stupid…' she said, letting the words hang like bait. It was up to him if he bit.

'I think I should go,' he announced coldly, chucking his cushion back at her before getting up onto his feet.

Frankie felt something snap inside of her. The desolation she'd felt all week from Jase's confession had curdled and she wanted to lash out. It was bubbling at her fingertips and before she knew what she was doing, she grabbed the cushion and walloped it against his thigh.

'What was that supposed to be?' he said, mockingly.

Furious, she unleashed a barrage of thwacks. 'Take that! And that! And… THAT!'

"What the hell— Ow!' he said, recoiling, with genuine pain after whipping him on the funny bone with the zip.

'Good,' she raged, 'GOOD. Because that's how I feel, but a million times worse.'

'Oh, is that right?' he said, protecting his manhood with cupped hands. 'It's always about you, isn't it. Well, I don't feel so fucking great myself thanks.'

He glared at her for a while, then darted to the side of her and before she had time to react, he'd taken another cushion and swiped it into her thigh. The sting set her off with a new onslaught but this time he was matching her every attack.

Back and forth, they traded blows, grunting with effort until Frankie decided to play dirty.

'What's that?' she suddenly asked, pointing out of the window. He stopped to look and she went for the backs of his knees, and shoved herself with it to make sure he toppled over. But because she'd used her entire body, she went over with him. He landed face down on the carpet and she fell onto him with an oomph, before rolling off. Floyd flipped over onto his back and made a grab for her leg, which she escaped by wriggling out of her joggers. Then she seized her chance, clambering on top of him to pin him down.

'How do you like that!' she said, panting, using all her weight to try to stop him moving. Her hands tightly squeezed his wrists and her groin pushed down onto his and she shouted 'Yes!' at her grand slam.

'That. Is. Pathetic,' he crowed, wrestling her off. 'It's your turn to suffer!' And he used one hand to lock both her wrists as he used the other to fake a yawn. 'Say mercy, go on!' he challenged her. She went limp, deliberately, and felt his grip loosen.

Summoning up every ounce of strength, Frankie brought up her knee and jabbed him in the privates and he fell off into a heap. Again she mounted him and trembled with effort as she held him still with the length of her entire body. 'I have you now!' she said, triumphantly, as her chest heaved from the effort of sucking in air.

He flopped his head to the side, baring his neck in surrender as if he was her prey. Frankie dropped her chin to recover – her heart was thumping and she felt his pulsing in between her own beats.

She raised her head just as he turned his and their noses were inches away. She was so close she could see flecks of hazel in his eyes and the curve of his thick black eyelashes.

'Finished?' he said, with a trace of a smile on his lips – his lovely red lips, Frankie noted – and his eyes glinting.

'Never!' she whispered, defiantly, before poking out her tongue.

He slowly freed his right hand and raised an eyebrow. She knew then he was asking her if she was okay with what was about to happen. She shut her eyes in acquiescence and a soft pat landed on her backside. She had no idea why but she gasped.

'Spanking,' Floyd said, still catching his breath, 'is the practice of consensual force for the sexual arousal of either or both parties. Pain in this context is an aphrodisiac, brought on both by the physiological reaction of blood rushing to the surface of the smack combined with psychological game play. For the giver, it's about control and for the receiver, it's submission.'

Her eyes burst open to study his – she abhorred violence, how could it be pleasurable? Although she had enjoyed their pillow fight. Oh my word, her longing was only growing at that thought.

Maintaining eye contact, he slapped her again, this time harder, making her bum smart.

'Properly done,' he said, quietly, 'the impact of a spank in this position makes the bottom squirm downwards, making contact between the erogenous zones.'

An ache which she'd been ignoring in her knickers had turned into a throb and she could feel Floyd's thing in the hollow of her inner hip. Another blow and she became aware that her panting hadn't stopped; her shallow breathing wasn't fear, she realized, but wholly unexpected excitement.

'It's said,' his voice now catching in his throat, 'women need to give themselves permission to let go and this is one way they can do it.'

Never had she thought she would enjoy this, but Floyd seemed to have a way of unlocking her reserve; when he explained things, it was as if he was speaking about her.

'But this isn't about anger or violence – it's about trust. It's a part of foreplay and should be mixed up with tenderness.'

He smacked her again and a groan came from inside her. His eyes were heavy with desire. Floyd swallowed slowly and waited. Frankie understood they had crossed a line.

She moved towards his face, pausing to see if he protested, but when none came she took his bottom lip in her mouth and bit into it, softly at first before she increased the pressure. A smack landed but this time his hand stayed in contact and he slipped his fingers underneath her knickers. The other hand stroked her hair and pushed down on her neck and she couldn't resist the pressure.

Her scalp tingled, her toes pointed in ecstasy and her mouth pounded as their lips touched for the very first time.

Monday Night

Em

'I'm thinking about changing the car,' Floyd said as Em struggled to fold herself into his Ford Cortina Mark III.

'Good,' she said as the ancient brown two-door motor spluttered into life.

'Bella has been a very loyal set of wheels, a bit of a head-turner too, you know, with the hipster chicks, but it's time for something more—'

'Stupid? Impulsive? Irresponsible?' she huffed as he turned the ignition.

'No, I want something a bit more reliable. To fit a baby seat, actually,' he said, seriously, 'to help you out. You'll need to borrow the car, won't you, when the little scamp arrives.'

Em was stunned by his thoughtfulness – and by her own tears which were welling up willy-nilly these days.

Clearing the lump in her throat, she said: 'Thanks, Floyd, I hadn't even thought about getting around with the baby. That'll be a real help. Oh, by the way, I'm going to tell Mum and Dad over dinner, now that I've got my head round it. I'm dreading Mum's reaction though – she'll be thrilled I'm going to be a single mum.'

'I bet they'll want to be called Sue and Albie rather than Nanny and Grandad,' Floyd said, tutting.

The pair settled into a companionable silence on the forty-five minute drive to their house, which was a windswept smallholding deep in the sticks, where they kept chickens and ducks. They'd moved there when they'd retired from lecturing at university, where they'd both been sociology professors. Em and Floyd had been born in London where their parents were from. As the car wound its way up into the hills, Em remembered the dislocation she had felt when they'd arrived in Cardiff. People spoke in a funny way and said strange things like 'by here' or 'by there' when they were explaining the location of something, even if it wasn't anywhere here nor there. Then there was the fear of starting secondary school knowing nobody. Floyd had settled straight in, proving a natural at rugby and football, which was all boys needed. The shift from England to Wales was a stepping stone for their parents, whose long-term dream was to live the good life in the rolling South Wales countryside. Having made it a couple of years ago, they had realized the ambition of growing their own, but had yet to work out how to generate their own power. On every visit, Floyd still liked to offer the contents of his bowels if they needed it. Actually, Em thought, Floyd usually mentioned it on the way. But so far, he'd said very little.

Something was up, which was odd considering how 'high on life, man' he'd been ever since he'd come home on Thursday night. 'Everything all right?' she ventured. There'd been a late phone call last night for Floyd but he hadn't brought it up. Perhaps that was it? But it could be anything – he might be fed up with her housekeeping rules – she could see how hard it was for him to remember to flush the loo – or he might be stressed at work. It must be hard listening to people's troubles all day, she thought.

'Yeah,' he said, absentmindedly, and that was that.

She tried to engage him with some chit-chat. Had he tried the new bar in Cardiff Bay? 'Nope.' Did he know Letty was loved up? 'Nice.' What about Frankie getting a sex teacher to win back Jason? He'd nearly crashed the car then – apparently just as Em had said that, a pheasant had run out into the roads.

He was the same over dinner too, which Mum took as a sign that his chakras were all out. Em noticed he didn't even take the piss when she said that; it was all very strange.

'This curry is lovely, Dad,' Em said.

'It's a veggie saag,' he said, then with triumph, 'featuring our very own spinach no less! The aloo gobi is made from home-grown potatoes and cauliflower too.'

'Amazing!'

Jingling with her arms of silver bracelets, Mum returned from the kitchen with warm naan bread. 'And this is from… the supermarket!' she laughed, holding it aloft like a trophy. 'I haven't quite got round to working the bread maker yet. Hey kids, listen, me and Dad have an announcement to make.'

Em looked at Floyd to see if he was going to chip in with something. This was the perfect moment for him to have a laugh: 'Are you pregnant, Mum?' 'Are you a lesbian, Dad?' But the only sign he'd heard Mum was he'd stopped mid-chew.

'Go on, Alb,' Mum said, looking mischievous, her ice-blue eyes dancing to a beat set by her hips which shook her hennaed shoulder-length waves and dangly ethnic earrings.

'You say it, Sue,' Dad said, his smile reaching up along his wrinkles to his still dark head of hair. 'It was your idea.'

They were like a double act, playing off one another, still clearly very much in love. In a world of their own, actually, and what the heck were they going to drop now?

'Right, well, here goes: we're going to spend three months living in a commune in Spain!'

Em was not in the slightest bit shocked. She sighed with acceptance. This was typical of them.

Floyd though just asked a blunt: 'Are you serious?'

'Albie,' Mum said, patting his arm as a sign to ignore Floyd.

'Well, we love living off the land here so much that we wanted to see what it was like doing it with other people, sort of in a community. Only for an extended holiday. There are some interesting techniques I'd like to learn which I can bring back here.' They'd bought a van, which they were picking up in the week and they'd booked their tickets. Mum beamed – it was really sweet the way she still had such an enthusiasm for things.

'When do you go?' Floyd said, with uncharacteristic sharpness.

'February the first…'

Two weeks before her baby was due.

'…So we've got ages. We'll be here for Christmas and back in time for summer before it gets too roasting there.'

Floyd inhaled dramatically through his nostrils and looked at Em with purpose. She was trying to hold it together. After all these adult years of finding Mum a bit of a pain, the one time she was going to need her, really need her, she wouldn't be here.

'Come on, you two,' Mum said, sensing the atmosphere. 'You don't need us like you used to, when you were small, you haven't done for years.'

Em didn't want to crush them with her sadness so she told them how happy she was and she'd help with whatever they needed to buy – sun cream and supplies – with her ten per cent discount at work.

Floyd suddenly stood up and his chair tipped back onto the

floor. 'This is a… bloody… fucking… folly!' he said in a voice which strained with anger. The table went quiet because this wasn't the Floyd they knew and loved. 'You two need to grow up, you're forever messing about and I just can't believe you're going when Em needs…'

Em shot Floyd a look of warning – don't you dare spoil this for them, it said, and don't even think about breaking my news.

Dad didn't lose his temper very often. But when he did…

'SIT. DOWN,' he yelled at Floyd.

Floyd did as he was told, realizing he'd overstepped the mark. But his face remained like thunder.

'We have never stopped you two from doing what you've wanted to do. Never,' Dad spat. 'We have always let you go your own way, encouraged you to do it, in fact. We've been deliberately hands-off to allow you to make your own choices. And we'd appreciate the same courtesy.'

Floyd pushed his plate away and put his heads in his hands.

'And apologise to your mother.'

Floyd hesitated as Em prayed he would say sorry. She just didn't understand where his tantrum had come from. Why did he care so much? It was so unlike him. Dad was absolutely right that they'd given her and Floyd plenty of freedom. They believed strict parenting gave teenagers something to rebel against. Neither Floyd nor her had had any need to do anything extreme – mainly because Mum and Dad would have liked it. There was the time Floyd was caught smoking a spliff out of his bedroom window when he was seventeen, but Dad had only told him off for not sharing it. That had put both of them off the idea that drugs were 'cool'. Their hands-off approach had taught Floyd and Em that only they themselves could do the hard work. And she never doubted her parents' love; Mum and Dad's worst crime was being a bit embarrassing in their sandals and hippy gear.

'Sorry, Mum. Sorry, Dad,' he said, getting up.

Em breathed a sigh of relief as Mum disappeared in a six-foot-something sandwich of a hug. His last comment, the bit where he almost said she would need Mum and Dad, had been forgotten. There was no rush to tell them; she'd do it in the week, when things had settled down. What would Mum miss in the first three months of her baby's life? She'd be back for the good stuff like walking and talking.

That night though, she lay awake trying to calculate how she was going to work through Mum's absence. Sure, Floyd was showing he wanted to be involved but he wouldn't be off work, neither would he have the experience she needed to guide her through the long days and nights she'd been told to expect.

It meant she'd have to reconsider her options, throw herself into mum-and-baby groups, which frightened the life out of her. She didn't mind being alone – she minded not having an instruction manual.

Round and round she went but, begrudgingly, Simon Brown's offer of moving in when the baby was born seemed increasingly to be her only real practical prospect.

Tuesday

Letty

'Attention, everyone!' Ross called as he went to Letty's desk, parking his backside next to her keyboard to make his announcement.

Her workspace was positioned at the top of the room, next to Ross' office, and looked out onto the rest of the team. So she rolled her chair to one side to see his audience, who were twenty-strong.

'Two things,' he said, rubbing his hands together. 'First, in three weeks' time we'll be going on a bonding day.'

He paused before adding: 'I said bonding, not bondage!'

A ripple of amusement went round the office. Letty noticed everyone laughed apart from her, Jools, the head of PR, and Sal, an account director. Ross really did do the sad middle-aged man act very well. Luckily though he had seemed to get the message and he'd not tried it on with her again.

'It's all happening at The Oaks, the splendid hotel in the Vale of Glamorgan we represent – special rates of course! We'll start off doing an assault course, crawling on our hands and knees through mud, that type of thing. Then we'll have a working lunch, a bit of role play – fnar, fnar – and blue-sky thinking. The afternoon will be free for some time in the spa, before we host a charity dinner in the evening.'

A mixture of oohs and aahs went up. It was typical Ross: flamboyant, generous, and all for a good cause.

'Letty, here, will send out the details later when I get the itinerary through from the hotel. All you need to remember is to bring joggers, bathers, your glad rags and a load of ideas.'

He crossed his arms and soaked up the smiles around the room.

'Second, the bonding day will coincide with the launch of our social media presence.'

Oh my God!

Letty exploded inside – she'd managed to impress him after

all! Just this morning she'd been wondering if he'd read any of her post-presentation emails – sending him links to masterful customer service and punchy campaigns online. Clearly, he had! Fucking hell, she wanted to do a lap of honour round the office.

She turned to him and waited for his smile. He was still looking straight ahead. She toned down her face a little because it might come across as a bit smug: he needed to explain it first.

'We'll be on all platforms – Facebook, Twitter, Instagram, YouTube, Periscope, Vine.' Yes, he'd definitely read her email, Letty thought. 'If it talks, we talk. This is a really important step for us and something that's going to take us to the next level. It's going to take an extraordinary type of person to manage it. I'm restructuring to reflect that to create a special position for that person to co-ordinate what we do, who we represent and how we get our message across.'

Letty stared at her lap: she was blinking dying here! Finally, everyone was going to see that she had ideas and she could execute them. This was the most cracking feeling ever: the anticipation of recognition that had eluded her made her heart race. And to think he was doing this in front of everyone – he could've had a quiet word in her ear but no, he obviously wanted to give her the credit she was due.

'So it is with great pleasure that I would like to present to you...'

Her feet twitched, her thighs were primed – she was all ready to stand up and take the applause! What should she say, she wondered quickly, her mind going crazy with buzzwords of brand-building, engagement and accessibility. And as soon as she got her first new and improved wage packet, she'd consolidate her debts and start paying them back properly.

'...our new social media lead... Dylan Gates.'

What?! Dylan Gates? Dylan fucking Gates? The scene accelerated away from her as though someone had pushed the wheels of her chair out of the way.

Dylan was walking up to the front now and shaking hands with Ross, sucking up the sound of clapping. How had this happened? It had been her project: she'd done all the work on it and it had landed in his flaming lap. Letty looked at Nick, Ross' deputy, who had tilted his head to one side. Through his minimalist rimless glasses, he was studying his boss with cool eyes. He had to be as shocked as she was – Nick had already complimented her on her presentation and would be backing her for the project. So what was going on?

The penny dropped. Dylan was the son of one of Ross' big clients, who had failed to bring in any business in the three months he'd been here. Rather than lose face and a cash cow by giving him the heave-ho, which was no less than he deserved but which wouldn't be favourably looked upon by his father, Ross had promoted him – and completely shafted her. Stolen her project and given it to Dylan, who was stood there in a fat tie and a wide-boy suit with all the gear but no idea.

'Cheers, boss,' he said, smoothing his footballer haircut. 'I'm mega happy about this. I'm gonna make sure we make a big entrance come launch day. Everyone will get their own accounts so we can all help drive the traffic. Letty will do the technicals for me. She doesn't know that yet but she does now!' He actually had the gall to give her a wink.

Being his monkey made it even worse, she thought, her eyes blurring with indignity. Just then she caught Ross staring at her: she could make out a vein in his neck which always stood out if he was getting a PR hard-on. It dawned on her then in searchlights: he'd done this on purpose. She thought she'd made stand, had shown him that she was professional and determined but obviously he'd taken very differently to her turning him down. His eyes were smirking: this was his revenge for her not playing the game. For reprimanding him for his casual sexism. For frustrating the hell out of his, probably tiny. willy.

She gulped and looked down at her hands, which were now shaking fists in her lap.

'Thanks everyone,' Ross said. 'Any questions? No? Okay, thank you.' Then he disappeared into his office with Dylan and shut the door.

Her head banging with outrage, she slid back behind her monitor and held her face. Think, Letty, think! She toyed with the idea of walking out. Of handing in her notice right then and there. But she'd have no way of paying off the interest on her credit cards, which she was behind on already. He had her over a barrel.

Lance couldn't bail her out – he was paying for his mortgage and maintenance. She'd never ask her friends or family. What the hell could she do?

With a stab to her heart, she realized those unworn Vivienne Westwoods were going to have to go back. Chucking money at stuff had never worked, she knew now. It was time to rein in her spending. If she could.

But that wasn't going to sort out Ross. Then it came to her.

What was it they said? When life gives you lemons, make lemonade.

If she was clever enough, if her instinct was right that she wasn't the only female to have been on his hit list, then she could make bacon out of her pig of a boss.

Wednesday Night

Frankie

Taking two steps at a time, Frankie felt as if she was flying up the stairs to Em's flat. Last week's session with Floyd had given her her wings – if only Jason could see her now, she thought, he'd say she had actually turned into Tinkerbell! The lessons weren't just practical in their value; Floyd was her sounding board and he had a way of putting things which gave her insight into her situation.

She ran through the lessons in a mental list to reflect the project so far, which was going well, on the whole. Not The Missionary had taught her the importance of touch and tempo. The Sixty-Nine advice of relax, take it slow and make a circle had worked. Spanking had been liberating, helping move on from the pain of Jason's infidelity.

Their to-do list was daunting: Something Risky, Dressing Up, Erotica, Talking Dirty, Orgasms, Sex Toys and Bondage.

But Frankie was sure her sex education would mean she would be unafraid when she got her chance to sleep with Jason.

How lucky she was to have a counsellor for a teacher! Not only was she starting to feel more equipped between the sheets, but in her head too. And Floyd said he was getting something out of it too; it was a distraction from Sasha, who he was missing very much, even more so because she'd gone AWOL this past week with no phone calls, emails or messages.

It was strange to think she hadn't had actual sex with Floyd yet. In fact, and she wasn't entirely sure why, everything they'd done so far had felt more intimate than what she remembered the physical act of sex to involve. But then, there had been times when she had slept with Jason when she hadn't really felt in the mood, out of a sense of what a wife's duty was. Perhaps it was because it was all new, not just the topics they covered, but Floyd himself.

Looking back to the spanking, she saw how sex could've followed on quite naturally. During that lesson, she and Floyd had ended up kissing – she still felt a rush of something when she thought about it. But then he'd put a stop to it, explaining it was unprofessional and he'd apologized profusely for 'unplanned snoggage'.

'These things happen,' Frankie had said, to soothe him, but she had felt less inhibited around him then. Yes, she was glad to have kissed him. Really glad because he'd been an amazing snog, actually, not that she liked to dwell on the deep, slow seduction of his lips. It had been different to pashing with Jason. They didn't tend to snog much; she supposed it was because they had been together for so long, and it had had less of an important role in their love-making as the years passed.

At Em's door, she knocked and waited for her friend. She was grateful Floyd wasn't in tonight; Wednesday was football night.

It'd be too weird to be in the same room as both Em and Floyd – once the lessons were over she would be able to pack away the secret forever and forget about it. It still felt wrong withholding information from Em, but Frankie didn't want to upset her; if she knew, it would only make things awkward. And it would mean the premature end of this arrangement, just as she was getting somewhere.

'Ready for your mum-to-be pampering evening, Em?' Frankie chirped when she stepped inside her flat. Em looked relaxed for the first time in her pregnancy; she was rosy-cheeked and her edges seemed rounded.

'I think so! I don't really do girly stuff, do I?' Em laughed, letting her in.

'Being pregnant is probably the ultimate in girly, I'm afraid,' Frankie said. And my, how she was blooming! Frankie still found it unfathomable that Em was pregnant when she was definitely 'the one least likely to' of the three of them. Her own broodiness had gone – it felt so far from being a possibility in her world now. Em's circumstances weren't ideal, but she seemed to have overcome that mental block. All credit to her, Frankie thought, taking in her friend's glow.

In the lounge, Letty had done a beautiful job warming up Em's functional and sparse living space. Where the surfaces were usually free from papers and cups and wrappers, Letty had arranged lighted candles, fluffy towels and scented oils. The curtains remained open, because it was dark and brooding

148

enough outside thanks to an approaching summer storm, and it gave the room an elemental feeling.

'Does it say "spa" enough to you?' Letty asked from the sofa, where she lay with slices of cucumber on her eyes. She spoke through ventriloquist's teeth because she'd already applied a face mask of avocado, coconut oil, peanut butter and an egg white which she declared 'bogging!'.

'The room looks perfect!' Frankie said, setting up her table of nail varnishes and hair products.

'What are you going to do to me?' Em asked nervously, sitting formally on the armchair she never let Floyd use because she was frightened he'd drop food all over it.

'I'll do a head, neck and shoulder massage, Letty will do nails and then we're going to eat cake. All right with you?'

'Not really, apart from the cake bit,' Em said, with a grimace. 'You know I don't like people touching me.'

Letty and Frankie swapped eye-rolls, pointing out she was going to have to get used to it with all that poking and prodding she was going to get at the birth. Then they got to work.

These make-over sessions – usually at Frankie's because with Dad being a bloke, he'd kept out of the way and left them to it – had been a constant since the threesome had met; only their problems and worries had changed. In the early days, they'd shrieked about boys while they'd tested each other's Rimmel lipsticks, tried out different hairstyles and practised French kissing on the backs of their hands. As they became women, they'd discuss men and work over waxing strips and eyebrow plucking.

Now they were each going through something different, yet they were still there for each other.

Letty was, in her words, 'farting rainbows', she was that happy with Lance. She was having a rough time of it at work, but she'd pledged to sort out her creep of a boss. Em was coping with the prospect of motherhood and Frankie was discovering things about herself that she'd never known she was capable of.

And it hadn't gone unnoticed.

'You look better than you have in ages,' Em said, licking the last bits of chocolate ginger cake off her fingers as Frankie trimmed her red bob, which was glossy and full from her pregnancy.

'Yeah, I feel it,' Frankie said, truthfully.

'Must be that sex teacher!' Letty sang.

'Oh, please, I've just got over morning sickness. Please don't make me feel sick all over again,' Em said.

'It's going well. I won't go into details, for Em's sake, but it's helping.'

'Are you ever going to tell us who he is? Your teacher?' Letty pleaded.

Em held up her hands. 'I don't want to know.'

Not on your nelly, she was about to say when a crack of lightning accompanied a rumble of thunder. The front door slammed and all three of them jumped. The hall echoed with what sounded like the clip-clop of heels.

Em murmured: 'Floyd.'

'Sounds like he's got stilettos on! The reprobate!' Letty whispered.

Frankie froze at the thought that perhaps he'd brought someone home with him. She had a desperate urge to hide or leave.

'Take your studs off! They'll mark the floor!' Em shouted.

'Football was bastard cancelled,' came his voice.

Exhaling slowly, Frankie relaxed and scolded herself for jumping to conclusions.

Em leaned forward conspiratorially and told them he was in a funny mood: Sasha had rung the other night, very late because she'd forgotten the time difference, to announce she was coming home. Frankie's heart pounded. She knew Sasha would be coming back at some point; Floyd had always been open about it.

Sasha had only asked if she could stay when she got back, here in her house, Em said.

Drawing a sharp breath in sympathy, Letty asked: 'Never! What did you say about that?'

'What could I say? He pays rent and he's allowed to have guests. I'm not running some old-fashioned B&B! But the strange thing is, Floyd isn't exactly jumping for joy,' Em divulged.

Frankie took some deep breaths; it was the shock, that was all. She had something at stake with Floyd, something good and she wasn't ready to give it up. There were six lessons still to go and if Sasha suddenly appeared, it would all have to stop. And of course Floyd would run straight back to her, Frankie thought feeling more than a pang of sadness, he'd only been helping her and it wasn't as if he was going to turn down regular sex with his girlfriend.

'Maybe he's just nervous,' Letty said, through a mouthful of lemon drizzle cake. 'He hasn't seen her for ages and he's probably built her up to be even more amazing than she is. Although I'm not sure how much more perfect she could be.'

The door handle rattled as Floyd barged in wearing a neon pink football kit. His entrance sparked off a series of crazy feelings in Frankie. Her tummy flipping, she wanted to laugh out loud at the sight of him. Next, she begged for the ground to swallow her up so she didn't have to fight the deep blush which was rising from her collarbone as she remembered how intimate they'd been.

'How's my favourite sister?' Floyd said, before icing up when he saw she had company. 'Jesus, what's that green stuff on your face?'

Letty poked her tongue out. 'You don't look too hot yourself!' she said, taking in his bright shirt, shorts and knee-high socks

'I'm very comfortable in cerise, actually,' he said.

Frankie was willing Floyd not to look at her. But when he didn't, she found herself thinking 'at least say hello'.

'I play for a gay side. The captain is a mate, his brother runs a gay bar which sponsors us. I'm the equal opportunities player, you know, their one token straight person. And I happen to think the kit brings out the colour of my eyes.'

'Why was it cancelled?' Em said.

'Most of them have gone to see a Dolly Parton tribute act, I think she's called Dolly Hard-On. I did know, I just forgot. Anyway, everyone all right?' he asked the room. Em and Letty sang a joint 'yep' while Frankie could only nod mechanically. Their eyes met and she pulled a smile which she hoped said 'oh, hi, I'm very cool with this'.

Was she imagining things or did his eyes flicker with amusement? They were warm, as usual, but there was something else there too. Was it a secret sign acknowledging that this was indeed an awkward situation in light of their arrangement? Was it mirth at her squirming?

Breathe in, breathe out, Frankie thought, but the air was hot and she needed to get out. But first, agonizingly, she had to speak because she couldn't just dash out. 'I'm just going to pop to the shop, for some chocolate for Em,' she said, flapping her top.

'Ooh, great, a Cadbury's Caramel, please,' Em said.

She'd got away with it, Frankie heaved, as she escaped into the hall. She lay her back against the wall to cool down. But the reddening all over didn't stop. She was out of danger so why was she the colour of... of his flushed lips when they'd kissed?

Her answer came when he appeared by her side as she let herself out of the flat. He'd go with her, he said, to get something for his tea. Holy sheep. It was his physical presence that was making her feel hot.

Meanwhile...

Letty

'So, what's happening with Simon?' Letty asked Em, once they were alone. She pretended to be preoccupied with the task of painting her nails bright coral, knowing this was her best chance of getting Em to talk. If she was too eager for information, Em would shut down.

'Not much,' Em said, shaking her fringe and examining her reflection in a hand mirror. 'Is it straight? Because I don't think it's straight. You can't see this eyebrow but you can see most of the other one.'

Letty peered hard at her friend. Fuck! Frankie had ballsed it right up, which was very odd. Normally she had a steadier pair of hands than a blinking surgeon. Em's usual style of fringe was Mary Quant but this was Mary Quirky. Although, hang on, she thought examining it intently, it was really lovely in a kooky way.

'It's not straight, no,' she said, tilting her head, 'But... I like it. Actually, I love it. It's edgy. Still angular, like you like it, but it looks great.'

'Okay.'

Bloody hell, Letty would've had a screaming fit if this had happened to her but Em was satisfied. This was one of her most lovely features, she would take your word for it; there was no fishing for compliments.

'Funnily enough, I feel a bit skew-whiff,' Em said as a flicker from the electric storm lit up the room.

'How's that then?' Letty said, returning to her nails.

'Simon Brown wants to move in to help with the baby.'

'Right. And how would that work?' It was quite an offer – above and beyond his duty – Letty thought, wondering if there was anything more going on which Em hadn't picked up.

'He'd have two weeks of paternity leave, so for that he'd be here all the time. Then a few months until I get the baby into a routine. Separate bedrooms. He'd do the cooking and washing.

I'd really wanted Mum to help but she's going away just before the baby's due. Floyd will be around but I need someone who's experienced, and it seems as if Simon Brown is my only option.'

Ah. It sounded that he was just trying to honour his role as the father. Poor love, Letty said to herself, she must feel so alone. 'Don't forget we're all here. We could all take a fortnight off in sequence so your first six weeks are covered and by then you'll have settled in.'

Topping up her glass with some fizzy water and refilling Letty's glass, Em said: 'That's so kind. But it'll be the blind leading the blind! I'm a godmother and I love kids, but babies, well, they're completely different. At least Simon Brown has been there, done that and got the sicky T-shirt with his six-year-old daughter. What do you reckon about his plan?'

Letty wondered if Em was actually seeking some kind of validation, permission even, to take him up on it. Perhaps Em had a gut feeling to do it but didn't yet trust it.

'Honestly? I think there'd be nothing better than you and him doing this together. It's natural to worry now about the effect it might have on you if he did move in when the baby comes. But I suspect when the time comes, you'll both be preoccupied with the baby. Besides, you get on still, you might not be together but you've got a good relationship.' She thought of Lance, who was finding it very hard not seeing Eddy every day. 'And Simon is the father – you're going to know one another for the rest of your lives now, so you have to consider him, build bridges. And kids need their dads. Dear God, they need their dads.'

Look how her dad's absence had affected her life. Yet she'd never try to find him: he didn't have the right to be part of her life now. It was too late but how she'd wished it had been different.

'But I'm scared,' Em said in a tiny voice. 'What if he hurts me all over again when he leaves?' Then she cleared her throat and smoothed her lap of creases. When she spoke she was her usual contained self again. 'No, I don't know what I've been thinking. I'm going to do this alone. I have my interview to think about and Simon Brown is a distraction. He is my rival. I have only known him a few months. I cannot put my life in his hands.'

This was standard Em, she was trying to protect herself, and Letty didn't blame her.

She narrowed her eyes. 'Perhaps he's doing all of this to distract me, so he gets the manager's job… would someone do that?'

'I don't think so, babes,' Letty said, frowning at her friend's neuroticism. 'He'd have to be a totally nasty piece of work to do that and he doesn't seem the type.'

Em sighed. 'I just wish I could rope off my private and professional lives, like I used to be able to. Like he can.'

'It'll all work out, babes,' Letty said, 'I refuse to believe otherwise. I mean, who'd have thought it'd work out for me and Lance?'

Em looked down at her thickening stomach and gave it a rub. 'I saw the midwife the other day. She said I should think about a home birth. It's all the rage these days. But Mum did that with me and Floyd, which is a good enough reason not to do it.'

'I'd demand all the drugs and a curtain at the neck so I didn't have to see any of it,' Letty said, firmly.

'Well, I fancy a nice sterile birth in a hospital with gas and air. Are you thinking about reproduction then, Letty?'

Letty reeled back in shock – truly it wasn't something she'd thought of. 'Christ no! I still can't believe we're together, properly together,' she said. 'It's weird enough to have a bloke there the next morning! But I'm really looking forward to having his son to stay once Lance has finished baby-proofing the flat, which by the way has completely ruined the look of the place. It's all gates and contraptions to stop fingers getting trapped. But it's going to be lush to see Lance as a dad. It'll be good training for me when you want some baby-sitting.'

Smiling, Em reached out her hands.

Letty felt a burst of love for her: she was doing so well for someone who found the unknown so terrifying.

'Oh, come here!' Letty said, leaping out of her chair to *cwtch* her.

'That's nice,' Em said into her ear. 'But I meant I was ready for you to do my nails…'

'I know!' Letty squealed. 'I KNOW!'

At the Same Time... Lesson Four

Frankie

Marching a fraction ahead of Floyd, Frankie was all of a dither.

'Talk about making it obvious,' she'd said when they stepped out into the muggy night.

'You're being absurd. They wouldn't guess I'm your teacher just because I've come with you to the shop.'

She'd stomped on for a bit, realizing that yes, he was probably right. But she felt all spiky and confused about her reaction to the news that Sasha was coming home – and for her physical flush in Floyd's company. Surely she didn't have a crush on him?

She had to think straight. She had no right to a breaking news heads-up on Floyd's 'relationship status update'. They had a professional agreement, that was all. And what she was feeling for him wasn't real. It was that 'trans-thingy' Floyd had told her about. Transference, that was it, 'an unconscious redirection of feelings from one person to another', he'd said, when he'd told how one of his patients fell for him. Frankie had simply diverted and projected her feelings for Jason onto Floyd. That was all.

Feeling calmer, steadier now she knew where she stood, her feet slowed down so Floyd could catch up. 'You must be so happy Sasha's coming home,' she said, trying to make amends.

'She wants to get a place together,' he said. 'It's all I've ever wanted.'

'There you are, your very own happy ending,' she summarised, because saying it out loud steeled her for what she had to do next – end their arrangement.

'It's just I never thought she'd go for it,' he said.

The thunder that had been in the distance crashed overhead – if there was ever a sign that a higher being was giving her a nudge, that was it. 'So... we need to call all of this off.'

'Yep, looks like it. Definitely. Absolutely,' he said, nodding ferociously.

They walked in silence for a bit.

'The thing is, though, she's always bloody late. Never on time for anything so it could be ages.'

Frankie's heart skipped a beat. 'Right, so you don't know when she's back?'

'Nope. She'll just turn up at some point, if she does at all. So there's no real rush if you, er…'

'Oh, right.' Oh my goodness, she thought, he's so lovely he's willing to help me right up until the last possible minute.

'And you're doing so well,' he said, brightening up, 'I really think the next few lessons are vital, you're almost there. Jason will be putty in your hands.'

'It'd be a shame to throw it all away, I s'pose.' She made it sound like she wasn't that bothered because she didn't want him to feel an obligation but inside she was jumping for joy.

'And we can combine some of the modules to speed things up. Like Dressing Up and Erotica, we can do those two together, plus Sex Toys and Bondage are virtually the same thing anyway. I'm hoping we can fit Orgasms and Talking Dirty in amongst them too.'

'That leaves us with three lessons because you've missed out Something Risky,' she pointed out, wafting the neckline of her skater dress because it was such a warm night.

'Right, so we should get a move on, then.'

'Cool,' she said, happy that they'd settled it.

'So, er, how about now?' he said, chirpily.

'Now?' she said, swallowing a scream and peeking at him quickly as they walked. Floyd was smiling broadly at her. He actually meant it!

'Why not? Time is of the essence,' he shrugged.

'Okaaay,' she said, laughing with nerves. And excitement. But then she began to see with new eyes. There was no way they could just stop and do anything here. They were on a busy road, there were people dressed up on their way to the waterfront and there were CCTV cameras everywhere.

Floyd clearly couldn't have cared less as he began. 'So, lesson number four. Risk in the sexual context is about the buzz of possibly getting caught,' he said, 'but it's also about taking things out of the bedroom and into the public arena to make it feel adventurous. It's a common fantasy and one which is fairly easy to act out in a park-'

'In the park? But the park's for picnics...' Frankie squeaked.

'On the train-'

'I just like a nice coffee and one of those baguettes, I do.'

'Or in the office.'

'Office? People put their bums on desks and things?' she said, horrified.

'Er... yes.'

'Oh. Right. Is it planned, then, like, do you go out with the intention of doing it? Because don't you have to make sure you're wearing the right clothes?' she said, worrying because she had pants on and surely you shouldn't be wearing any.

'It can be or it might happen spontaneously, like, you're out together and you feel... aroused and you just want that girl right now,' he said in his loud lecture voice. Frankie looked around to check no one could hear. 'For example, say I was feeling that about you...' he said, touching her arm to indicate that yes, indeed, he meant her.

Frankie laughed then apologized when he gave her a stern look.

'So, as I was saying, we'd be walking to the shops, as we are, and then we'd have a flirt – some teasing, a bit of a giggle, a bit of ooh-la-la lingering eye contact...'

'Got you,' Frankie said, with complete attention.

'Then I'd take your hand, like this...'

Frankie's whole body rippled with pleasure; she adored holding hands. Jason had always been a bit shy to do it in public, in case his mates saw him. So doing it now made her skin tingle. Floyd's touch was warm and steady and their hands met perfectly, despite their gaping difference in height. She didn't care if anyone saw them – she'd develop a hobble if they bumped into somebody, but it was dark enough to feel safe but thrilling at the same time.

'Then I'd be imagining how it would feel to kiss you, to press against you, to feel your bumps squashed against me...' His voice was softer now and she turned to him, biting her lip. Floyd blinked slowly, his intense eyes checking to see if she was feeling it too.

She gave a small nod and he continued.

'Maybe,' he sighed, 'you'd do some... touching.'

Frankie began to throb as she saw the scene in her mind. His grip became firmer and her heart was there in her groin.

But they'd reached the shop! Going inside, Frankie felt fizzy and heady – buying groceries was the last thing on her mind but if he went back empty-handed the girls might twig. So she grabbed at random bars of chocolate before fiddling around in her purse for a note, then waited outside for Floyd. But he couldn't come soon enough – she was dying to get to the good bit. When he stepped outside, he too had a hungry look on his face and they walked quickly, their glances smouldering, tripping over themselves to go wherever it was they were going to do this.

Rain began to fall in heavy, loaded drops and the streets became deserted. Floyd had ditched his glasses and his eyelashes were gleaming. Her chest felt shiny and her hair was now a mess of dirty blonde ringlets. Swept up by the anticipation, she couldn't have cared less.

'What now?' she said, urgently, feeling nervous excitement. They weren't touching but an electricity bounced between them, as if their anticipation was tangible.

'Soon,' he said, picking up the pace and holding his bag in front of his groin – Frankie felt a wild shot of lust go through her as she saw his shorts were straining.

Using a fob key, Floyd opened the glass door to Em's block of apartments and took Frankie by the hand into the wide hallway. How many times had she passed through, not stopping to soak in its minimalist, modernist style? Now she noticed the muted lighting which fanned erotically up the matte dark grey walls. On the right, there was a winding industrial-style metal staircase which made her feel raw. At the back was a bank of steel rectangular letter boxes. And on the left, the wall was an entire mirror in front of which sat an armless creamy leather loveseat.

Floyd threw his bag then hers onto the petrol-coloured slate floor. 'Ready?' he said, hoarsely, pulling her towards him.

'What if someone sees us?' Frankie whispered, resisting his tug, holding onto the thrill of their charged longing. 'Em and Letty are just upstairs, what if they come down, what if someone walks in?'

'That's the point.' His voice was like gravel, coming from somewhere deeper than his chest.

She knew they didn't have much time, so quickly, Frankie took it all in again. The hallway could almost be watching them.

Anyone could walk past the door. There were people above them oblivious to what was about to happen – and the thought thrilled her. Just then, she caught sight of her reflection. She hardly recognized herself: it wasn't just because she was sodden from the rain, in fact she hardly saw that at all. What struck her was her tousled hair, ripe lips, excited eyes and shining skin. Frankie shivered and stared up at Floyd with hungry eyes. Instinctively, they moved together. He picked her up, she drew her legs up around his waist and they began to kiss. Tenderly, slowly, at first, making the fantasy they'd shared real. He carried her to the stairs, where he placed her onto the coiled end of the bannister so he could free his hands.

'Anyone could see us,' she whispered, turned on by the thought. And then she gasped as she saw her and Floyd in the mirror. She was the voyeur.

'Can you feel the danger?' he breathed.

She could and they got lost in each other. Frankie was floating in a deep luxurious velvet to the soundtrack of the downpour outside. All of the hurt and humiliation and doubt was starting to be erased. In its place was a delicious, insistent and overwhelming pulse – holy moly, it was the same feeling she'd had when they had covered the sixty-nine. Was this how an orgasm began? In the mind?

But there was no time to find out. A door slammed high above them, making them seize up. Then footsteps gradually got louder, echoing Frankie's disappointment: she could've gone all the way tonight.

'Custard creams!' Frankie said as they recovered themselves and played at searching through their bags when a woman appeared and went past them unaware.

'That was close!' Frankie whispered, on a high from the experience.

'Too close,' Floyd said, white-faced.

'So I'm guessing that getting off on the thought of getting caught is an entirely different matter to actually getting caught.'

'Correct. Safe to say, you get an A star for that assumption.'

'You know, Floyd, it's down to you! You're ever so good at this. How you manage to act all of this out, it's so clever. And if it's like this with you then I can't imagine how it'll feel with Jason!'

Floyd opened his mouth, thought about it then shook his

head. She didn't wait for him to explain because suddenly she was aware of the time.

'Come on, we better go,' Frankie said, taking the stairs two at a time. 'They'll be wondering where we are.'

Em was on standby with towels, making sure they stayed on the doormat so they didn't drip on the floor.

'You took your time,' she said, making a grab for Frankie's bag. 'Did you pop to Cadbury's HQ? Wow. You seem to have bought the entire shop. Apart from my Caramel. But thanks.'

Then she turned her attention to Floyd's carrier and began rifling through it. 'Pesto, beef burgers and a Tex-Mex sauce? Interesting combo.'

'It's a, um, a fusion cuisine sort of thing,' he snapped, before swiping it off his sister and heading to the kitchen.

Frankie was grateful for the hair towel so she could hide beneath it and breathe. The pride she felt at nailing the lesson in risk was gone; now she felt guilty that she was doing this behind Em's back. It's just that she wouldn't understand, Frankie truly believed that. But it still felt a betrayal of sorts.

As she resurfaced through a tangle of curls, she heard Floyd saying: 'You look hot!'

Whirling round to confront his indiscretion, Frankie smiled at the thought of whipping him with her towel. But he hadn't been talking to her. He was grinning into the screen of his phone. She felt a stab of jealousy that he had been talking to… who?

'It's 3 a.m. and it's still 30 degrees,' said a familiar girly voice.

Oh, right, he meant she looked 'hot' hot. Frankie's envy stood down – but then she corrected herself: her reaction had been out of raging hormones, nothing more.

'Why are you up so late?'

'I've just got in from a beach party, it was the most amazing thing with fire-eaters and a UV bar – you'd have loved it. It was sort of a leaving do for me, well, one of them!'

Sasha. She was definitely on her way.

Friday

Letty

'This makes a change from the canteen!' Em said, her fingers itching to dive in as she eyed up slim crustless sandwiches, scones, custard tarts, eclairs and mini chocolate muffins piled high on cake stands on the table.

'It's SO posh!' Frankie squeaked, pouring Earl Grey into the most beautiful mismatched china cups and saucers.

'Letty said you'd like it,' Lance said. 'It's on me too so tuck in, ladies!'

Letty allowed herself a self-satisfied smile as she surveyed the scene: here before her were the most precious people in her life. She was so proud of Lance for making exactly the right impression on the girls here in The St David's Hotel; it hadn't been her idea as he'd implied. He'd come up with afternoon tea himself – so very British, Pommie perfect, he'd called it. And it was – it felt special but not over-the-top. They'd even dressed up for it, the total babes: like Letty, Frankie was in a tea dress and heels, and Em had worn her best suit to work so she could look the part when she nipped out for lunch.

An hour was just long enough to introduce him, and Letty hoped with all her heart they'd like him. How could they not! He looked mind-blowingly gorgeous in his navy blue suit which sat just right on his Herculean shoulders.

'So, Lance, how's it going sharing a house with Little Miss Tidy?' Em asked, already on her second egg and cress sandwich.

'Yeah, she *is* a bit of a neat freak,' he laughed.

For a forty-year-old who was brought up Down Under, he still had the most amazing skin, Letty simpered, before changing her expression to a fake-frown when she realized they were taking the piss. Look at yourself, she thought, you big wet fart!

Lance continued: 'God knows what she's going to be like when my son comes over, she doesn't realize how destructive little tykes are.'

'Ooh, any news on that front?' Letty said, squeezing his hand beneath the table. She didn't want to rub it in that they were basically Completely In Love.

'Yes!' Lance said, punching the air. 'She messaged on my way here. We're having him next weekend!'

He was overjoyed. 'Oh, amazing,' Letty said.

'There's nice,' Frankie said. 'What's his name?'

'Eddy, he's twenty-one-months. He's coming Friday and then I take him back Sunday. I can't wait.'

'You better think of some things to do then, Letty,' Em said, selecting a miniature beef and horseradish brioche.

'Well, funny you should say that. I've already started clearing the box room for his travel cot and I thought we could go to MacDonald's, the cinema, you know, the stuff kids love.' Letty nodded satisfactorily to show she was on the ball.

Lance guffawed. 'You reckon?'

'Why not? I used to love that shit.'

'I'm a personal trainer, I can't feed him junk! It's organic all the way for him. And he needs to be outdoors! Have you ever tried to get a pre-schooler to sit still for longer than five minutes? It's impossible. Besides, Helen would kill me, she's a bit of an earth mother.'

'But we want him to have fun, don't we?' Letty said, pulling a face to cover up her hurt. Even though she knew he wasn't trying to make her feel bad, she felt stung.

'Kids need routine, Letty,' he said gently, realizing something was up. 'We need him to feel comfortable first, that's all.'

Letty felt a complete twat and she could see the girls had noticed it. Fuck, she'd been so desperate for it to go smoothly too.

'You'll be a great stepmum,' he added, 'trust me.'

'With any luck, he'll be asleep in his room by 7 p.m.,' Em said, 'then you'll have the evening to recover.'

'Yeah, that's another thing,' Lance said, looking apologetic, 'he'll have to come in with us in case he gets scared, waking up in a strange place.'

Dear God, this was getting worse, Letty thought. She really hadn't understood what parenting entailed. But she had to regain her poise. 'Of course,' she said, 'there's plenty of room for the cot in our room.'

'No, I meant he'll be in between us. He co-sleeps with Helen, it's something she insisted on and it's really worked. He had terrible colic when he was small and it was something we looked into and it calmed him down, so we stuck with it.'

Jesus Christ, what the hell? The prospect of playing 'mum and dad' suddenly didn't appeal to Letty: the pair of them were insane! They were like those idiot parents you heard about who treated their kids like little buddhas. In her mind, there was little people's time and adults' time.

'I might go in the spare room, then,' she said, making light of it but praying someone would change the subject.

Luckily, Lance needed the 'dunny'.

As soon as he was gone, Letty asked what they thought of him. If they didn't like him, she would be gutted. None of her boyfriends had ever made the effort with her mates like this before.

'So?' Letty said, her eyes wide.

'He's lovely!' Frankie said, refilling their cups. 'Like James Bond!'

'I like him too,' Em said. 'Although strange parenting ideas. This one,' she said, pointing to her tummy, 'will be highly trained. I've done the research and it all points to routine. Self-expression and exploration is very important for their development of resilience and independence but I will never share my bed with a baby.'

Letty shuddered at the bonkers of Lance expecting his son to sleep in with them. The boundaries were non-existent: it seemed as if he sacrificed his own sense of self so the child would rule the roost.

'By the way,' Em continued, 'I've been thinking about your boss. You should take legal advice. Talk to someone.'

'Yes, I've been thinking the exact same thing, babes,' Letty said, having so far devised half a plan.

'Because say you felt you had to resign, because you'd been overlooked, forced out, there could be a case for constructive dismissal. Or discrimination.'

'It won't come to that, I promise.' She tapped her nose – if only she was so sure. The revenge she had planned was taking up her evenings but it would be worth it – her gut had been right: Letty hadn't been the only one at work who'd been seen as fair game for Ross's unwanted affections. He'd sent dirty texts to Jools and felt up Sal in the stationery cupboard. While the first stage of any complaint was to report to human resources, Gittings PR didn't have one – it was a perfect arrangement which gave him free rein to harass whomever he chose. But not for much longer if her plan came off.

Luckily, Dylan was so clueless that he'd given her control of the mechanics of the social media project: she knew every password and log-in. Plus, Ross had put her in charge of arranging the technical side of the charity dinner: he wanted to present the social media launch in a flash video in front of his guests. Not once had he brought up security or the prevention of hacking – well, more fool him.

'If it was up to me, I'd cut off his balls and feed them to a crocodile,' Lance said, returning to the table. 'I wish I could take her away from all of this.'

Frankie and Em gawped at him.

'I hope you're not plotting to move to Australia with Letty?' Frankie said, suspiciously.

'Of course not! My son's here, my life. Letty.'

He gave her a look of love which melted Letty's heart – and with it, made her forget her cynicism over his walkover parenting style.

'I saw a programme the other day on the Great Barrier Reef. I'd quite like to go, I must admit,' Frankie said out of nowhere with a gooey look on her face.

Really? Letty thought, the farthest she'd been was Spain. But hang on, there'd been other little changes in Frankie which Letty had noticed too – her clothes were a tad more out-going and there was a sway to her hips too.

'It is beautiful,' Lance said, misty-eyed. 'Bright shoals of fish weaving in and out of pink coral…'

'Hmm. Sounds nice,' Em said, picking a piece of bread from her front teeth. 'But the trouble with that is, you might come face to face with a shark.'

Sunday

Em

Em slipped out of the house at 9 a.m. in sensible footwear and a rucksack. She was just as prepared on the inside too with what she was going to say to Simon Brown. The heat of the city was closing in on her. The heat of carrying another human being was getting to her too, and she needed some air and a view.

In Floyd's Cortina, she took the scenic route, there was no rush, and twenty minutes later she was standing in the shadow of Penarth Pier, looking out to sea.

The morning chill had gone and now a faint breeze played with her hair and flapped the edge of her shorts. The overlapping hills wouldn't have been enough today; she'd wanted a horizon that went on and on.

Breathing in deeply, she could smell seaweed, wet stones and bacon. Her favourite cafe in the world was on the prom where runners and dog walkers were the only traffic.

Down the coast was the brash kiss-me-quick of Barry Island, but here was quieter and calmer. She looked at her watch, turned and crunched up the stones to pick a blue wooden table and chairs at The Beach Shack.

'Ready for a coffee?' the waitress asked, tying up her blonde hair to show she meant business.

'Decaf latte, please, and I'll order food in a sec when my friend gets here.' Friend. The word still cut her to the core.

'Cool, coming right up.'

She shut her eyes and held her face to the sun – now and late evening were the only times of day she dared to expose her pale skin. Seagulls squawked and knives and forks chimed on plates. A girl's high-pitched voice squealed 'Daddy!', he'd obviously done something funny, and Em smiled at the unfettered delight in her voice. She felt okay, she realized, capable even. She could do this alone.

'Sorry… you look so peaceful there.'

She opened her eyes: it was him. Simon Brown. With a

child.

'This is Megan, say hi,' he said, looking down at the girl who was holding his hand. 'Mum's poorly, isn't she, Meg, so Meg's been staying with me and Grandma. I hope you don't mind...'

His daughter, he'd brought his daughter, and instantly Em saw it. Curious eyes, the same brown as his of course, ditto the hair, although hers was down past her shoulders with sandy streaks, and she had the rosiest cheeks, just like him. Her joining them actually made things seem less complicated.

'Hi, Meg, I'm Em. They do the best breakfasts here, do you like milkshake?'

'Strawberry but not chocolate, it makes me feel sick,' the little girl said, nipping onto a chair beside her.

'What have you got in your backpack?'

'Pens, smelly ones. A notebook. My iPad Mini,' she said, unpacking the contents onto the table.

'You never go anywhere without your iPad Mini, do you?' Simon Brown said, smiling as he sat down.

'Is this your girlfriend, Daddy?'

'Meg! You can't say things like that! It's rude.'

'No, I'm not, we're friends,' Em said, happy to get things straight. Children needed answers in black and white.

'I'm six,' she said, obviously content with the answer, and moving on without a worry. 'How old are you?'

'Thirty-and-a third,' Em said.

'Not ancient like me, Meg,' Simon Brown said.

She hopped off her seat and gave her dad a hug. 'Don't worry, Daddy, I'll look after you when you're old.' Then she twirled round and pretended to be an elderly person hobbling with a stick. 'That's grandma, she's really old. She's seventy-two.'

Em felt herself soften in this little girl's company: seeing Simon Brown as a father made her a mess of tenderness and regret. She had to pinch her nose to stop a sniff.

'Right, now we all know how old everyone is,' he said, in captive amusement at his daughter, 'can we order?'

Several minutes passed as they argued about what constituted a sensible breakfast. Meg wanted cake and sausages in that order but got bartered down to a waffle with fruit and whatever she fancied off her dad's plate, a full English, while Em went for poached eggs on toast, wholemeal, with a side of mushrooms and tomatoes. It was all so hard to watch – she wouldn't witness him like this with their child because she wouldn't be there when he had access.

While they waited, Meg scampered down to the water's edge, to throw stones.

'She's full of life. Does she know she's going to be a big sister?' Em asked.

'Not yet. She'll love it though. Sarah, her mum, she knows and she wanted to leave it up to you and me.'

Em was taken aback that her body had been discussed in her absence. 'You get on then, with Sarah?' Or did it rankle that he had brought up his former wife?

'Just because we aren't together doesn't mean we can't be grown-ups,' he said, gently. 'We never had a bitter break-up, we just weren't right for one another. Some people treat their kids like pawns when they split up – we would never have done that with Meg. And Sarah's bloke is on board with it, he's as much a father figure as I am.'

'What? Aren't you perturbed by your daughter being brought up by someone else?' To her, it was clear cut: children had a mother and a father and that was that.

'He's a great guy. Meggy adores him. No kids of his own so they're really close. Meg's being brought up by all of us. What kind of message would we be giving her if we were having petty fights about access? As Meg sees it, she's got three parents who love her rather than two or, worse, one.'

Em found herself nodding even though she had never considered this before.

'We even spend Christmas together. Not the whole day but we're all there for dinner. It's important.'

'But how does it work?' Because perhaps it might work for her too.

'Meg comes first, always. Whatever decision we make, it's in her best interests. For example, they're buying the house off me and he'll move in when it's gone through. They thought about a new place but it's her home.'

'So where will you live?' Em asked, wondering where he fitted in.

'I'll stay at Mum's for a while. I don't want to rush into anything. I need to be near Meg plus there's the baby. And work. It'll sort itself out.'

He made it all sound so easy.

'Anyway how are you and the Work In Progress?'

Em failed to control a burp which came up without warning. She was mortified in the face of his composure.

'Full of indigestion?' he said, trying not to laugh.

'Yes and I need to wee all the time too. I can't remember the last time I slept a whole night without having to get up for the loo. The afternoons are hard; I get so sleepy.' She'd intended to keep it formal but as ever, in his company she became quite natural.

'I was going to say to you, about the job interview next week, if you wanted to swap your observation to the morning so your legs are fresh, you know, take my slot, I'd happily do it.'

"Why would you do that?' she said, narrowing her eyes, because that part of the interview was by far more challenging. After all, she wouldn't give a rival the edge. Although at this moment he was as threatening as a piece of cotton wool.

'Because it makes no odds to me. You deserve the best chance. It's your job, I'm just going for it for interview practice. I don't think for a second I'll get it.'

'Seriously? I think you could pip me at the post. I'm not taking anything for granted.'

'That's why you'll get it.'

Em was astounded: he wasn't out to ruin her at all. He wanted to be friends and, while she wanted more, it was better than being her enemy. The way he simplified things and made her believe it. No one else could make her feel able to take a risk apart from him; that's how they had ended up here. Would it be the height of stupidity to take one again?

For the second time in his company, she stepped into the unknown. 'I was coming here to tell you I wasn't interested in your offer to stay with me, us, after the birth,' she said, laying her hand on her stomach. 'There's something too unconventional and odd about it.'

He nodded slowly as if he'd been expecting it and she saw his mouth turn down.

'But hearing how you manage with Sarah...'

'Really?' he said, his face brightening.

'I'm unconventional and odd so I think it might be appropriate,' Em said, aware that again she was so open with him.

'They say it takes a village to raise a child.'

The saying struck her – it was one of Mum's favourites but it had meant nothing before now. Yet Em saw how it applied to her situation: this baby would be cared for and loved by an extended family. Yes, it meant letting Simon Brown into her life, but it was for the greater good: to pull together not apart. Maybe compartmentalizing life made things harder? Perhaps consolidation was the answer. It would need flexibility, but as she rolled the word on her tongue, she realized she quite liked the taste of it. 'I'll take your slot too, if that's okay?'

'We'll make this work,' he said as a blur of colour, energy and happiness landed on his lap and announced she was starving.

'It won't be long,' Em said, imagining her hand rocking a compact buggy by her side. 'It'll be even better when it comes.'

Tuesday

Frankie

'I was thinking, we'll do your usual set but why don't we go for a bigger curl?' Frankie said as she combed through Phyllis' wet hair.

'As long as you don't make me look like Maggie Thatcher, couldn't stand that woman, what she did to those miners.'

'I promise! It'll be a softer look, more glam. It's nice to try something new every now and again.' Frankie felt the words roll off her tongue as if she had always been so adventurous.

'I'm only going to the Harvester!' Phyllis laughed, then she waved her hand and told her to go for it – she was meeting Norman's daughter for the first time and she didn't want to look fuddy-duddy.

'Ooh, so you're being introduced to the family, sounds serious!'

'He only wants us to get a double unit so we can live together.'

'Never!' It seemed quite daring seeing as they hadn't been dating or 'courting' long – but then time wasn't on their side. It was rather romantic actually.

Phyllis pointed to a photo on top of the TV which showed her and a silver-haired man both in whites holding a trophy. 'That's him there, it was taken when we won the bowls last week. Norman had it framed. You can see he would've been a looker in his day.'

'What are you going to do?'

'Stay put! I'm not doing another man's smalls! No, I'm happy as I am, thank you very much. I'm very fond of him and he can stay over as often as he likes, but that's as far as it goes.'

'He stays over?' Surely she didn't mean they slept together?

'Of course he does! You don't stop wanting a cuddle just because you're old.'

'Oh, right, yes! For a second I thought you meant—'

'I do,' Phyllis said. Frankie had to put her hands on her

171

client's shoulders to steady herself.

'I thought that sort of thing… dried up when you…' She fought the urge to pull a face because the image of them at it, doing the things her and Floyd did, well, it was a bit urgh.

'God, no, desire never fades, it's the glue that holds a relationship together, otherwise it'd be a friendship. It's true all your life, although you might have to take it more slowly when you're getting on. Going to bed isn't something to be ashamed of or embarrassed about, it's an act of love, respect and trust between two people; you bare your soul when you bare your bum!'

Frankie nodded at every single word Phyll said. That was exactly it. She'd discovered this for herself. The act of letting go was liberating because when you were letting someone inside your body, you were letting them touch your heart too. Not that Floyd had done that, of course.

'It's weird because I've only just sort of realized that,' Frankie said before she understood what her confession meant. But that couldn't mean she liked Floyd more than she knew… could it?

'Ah, has Jason come to his senses then? Are you back together?'

'No,' she whispered, before clearing her throat. 'Jason wasn't the one who taught me all that.'

'Oh, it's like that is it!'

'Not exactly,' she said, truthfully because how could Floyd be that 'someone else', 'it's complicated.'

Phyll raised her left hand to her shoulder and put it on Frankie's. 'Let me tell you this: if you don't know what your true feelings are, then sit on them. Ignore them, bury them. That's how you'll know what they are, because one day they'll out.'

Frankie wasn't sure what she meant, but she squeezed her hand anyway because she was a treasure. Then Frankie noticed Phyll's modest gold band which she'd worn for 50 years was gone. 'Where's your wedding ring? You haven't lost it?'

'I've taken it off, it didn't seem right when I'm with Norman. It'll be buried with me, I've made sure of that. Life moves on and while I love Dai and always will, I felt I was living in the past.'

The old lady's honesty struck Frankie then and all the way

on the drive to Dad's, where she dropped half of Phyll's home-made Welsh cakes. He wasn't in but he must've guessed she'd call by because there was one of his notes, which he always left her if he was going out on the off-chance she'd visit. *Gone to the butchers xxx*, it said. It made her sad to think she was so much in his thoughts: of course, it was lovely to be loved, she was very lucky, but how she wished he had someone special in his life.

Back at hers, she unwrapped her half with Phyll's words ringing in her ears. 'They're nothing fancy, not showy. But they're made from the heart and perfect with a cuppa,' Phyll had said, so Frankie made a brew and gave Leonardo a fuss.

He swished his tail though when she announced she had to get her laptop because she wanted to email Jason to explain her wall of silence had been because he'd slept with someone else. Keeping the communication going was essential if she was going to get inside his head again.

She opened her emails and scanned through the offers of hair product discounts and messages from customers; she'd deal with them first so she could devote herself to Jase. There was one from Floyd, which was strange, he normally texted. She knew she should get on with her work but the subject line of 'Lessons Five and Six' was too intriguing. 'Dear student,' it began.

> As you know, we previously agreed to combine lessons five and six. I would like to take you on a field trip on Saturday night to educate you about Dressing Up and Erotica. There is a link beneath my signature to a website from which you should choose an outfit. Please confirm your attendance ASAP. Kind regards, your teacher.'

She smiled at his silly tone and wrinkled her nose at the thrill of a night out. Clicking on the URL, which was www.frenchfancies.com, she wondered what the heck cakes had to do with it. Absolutely nothing, it turned out as the screen went black then flickered into life.

A short film showed a series of women who were apparently getting ready for a glamorous evening. But instead of getting dressed, they were peeling off their clothes to reveal some of the most breathtaking underwear Frankie had ever – or more aptly, never – seen. Extravagant but tasteful, erotic but elegant, the luxurious lingerie hit her right between the thighs.

These women weren't size-zero clothes horses; they were all

shapes and sizes. Voluptuous dark-skinned beauties, petite pale redheads and boyish blondes were posed artistically, opposite to the straining chests and bulging booties that you couldn't avoid on billboards, in magazines, online and on TV.

Her breathing quickened as she scrolled through peephole bras, panelled surprise knickers, barely there playsuits, sheer baby-dolls, boned basques, elbow-length gloves, sequinned masks, diamanté paddles, old-fashioned stockings, ornate suspenders and stern hold-ups.

Teasingly shot, you might think you could see a nipple or two, but it was the design of the underwear playing tricks on you. This was all about what you didn't see; it was about the power of suggestion, the art of conceal and reveal. Floyd had understood what would appeal to her. The pouting vamps and showgirls were as far from her tacky and synthetic 'let's play naughty nursie' nightmare as you could get.

But what to buy? Frankie decided to let her body decide: whatever aroused her, she would go for.

Clicking through the images, she went deeper and deeper inside herself, seeking a fit for her desire.

When her legs squeezed together she knew she'd found the right pair of knickers. Low-slung and black, they were see-through at the sides with a fan of lacy embroidery over the crotch and the backside was dotted with miniature feathers. The throbbing grew when she saw a waspie, a delicate ribbon-tied black corset which began below the bust and sat on the hips, giving the illusion of a dramatic hourglass shape. Frankie picked a strapless sheer scallop-edged peek-a-boo black bra which made her mouth go dry. She thought she was done – until she spied something so beguiling, she had the urge to touch herself. Called pasties, two circles of fabric covered just the nipples, giving a false sense of modesty. What's more they gave a lift to the breast's silhouette in a nod to old-fashioned glamour.

There were tassled ones, heart-shaped ones and sequinned ones, but the pair she fell head over heels with were more delicate: simple on first sight, when she zoomed in she could see an ornate lace trim centred with a tiny ribboned bow. What she loved about pasties was their surprise element: you might think that once the bra was off, that would be it. But no, the illusion remained with another unexpected layer of torment.

Aroused and pulsing, she exhaled as she closed her laptop; she couldn't possibly do her work now, she needed a lie-down. As she did, she realized this had been a lesson all by itself. The act of blending into one person with another wasn't an act of confinement to the boundaries she'd always lived by; those of seeking approval and taking care of others' needs. She was discovering a sensuality of her own.

Saturday

Letty

I do not fucking believe this, Letty said through gritted teeth, as the state-of-the-art buggy jammed yet again.

State of the art? she thought, trying not to ram it so hard over a bump in the pavement that Eddy would be bouncing about. Like bollocks it was: the pushchair seemed to jar at the hint of a bird fart.

'It's a running buggy,' Lance had said when he wheeled it in to the flat. It was the size of a tank and stupidly heavy. It wouldn't do to leave it in the communal hallway, oh no. 'I'm worried it'll get nicked,' he'd said. By whom? she'd asked, the British Army? But Helen would go mad, he had pleaded, and, as Letty was learning, What Helen Wanted, Helen Got. Whenever her name was mentioned, Lance seemed weaker and less of his own man. It broke Letty's heart every time. This woman wasn't an earth mother, she was a sergeant bloody major, not just in charge of Lance, but now her too.

How apt it was that Helen ran a fitness class for new mums. Letty could just imagine her bellowing at 'Buggy Body', which invited poor victims to bring their babies along in their prams. The clever thing about it, Lance had said, was that not only did the little ones get some fresh air but the mums could use the weight of their buggies as part of their training. Letty though couldn't understand why new mums couldn't just enjoy tea and cake for a while rather than have to get their bodies back. What was the rush and the obsession with that? Why couldn't people just let them be?

And how exactly had she ended up spending her Saturday afternoon looking after Eddy by herself? she wondered, as she made her way to the kids' play area up the road from her flat.

She stomped the rest of the way, harrumphing with every step, until a little hand appeared, dangling a chewed-up bunny. Stopping to check Eddy was okay, Letty squatted down at the front of the pushchair and was rewarded with a smile.

'Hello, little fella,' she said, softly nipping his nose with her fingers because he was a lush little thing, 'we're nearly there, it's not far.'

The adorable little cherub, who had his dad's eyes and mouth, began jabbering at her and then pulled at the straps holding him steady. 'Up! Up!'

'We'll be there very soon, babes, don't you worry.'

The interruption gave her a pause for thought: she'd been spitting venom because she was tired. She felt bad for her damning stream of consciousness just a few minutes before – she hadn't even met Helen so how could she say she was an ogre? And Lance was just trying to do his best. Give everyone a fair go, she thought.

Lance was working so hard, that was why she was in charge now. Weekend PT sessions were a fact of life: he'd told her this would be how it was, and she'd taken him on knowing it.

And it wasn't as if he didn't make her feel appreciated – he bought her flowers and chocolates and paid for everything when they went out.

This afternoon was a chance to get to know Eddy – a good job because it hadn't started off well. Even before she'd set eyes on him she hadn't felt reassured by Lance that it would go well. He was touchy as if he was preparing to welcome Prince George. In the week leading up to his visit, Lance had become obsessed with getting everything ready. Disinfecting everything within reach, moving 'dangerous' things out of harm's way. Plug sockets were sealed, cupboards were screwed with locks, corners were cushioned with foam guards, and the doors had bumpers to stop fingers getting trapped. He'd put up baby gates and put together a kiddy workbench and a kitchen – because Helen didn't like gender-specific toys – both of which took over the lounge. Baby-proofing, he called it, but it seemed more than that: like he wanted to make up for leaving him. She had tried to tell him that love was all Eddy needed, but he would always answer her with the undeniable fact that 'how could she know seeing as she wasn't a parent'.

Something had altered in their relationship, she could see that now. The intimacy had disappeared. Her cup of coffee was still waiting for her when she got out of the shower, but he never was. They hadn't had sex for a week – she'd tried to initiate it, to tell him it would bust his stress but he'd given her the line 'is that all you think about?' She'd been hurt because that wasn't it at all – sex was how they soothed and supported one another, there was nothing wrong with that.

So when Eddy turned up, Letty was hopeful that it would mark the end of Lance's worry: his son would be here, right, the wait was over, therefore he'd relax. But that was when Letty discovered how unprepared she'd been.

Stupidly, she'd rushed to the door and been too in his face when he'd arrived last night. She'd only wanted to make a good impression, but it had backfired with Eddy bawling.

Had she left it there, it might have improved. But no: she waved toys at Eddy like a moron and tried to pick him up before he was ready. Cue more screaming.

Fair do's, Lance was brilliant, understanding that in spite of reason, she was taking it personally. 'He's just a bit unsure,' he had said gently, over his shoulder so she was out of Eddy's eyeline, because for fifteen minutes just the sight of her made him cry. The plan had been to settle him in, put him to bed at 7 p.m. then for Letty and Lance to share a bottle of red over paella. But it took two hours of children's telly – 'Don't tell Helen, it goes off at 4 p.m. at hers,' Lance had said – for Eddy to chill out. Thankfully, he went out like a light by 9.30 p.m. – she didn't care by this point that he was in their bed she was so tired – so they reheated their tea, wolfed it down then called it a night by 10 p.m. A cuddle, of course, was out of the question.

Eddy was up twice in the night, and by 3 a.m. Letty decided to sleep on the sofa. Then she was awoken by a pudgy finger in the eye three hours later, which on a weekend was practically still the middle of the night for Letty. Maybe it was because she was sloth-like and didn't leap up for him, but he went up to her face and gave her a big sloppy kiss. She had felt as if she had been forgiven, that things would be okay. Thank you, God, she'd thought, as he pulled her out of the duvet and spoke mumbo-jumbo, which Lance translated as him wanting to play hide-and-seek.

Over and over, he'd hidden in the exact same spot, behind the floor-length curtains and laughed hysterically each time she found him, the cherub. There was a minor altercation when he didn't want to go in his high chair, but when he finally relented he ate up all of his breakfast. Although, by the taste of the spoonful of organic sawdust posing as porridge he shoved in her mouth, she wouldn't have blamed him if he'd chucked it on the floor.

She got a chance to tidy up and recover when Lance took Eddy swimming for a couple of hours. They had lunch, Eddy had a nap and then, as Lance left for work, he strapped Eddy into the tank so Letty could take him to the swings.

And that was where she found herself now, in the sunshine with a rabble of other knackered-looking mums and dads pushing their poppets.

Eddy's little legs kicked with excitement as she got him out of his pushchair. Immediately he ran towards the rising and falling legs of children who were going as high as possible. She almost had a heart attack and rushed to get him. He had a meltdown when she scooped him up – luckily she had some chocolate buttons in her bag for bribery purposes. Undisclosed chocolate buttons, that is, because Lance would've gone nuts if he'd known. 'We don't reward bad behaviour,' he'd said yesterday, 'we believe in positive reinforcement of good behaviour.' Whatever the hell that meant.

In to the swing seat he went and she began to relax. At least he was caged in there and couldn't come to any harm. The responsibility of looking after a child was all-consuming, Letty thought, God knows how Mum had managed with two of them by herself. And Em had this all to come.

Eddy was shouting out in happiness now, and she accompanied every shove with a 'weeee!'. It made her feel less useless.

Once he'd had enough, they went for a snack. But only after he'd gone rigid when she'd tried to crowbar him back into the buggy. So they walked to the cafe hand-in-hand.

Inside, his little face beamed when the waitress brought chocolate cake.

'I'm sorry, this isn't for you, babes,' she said, looking through the enormous changing bag that contained nappies, wipes, cuddly toys and probably the cure for the common cold if she looked hard enough. 'Daddy has packed something for you.'

Finally, she found it – an organic gingerbread sweetened with grape juice. What a disappointment for Eddy. His bottom lip quivered as he threw the biscuit on the floor. I'd do the same if I was you, fella, she thought.

'Dat!' he said, angry and sad and covetous all at the same time, as he pointed at her double chocolate fudge cake brownie.

Letty sized it up. She knew she shouldn't let him have any. But she didn't want a scene, seeing as she'd never know how to stop the screaming. And she wanted to make him happy. She broke off a bit of her brownie and handed it to him. His watery eyes lit up and he beamed his sunbeam smile at her. Then he proceeded to wipe most of it over his face.

'Jesus H Christ, little man,' she said, 'try not to get it on your shoes, will you?'

He giggled then and slapped the table with a mucky hand, clearly on a sugar high. But this would have to do – these would have to be the building blocks of their relationship. She couldn't become a stepmum overnight. This seemed a much more attractive and instinctual option than being a role model. And it was pretty much guaranteed he'd like her more for it than if she stuck to Lance and Helen's boring rules. So she handed him a bit more of her deliciously squidgy cake.

'We friends now, fella?' she said, as he answered her with a chocolately grin. For that was the best she could hope for.

That Night – Lessons Five and Six

Frankie

Frankie had been surprisingly pleased at the way she looked in her underwear. She'd felt like a different person: an exotic and erotic creature as her body naturally fell into coquettish poses in the mirror. The pasties were suggestive beneath her peek-a-boo bra, her waist was cinched in by the waspie and her knickers were oh-so tempting.

But the idea of herself as a sensual woman had given way to the fear of being ridiculous as she walked to meet Floyd. What if she was run over? What if she was trollied into A&E in a neck brace and decorative boobs? How would she explain it?

So she was initially relieved to arrive at the designated meeting place, at the end of an alleyway in the city centre that she'd walked past a million times on the way to a club or the shops. Not that she'd thought there'd be anything there; she'd assumed it was a starting point for their adventure. But as she peered down the dank and dark narrow passageway, she saw a red lightbulb above a door halfway up, which cast a glow on the people going in. Frankie couldn't see any faces but she could make out very high heels, feathers and headgear. What a bunch of weirdos! What was this place? The sooner Floyd got here, the sooner they could move on to the venue he had in mind.

Then the terrible thought struck her – what if Floyd was taking her there? What if it was a fetish club? Oh my days, Letty had once been to one with an ex. She'd worn a crotchless PVC cattleman suit and the place had had a dungeon ruled by a dominatrix. Even Let had found it disturbing. Where was it? Feeling uneasy, she clutched the neck of her denim jacket with one hand and tried to pull down the hemline of her little black dress with the other. She wracked her mind for a titbit of a memory. It was definitely in the city centre, hidden away behind a normal-looking door. And that door up there looked normal. Dear God, she was going to be eaten alive. And where the heck was Floyd?

Trying to douse the panic, she reasoned that Floyd knew her well enough now. But what if it had all been a ruse to induct her into some kind of warped and depraved—

'Miss Frankie Divine, I take it?'

She swivelled round on her scrappy silver heels and saw a bowler hat, a cravat and a waxed beard.

'I'm not going anywhere where there's whips or nipple clamps or chains,' she hissed at Floyd.

'And good evening to you too,' he said, his eyes wide at her distress. 'What are you talking about?'

'That place up there,' she said, gesticulating with her elbow because she daren't drop her guard. 'If you think for one minute I'm into that sort of thing…'

'Calm down, calm down,' he said. 'It's not Kinky!'

Kinky. That was the name of the place Letty had been to. 'Promise? Because I'll never talk to you again.'

'Of course it isn't! Would I be chapped up like this if it was? They'd never let me in. I'm in brogues, for starters.'

Frankie took a moment to check he was telling the truth. Yes, indeed, his footwear matched his description and he didn't appear to be carrying any instruments of torture. Relief flooded through her and she began to shake with laughter.

'I was so scared!' she said, gasping for air, bending double and slapping her thighs. 'Soooo terrified. I was going to pretend to go along with it then run off!'

'As if I'd take you somewhere like that.' He shook his head and smiled.

'Anyway, you look brilliant!' she said, admiring his skin-tight jeans and styled moustache.

'This is what they call "chapping up",' he said, lifting his hat. 'It's a movement in which followers decry the vulgarity of the twenty-first century and pine for the days when men were gentlemen. Think Oscar Wilde and dandies.'

She clapped her hands together in delight, still feeling the buzz of having got it completely wrong.

This version of dressing up didn't feel shameful or fake or stupid or sleazy: it felt fun, thrilling and on the right side of sexy.

'Shall we?' he said, presenting the crook of his arm through which she threaded her wrist.

Then she realized she was still in the dark. 'If this isn't a dungeon, what the heck is it?' she asked.

They crossed the threshold into a small and entirely black room where a tattooed and pierced rockabilly girl was sat in a peephole taking the money.

'Wait and see,' he said, drawing a thick curtain to unveil a circus of a nightclub. Everything was a reddish hue by the dim standard lamps dotted here and there, and as her eyes adjusted she made out a zoo of people. It was a total mishmash of 1940s sirens, magnificent facial hair, heavy fringes, feather boas, sequinned wings and even top hats. On the left, a giant birdcage containing a plumed dancer wearing just knickers and nipple tassels hung from the ceiling. To the right, a man in tight leather shorts flew back and forth on a trapeze. A raised mini-stage was sat in the centre, above which was a beautifully ornate chandelier. Plum velvet seats were arranged around dainty circular silver tables each with low lamps, and the staff, all of whom had gelled-back hair, were all in black tie, including the girls. Big band music played but not too loudly so you couldn't think. It felt seedy but it was glorious and Frankie was transfixed.

'What on earth…?' she said as Floyd took her to a table and ordered them Martinis.

'It's a burlesque club,' he said, 'it's like a variety show, with comedians and striptease, both men and women. It's not the usual squirty-cream thing, it's theatre.'

'Wow. I had no idea this place even existed.'

She took off her coat to reveal a figure-hugging off-the-shoulder dress with a Latino burst of a skirt which she'd bought especially from a boutique rather than her usual Next, Topshop or M&S.

'If only Jason could see you,' Floyd said, before holding up his cocktail glass and demanding a 'chin chin'.

'I'm thinking of wearing this when I get my chance to seduce him.' Frankie wasn't fishing for compliments but she wanted to know if Floyd thought it was suitable. That it sent out the right message of sexy sophistication.

'You look… stunning,' Floyd said, 'He'll be hook, line and sinker.' He looked a bit… what? How did he look? It was a funny face, one she hadn't seen before – it wasn't the same as the way Dad had looked on her wedding day, because that would be weird, but it was quite close. Maybe it was fulfilment

Floyd felt, for getting her to this stage? Whatever it was it was only fleeting and he was back to his usual self as he asked: 'How are your plans going to seduce Jason?'

'Still on the drawing board,' she admitted. She'd been thrown by his infidelity, which still played on her mind but which she'd started to accept or she'd never get anywhere. 'I've got to ring him, suggest a night out somewhere but it's got to be the right place. Not anywhere we've been before, I want to show him I'm not the same person. This might be stretching it,' she giggled. 'What about Sasha? Any news?'

'Nope. I can't stop thinking about it,' he said, playing with the rim of his bowler. 'Anyway, let's get on with the lesson. Dressing Up and Erotica. Is this a suitable venue?'

Frankie looked around her and threw up her arms. 'It's a spectacle! It's like we're in a film,' she said, grinning. Then she bent in towards him to explain. 'I'm wearing some stuff from that website you sent me.'

'And?'

'It makes me feel excited,' she said, 'like I've got a secret. And it's making me feel all sorts of things.'

Frankie crossed her legs to squeeze the thrill and she felt her calf make contact with Floyd's. Sparks shimmered inside her as she began to imagine revealing herself to him later. She hadn't been able to put her almost-orgasm out of her mind: it was as if the sensation hadn't left her and she could feel it building up again just being sat here knowing she would get to try again tonight.

'That's the anticipation,' Floyd said as if he'd read her mind, 'the psychology of it is also about being able to play someone else, it's like acting and through that we can lose inhibitions.'

'Have you done this before?' she asked. 'Is Sasha into this kind of thing?' For some reason, she wanted to know how she compared.

'Sasha? Jesus, she'd have turned her nose up at this. Not adventurous enough for her.'

Frankie gulped and immediately felt her desire shrivel because it made her feel such an amateur.

'She tried to get me into swinging. We went to this club and there were three floors. The ground floor was a bar for everyone "to get to know each other",' he said, with his fingers making air quotes. 'Upstairs was a room with a giant plastic mattress with people doing it and others watching. It was horrific.'

Frankie's shoulders relaxed – at least she wasn't alone in finding the thought of that unsavoury.

'Don't get me wrong, I like a bit of fantasy but, to be honest, I'm more into the stuff we've been doing. And the majority of the women I've slept with are too, I think.'

'How many people have you slept with?' she asked, suddenly desperate to know more about his past.

'Dunno. A few. A fair few,' he said, scratching his beard in thought. 'Fifty? Sixty? God knows.'

Frankie choked on her drink. She was glad she hadn't known this at the start. Blimey, it really did make her feel even more of a beginner. And he must still think of her as such a Sunday driver.

Floyd pulled out the burgundy handkerchief which had been poking out of his shirt pocket. 'Here, use this,' he said. 'But numbers don't matter, honestly. There were some dreadful shags in there, and I include my own performance in that. I've learned it's about what's up here,' he said, tapping his head, 'not just what's down there.'

Frankie felt the warmth return now that he'd made it clear it was quality not quantity.

'The brain is the biggest sexual organ,' Floyd said. 'Openness creates intimacy. Dressing up can challenge the views you have of yourself and your partner, say the submissive person in the relationship takes control, that sort of thing. But whatever you get up to, it's about trust, respect and confidence.'

'I think I'm getting there,' she said, 'thanks to you.'

Floyd shook his head and held up his glass for another toast. 'You, baby, it's down to you!'

'LADIES and gentlemen…' A ringmaster had taken the stage and the crowd applauded as she whipped the floor and announced Miss Dallas D'Amour.

The lights went off, creating a murmur of expectation, and then a single spotlight shone on an exquisite brunette straddling a chair. Pale with bright red lips and rolled hair, the dancer held her pose for a minute before she began to perform a tantalizing striptease. She pulled off her elbow-length gloves with her teeth, shimmied her boobs so they threatened to spill from her basque, and pushed out her backside as she unhooked her outfit.

By the end, she was down to her sequinned groin and a beaded open bra which just covered her nipples – nothing 'rude' was exposed. It was a clever illusion and Frankie was sucked right in. Spell-bound and drunk on lust, she felt something animal take hold of her.

'Let's go,' she whispered into Floyd's ear, grabbing his hand.

'All right?' he asked, looking concerned as they stepped out into the night.

'Yes,' she said, hailing a cab, 'I want to show you…'

His nod showed he understood. Their silence heightened her feeling – all of the lessons she'd had had shown her the way, and burlesque had been the perfect turn-on. Her self-belief was soaring; she could do this now without instruction and direction. Frankie's heart was galloping but not with nerves. It was wholly from a lust which she could finally let loose.

When they reached her house, she let them in without a word and took Floyd upstairs by the hand. She pushed him onto the bed and closed her eyes, losing herself in the moment. With her back to him, she swayed as she unzipped her dress, letting it drop to the floor. The feel of the fabric slipping down her thighs and onto her feet felt euphoric; every inch of her was alive. She could hear their breathing, hers was quick while his was deep. She looked over her shoulder, her eyelashes batting down. Around she went, pushing out her chest, and with teasing fingers she took off her bra. Her hands went up behind her head and she gazed down at her covered nipples. Then she untied the ribbon of her waspie and watched it give way to skin, which ached to be touched. She was naked but for her knickers and pasties. Floyd cleared his throat. It brought her out of the moment: she had been lost in lust. He looked mesmerized: his eyes were fixed on her and he was biting his lip. So she moved towards him, feeling a force at work, something inevitable and magnetic. She mounted the bed and crawled on her hands and knees towards him.

So close now, she could see his pupils were wide. She wanted to climb into him and get lost, to breathe his breath and taste his mouth, to have his lips on her breasts and in between her thighs and to be free of the frustration and pain. To chase it all away with an all-consuming swell, to surf the crest until she shuddered in ecstasy.

'Frankie, I can't do this,' Floyd said, tracing a fingertip from her collarbone to the valley between her breasts.

She smiled and shut her eyes: the tease was all part of it. On she went, arching her back, rolling her shoulders, dipping her chest into his face, feeling his breath hot on her skin.

'Frankie,' he said, again, making the throb harder. His jeans were drawn tight and she felt him pulse when she put her hand on his crotch. He thrust forward and moaned. 'Fu-ck. Frankie, I can't – we mustn't. I mean it. This is killing me but… custard creams. I'm sorry.'

'What?' she asked, pulling away so she could examine his face. Surely he didn't mean it? But his eyes were downcast and he was grinding his teeth.

'This isn't part of the lesson,' he said. His voice was weak and hollow. She backed off slowly, waiting for him to announce it was one of his jokes. When it didn't come, she crossed her arms, feeling vulnerable in next to nothing. Then as he looked away she knew it was all over: she'd let it go and it wasn't enough.

What a fool she'd been, she thought, holding back the tears as she reached for a T-shirt on the floor. To think she had thought she'd been capable of this. She felt the same kick in the stomach of rejection that had started her on this journey. Worse, she had uncovered a longing she'd never had before, not even one she'd had with Jason; it had been Floyd she'd wanted tonight and he'd turned her down.

'I'm sorry,' she said. 'I got the wrong end of the stick.'

'No, no, no, it's my fault,' he pleaded. 'I'm your teacher. It has to be the way we decided at the start – we stick to the lesson plan.'

So why did he come back here? she wondered. Why did he let her undress? What was the point of a sex teacher if you didn't have sex? Yet there was no point being angry; she was the one who had misread the situation. No one had forced her to do this: it had been entirely her doing. Frankie had imagined there was a mutual attraction and a willingness to go further. She had got carried away.

But how had he slept with so many people yet turned her down? It could only be because she was useless and untrainable, like an old dog who couldn't be taught new tricks. She put on her dressing gown as extra armour: perhaps there were some abnormal bits to her body after all. Her right boob was slightly larger than her left.

'I really wanted to, you know,' Floyd said to her back. At least he had had the decency to pretend, Frankie thought, but it didn't make her feel any less of an idiot. 'It's just... there's Jason... and Sasha, and maybe we forgot why we were doing this.' She nodded, staring at the floor, knowing he was right. And if you have a racehorse lined up, like Sasha, then why would you want to ride a donkey? 'You looked amazing tonight,' he said, 'I really, really, really mean that.'

Frankie turned around and gave him a brave smile.

'And guess what? You're student of the week – again.'

'Yey, go me,' she said, rolling her eyes but grateful for his kindness.

'Come here, gimme a hug,' he said. As they embraced, Frankie noted how snugly she fit into his arms: her head tucked in under his chin as if it had been created with that in mind and his shoulder had just the right amount of padding to support her cheek.

'I think I'm done with all of this,' Frankie said, knowing she'd have tumbled over the edge had she really slept with him. She didn't know exactly what she would've fallen into, but it was bound to have been dangerous. As it was, he had just saved her in time. Whatever this emotional tug she felt towards him was, it was better they remained on good terms. And if there had been any fallout, it could've messed up the happy equilibrium of their group; Em might have found out and Letty would be dragged in. Still, that didn't mean she didn't wish he'd at least make a play of trying to get her to change her mind.

'Yeah, that's probably a wise move.' He rubbed her back and rocked her slowly.

'I nearly came at the last lesson,' she said in a tiny voice, 'and I've learned so much. I don't think sex toys, bondage and talking dirty are me, to be honest.'

'You never know, Frankie, you never know. We'll have a post-course evaluation another time, eh?'

Suddenly she felt an overwhelming tiredness. That was the last thing she was aware of until the next morning when she found Leonardo sprawled asleep beside a note on the pillow which smelled of Floyd. *You need oil and Q-tips*, it read. *Don't rip off your pasties like a plaster. I did that once and, put it this way, my chance of breastfeeding is now zero. You should be proud*

of yourself. You've worked v. hard. I am pleased to award you a
highly commended pass. Love, Sir XXX

She laughed as a single tear rolled over the bridge of her nose and into the other eye before it soaked into her pillowcase.

He was such a lovely man; it was amazing the way he touched her. Okay, they hadn't done it, but it was as good as, she realized, because she'd got to the stage where she was ready. Maybe that had been the point all along? If nothing else, that's what she had got out of her sex education.

Monday

Em

Em slammed the door of her locker. That was that. There was no more she could do but wait to hear if she'd done enough to get the job.

Interview day, and the first day of week sixteen of her pregnancy hadn't started well: her stomach had popped overnight into a proper bump, so she couldn't do up her trousers. She'd scrambled through her wardrobe for something looser, but she'd been the same stick insect all her life. She could hardly turn up in her stretchy waistband tartan pyjama bottoms. So she had crafted a loop through the eye of the buttonhole of her trousers using a hairband and curled it over the button. For the first time in her professional life, she noted, her shirt had been untucked and her suit jacket undone. Before, she knew, this would've thrown her. But having dealt with all that had happened with the baby and Simon Brown, even with her Mum and Dad's decision to go away to Spain, she had felt at ease. Spanners in the works and upsets were still an inconvenience, yet she had learned to go round them. Her heart had still jumped when Simon Brown had wished her good luck, but instead of shutting it down she allowed its warmth to flow into her hand when she shook his. She must've covered miles on the shop floor under the observation part of her interview.

Her task had been to roll out the Back To School range – September was only round the corner. It wasn't just a case of putting out uniform in the clothing section: Back To School was a state of mind for the entire store, from signage in fresh fruit for break-time snacking and stacks of lunch boxes in household, to new lines in stationery and frozen meal deals for busy parents. Through this, she had been problem-solving, project-managing, leading and developing her team as well as directing shoppers to the cat food aisle. It was a typical day and she had felt so at ease that she had forgotten the area manager was watching.

She had been glad to put her feet up for the afternoon with her presentation before the panel. It was on introducing 'smart shelves' which suggested how to surmount the challenges facing the walk-in retail sector in the light of growing online sales. The market was changing; supermarkets would soon be depots dedicated to deliveries. That meant customers needed a reason to go in-store – and other than smart tech, she also recommended 'artisan products' and grab-and-go counters. The presentation had been on PowerPoint, so she had had prompts to help her tired brain, and the panel of two men and a woman had nodded and smiled at all the right places.

The last but one question had asked where she saw herself in two years. It had been a dilemma whether to bring up the baby. It wasn't a secret but, by law, she knew they couldn't ask. And she was pretty sure Simon Brown wouldn't have considered that fatherhood had any impact on his ability to do the job.

That's what had convinced her to keep quiet. 'I have my sights on area manager,' she had said, 'but my focus would be becoming the very best store manager I could be.'

Finally, they had asked what she would do if someone junior to her got the job. It had been a reference to Simon Brown and she'd expected it. She'd trotted out the line of respecting the decision and wanting to do what's best for the company, but the truth was she didn't know how she'd react: disappointment would be in there, yet it might give way to acceptance or a determination to find another role.

Now, with her interview day over, she was feeling drained. Em sat down on the bench in the ladies' changing rooms to swap her heels for trainers.

'Em, my darling,' Sly said, as she appeared from the loos and washed her hands. 'You did well, I hear, very well.'

'I did my best,' she said, shrugging. 'What about Simon Brown?'

'Very strong too. Hey, by the way, did you agree beforehand to tell the panel about the baby?'

Em span around. 'What do you mean?'

'Apparently he raised it because, even though there's no policy regarding staff relationships, he wanted it out in the open. And he was brimming with joy, so they said.'

Her head exploded that he'd told them that he was the

father. What a bastard. 'But I didn't mention it! Simon Brown and I, we never discussed it beforehand. I need to explain,' she said, grabbing her stuff and getting up.

'I'm afraid they've gone, darling,' Sly said. Then she began to backtrack: 'I'm sure it won't make a blind bit of difference.'

As she left, Sly gave her a compensatory smile as she left. Em threw her a sceptical look.

The door swung shut and Em sat down, alone with her thoughts. How bad she had felt the other night when she'd questioned his kindness. Even Letty, who had more reason to doubt men, had thought Simon Brown wouldn't be capable of such deviousness.

But it was clear now: crystal clear. Counting the ways he'd betrayed her, she began with his oh-so innocent explanation why he couldn't get involved with her. His heart-felt confession that he had a responsibility to Megan, she saw now was just an excuse. The offer to co-parent was a way to appear considerate and supportive, which made him look the caring gentleman. When he left her holding the baby, he would be able to justify to himself and everyone else that he'd been there.

The reality was he would flit in and out of her life, just as he did with Megan's mum. Not once had he said he'd be there for her emotionally; practical help was all he had to give. He knew she loved him and he was toying with her to knock her off balance.

Then by getting her to swap her observation with him so he could go first before the panel gave him the upper hand. He had brought up their baby to spoil her chances – it made him seem accountable, trustworthy and touchy-feely. He would've known she was too private and too professional to have raised it at interview. The panel could read whatever they liked into his disclosure and her concealment; she feared his supposed warmth would make her appear detached, which was just what a manager shouldn't be.

Em imagined Simon Brown ruthlessly rubbing his hands together right now: he'd leached all of her know-how during his secondment and he was almost there. He would get the job.

She had been played good and proper by a wolf in sheep's clothing. Em shook her head at this schoolgirl error: she had allowed her emotions to get in the way. Well, never again. Never. There could be no going back.

How could she trust him? She realized then that she didn't really know anything substantial about him. Em had never been to his house – or his mother's, to be exact. Was it even true that he lived there? Perhaps he'd stayed there when Meg had come over because he could shirk his duties and let grandma take the strain. For all she knew, he might have a bachelor pad with the latest everything.

Em leant down and finished off tying her laces. Or at least she tried to, but her tummy, although it was small, was protruding enough to get in the way. 'Budge up, prawn!' she said, without even thinking, 'I can't reach my feet!' Then she stopped.

It was like the sun suddenly coming out after a rain storm, when the earth sighed with happiness. Her brain whirred as it computed what she was feeling. There was a refreshing certainty now after weeks of confusion, which was always a relief. But more than that, Em realized she had reached a depth of understanding she'd never had before. She had dissected her emotions without anyone else's help. This awareness – that's what Letty calls it, she thought, scrunching her brow – meant that she was going to be okay.

She would survive no matter what happened with the job. I've been looking for love all this time, she thought, and it's already here, inside me in this baby. Simon Brown would be permitted his paternal rights without a hint of drama. But she was done with someone who didn't want her.

She nodded once to show that business was taken care of. Then she moved on and started a new list in her head, titled The Baby.

As she began her journey home, Em smiled with pleasure at the prospect of drawing up a lovely spreadsheet with sub-sections such as Things To Buy and Hospital Bag. She had come so far, but there was always room for a list.

Tuesday Night

Frankie

Frankie was breathless and slobbed out on the sofa, recovering from an attempt at a run. Flicking through channels, there was absolutely nothing on – the evening ahead would be empty so she might as well fill it doing her accounts.

Just then a scrunched-up face appeared at the window. Floyd's! One hand shielded his eyes from the light and the other waved madly.

Frankie cracked up at the sight of him and she returned the wave like an idiot. Her bruised ego from Saturday night's rejection had faded from purple to beige: but now it was concealed all together by the flush of her belly laugh.

No matter what had happened between them, they had survived it: there was no rollover of negativity, no embarrassed hangover. And let's face it, there had been plenty of opportunity. He'd been true to his word and helped her get through a bad time: they'd had an experience and they'd come out of it as mates. Floyd was just a lovely guy: what she had for him was a soft spot, a platonic affection which burst like a fountain when she saw him.

She jumped up and opened the door.

'Sorry if I'm a bit sweaty. I've been working out!'

'Why on earth would you do that?' he said, grimacing.

'To tone up,' Frankie said loudly and slowly because she was speaking the obvious. 'Got to look my best for Jason!'

'You're mad,' Floyd roared. 'You've got a lovely—'

Then he stopped. He was blinking rapidly and rubbing his neck. Oh my word, he was only flapping!

'...lounge. You've got a lovely lounge,' he said, looking everywhere but at her. 'It's all cosy and welcoming, but that makes it sound like it's a bit mumsy and I don't mean that.'

He was blushing now – it was the first time she'd ever seen him flummoxed. Frankie felt a smirk on her lips – how she wanted to tease him! But that'd be cruel and he was suffering enough. It was hardly a crime to pay someone a compliment, and secretly she was thrilled; who didn't like to be flattered?

Then he stared straight at her, knowing he was rumbled. He rolled his eyes and shook his head. 'You have lovely furnishings,' he said, putting finger guns up to his head to show his embarrassment.

She wanted him to know she was fine with it: that she hadn't thought he'd overstepped the mark or she'd read anything into it. Here she was, after all, with a red face and a shiny topknot; she would hardly think he had the actual hots for her. So she wrinkled her nose and thanked him in code. 'Once, Jason said he'd pay if I wanted a pair of larger cushions. He didn't mean it nastily. I'd been complaining about the size of mine and he'd offered, as a present. But you know, looking back, I think I'd have preferred it if he'd said my cushions were perfect as they were. So I really appreciate what you said.'

'What an idiot. Larger cushions would look ridiculous on a sofa that size,' he said, incredulously. Then he remembered why he was there and held up a plastic bag. 'So, anyway, I've brought you something,' he said, dumping it on the carpet and sitting down, 'sort of a good luck present. Now that the lessons are over.'

'Oh, thanks! That's nice of you. Shall I open it now?' He really was a sweetie, Frankie thought, and she had nothing for him. Not even an apple.

'Nah. Wait 'til I've gone. I won't be long... Yeah, so, I just wanted to, you know, make sure we were good.'

'Yes, of course.'

Floyd rubbed the thighs of his jeans, adjusted his T-shirt and then began huffing on his specs to give them a clean. He was faffing for some reason. Ah! Now she got it. He was waiting for her to notice!

'Your beard! It's gone!' Frankie had the urge to touch his face then, which was so silly – it'd feel as smooth as any other shaved face, like Jason's, so why bother? Besides, she couldn't just touch him anymore – their arrangement was finished. She waited for him to make some kind of 'back, sack and crack' joke – this was pure Floyd territory. How did he put it? 'You set 'em up, I'll knock 'em in' complete with a header action. But he only rubbed his chin with his knuckles.

'I decided it was time. A new beginning and everything.'

195

'It suits you!' Frankie said, noticing that while he looked younger he seemed older, more serious.

'Thanks. I hope Sasha likes it. She's back tomorrow,' he said, watching himself pick at a nail.

Frankie's insides lurched. This was the moment she'd been training for. It marked the end point of their journey, and her start line to fly solo without an instructor.

'It's meant to be a surprise but Em told me. She wanted to give me some notice. Breaking news: Em has insight into human emotions.'

He gave a snort through his nostrils. Then he looked up and his big brown eyes seemed clouded, fearful even.

'Don't be scared,' she said, softly. 'It's natural to be nervous but it's not as if she's a stranger. You're getting her back! Be happy!'

He nodded deeply then clapped his hands in preparation to leave. They shared 'right then, better get on' smiles. But he didn't move.

'So time to say goodbye,' she said, wanting to liberate him from being on loan. He probably felt a responsibility towards her. That's how lovely he was. So she added 'go!' for emphasis.

'Yes, I… er… so… this is it! Bye! Shall we, er…' Floyd stuck out a hand to shake. She felt her shoulders sink with disappointment as she produced hers. Professional to the last; begrudgingly, she admitted, it made him even nicer. But as she went to take his palm, he pulled it away and stuck his thumb on his nose and wiggled his fingers.

'Got you! As if I'd say goodbye like that,' he said, smiling, stretching an arm out to pull her in. 'Come here, you silly sausage!'

She felt herself fall into his broad chest.

'There you go, you lovely, lovely… person, you.'

She breathed in his musky smell for the last time, trying to store a memory for when she found herself needing some courage and self-worth.

He was sighing now and she was too. Her arms were around his tight waist and he was stroking her back in a large circular motion.

'I just want to say thanks,' she said, lifting her face so she could snuggle into his neck where his pulse boomed against her ear. 'You've been wonderful. So good for me.'

'No, I should be thanking you,' he said, rubbing her shoulder. 'You've taught me a lot too, made me grow up.'

Frankie was moved: he didn't have to make a show of it but she was glad he had.

'And you've done brilliantly. You don't need any more help. Don't worry about what we didn't do – you had it all along. You just had no confidence. Jason won't be able to resist...' His voice tailed off into a little cough.

'Why did you call him a wanker that time?' she asked, seeing as he'd brought him up; it was a question that had been nagging away in her mind ever since he'd said it. Everyone loved Jason apart from him, it seemed.

'Because,' he said, as he started to rock her slowly, 'he was stupid enough to let you go. That's why.'

She was so affected by his confidence in her that Frankie gave him a squeeze – he hadn't been slagging off Jase all along, it had just been his way of trying to make her feel good.

'Keep in touch, eh?' he said, holding her tight as they sealed their friendship.

'Yes,' she replied, becoming aware of an ache growing: the one he'd helped her mine, which she couldn't stop. And didn't want to. This was the last time they'd be together and her body had been so used to reacting to him that it just seemed to do it of its own accord. Still the hug went on and now her cheek was on his; without bristles, it was even smoother than she'd imagined and she could feel the flutter of his eyelashes as he blinked.

'I'll miss you,' he said, his hand on her neck.

'Me too,' she said, feeling the muscles at work in his back. Her heart was racing, her groin thumping. The pleasure was spiralling up and down until it reached her toes and fingertips.

She wasn't sure who moved first. But suddenly their faces were inching back and their lips were on each other's skin; they were tilting, sliding, unable to stop their fall, their noses side by side, their mouths touching. Soft, plump lips, the warmth of his tongue, entwining with hers, setting off slow throbbing pulses all over her body. They fell to the sofa, melting in their own heat, and their hands began to explore, tugging at clothes in desperation. The soaring was starting, her need to blend into one was overwhelming. Their top halves now naked, his mouth began at her neck then kissed its way down. She had never felt such bliss as he outlined her breasts with his tongue. Her hands explored the expanse of his chest, the sinew of his lean, defined stomach. Touching his warm and smooth skin wasn't enough. She began to undress him, pulling at his jeans, unravelling him, her grip finding his cock as she began to stroke him. He groaned at her touch and then again as he felt her wet insides, his fingers hot from her lust. Their eyes never parted in their abandonment. This time there were no boundaries, no set guidelines and no full stops as they moulded into one. Frankie gasped as she received him whole, wanting him deeper and deeper, and his mouth hungrily sought hers. They moved to her rhythm, tenderly at first, then she set the pace with a confidence as her pelvis pushed into his, grinding towards ecstasy. Rolling waves were coming to her and she was thrown around underwater. She turned her back on the surface, only wanting to go down, down; her senses blurred, she was tasting him with her eyes and feeling his moans. Feverous, she was soaring, tumbling, gliding and riding as her orgasm lapped at her pointed toes.

She'd never been this close before. Steadier, stronger, she felt the tide crashing over her and he responded with an urgent strength, on her heels, sharing her glow. Then Frankie was possessed, trance-like, blinded, sucked under but still able to breathe in Floyd as a violent softness exploded – and kept exploding until the tremors took over completely when her cry became a blissed-out duet. Together they stilled; their heartbeats banging as pleasure trailed their veins, slowly subsiding, receding until the air held the magic like fireflies before it was extinguished and they were in darkness, silent and motionless.

Frankie's euphoria of finally experiencing an orgasm had settled into a serenity of fulfilment: this was what it had all been about. It had had nothing to do with position or pretence, she realized. She had let go – the fear of losing herself hadn't materialized. Instead, she had been empowered, but it hadn't been selfish or violently passionate, rather it was a resounding awakening. This simple act – in the missionary, no less – she had done on instinct without instruction or direction. But what was behind it? She knew the only way she could find out would be if she tried it with Jason.

'Well, that was some goodbye,' Floyd said from up above.

'I'm not sure I could do that every time I bid someone farewell. It'd be exhausting not to mention a bit too… nude.'

'I know!' Frankie laughed. 'To think that's what I've been missing out on all this time. And for you that's completely normal.'

Floyd pulled his face back and shook his head. 'Er, no. I'm having a think but… nope, it was quite a bit more than that.'

He was very cute, saying that, but she didn't believe him, what with all of the hundreds and thousands of times he'd done it. 'How the flip did that happen?' she said, asking a metaphorical question. Then she felt sheepish. 'I didn't mean it to. I didn't force you, did I? After what you said on Saturday night.'

'You have used and abused me, Frankie Green. For your own wicked, depraved ends… Nah. I wanted to. I could because I wasn't your teacher any more. Just Floyd. Named after Dad's favourite band Pink Floyd.'

The tension whooshed from her in a high-pitched squeak. 'And I'm not your student. I'm just Frankie, after Dad's favourite singer Frank Sinatra,' she giggled.

'I think it happened because it had to happen,' he said, now contemplative. Frankie knew exactly what he meant: weeks of build-up, it was like closure. An end to that period of her life.

'And we had to do that before we could move on,' she said. 'What with Sasha home tomorrow and Jason…'

'Absolutely,' he said. They were both being very emphatic about this.

'Um… Floyd…'

'Yes?' he said quickly, his eyes searching hers.

'There's something I have to tell you…'

His eyes bored in to hers now; he looked pensive for some reason. 'What is it?' he said, quickly.

'The thing is… I can't feel my legs now. You're a dead weight.' She snorted at her joke, feeling pleased she'd caught him out the way he had with her so many times.

'Right, yes, of course,' he said, giving a weak smile as he moved to her side and reached for the sofa's throw, which was in all sorts of tangled trouble. Pulling her in to get comfy next to him, he said: 'Isn't it funny, that after all these years, after what nearly happened at Debbie Yates' fifteenth, that we're here now, doing this.'

199

'You remembered! I never thought you would!' she said, sitting up with shock before settling down again. 'I was a bit teenage and confused, I think.'

'Charming!' he laughed. 'Course I remember. How could I forget the biggest Em bollocking of my life?'

'I wonder why she was so cross? I mean, I get why she was grossed out but… we were just kids.'

'She's very black and white. It didn't fit into her categorized perspective.'

Frankie nodded. That was Em all right.

'Before all of this,' Frankie said, 'I was a bit like that. Very certain about things. But now…'

'It's called experience, Frankie,' Floyd said, 'When you love someone, you love them for what they are, not what you think they are.'

'Maybe that's why it all went wrong with Jason. He had been my knight in shining armour. I'd had such a rough time growing up that I had looked at him as my saviour. Not as my husband.'

'And perhaps he saw you as helpless. So instead of discussing how he felt about the way things were going in your relationship, he bottled it up because he didn't want to put it on you. In his eyes, maybe, you were a glass princess. When in actual fact you have more balls than Manchester United.'

Floyd was bang on. If only Jason had spoken to her about it all. Yet she had been just as responsible in her own way for idolizing him rather than acting as his equal.

'Yes! And knowing this, knowing our mistakes, means we'll have a stronger marriage.'

Her words were steady and clear because she was convinced she had grasped where things had gone wrong, and how she could fix it.

'Do you ever doubt you're doing the right thing, wanting Jason back?' Floyd said, playing with her hair.

'Of course not!' Frankie said, playfully slapping his chest. 'Why else would I have put myself through all of this? I can do this, Floyd. I'm certain of it. I've changed. Why? Do you wonder about Sasha?'

'No. Yeah. A bit. Just… I worry we're not the same people we were.'

Leonardo suddenly appeared on the back of the sofa then

jumped down and stood with two paws on her lap and two paws on Floyd's.

'Wow, he's quite choosy, he is.'

'I'm touched,' he said, smoothing the cat until he settled into a tight ball between them.

Then, wrapped up in each other, they fell into a silence. But Frankie wasn't quiet inside. She was wondering if Jase would appreciate how she had grown. He'd wanted some excitement, that's why he'd suggested the separation. Well, what wouldn't he like about the new her? She was more adventurous in every single way now, not just in bed. Not exactly Bear Grylls, but you know... And he was bound to have had a journey too. An excitement grew as she considered what she'd find changed in him. All the good bits would still be there, but what would she see different about him? Perhaps he'd be more open to discussing things rather than hiding his thoughts as before. She could see now they had fallen into the habit of not communicating.

Unlike Mr Snoreypants here, she smiled. If she could just move Leonardo, she could get up... but Floyd looked so still. What was the harm of just lying here for a bit until he woke up to go?

Staring at the moon, she decided to enjoy the company; it's not as though this would ever happen again.

Wednesday

Letty

'Oh my GOD!' Letty said, closing her eyes as her head rolled back. 'That's heavenly.'

'Let me try!' Frankie demanded, swiping the cup off her for a swig. The effort rocked her momentarily on the edge of the worktop on which they were sat, but Frankie just about saved herself from a fall and gasped with laughter.

Letty licked the green foam off her top lip and watched her friend with curiosity. Did she seem brighter than normal? It was hard to remember when Frankie last seemed so alive. But that could be because Letty's mind was an unmerry-go-round of niggles about work, her massive overdraft and Lance's depression after he'd dropped Eddy back to Helen's, which were increasingly keeping her awake at night. Frankie was pissed, that was all.

They were having a ball of an early evening – a trim from Frankie had turned into an impromptu drinking sesh, which they hadn't done for yonks. It was just what Letty needed; everything had been so sensible of late. They were on their fourth cocktail, made with Lance's beloved NutriBullet. It was lucky he was at work because he'd never approve of boozy smoothies; his body was a bloody temple. She didn't mind but, come on, everyone had to have a blowout now and again.

Their first creation had been virgin, but then, with naughty giggles, they'd splashed rum, gin and Bacardi into combinations of blueberries, spinach, beetroot, banana, ice and berries.

'This one,' Letty explained as Frankie knocked it back, 'I've called the Vitamin V, which is kale, apple, mint, cucumber and a shitload of vodka. I tell you, babes, it's a liquid orgasm!'

'It's good,' Frankie said, her eyes glassy, 'but… not that good.'

Letty drew a breath until she saw Frankie doing comedy eyebrows, waggling them up and down in a sign she had news.

202

'You haven't! Have you?' Letty shouted with glee.

'I have!' Frankie grinned back.

'No. Way. When?'

'Last night!'

Letty stared at her friend. Frankie wasn't covering her face or blushing. She was slapping her thighs and laughing. Frankie had had her first ever orgasm and she was still on a high. The irony didn't escape Letty's attention: she was supposed to be the siren but she'd had not a squeak of action since before Eddy's visit. She sympathised with Lance's misery over not seeing Eddy every day – she'd seen how much he adored his son, it was a love that rivalled no other, as it should be. As her father should've felt about her. But it had taken him away from her: he was withdrawn and anxious, monotone and unresponsive. When she tried to speak their language, the reassurance of being desired and paying homage to each other's bodies, it fell on deaf ears.

'With your sex teacher?'

Frankie nodded with a beam that lit up her entire body. 'I'm a newly qualified sex kitten!' she said.

'Well, hallelujah, babes!' Letty was chuffed to bits for Frankie. Not that she didn't think she had it in her, but that it would be buried so deep, she'd have needed a lot to find it. Like a JCB rather than a few lessons. She'd followed Frankie's progress from the beginning and it had increasingly looked like Frankie wasn't even going to do the deed because the guy was too much of a gent. That or he had some major issues going on. 'Come on then, tell me!'

'It was amazing. I can still feel it if I do my pelvic floors.' Frankie shut her eyes and giggled.

'Are you going to explain how this bloke finally succumbed?'

'Sorry, yes,' she said, pulling herself together. 'So, as you know, he had stuck to the lesson plan every time with no deviation. Then we had to finish the course all of a sudden – I can't say why, so don't even ask – but last night he came round to say goodbye and it just happened. On the sofa. And the funniest thing is, even though we'd covered loads of exciting stuff, we did it in the missionary!' Frankie was pink with the glow of the memory. 'I wasn't sure at first but then I had this feeling, like I was on the crest of a wave, and then I was riding it, on and on it went and… well, if it was that fantastic with someone I have no feelings for then I think I might die when it happens with Jase. See, what I've realized is the lessons weren't about sex but about unlocking the bit of me which wasn't safe and boring.'

Letty nodded supportively but she also noted Frankie's unnecessary acknowledgement of having 'no feelings' for this guy who had brought her out of herself. Hadn't she done the same thing when she was falling for Lance?

'But what about this teacher? Did you have any chemistry? You must've!'

Frankie stopped to think then shrugged. 'I don't even know what chemistry is! I trusted him and he was really understanding and helpful… and funny and handsome in a sort of odd way. He's a really good listener too. Really insightful.' Then, finally, Frankie had the decency to acknowledge she was gushing. 'God, listen to me! But I don't fancy him. I mean, he stayed over accidentally, he fell asleep on the sofa and then in the morning there was no attempt at doing it again, like you would if there was more to it. We had breakfast and there was no atmosphere or cringing or anything. He's not my type. Too… dunno, just not…'

'Jason?' Letty said, dangling his name in the hope she'd realize she'd never spoken about Jason like this. I mean, was Frankie stupid?

'Completely. That. I mean, I did have a little crush on him in the middle but it was just me putting all my feelings for Jase onto him.'

This was a possibility, Letty conceded. But something puzzled her. 'I'm not being funny, right, but I don't understand why he did it this time?'

'I can answer that!' Frankie said, triumphantly pointing a finger at her. 'Because he wasn't my teacher anymore!'

'But why did that matter?'

'Because… there was no lesson plan last night so we could just do it. That's why!' Frankie looked at her as if she was thick. Letty bristled with a prick of indignation at the insinuation that she was the idiot not Frankie.

'I'm sorry but I don't get it. He won't do it when he's supposed to, then does it when he isn't.' She sincerely hoped he wasn't a player.

'It just felt right. Completely natural. Like it was meant to be.'

'And you say you haven't fallen for him?' Letty said, laughing, wondering who the bobbins this sex guru was. She would ask, but Frankie would only refuse to tell.

'Don't you understand? I've been training for this make-or-break moment for weeks. I'm ringing Jase tomorrow to set up a date. I have to do this.'

'Fair play,' Letty shrugged. 'Just keep an open mind about things.'

But Frankie's chest started heaving. 'I'm not that naive, you know. I know what I'm doing.'

'I just want you to be happy. I kind of thought you'd get over Jason, if truth be told. Not that he isn't a great bloke, but you're braver now than I've ever seen you. As if you've thrown off the chains of whatever it was that was holding you back.' She was beginning to think a return to her husband would undo all of the work Frankie had achieved.

Frankie broke into a smile. 'Please, don't remind me of chains. That's what got me into this in the first place! Look, this is my last shot, I have to do it. I have to see if I can save my marriage.'

'How you going to do that then?'

Letty listened as Frankie ran through her planned repertoire and was astounded to see how far she'd come. From nowhere, a sob came from deep inside her.

Frankie jumped, wide-eyed. 'Christ. Is it bad, Letty? Do I need to change it?'

'No, babes, it's perfect,' she whispered. Listening to Frankie, animated and happy, had reminded Letty how far she was from that herself. 'It's me, it is.'

'What's up?'

'Lance and me, it's just not what I expected,' she admitted. 'It's like we're an old married couple already. It's not the sex, it's the intimacy that came with it. It's gone. For the first time, we went to bed last night with our backs to one another. We'd had an argument about Eddy. He wanted to see more of him, have him mid-week but how can we when he works evenings? He can't expect me to have him after work, feed him, put him to bed and all that. It's not fair on Eddy, that was my point, he doesn't really know me. And I'm not sure I'm prepared to do it.

I dunno, Lance has got so much baggage and I know I have too, but it feels like I'm not strong enough to hold his as well as mine. I'm not sure I've done the right thing.'

'Oh, my love,' Frankie said, holding her tight, 'things have changed so quickly for you, no wonder you're confused.'

'And I'm finding it hard to cope, not being the most important person in Lance's life. I know it's selfish and stupid but...it makes me feel like I'm still that little girl who craved her dad's attention. That I'm worthless without a man.'

Saying it out loud, Letty realized she had uncovered something important about herself: all this time she had thought she was the worldly one out of the three of them. But all those notches on the bedpost weren't a sign she was more mature and more knowing; in fact, they were just endless one-dimensional repeats of her need to be loved.

The realization that she was still basing her self-worth on her success with a man spurred her into action.

'I've got to do something for myself, for me, Frank,' she said, feeling sober. 'That's the answer. I've been thinking it for a while and now I've got to act on it. Then I'll know if I'm with Lance because I love him or because I'm not bold enough to be on my own.'

Meanwhile...

Em

Irritated by Sasha's sunny 'hiya!' over the intercom, Em crossed her arms as she listened for footsteps on the stairs. She wanted to hear heavy shuffling jet-lagged feet, but in their place came a light two-steps-at-a-time tap dance. Well, of course Sasha's dainty toes would sound like that, Em thought. She could've walked back the six-thousand-and-forty-four miles from Bangkok to Cardiff and still be as fresh as a daisy.

Ugh, why hadn't she gone back to her mum's place? She'd left Floyd in the lurch. Why did she have to turn up here? Because she needed to make an entrance, that's why, she thought, as nervous bubbles rose in her stomach. Well, Em thought as she saw the top of Sasha's head coming round the bend, there was no way she was going to be in the audience this time because—

Em was pole-axed when Sasha dropped her enormous rucksack on the floor then came at her with arms spread. She was even more beautiful than Em remembered. Her thick golden wavy hair was almost down to her waist, her oval green eyes shone and her teeth were even whiter next to her honey-coloured skin. A tight black vest and tiny cut-off denim shorts caressed her slender body, and the straps of her silver gladiator sandals curled round her calves like angels' fingers.

Em knew it: when Floyd got in from work he was going to be absolutely smitten all over again. The poor dab didn't stand a chance.

Sasha took Em's face in her hands, pausing to gaze at her, before she rubbed noses, just like old times. Irritated, Em was transported back to the days when she'd been her confidante.

'It's so good to see you! I've missed you so much,' Sasha breathed into her hair.

Hours on a plane and she still smelled as sweet as icing. Em had intended to give her a stiff air peck but Sasha was oh so impossible to resist. And she didn't want to be rude. She sank her chin onto Sasha's shoulder and rubbed her back. Just to be nice. 'Welcome home,' she said, hearing the echo of her words repeated inside her head in a mocking, scornful tone.

Well done, Em, you lasted three point eight seconds there. I'm doing this for Floyd, she said to the voice. Course you are, it whined back, talk about shallow. What's the point in causing a scene or being antagonistic, Em mentally replied, when things have changed? I've opted out of matters of the heart – I just want a quiet and simple life for me and my baby, that's all. Whatever you say, her mimic said.

Sasha stood back, taking her hands in Em's. 'I'm so happy for you, you're going to be a fantastic mum.'

'Floyd told you...' Em wasn't sure how she felt: Mum and Dad still didn't know. She hadn't yet found the moment: there had been so much to work out. Should she be angry at Floyd? Yet it was easy to entrust someone with a secret if they were in a different time zone. And who knows, had Sasha been here from the beginning, maybe Em would've told her from the off herself.

'Of course he did! Nearly halfway, aren't you?'

The way she said it revealed Sasha still thought of her as a sister. It left her stumbling for a response. Damn her! She manoeuvred herself back onto solid ground. 'How was the flight?'

'I was upgraded so I had a flat bed.' Sasha shrugged as though this sort of thing happened to everyone. She had never had it hard; fortune followed her around like a loyal fan. 'I grabbed some of the business-class products for you, fluffy socks, an eye mask, some posh skincare stuff. Oh and there are some Thai spices in my bag. For the kitchen. And I hope you don't mind, but I bought a little buddha for the baby.'

Em took a deep breath, thanked her with a hug and then showed her in, pointing at Floyd's door so she could put her bag out of sight.

'You haven't told him I was coming back today, have you?' Sasha asked, tying her hair up, which revealed more grace; breathtaking cheekbones, a long elegant neck and narrow but assertive shoulders.

'I've got an ambulance on standby for his heart attack, the great big wimp that he is,' Em said to get out of telling a lie. Floyd was so together, except when it came to Sasha; she'd let him know it would be some time in the next couple of days so he had the chance to gather himself.

Sasha laughed her generous laugh, covering everything within hearing distance in happy confetti.

'Tea?' Em said, needing something to settle her dancing stomach. Perhaps she'd eaten too much fibre lately, she thought. 'Green, white, jasmine, Earl Grey? I'm having peppermint.'

'Have you got PG Tips? I've been dreaming of a proper cup of builder's tea for a year.'

'Yep. Floyd's got some. Still like it strong and sweet?' Em berated herself again for slipping back into their once-familiar patter, rather than making a stand that Sasha had chosen the world over her brother.

'Just like I like my men!'

At the same time, as if it was a well-rehearsed joke, they both announced: 'Not like Floyd, then!'

Em knew she was doomed. In the past year, she had refrained from liking any of Sasha's schmaltzy hashtag blessed Facebook updates – wishing instead for a dislike, no, a 'grow up' button – and had only sent the odd pithy response to her emails. But in spite of that minimal contact, they were still on the same wavelength.

She flicked on the kettle and sat down opposite Sasha at the breakfast bar. Had Em put her hair up, her ears would be doing their pixie impression. But even Sasha's ears were lovely and flat and neat. Em searched for a flaw, an indication of ageing or tiredness, but a year in the sun had done nothing except kiss her. Even nature wasn't immune to her charms. They were both thirty-one, but Sasha could pass for being in her early twenties. Em hadn't been asked for ID since she was fifteen, such was her mumsy look which had long pre-dated her now tubby torso. She played with her fringe and panicked about how she was going to broach their lack of contact.

But Sasha got in there first. 'Listen, before Floyd gets back, I just wanted to say something,' she said, earnestly. 'I'm sorry I haven't been here for you. I had to find out for myself that I already had everything I needed with Floyd and you. I went on this yoga course thing in India – it was a nightmare to be honest, full of stressed-out executives seeking nirvana, trying to chuck money at their problems – but it made me realize all that searching was actually a waste. I had it here all the time.' Sasha put a hand on her heart and allowed the silence to magnify her words.

Em had imagined this moment ever since Sasha had deserted Floyd. She'd be spouting off and Em would rip into her and tell her how she'd let everyone down. But now the opportunity was here, she didn't feel the rage she had expected. She was astounded to see now that she had found an acceptance that there were shades of grey. Floyd wouldn't thank her either for raking over old coals. Em wanted to let the past go.

'I owe you an apology too. I should've been in touch but…' Em said, as any remaining awkwardness disappeared. '…Well, I was hurt, believe it or not, not just on Floyd's behalf but on my own too. I thought of you as more than just his girlfriend. I thought of you as my friend. So when you walked out, it felt as if you'd betrayed me too. And so I couldn't bring myself to stay in contact. It was silly of me to be so uptight, I know that now.'

'I'm going to make it up to you both. Just wait and see!'

The ceasefire set off popcorn in Em's belly. It looked as if Floyd was going to have his happy ending and she would have a friend back, just when she needed her.

A bang, bang, bang came from the hall.

'EM! I'VE FORGOTTEN MY KEY. LET ME IN.'

It was Floyd!

'OKAY,' Em shouted to him, flapping her hands. Then she whispered to Sasha, 'Go on, you do it!'

Sasha pulled an 'aargh' face, crossed her fingers and then nipped to the door as Em hovered behind her. He was going to collapse, Em knew it. And by the way Sasha had been talking, he might even die of happiness! All his waiting had paid off, all of his mooning about and funny moods. The popcorn turned to fireworks in her stomach when Sasha flung open the door and threw her arms up in the air.

'Misery Guts from upstairs buzzed me in,' Floyd said, looking down at his phone, before mimicking Rhys, the killjoy civil servant who lived in the flat above. "Do it again and I'll report you to the residents' committEEEEEE…" Jeez, Sash!'

Floyd stepped back in a double-take. He had actually forgotten Sasha would be here, Em could tell by his eyes, which were bulging out of his head. What a moron!

Sasha leapt off the floor and jumped up to cuddle him with her arms and legs. He was actually speechless!

But before he could say anything, Sasha had let go of him and was on the floor. On bended knee.

No! Em couldn't believe it – was Sasha about to do what Em thought she was going to do?

'Floyd Good-Fellow…' Sasha began.

Her brother froze, open-mouthed. Em held her breath.

'Would you do me the pleasure of becoming my husband?' she asked sincerely. 'I love you, Floyd. I want to be with you for the rest of our lives. And hurry up because my knee is starting to hurt.'

'Well, when you put it like that…' Floyd said, pulling her up into his arms. He looked solemn, which must have meant he was deeply touched, Em thought. So she cheered and she was bundled into a group hug which turned into a jig.

But it made Em want to belch, she'd been struggling with a gassy feeling on and off all day, so she stepped away to still herself. But even though she was motionless, something inside of her was still moving. Oh, please don't let it be a fart, she thought, clenching her bum cheeks.

Then a few seconds later it dawned on her and she gasped and held a hand over her tummy. Floyd had seen her.

'What is it? Everything okay?' he said, peering with concern over his specs into her face, holding her arm to check.

Em nodded, stunned. Talk about timing.

'I thought it was trapped wind. But it's the baby. I can feel it kicking!'

Thursday

Frankie

'Anything in particular you fancy, love?' the stylist said to Frankie's reflection as she gowned her up and combed through her long, tired-looking locks. Oh, not much, just something that will match the wow when I save my marriage!

'I'm a hairdresser, so, I'm not going to ask you to make me look like Taylor Swift.'

'Why do they do that? "Tammy," my clients say to me, "you couldn't trim off three stone and perform a face lift too, could you?" We're not miracle workers, are we?'

'I just want a change. Something a bit less boring, more sophisticated, you know?'

'I do, love, I do. You've got the right texture for it.'

'A bit like yours actually. In fact, exactly like yours,' Frankie said, pointing her fingers at Tammy's long choppy bob.

'Easy!' she said, taking her to the sinks for a wash.

The hot water soothed away the day, which she'd spent dashing round South Wales to fit in eight clients plus a warehouse run. Then she'd come into town to find The Dress to knock out Jason – a black silky tunic which covered her front entirely but revealed a bare back all the way down to her waist, a style she'd never have dared worn a few months ago. She hadn't had a minute to ring him yet but she was building up to it; only when she could see the woman she'd become would she dare.

She had plenty of mates who could've done her cut but they'd have given her the same old thing. In here, in this cool city centre salon with dark walls and ethereal lighting, she was anonymous.

As the sweet scent of shampoo then conditioner reached her nose, she knew what she desired – a new chapter after the biggest adventure of her life. And it started now, with the most tingliest of scalp massages. Frankie responded by pointing her toes in delight; she realized she was reacting to another person's touch with a deeper level of awareness. It was a reminder that this was the first Thursday night she'd been without Floyd in weeks; she had a pang for him then, just like the one she'd had on her way into town when Em messaged to say Floyd was getting married to Sasha. It had been the most unsettling feeling – a great sadness that he wasn't part of her life anymore, combined with a soaring happiness for him having his wish granted. What would they be doing now? Probably in bed. Floyd relieved to have an equal rather than a trainee to play with.

As wet chunks of hair fell this way and that, she concentrated on her reinvention instead. From shy and frightened to confident and brimming with self-belief.

Once the blow-dryer had done its thing, Frankie knew it was time to call Jason, for there before her was a sassy lady with the most gorgeous of swishy bobs.

She had to seize the moment – but where should she go to call him? What would a sassy lady with the most gorgeous of swishy bobs do, she wondered, and then she knew. She would go into a bar all by herself – for the first time ever – and order a posh cocktail!

So she set off down Queen Street, swinging her shopping bag, and found the perfect place for a balmy evening; a rooftop terrace playing sundowner beats, containing grand leather wingback chairs, and tables of railway sleepers bordered by potted palm trees and Mediterranean grasses. Feeling a tad self-conscious but doing it anyway, she found a spot and perused the menu, settling for a Sour Cosmopolitan, and waited until she had had half of it for luck before daring to pick up her mobile. This was it, the moment she'd been working towards since her barbecue. Eight weeks had passed since then and in that time she'd put everything into exorcising the ghost of being boring in bed. She'd confronted embarrassment and humiliation and, to her surprise, she'd found out she wasn't frigid or useless; she knew what turned her on now. She was all woman. She tapped on Jason's name and waited, holding her breath. Please don't go to answerphone, she prayed, because she couldn't ask him out like that. It had to be done directly, in the way she'd learned to speak with Floyd.

It rang once, twice, three times – where was he? He usually picked up straight away – four, five – he was avoiding her, she knew it, oh God – six, seven – all of this for nothing – eight… 'Frankie!' He sounded pleased to hear from her, but he also sounded breathless. Her mind began to accuse him of doing all sorts of things. Quick, say something!

'Hi! Yeah, it's me. Okay?'

'Yeah, great! I'm in the gym, doing some weights.' Phew. 'You?'

'Good. Um, I was wondering if you were free on Saturday night?'

Was there a slight pause? 'Yeah, I've got nothing on.' Her stomach fell all the way down to her knickers as she thought of him naked.

'Cool. I thought we could get a bite to eat.' This was going amazingly well! 'Shall I message you where? I'll have a think, we could try somewhere new.' To show she was different.

'Nice one, can't wait.'

She'd done it! Her heart thumping, she threw her phone into her handbag, knocked back the rest of her drink and skipped her way down the stairs. She was going to think of nothing else for the next two days! How she was going to concentrate, she had no idea. There was so much to do – leg-shaving, moisturising, exfoliating, fake-tanning, nail-painting, eyebrow-plucking. And so many decisions to take. Should she get a Brazilian or was that too much? A new perfume or her old one? Earrings or a choker – she had to figure out what would work when she was naked. Then there were the shoes, which ones would go with her dress? No more the sweet innocent wife but a self-assured lover.

Her dress... She'd only left the bloody bag in the bar. Racing back, she burst through the doors and up the steps to where she had sat. But the bag was gone – oh no! She'd spent hours looking for the right thing to wear and it had been the last one in her size in the shop. Frankie went up to the bar to ask if it had been handed in. The barman, who was serving, caught her eye and indicated he had what she was after. Hallelujah! Frankie felt her shoulders relax as she caught her breath and she looked around at the dimmed faces wanting to explain to someone, anyone, in a British reflex of embarrassment why she had dashed in like that. Just then she saw a very familiar someone over in the far corner, obscured by the pointed leaves of a yucca plant. It was Letty! What a lovely surprise; she'd love to share her good news about Jason. Once she'd got her bag – she didn't want to forget it again – but... hang on... she was with a man...

a man who wasn't Lance! Their heads were close together, she was touching him on the knee and they were laughing, looking very comfortable. Oh, Letty, she thought, what had happened to the woman last night who'd declared she'd do something for herself? That she wouldn't depend on a man for self-esteem?

Frankie felt disappointed and sad that Letty had been on the cusp of a discovery yet hadn't had the courage to go through with it. So who was he? She strained her eyes to get a glimpse as a breeze jostled the leaves. And then her heart stopped at the sight of his profile and the way he was ruffling his sticky-up hair. Letty was with Floyd. And they looked intimate and involved, deep in conversation, oblivious to anyone else. What was going on?

Frankie had to get out of there. Not waiting for the barman to act, she stood on the foot rail and leaned over the bar to find the bag for herself. Then she fled.

Saturday Morning

Em

Making canapés was right up there on Em's Top 5 Things To Do List, she calculated as she mashed up the ingredients for pea and feta toasts.

Not that she'd admit it to anyone because they'd laugh. Theirs were brimming with clothes shopping, eating out at posh restaurants, competitive exercise, wild holidays and getting drunk; all of which were about extravagant behaviour, which she just didn't get.

Hers were simpler, more self-sufficient, and she was glad of it. Number five was going to work for fulfilment and satisfaction reasons, number four was geeky telly – whether watching it or living it at the Doctor Who Experience in Cardiff Bay, which she'd visited nine times. At three were crosswords, sudoku and jigsaws. But it was tough to choose a number one and two out of walking and cooking. Walking had its obvious health and head-clearing benefits, while cooking was good for her soul and she liked eating very much. Could she cope with a tie? She mulled it over, weighing up the pros and cons, then thought 'oh, to hell with it', it was her list so yes, she could!

Em breathed in the sunshine; today was so clear she could see the Severn Bridge shimmering in the distance. In the lounge, she'd flung open the doors of her little balcony, and the muted buzz of people enjoying drinks in the Bay would occasionally come in on the wind. Em sighed with happiness.

She wouldn't be anywhere else in the world right now, she thought, as she prepared amuse-bouches for the gathering she was hosting tomorrow in a joint celebration of Floyd and Sasha's engagement and her pregnancy. Sasha had been the one to persuade her to double up – she'd known Em would never go for a baby shower nearer the due date when all eyes would be on her. 'But don't you just want your own special moment,' Em had asked. Sasha, so thoughtfully, had said she wanted to share it.

It had also given Em the shove she'd needed to tell Mum and Dad they were going to be grandparents. Although she'd have preferred to do it over the phone – it would be less dramatic – it had rung out. This wasn't unusual – they had an unreliable old-fashioned phone which made two plastic cups and a piece of string look sophisticated. You could forget about any mobile service out there too. Fancying a drive, she'd gone up there and faced the mad music of delight and tears and hugs. What had she always said, she'd laughed, that Mum would've been proud of her for doing something out of character for once! Mum had denied this, obviously. But in a glimpse of the depth of the love that Em knew she would feel for her child, her parents had cancelled their trip to Spain – they wouldn't want to miss the baby for the world. And of course Mum would stay for the first fortnight. It was such a relief to know she wouldn't be alone.

'Not to worry about the commune,' she'd said, 'we'll have our own one now! Maybe we can go on a month-long cruise before February.' Who'd have thought they were capable of doing something so normal? For all their quirks, they knew the importance of family.

With Floyd and Sasha out buying a ring, Em had the flat to herself – well, almost, what with the baby kicking along to the tempo of her chopping and slicing.

She'd feared Sasha's presence would be overbearing on top of Floyd's giganticness, but she fitted right in. Sasha talked of her travels but not too much, allowing her spectacular photos of deserted beaches, crowded cities and the obligatory selfies to tell the tale of her year out. Instead, she was an eager ear to Em's situation, listening attentively while she caught up on twelve months of gossip. Floyd wasn't quite himself, he seemed quieter than usual, he was more thoughtful rather than troubled, but Em presumed it was because he was metamorphosizing into an adult and deliberating his future with Sasha. Or Aunty Sasha as she called herself now 'to practise for when the baby comes'. Sasha hadn't mentioned job-hunting yet, but there was no rush with Floyd's decent salary, and Em suspected, with quite unexpected sadness now that it was on the horizon, that it wouldn't be long before they moved out together.

Everything, finally, was slowly slotting into place. The job would be the icing on the cake. But, as Sasha had said, life was better lived in a mindful state of mind. Enjoy the now, Em said aloud, holding tight to the doughy feel of breadcrumbs between her fingers.

Her telephone rang and she craned her neck to see whose name flashed up. Simon Brown.

Yet again.

Since she had mentally backed off, he had begun to pursue her, no doubt out of guilt and shame that he'd used underhand tactics at the job interview. At first, he'd left voice messages asking for her to ring, which she'd ignored, then a couple more stating he hoped her interview had gone well. Still she resisted, even though his friendly voice still set off goose bumps.

He was simply proving all that Em thought of him now: his ego couldn't stand her radio silence. And he wasn't genuinely concerned about her, he was only trying to begin the damage-limitation strategy to justify his loose mouth about the baby before the panel. As her phone fell silent, she vowed she would only communicate with him when it suited her; and then there'd be no chit-chat and no pleasantries. He deserved nothing more – what had he ever done for her?

She had better things to do, she knew now. Like getting on with the important matter of making smoked haddock Scotch eggs, mini New York cheesecakes and Thai chicken skewers.

Later

Frankie

Frankie put a hand on the metal pole of the glass door and paused when she saw herself. Her chunky shoulder-length bob framed silver powdered heavily black-lashed eyes, sun-kissed cheekbones and a slick of lip gloss. A slim chained choker glistened above her bronzed collarbone, beneath which scooped the neckline of her sleeveless black dress. Smooth, soft and bare knees and legs fluted down into heeled sandals which had a simple strap across her pink toes. And there in her hand, she carried a green clutch bag – and months' worth of hope.

She dropped a shoulder and twisted slightly to get a quick flash of her naked back so she could give herself a thrill at daring to go without a bra. Without being big-headed, she knew this was the very best she'd ever looked. Flawless and composed but with a hint of sexy was how she seemed on the outside. Inside, it wasn't quite as neat; she'd barely eaten all day, save for a sensible cheese sandwich and a mug of tea before she left the house. Her heart was going like the clappers and her mind was even faster, trying to control random panicky thoughts – such as what if he doesn't turn up, and what if he says he wants a divorce? – with mantras of calm, 'you can do this' and 'stop sweating or your make-up will slide off'.

When Frankie was hatching this plan, she had intended on asking Letty for some last-minute advice, but she felt confident enough to play this her own way now. Not to mention the fact she was lying low after spying Letty with Floyd. Frankie had reprogrammed herself to think that whatever she'd seen was their business. Okay, she felt very uncomfortable about seeing their heads together, but getting stressed over what may or may not be going on was a distraction; and if anything was, then the overriding feeling she had about it, she told herself, was that of the disappointment and hurt of being left out. And that just highlighted what she really did want: to be reunited with Jason. It was a sign that her and Jason were meant to be.

She simply had to play it cool, to hint at how she had changed.

Her hair was a clue, obviously, as were her clothes; conversation would show the substance of her transformation, but the starting point was here at this door which belonged to a champagne and oyster bar in a swanky five-star hotel in town. The kind of bar she'd have once found intimidating.

As her eyes adjusted to the candlelit restaurant, she scanned all of the heads for Jason, who was always on time. Excitement sprinted up her spine as she prepared herself for the lurch which would come when she saw him.

But after a circuit of the floor filled with New York-style metallic high stools and tables she realized he wasn't there. With a dry throat, she checked her phone to see if he'd rung. Nothing. She could feel her whole body wilting at the thought she'd been stood up. Then there was a light touch on her shoulder and she span around to see his irresistible smile. Jason! He was here! Her heart swelled at the sight of him: his dark hair had grown into baby curls, his wide brown eyes were sparkling and he had perfectly trimmed manly stubble which made his full lips seem even more red. Dazzled by his new look and thrown by his sudden arrival, Frankie felt her legs go weak.

A black V-necked T-shirt emphasized the bulge of his even more muscular arms and hinted at his hairy chest and six-pack beneath, while expensive jeans kissed his hips. The carefully manicured poise she'd spent months cultivating deserted her, and she virtually threw herself at him in adoration – and gratitude that he'd shown up.

It was the worst possible start.

'Hi!' she squeaked.

'Sorry I'm late,' he said with feeling. 'Work.'

'On a Saturday?'

'Paperwork and a contract to finish off.' Her heart raced at how easily the business jargon fell off his tongue. 'Anyway, that's not important. Shall we get a table?'

She nodded, like a lovesick sap, and felt all floaty. He weaved off and Frankie trotted behind him like a faithful dog.

Frankie was vaguely aware of something she had to be doing, but all she knew right now was the way his broad shoulders tapered into a strapping back which curved into his strong and athletic bum.

'This place is a bit posh!' he said as he pulled out a seat for her. A helpless damsel, she took his arm – a million fireworks going off at his touch – and hopped up and grabbed onto the circular table edges to steady herself. Her eyelashes batted in agreement and he waved at the waiter to order drinks. This meant she'd have to talk. The jolt was like being attached to a pair of jump leads; she was going to have to form some words into a coherent sentence without stuttering or drooling.

'Are we doing champagne and oysters then?' Jason said, picking up the menu. He looked around and she followed his gaze to see flutes of bubbles and plates of grand orange crustacean, with claws and people using pliers to crack through their shells! What the hell had she been thinking, coming in here like she was some sort of sophisticate? She hadn't managed to try octopus at the tapas bar with the girls, so why did she think she was up to this?

Think, Frankie, think, she told herself, remember why you're here. Everything hinged on how she reacted now – if she regressed to her former self, she would never be able to return.

But if you go for it, if you go with the flow and open up, then you can go forward. And if you show who you have become, then you will have Jason by your side. She knew what she had to do. 'I've never had oysters, but I'd really like to try,' she said clearly and tremor-free. 'Why not?'

Jason laughed and gave her an impressed smile. Hot damn! She'd done it – she'd cleared the hurdle with ease and he'd recognized it. What's more, judging by his encouraging face, he was going to join her – she anticipated the thrill of them trying something new together…

'Christ, no. You won't catch me having oysters,' he said. 'I've always thought it was a bit weird, you know, swallowing them without having a good chew. Winkles. I'll have winkles. I like them.'

'Winkles?' she said, incredulous. He was the adventurous one, not her!

'Yeah, you know where you are with winkles.'

Jason pointed at exactly what he wanted to the waiter, and ordered two glasses of the house prosecco.

Prosecco? Frankie hadn't come here for prosecco! She could have that any day of the week. 'Actually,' she said boldly to the waiter, 'we'll have a bottle of this champagne, here, the

221

cheapest one, and I'll have six oysters in pickled ginger, spring onion and soy sauce. Thank you very much.'

Jason waited until they were alone again to raise an eyebrow at her.

'What?' she said, lightly, neither wanting to show nor acknowledge the hint of indignation she had felt at Jason taking over.

'Nothing. I just assumed you'd want the prosecco, that's all.'

'Well, I would normally but not tonight. I just fancied a change.'

She grinned at him as he nodded slowly.

'You look great, Frankie, by the way, really great. Your hair…'

'Yes, I had it done the other day. I just—'

'Fancied a change?' he said, smiling.

She laughed and held up her hands. 'Yes, exactly!'

When the champers arrived, she savoured the bubbles tickling her nose and throat – it was like the feeling she'd got when Floyd had kissed her. No. She stopped herself. It was like the feeling of the high she had from taking control of her life.

'What are we drinking to then, Frankie?'

She wanted to say 'to us, to you coming home with me, to love'. Instead, she came up with 'To fancying a change.'

As the alcohol sank in, she began to focus on the now: to soak up her surroundings with each of her five senses. It was as if Floyd was on her shoulder, giving her direction, in a mindful masterclass of zen.

Then came the oysters. This was a test of her daring and with Jason's eyes on her, she went for it, forking one in its shell. The nerves had gone: she felt decadent. With a one-two-three, she swallowed it whole. Whether it was the aphrodisiac effect or the buzz of stepping into the unknown she wasn't sure, but Frankie felt divine. Sliding down her throat, it had tasted silky, elegant, salty and spicy – it was the most sensuous eating experience of her life.

She took another and presented it to Jason's mouth. 'I dare you,' she said, feeling flirty and fantastic.

He looked at her and appeared to be sizing up what this offer meant. Of course, it meant everything: from the childish laying down of a gauntlet and letting her take charge, to the intimate invitation to follow her down a path and to give in to pleasure. 'Frank, there's something I need to say before…' She lowered her hand. '…about me sleeping with someone else. It was meaningless. I just wanted you to know. I wish I'd never bothered.'

Frankie waited for the pain to hit her again. But it didn't come and neither did any jealousy: instead she felt sorrow and a disappointment on his behalf that he hadn't had the journey she'd had. 'It's okay,' she said, really meaning it, 'I've learned a lot too.' But that was as far as she wanted to go; she wanted to feel the now not the past.

'I just don't want you to think I ever stopped loving you because I haven't. And I never will.'

Having Jason's undivided attention was like having the sunshine all to herself.

'If you give me the chance, I'll make it up to you, Tink,' he said.

Her heart soared as she considered just how wonderful it could all be. 'You don't need to explain,' she said softly. 'Tonight's all about fun. Let's just forget we're husband and wife; let's pretend we're on a date and get to know each other all over again.' Then Jason closed his eyes and opened his mouth to receive the oyster.

Meanwhile...

Letty

Letty's eyes went round and round, following the tray in the microwave in a circle going nowhere.

Just like me, she thought, yawning, as she leaned her head on the machine's glass door, waiting for the ping to make her jump and prove she was still alive. She felt anything but at the moment, for she was trapped in a flatlining malaise of boredom.

Saturday night and she was alone, reheating a meal for one. It wasn't meant to be like this, she thought. Or was this sluggish can't-be-arsed a common taboo of coupledom that no one talked about? No fucking wonder, she thought, who'd confess that?

Lance was due back late after a PT course to learn some new technique or other. He had told her what, but Letty hadn't been listening. He'd said for her to go out and not to wait in for him, but she didn't want to see anyone or go anywhere. There was nothing on telly, she couldn't find a book to read on her Kindle, and she had no energy for a run. She felt vacant and empty. Lonely too, even though she was living with someone. It just didn't make sense.

PING! Sighing at the prospect of eating a crap lasagne, she took out the black tray with her fingertips, examined its plastic melted cheese surface and chucked it straight in the bin. Food wasn't the answer. What she needed was to feel something other than this drab is-this-it? Something that would get her adrenalin going and her pulse pumping – to make her cheeks pink and her chest flushed. With a burst of longing, Letty knew exactly what would do all of those things. But she couldn't; she was in enough trouble as it was.

Her hands twitched and she stuffed them into the back pockets of her skinny jeans. Dampen down the urge, wait for the desire to pass. But oh, how she yearned the thrill of the chase, closing down on a target and seizing it whole. The acquisition was the perfect moment, before you had the chance to see its flaws; it represented the thing you most desired in the world and it made your life complete.

'Now look at that, Letty,' she said out loud, 'one mention and you feel alive again. How can it be harmful if it makes you feel so much better?' Just one go, she told herself, as a treat because you did take back those Vivienne Westwoods. She went to the drawer where she kept her important bits and pieces. She rifled slowly through batteries and screwdrivers, lighters and paperclips, but there was no sign of it. It was an envelope she was looking for, had it slipped out the end? Feeling irritated, she opened the cupboard beneath to check: nope, not there. Back into the drawer, her fingers now busy and fast. Cross as she caught herself on a drawing pin. Where the fuck was it? I need it. For FUCK'S SAKE. Hang on, was this it? She got down to eye level to assist her search and there, at the back, was the slightly raised envelope, the one she hid just in case. Her breathing sharp and quick, she threw anything in the way out onto the floor in a shower of Ikea pencils, fake nails and blobs of Blu-Tack.

Scissored between her fingers, she grabbed it and held it up triumphantly. 'Ta-da!' she sang, ripping the envelope open to get her hands on the emergency credit card, and she raced into the lounge for her laptop. Just a few taps and she was on the ascent. Scanning her favourite designers' websites, she began the search for the thing that would make everything right. It might be a pair of shoes or a dress; whatever it was, she'd know as soon as she saw it. Click, click, click, her eyes flicked quickly from image to image, waiting for the explosion in her brain.

And then, boom, there it was, a beautiful camel-coloured soft woven leather handbag, reduced from £900 to £500. It was expensive but then it was suede-lined and hand-stitched. She could smell the luxury, touch it even – and she saw herself in a crowd of people, all eyes on her as she held everyone's attention; not because of the bag itself, which she wore across her body, but because it was a garnish, signalling she was complete and happy. On top of its beauty, it was actually a bargain if you calculated cost per wear. It would last for years! She could make a few savings here and there to cover it – take a sandwich for lunch rather than buy one, give up her morning latte, ditch the gym membership – she had Lance now after all! And even if it was a bit too much in one go to pay off, she'd have no problem meeting the minimum payment.

Add to basket, the screen told her, which she obeyed submissively, unable and unwilling to turn back.

As she went to sign into her account, remembering her username and password like old friends, she countered the guilt and the shame with feel-good affirmations: *I deserve nice things, I work hard, they make me feel good…*

'Enter credit card details' popped up. She inhaled deeply – this was the bit that hurt, every time, it made it seem dirty. They're just numbers, she said, hitting the buttons with force. Then her address, which brought her back on track – the bag will be mine, all mine! Confirm purchase… she closed her eyes and felt them roll back, ready to reach the peak. Her fingers hovered on the mouse pad; her head filled with noise as the demons of doubt – and debt – fought with her desire. The banging got louder and louder.

Shit. That was someone's knuckles. Fuck, she said through gritted teeth, who the hell was that? She had been on the verge of a shopping orgasm, and now she was angry and frustrated.

Throwing open the door, she shouted: 'Yes?'

'Hi, I'm really sorry to disturb you…' a woman said, with a sheepish smile. She looked vaguely familiar and Letty tried to place her. She was small – a petite size, Letty guessed, because only tiny women could pull off mini dungaree dresses – and good-looking with long dark straight hair and big blue eyes. And there was a trace of an accent – where was she from? Letty needed more clues. Then she followed the woman's head which turned anxiously to a car parked outside. She was checking something. There was a movement in the back of the old banger and then she saw a mop of blond hair. Eddy was waving, which meant this could only be Helen, whose face she now placed from a photo on Lance's phone. This was a fucking disaster. Her body, which had been ready for pleasure, now turned on itself with fear, panic and guilt.

'Oh, hi,' Letty said in a much softer voice, feeling very uneasy. Quickly, she tried to assess what Helen was doing here. Had she come to punch her lights out? To have a slanging match?

In a way, Letty wished Helen would go for her – she deserved it.

But it was unlikely, seeing as Helen had apologized when she'd first spoken.

'It won't take long. Eddy's okay in the car,' Helen said humbly in a lighter version of Lance's fair dinkum, looking back to make sure her boy was safe. There was no point in making an introduction; they both knew who they were. 'He used to be in a routine until…' Helen stopped. She placed her hand on her forehead, and her eyes communicated a million apologies for putting her foot in it.

Cringing inside, Letty shook her head – there was no need to express remorse.

Helen started again: 'I wouldn't just turn up, you know, if it wasn't important. I've been trying to get hold of Lance all week.'

Her face was tortured at the inconvenience. Letty wished she'd been smacked in the chops instead because Helen's dignity was making her feel terrible.

'Oh, right, okay,' Letty said, wanting to explain how busy he was and how little time he had between clients. But Helen would've known that herself from when they were together. 'Can I help?' Letty gulped at her own arse-aching stupidity then; here she was, the other woman giving a trite offer of assistance.

Helen hesitated. Then she cleared her throat and looked downwards for a split second, which revealed a chink of hurt. Letty couldn't bear it. Her dignity and reserve were nothing like the woman Lance had made her seem.

'It's okay, you don't have to tell me, I'll just tell him you want to speak to him,' she said.

'No, no. You'll know all about it anyway so…' Helen said, nodding to show she understood they were a couple and couples shared everything. 'It's about me going back to Australia. With Eddy. Lance isn't very happy about it, as you'll know, but my mum, she's not well, it's cancer, and I need to go back. Sooner rather than later, before Eddy starts school.'

It wasn't the punch Letty had been expecting – it was far worse than that. Lance hadn't told her about any of this. That had to be why he'd been so absent.

She couldn't speak; she could only nod.

'I want to do it properly, with his backing. But he won't talk to me about it. He says he'll go to court to stop me. That's the last thing we all need.'

It dawned on her then that Helen might have called round

to see if Letty could persuade Lance. Which would make her very desperate. Letty felt exhausted then ashamed of all the times she'd judged Helen – from cheating on Lance before Letty came on the scene, to criticising her parenting. It was clear she was just an ordinary woman who was trying to do her best for her son, and spend as much time with her mother before it was too late. Letty had a chance to atone for it.

'Of course, I'll talk to him, I promise.'

'Thanks so much,' Helen said, putting her hand over her heart. 'I'd really appreciate it. I don't think Mum's got much time left.'

Letty stood motionless as she watched Helen walk back to the car, waving at Eddy, before she got in and pulled away.

Doing the right thing, trying your best to be a good person – that's what Floyd had said when they'd met in the bar the other night.

Floyd had given her the opportunity of a new future. Her heart bloomed not with the pump of the high she was familiar with, but in a slow release of warmth which went on and on, offering sustenance and hope. She knew what she had to do.

Striding back inside, Letty went to find a pair of scissors. Then, once she'd switched off her laptop, she took her credit card and cut it into dozens of tiny pieces.

The Early Hours of Sunday Morning

Frankie

Jason let out the most enormous groan then stared up at her with heavy eyes.

No, please God, no, she thought. He hadn't, had he?

A woozy smile spread across his lips – it could only mean he had.

'That was amazing, Tink,' he sighed in ecstasy.

'But I'd only just started!'

It was a crushing disappointment for Frankie whose game of 'let's pretend we're not married' had worked wonders in the restaurant. They'd played a Q&A that she'd revised from a dating tips website: What would you do on your last day on earth? He'd skydive over the Monaco Grand Prix, eat steak in New York, surf in South Africa then finish up with one of his mum's roasts. She'd do Victoria Beckham's hair, lunch with Princess Diana then watch a show – *Grease* – on Broadway. Perhaps we could meet up the Empire State Building, he'd asked, which had made her giddy.

There was not a single mention of kitchen tiles. Gradually, they had become closer, physically and emotionally, blocking everyone else out, and flirtatious fingers on the arm lingered longer every time.

When the waiters began to cough, Jason had posed the last question: 'Can I take you home?' He hadn't dropped her hand as they hailed a cab. She was certain they had reconnected on a new level of understanding; that things would be different. They had shared a charged silence on the drive back, only swapping long heated glances; there was no need to speak when their eyes and touching thighs were doing the talking.

Even right up to when she'd let them into the house, he'd gone along with it, asking if she'd lived there long.

So when she'd led him upstairs, she had no nerves: she'd

done all the homework and she'd just wanted to do the job. At the door of the bedroom, Frankie had pulled his waist to her body: a surge of arousal, so basic, so innate, had hit her in the stomach. Swept along, she placed her mouth on his, setting off bursts of bliss as his longing mirrored hers.

Then it had been time: her routine, which wouldn't be rigid but fluid, began with a slow striptease to reveal the waspie which sculpted her midriff and trophied the arc of her bare breasts. She turned him upside down to make a circle then reached for the silk ties from Floyd's gift bag. This was what he'd craved and she'd denied: she was going to turn the pain into pleasure.

Once she'd restrained him on the bed, she climbed on top of him. The heart-stopping sensation of their reconciliation, which felt familiar yet audaciously indecent, was compounded by a mental rush of pride and affirmation: she was doing it and she was doing it well.

But then within a few seconds, Jason had gone from nought to sixty.

His face now was like a marshmallow, all pink and fluffy.

'Wow,' he said, panting.

'But I hadn't finished! I had so much more to do. Like, I was going to change position, spank you, talk dirty and orgasm,' she said, ticking the items off on her fingers.

'What?' Jason came to with a splutter. He'd gone cross-eyed with the effort of thinking in his fog of euphoria.

'Still, I suppose we did the sixty-nine, dressing up and bondage,' she continued. 'That's not bad.'

'Not bad?' Jason's eyes bulged. 'We've just done something... we've never... I've never... you're acting weird. What's going on?'

Frankie didn't want to keep anything from him: their marriage would only survive on honesty and communication. 'So when you dumped me—' she began.

'When we separated.' His correction annoyed her and betrayed the reality.

'Whatever. I decided to broaden my horizons to show you I wasn't a dead loss, and you'd be so impressed we'd get back together. I had a few lessons.'

Jason turned puce. 'You mean you've shagged someone else?'

'That's a horrible way of putting it. I took some advice, that's all.'

'Jesus, Frankie, you could've told me.' He sounded hurt and humiliated.

'Oh, come on, Jason, don't be like this,' she said, rolling off him. 'You enjoyed yourself didn't you?'

Jason sniffed as his deflated penis retracted like a snail. She had the urge to laugh out loud – this was ridiculous! 'You slept with someone before I did!' she said, holding her arms out in protest.

'Who was he, anyway?' Jason asked. 'This Mr Lover-Lover.'

Frankie stopped for a second at the thought of Floyd, the one who'd turned her life around. It felt wrong to have him here in the room with them so she pushed him out of her mind as she stood up. 'No one you know,' she said. It was the first time she'd lied to Jason, and surprisingly it had been easy: but then it wasn't to deceive him, it was to prevent a bomb going off. Floyd and Jason knew one another; not well, but enough for Jason to confront him if he had had one too many and came face to face with him. It just wasn't worth the risk. Besides, it was her business: a very special kind of business, for which she felt warmth and protection. If it got out, it would seem dirty and ruin the memory. 'He was in the same boat as me.'

'Sounds weird to me.' Jason's eyes seared into her like hot coals.

'Well, it might look like that but we'd both been dumped,' she said with an accusatory chin, 'and he was very kind to me actually.'

'Sounds like you have feelings for him.'

'He's a friend, that's all,' she said softly, remembering Floyd's freckles and the way he ruffled his hair, and how he made her unafraid. 'I've never imagined he was anything else.' They had been there for each other for a reason, not because Cupid had shot them with arrows. It had been practical not romantic – it wasn't the kind of love story you told your grandchildren, after all.

Jason raised his eyebrows. His scorn knifed her composure.

'You were the one who wanted some space! Not me! You were the one who said I was boring in bed,' she said, pointing at him, her voice reaching a crescendo. Weeks of pressure began to escape – and it felt good. Very good. 'I only did this for you. For us. Talk about double standards! I have tried to better myself, to discover that the part of me which I thought never existed was just suppressed. I've blossomed, Jason! Can't you see? I'm happier than ever – I feel liberated. How could you not have noticed? For God's sake, couldn't you tell by my hair?'

Shaking her now messed-up mane for dramatic effect, she felt better for letting it out. Better than she had all night.

'Yeah, well, I preferred your hair longer actually,' Jason pouted.

Frankie waited for the hurt – but it didn't come. She found that she didn't give a damn.

'And some of that stuff you wanted to do,' he added, 'well, it's verging on kinky.'

'Kinky? KINKY? It's not glory holes and dressing up in babygros!'

Jason eyed her with alarm now. 'What's happened to you?'

She was outraged by his accusatory tone, but she resisted the urge to inform him of the X-rated details.

'Look, all I want is a nice life. I don't need all of this,' he said, rattling his wrists against the bedpost.

Frankie went to untie him. 'But you said…'

'I know I did. I'm sorry, I'm so so sorry. I got it wrong. I slept with someone because I was a fool. I was looking for what we used to have, that excitement when we first got together. I thought I'd get it with—'

'That surfer chick?' Frankie said, snapping because all of this could've been avoided had he simply talked to her; they could've worked it out. Now he was putting it all on her as if she was the one who had messed up.

'Yes,' he said, hanging his head in shame. 'She was all wild and crazy, then when it happened it was awful, the least enjoyable moment of my life. It was my fault, I put all these expectations on her and me and then, well, it was just wooden and flat and there was no feeling in it. That's when I knew I'd fucked up. But I couldn't come running back to you straight away.'

Feeling drained all of a sudden, Frankie sat down on the bed next to him. 'But why didn't you just tell me all of that?' she asked.

'Because I felt... not worthy. And you were changing, so alive and beautiful and I thought you wouldn't want me anymore.'

'Oh, Jason.'

'That's why I took the job when Dad sold the business. To prove myself.'

'And I'm really proud of you,' she said, turning to him. She wanted him to see that he had a reason to feel he'd moved forward too, not just her. However much he had damaged her, she still loved him.

'But that's been a disaster too. I just haven't got what it takes. I wish I had, but I'm no good with the business side of it. I've tried, I really have. I've told the directors that I'm stepping down. Once they've found a replacement, I'm going back on site, with the boys, that's where I'm happiest.'

Frankie's heart sank. She felt deeply sorry for him.

'I think I'm going to go,' he said, looking half the man he'd been at the oyster bar.

'You don't have to,' she said, feebly because what she needed right now was some room to process the events of the night.

'No, I do. You need the space, not me. I want you to come first from now on,' he said, groping around for his clothes on the floor.

He got dressed and turned to her. 'You looked amazing tonight,' he said. 'And what you did, in bed, was incredible. But I don't need you to be like that. I love the old Frankie.'

She went to get up to show him out.

'I think I know where I'm going,' he said, smiling, 'You stay there. You know, I wish I could turn back the clock to our anniversary. I'd never have said what I said if I'd known all of this now. I'll ring tomorrow, okay?'

He bent down to kiss her on the lips and then left. She waited until she heard the door close before she went downstairs. What she needed was a cup of tea and a good think. It hadn't been the night she'd expected – yet why, because she'd dazzled him and he'd practically confessed his undying love? So why wasn't she jumping for joy?

She sat at her kitchen table and slurped her way through the best brew she'd ever tasted, trying to work it out. A tail brushed against her legs.

'Coast clear now, is it, Leonardo?' she said, as he jumped up to kiss her nose. She was beginning to think he was trying to tell her something. Frankie replayed Jason's confessional in her mind, looking for clues. He'd loved the old Frankie, he'd said,

233

but she was fast disappearing. And he'd said he'd wanted her to come first. Pah, he'd made little attempt to make her come at all.

It wasn't that sex was the be all and end all – but as Floyd had said it did reflect the state of a relationship. She had never had an orgasm with Jason – what did that say about them as a couple?

As she sat there, topless in a waspie, she realized she was at a crossroads. To be with Jason could be a wonderful thing. But to have a future with him could also mean she might have to go backwards, to the old Frankie.

She wasn't sure if she wanted to, or even could. Yet he had been open about his disastrous experience with that girl – was it possible that he had developed a new level of awareness?

If he had, then she could love him with her everything because they would walk a path of openness as equals.

The remaining question in her mind though was this: would he, could he, be able to love the new her?

Sunday Afternoon

Em

Soaking up the happy faces around her, Em conceded she had underestimated everybody.

The gathering of aunts and uncles and friends and cousins had chomped through most of her buffet – thank goodness she had had those oven bake baguettes in the freezer. But more than that, they'd congratulated her on her pregnancy with tactful restraint, knowing that she hated a fuss. It was yet another lesson to her that she had to be more forgiving when she was prone to assume the worst. These people were her allies, and while it would grate to have to accept help when the baby came, she just had to live with it. Hell, she might even enjoy it, she told herself, as she squeezed through a gap in her full-to-bursting flat to get some ice in the kitchen.

The excitement had been unleashed on Floyd instead, who was far more capable of handling the spotlight. As was Sasha, who had a way of reflecting their smiles, making them feel included and appreciated, as she flitted around refilling glasses. Mostly Floyd's, by the looks of him, who was well on his way to being drunk.

It was probably a good idea that he did a speech sooner rather than later; not just because he was on the verge of slurring, but two hours of hosting had seen her reach her limit of sociability. As lovely as they all were, she wanted them to go.

Em went to find Floyd – he wasn't in the lounge, on the balcony, in the hall or loo. Pausing outside his room, she heard his voice and Sasha's. How sweet, she thought, they're having a moment to themselves; true love was all about wanting to be alone with your special someone. But hang on, she'd just seen Sasha in the lounge. Peeking through the gap in the doorframe she saw Floyd with his hands on Letty's shoulders. What were they doing?

There was no time to ask. She banged on the door and demanded he come out at once.

'Speech time, Floyd. It's about time you added something to this – you haven't brought anything to the party so far, not even a tube of Pringles. I'll wait for you in the lounge.'

Floyd staggered in, his hair a total mess. She widened her eyes at him to tell him to sort himself out but he poked his tongue at her. He waited until he was in the centre of the room and next to Sasha's elegant mother, then, horror of horrors, he bent forward and started twerking the room. Em closed her eyes wishing she could unsee his disgusting rear-end jerking into people's groins.

'So, as you can see,' Sasha said, leaping into action to draw everyone's attention to her instead, 'Floyd is using the medium of dance to express his joy at you all being here today!'

Everyone laughed and Em exhaled through her mouth. Thank God for Sasha, what a saviour!

'Clearly the excitement is all too much for him! Anyway, we'll make this quick, but on behalf of the two of us, I'd just like to thank you all for coming to celebrate our engagement.'

She held up her ring then – a rock the size of a sugar cube – to a whoop.

'And no one look at Em but we're all wishing you the very best and thanks for the amazing spread!'

Everyone turned to her then and she gave an uncomfortable smile. While she hated being looked at, she was touched by Sasha's thoughtfulness.

'Right so you'll all be wanting to know about the wedding details…'

A murmur rippled around the room and Em squeezed her shoulders because she had been dying to know where they'd do it. They might relish surprising everyone with a church wedding and a formal sit-down reception, or perhaps they'd please themselves with a quirky ceremony on Penarth Pier, and then cross the prom to the open top roof restaurant for fish and chips and a DJ.

'Floyd and I, we've decided that we're going to do it barefoot and on the beach!'

Applause broke out and Em nodded her appreciation: it was so very them.

'On my travels, I went to a gorgeous little place in Thailand which I promised myself I'd return to if I was ever lucky enough to convince Floyd to marry me.'

How romantic! She must be talking about the honeymoon, Em thought.

'The thing is, we've decided to make it very low key. By ourselves.'

Em felt her jaw drop. How could Floyd have agreed to this? Mum and dad would be absolutely gutted. She stole a glance at their faces and the pair of them had plastic smiles. And even if close family was allowed to go, Em wouldn't be able to seeing as she'd either be massively pregnant or with a young baby. It was just unbelievable. She'd always assumed she would be there with Floyd on his big day – he loved family and he was so gregarious that only a big bash would do.

'I know it's a shock and I wish we could fit in with everyone's wishes, but we want to do what feels right for us. We'll have a party before we go, we can pretend it's our wedding so don't fret about missing out. Anyway, that's all for now, we'll let you know our plans. Thanks again. Oh and by the way, we're all going to the pub now, to give Em some peace, so please join us there!'

She didn't want to acknowledge it, but Em felt wronged. She'd completely fallen for Sasha all over again and then off she'd gone at a tangent, like a rubber ball. How could she consistently read people so badly? No matter how far Em had come this last few months, it was damned obvious she would never understand the human race.

Busying herself tidying up to hide her disappointment, Em didn't show anyone to the door. Letty and Frankie silently collected the glasses and stacked the dishwasher in record time, then gave her quick pecks on the cheek before they disappeared.

Soon it was just her and Floyd in the flat.

'Aren't you going to the pub?' she asked him, as he held his head in his hands at the breakfast bar.

'Nope.'

'Why not?'

'I've had enough,' he said, sinking a whisky in one.

'Are you all right?' she asked, more out of duty than concern. She would raise their inexplicable decision when she'd had a chance to let it sink in. And when he was sober – she was sick to the stomach of people acting oddly, and for now she wanted nothing more than to sit down with her new Lakeland catalogue.

'No, I'm bloody not,' he said. His eyes were bloodshot and googly from the booze.

Em ignored him and turned to wipe the surfaces of sticky rings and crumbs.

'I don't know if I love her,' he said.

'Of course you do,' Em replied, knowing he'd be collapsed on the sofa snoring within five minutes. He had to love her to go along with the plan to tie the knot away from home. It was just pre-wedding nerves.

'You've always said she's the best thing that's ever happened to you. You're going to be very happy together,' she said, scraping at a stubborn stain, 'marriage, living together and you'll be an uncle too.'

'No I'm fucking not. Slasher is like a sixth-form poet or an art student. She's full of total and utter shit.'

'Are you being serious?' Em said, swinging around, unsure she could take another surprise.

'Yes. She wants us to get married in Thailand so we can go to this island she likes to set up some kind of hippy backpacker hostel, where we'll play flutes at dawn and do chakra meditation classes. That's why she wants a party before we get married – we're not coming back.'

Em reached out for the counter because it felt like her Birkenstock sandals had become ice skates.

Howling, Floyd broke down with his entire body. His chest heaved, he was gasping for air and grasping his hair tightly like a crazed lunatic.

'Her version of settling down is running away and I was so looking forward to changing that little nipper's nappies,' he wailed.

She wanted to go to him but she couldn't trust her legs. It was a good job, she realised seconds later, because in a convulsion so severe, Floyd threw up a fountain of vomit so spectacular it went across the breakfast bar and splattered across the tiles.

The Early Hours of Tuesday

Letty

'Come with you?' Letty whispered.

'Why the bloody hell not!' Lance said sitting up in bed, his eyes shining like blue infinity pools, as if it was a eureka moment.

Stunned, Letty realized that all she had to do was dive in and they'd have forever. But what he was suggesting, what he obviously wanted to do, was life-changing.

'To Australia?' she said, 'You're going to go?' She needed him to spell it out.

He shrugged. 'What else can I do? I can't live in a different hemisphere to Eddy. Saying goodnight to him when it's morning there. I'll be a stranger. But it doesn't have to be the end of us.'

Letty's head whirled from two days of worry. Lance was in full 'get your beach body' mode, rising before she was awake to do early PT sessions and not returning until she was asleep. There hadn't been a moment to raise Helen's visit. It hadn't stopped her wondering though: why he'd kept it from her, how they were supposedly in a serious relationship yet he knew nothing of her money problems. They both had secrets – it wasn't how things should be. Their first chance to discuss it all came just after 10pm when he came in. Incredibly, they'd avoided a row. She'd understood she couldn't criticise him for holding things from her when she had done the same.

They'd both cried though: he hadn't told her about Helen's plans to leave because he was so in shock. He'd felt sick with the guilt of thinking of himself rather than Eddy's dying grandmother. And of thinking Letty wouldn't understand because she wasn't a mum. This had set her off: she felt she was falling short of who he needed. Her anguish that their intimacy had gone. Then her debts came tumbling out and she heaved sobs of grief that she had filled the holes in her life with material goods. In an instant, he'd offered to turn her red statements black: they were in this together.

Their make-up sex had been slow and adoring – they promised over and over never to let go of each other. But now Letty could see it wasn't that simple.

'Come with me,' he repeated, taking her hands into his. 'As my partner, you'd be eligible to apply for a visa if I acted as your sponsor. Or we could get married. Whatever you want, however you want to play it,' he said, desperately.

'Not the most romantic of proposals there... I dunno, babes.' She shut her eyes and held her head. This wasn't a tea or coffee, brown or red sauce dilemma. This was bloody massive.

'It's a great life out there, beaut. The sunshine, the sea, the barbies. We'd have a pool and Sydney would be our doorstep. You haven't lived unless you've had a barramundi fillet at Doyles On The Beach.'

'I can go to Barry Island for fish and chips, you know.' She needed a lot more persuading than a naff postcard from *Neighbours*.

'Yeah but can you see the Opera House and the harbour from there? I think not. Then there's the surf. Manly is the place. And the food – there's pan-fusion-everything. Sydney is where every culture meets – you could have anything you can dream of. Vietnamese, Lebanese, Chinese, Japanese, American, Indian, Spanish.' He was holding her in his arms now, begging her to picture it.

'What about chicken curry half-and-half? I'd miss that Welsh delicacy of rice and chips from Dorothy's. There is no better takeaway after a night on the pop.' She couldn't take it in.

'I'm being serious,' he said, cuddling her. 'Stop making jokes.'

'I can't help it. It's what I do.' Even though she found comfort in him, she also felt the wrench of everything she'd leave behind. 'The hills, I'd miss the green.' The Valleys where she'd grown up, the parks of Cardiff and the countryside.

'There are mountains a day trip away, you know. There's the Botanical Gardens too, right in the centre. We've got cockatoos, galahs, kookaburras, flying foxes, lizards, yabbies'—'

'SNAKES! Scary poisonous ones and big bitey spiders.'

'Yeah, but they don't like Pommies. You taste too bitter.'

They shared a laugh, collapsing onto the bed on their backs.

But she was troubled by the wonder of where she would fit

in. 'What if you're only asking me along because you'd feel too guilty to go off without me after everything that's happened?'

'Look, I won't lie to you,' he sighed. 'Eddy comes first. I won't live thousands of miles away from him. End of. I have to be there to see him grow up.' She got this, a million times over. 'It's hard to say that to you when I love you so much. But I'd be miserable without you. We can make this work.'

'I've no money, you know that...'

'I told you. I'd look after you.'

'I just don't know,' she said, snuggling into him, hiding from the decision.

'What's stopping you?' he said, smoothing her hair.

'My friends. Cups of tea with Em, drinking sessions with Frankie, our pampering evenings, they would all end.'

'Haven't you said their lives are changing?'

This was true – Em was going to be a mum, and in all likelihood Frankie would end up back with Jason. Where did that leave her? Single and a spare part.

'They can visit, you can FaceTime and you'll make new mates.'

Damn him, Lance was setting out a very persuasive stall.

'I don't want to be trailing you around, depending on you. Like, I've made a promise to myself, that I was going to start being more assertive for myself, starting with my spending. Address my feelings of worthlessness. But how can I be independent when I'd be so dependent on you?'

'You'd make your own life out there. You'd have a head start too being with an Aussie, you know, you wouldn't be an ex-pat. And one day we might have a baby and that's a social life of its own.'

Letty's heart leapt at his projection into the future, their future. Then it crashed when she thought of what she'd do all day. 'But what about work? I'm just a PA.'

'There's college. You can get this qualification you're after. You'd get away from that creep Ross too. Imagine telling him to stuff his job – you're off Down Under.'

'But I'd be running away.'

'Nope, you'd be free.'

But no matter what Lance said, no matter how amazing it sounded, she'd be going because of him not because she was doing it off her own back. Playing third fiddle to Eddy, Helen and Lance.

She was facing an ultimatum. He would go whatever.

Taking control, that's what she'd promised she'd do, could that happen if she followed him? Could she make it her own?

It was her choice to make: stay here and then what? Or make a go of it and start a whole new adventure?

It all depended on one thing, she knew as their entwined bodies moved towards sleep, and that was whether their relationship was strong enough.

That Morning

Frankie

Dad is bright this morning, Frankie thought as she watched him pacing a spot of carpet while he took a quick call on his ancient brick of a cordless phone in the lounge. Even though she'd only just arrived, he seemed less creaky and more lively, as if he was taking a role in life rather than watching from his armchair. It must be having her round, she thought, feeling guilty that she hadn't been over sooner.

'Clifford Rogers speaking. Oh hello, ye-es, yes…' He winked at her with a creased hazel eye as he spoke. '…no… a bit later.' He pulled a funny face to make Frankie laugh. 'Okay, ta ta, bye for now.' He examined his immaculate fingernails as he ended the conversation. Despite his DIY projects, Dad always had lovely clean hands. 'Sorry about that,' he said, turning to her. 'Right then. Tea? Coffee? Fairy juice?'

'Whatever you're having. Who was that then?' she said, perching on the worn sofa that had been around for as long as she could remember.

'Gareth. We'll be having a pint later. Tuesday night is Legion night.'

Frankie's smile hid her sadness that he hadn't been talking to a lady friend. But she had suspected as much. That was why last night she'd asked if she could pop in for a couple of hours in between clients – to encourage him to try online dating. He had been stuck in the past for too long. Like the old her, he resisted change – the evidence was all around her; from the furniture and the shelves lined with crafts she'd made at school to the hideous orange clock above the fireplace dating back to 1983 when Mum discovered Habitat. But he had to move on from mourning, and she was in the right place to support him.

'I've got you some new trousers,' she said, jiggling an M&S bag at him.

'Oh, God, they're not those skinny what-nots are they?' he said, holding his once-dark now greying short back and sides in alarm. 'I'd be worried they'd cut off my circulation.'

'No! They're just trousers. A bit more up to date, though.'

'And what's wrong with how I dress?' he said, crossing his strong and capable arms in mock offence. 'I'll have you know these utility shorts and this T-shirt are new. Ish.'

'You always look nice, Dad, I didn't mean that. I just think you could try something a bit different. Something subtle, but it will make you look younger, more trendy.'

'I'm fifty-bloody-eight, love!' Then when he saw her face had dropped, he promised her he'd try them on. But not now with an audience. He wasn't one of those supermodels, you know, he added as he led them along the dark corridor into the light of his new kitchen, which he'd finally got round to finishing.

'It's only because I think you hide a bit,' she said, to his back and bald spot. 'It's like you've given up on things. Fifty-eight isn't old – you've still time to meet some— Wow! This is amazing!'

She stopped to take it in: the terracotta-tiled back wall had been replaced by French doors which were pulled open all the way and led straight onto the sunny patio. On the right was a black two-seater sofa facing a wall-mounted flat-screen TV on the left. The grey floor tiles contained sprinkles of quartz which twinkled in the light. A wooden-topped island floated in the middle of a brand new country-style set of white units and there was even a vase of tulips on the side.

'Given up, have I, love?' Dad said, smiling from the sink where he filled the kettle.

'Dad,' she gasped, 'when you said a bit of an update I didn't think you meant this! How did you get it done so quick? I was only here…' She stopped when she remembered she hadn't dropped by for at least a week. 'I'm so sorry, I've been caught up with stuff,' she said, explaining.

'Oh, I had some help. And listen, you've got a life and I'm glad you're busy. What do you think then? Look, I even kept a space for Judy. And there's underfloor heating to keep her old bones warm.'

Judy, who was lying on her back with her bent paws hanging in half on top of her chest, opened an eye and wagged her tail half-heartedly.

'Don't get up, old girl,' he said to the dog, 'her arthritis is getting worse, Frankie, I'm not sure she'll be around much longer.'

'Oh don't say that,' Frankie implored, then before she had time to think, her greatest fear spilled out, 'You'll be all alone.'

Dad shook his head at her. 'Now look, I'm very happy, don't you start with all that.'

'I've been thinking, Dad,' Frankie said, seizing the moment.

'Dangerous,' Dad said, opening and closing cupboards because he couldn't find the teabags.

'Internet dating. There are loads of sites for older people, divorced people like you with kids and…'

He laughed and announced there was no need for her to feel sorry for him. Honestly, he added, which meant he didn't want to hear any more.

Frankie sighed but having said her bit she respected his right to shut her up. If she went on, he would be even less receptive next time she mentioned it. She had to go softly-softly with Dad.

'Why don't you tell me about your stuff, love?' Dad said.

Frankie sank into the squishy settee and took a mouthful of tea. 'Oh, it's nothing really. Just Jason, as usual. We went out Saturday night and he stayed over,' she glanced up at him to make sure he understood her coded revelation.

He joined her and nodded. 'Go on,' he said, showing he knew what she had implied. It was incredible how much empathy he had for a man of his age; he must just be very observant, seeing as he was single.

'Well, I'm just really confused. He told me he had made a mistake and he hinted at wanting me back. And I thought that's what I wanted, and I do, but there's something stopping me…' Frankie couldn't quite believe what she was about to say but it was coming over her and she was helpless. '...There's this other guy, you see. It's not like anything has been said between us,' she said, quickly to stop Dad drawing the wrong conclusion, 'but I feel comfortable with him, more comfortable than I do with Jason. He gets me and…'

Dad placed a hand on hers and nodded deeply, which showed the depth of his generous nature, to accept her dilemma with heart rather than scorn.

'...and here's the thing, I'm not sure Jase does anymore. This other guy, he's engaged, and it's purely platonic but his friendship has made me see things through different eyes. It's made me question everything that I thought I knew. Not that I'd be with this guy, just that what I want and need in a partner isn't what I wanted or needed before. Oh Dad, I just don't know what to do.'

He looked long at her face as if he was thinking of a solution. He took a breath and her soul leapt that he was going to console her; she knew it was pathetic, she was a grown woman, but she needed his wise words. 'Frankie, I'm going to tell you a story now and it might help you,' he said. His eyes changed to brown as the sun went behind a shadow. He cleared his throat and began. 'Once upon a time, there was a man who lived a lie, only for a woman to save him. She stood by him, her husband, for years. She stayed with him so he could be with their daughter. Then she had a chance of happiness, she met a good man and moved out. She left the daughter with her husband, not because she was selfish, but because the daughter had asked to stay with her dad. She made the ultimate sacrifice.'

Frankie felt alarmed at the parallels to her own life. But this wasn't about them: Mum wasn't one for personal sacrifices.

'Why was he living a lie?'

'Because, Frankie, that man was gay. He knew it all along but hid it. He was so close to the girl, he was more like a Mam than her own mother. She'd always found it harder to connect, the girl would always go to him for everything – it was as if their roles were reversed. Do you understand what I'm telling you?'

'Sort of,' she said, getting the moral of being true to oneself or at least the truth will out, which was what Phyllis had meant too. 'But who are you talking about? It might fall into place then.'

Dad paused and put his hand on her shoulder, his eyes turning green and golden as the sun broke free. 'Me, love, I'm talking about me and your mother and Colin. I'm gay, love.'

'What?' she said, screwing her face up in utter disbelief. She must've misheard, surely. She waited for Dad to tell her it was a joke or that he'd got his words mixed up. But he held her stare and nodded slowly. The kitchen seemed to swivel then as the shock shook her by the head.

'But you can't be! You play darts and you're a plumber!'

Dad gave a small smile. 'That is true, I do and I am. But it doesn't make me straight. We're not all air stewards or Elton John, love.'

But where had the clues been? She rifled through her memories but there was nothing. No shouty signs she associated with being gay, but then, as Dad said, not everyone wore it on their sleeves. He had friends, blokes he went to football with and the boys at the working men's club. He was just one of the lads.

'How long have you known?' she said because she needed more to accept this new version of the truth.

'Forever, but in those days, especially here in Wales, it wasn't like it was now. There was no Pride march. You ignored it, you were at pains to fit in. I met your mam, we were great friends and we fell in love. A love of sorts anyhow, which is not to lessen it, because we still have a very strong bond and always will. We just did what we were expected to do. Got married and had kids. It was all I ever wanted. Your mother, she had terrible baby blues after you, what they call post-natal depression now. And it brought you and me even closer together. One day she found me in tears, it was such a struggle denying who I was and I told her. Yes, she flipped out, but after a bit she was marvellous. We made it work for you. Occasionally, to my shame, I couldn't take it anymore and I'd... you know. I'm not proud of it, your mother was an angel, she turned a blind eye for years. So when she met Colin, I was the one who told her to go. She deserved it.'

Frankie's eyes filled with tears at the way she had always sided with Dad.

'I'm very sorry we didn't say anything sooner. I thought you might perhaps have guessed, not many straight men name their dogs after Judy Garland, do they? But it's not all bad...'

She looked up quickly. 'What do you mean?' Because if there was any good to have come out of it, she was so sad she needed to hear it.

'Well, I have a friend.'

Frankie's jaw nearly fell on to her lap. To hell with the years of not knowing, Dad had a boyfriend! So thrilled he wasn't lonely, Frankie bear-hugged him.

'That's why you didn't want me to bang on about online dating!' she crowed, clapping her hands. 'So who is he?'

'Well, believe it or not, it's... Gareth.'

Frankie swooned at the sweet sight of her dad's bashful blush as he'd said his name. 'Gareth? The painter and decorator? This is classic. I thought you were just mates!'

'No. Well, we are but it's more than that. We're coming up to our five-year anniversary.' He was brimming with pleasure and pride.

'Five years!' Her parrot impression was coming on very nicely, she realized.

'He's got his own key. He lives with his mam, she's not too good so he's her carer, but he stays over twice a week and he can come and go as he pleases. It suits us very well. One day, he'll move in I'm sure, but not yet. We all need to get used to the knowing.'

Frankie hit her forehead with the heel of her hand. The complete opposite of what she'd first thought, it all made sense – all of it. Dad was a messy so-and-so yet the house was always spick and span thanks to Gareth. Dad had no style yet the new kitchen was tasteful. That was Gareth's influence. And the notes Dad left when he went out weren't for her, they were for Gareth. It was just like any other established relationship, yet by the looks of Dad they still had a spark.

'Does Mum know?' she asked.

'Yes, love, she does. And she's very happy for me, for us. You see, your mother and I, we know we've made a mess of it but, believe me, we only ever had you in mind. That's why we meet up, to talk about you, we'll always be tied together in that way. Your mother will forgive you, she's a wonderful lady.'

'I need to see her,' Frankie said, bursting from her seat, kissing Dad and racing to the car. The ten-minute drive to Mum's was usually one she did reluctantly, but now she was pressing down on the accelerator, desperate to see her, nipping left and right on the fly-over to Penarth Marina.

She screeched to a halt outside her townhouse and beat the door with the palm of her hands. Mum's face appeared, she looked bashful.

'Did Dad ring?' Frankie breathed.

'Yes, love...I... We should've said.'

'It's okay,' Frankie said, hesitating before making a move then throwing herself into the arms of the woman who'd been Dad's rock, who'd stayed put when she could've turned him into a freak show. To the woman who'd suffered depression and humiliation to keep her in a family unit. To the woman who struggled to be maternal but who was still her mum. She wasn't a model parent, far from it, but she was stoic and selfless, had put everyone else's needs above her own for years – without once making profit from it when she had every right to slap Frankie down when she gave her a mouthful.

Her mum's body was bony and stiff, as if she didn't know what to do. Then, as Frankie hung on, she felt her mother slowly relax.

'I'm sorry, Mum, I really am,' Frankie said, feeling the deepest sorrow for taking sides. Had she been told, she might have behaved differently but then, even worse, she might've blamed Dad.

As she sobbed into her mum's hair, Frankie realized she'd run to her mother for the first time in her life.

Thursday

Em

Em felt like a dried prune after four hours of talking in the windowless, air-conditioned training room.

As part of the indoctrination of new recruits, the sessions were always conducted within these four white walls, complete with deliveries of polystyrene coffee and biscuits. There was so much to get through and if they were 'released' for anything more than loo breaks, someone would always get lost. The intensity of it helped bond the staff and Em got to identify those who showed promise.

Afterwards, she always wanted some air. Shuffling papers and shutting down her presentation software, she promised herself – and the baby – a lunchtime walk. She felt a little flutter in her tummy, which she took as a high five; the prawn was going to love the outdoors, just like her.

'Sorry, not just yet,' she said to her bump, 'I've got to drop this lot back in my office first. Then we'll be free!'

'Talking to yourself is a sign of madness,' said a voice behind her.

Her heart skipped at the same time as her insides recoiled.

Em looked over her shoulder to see Simon Brown grinning at her from the doorway, resting on it with his arms crossed, looking very pleased with himself. What was he doing here?

'I was talking to the baby,' she said, coldly. 'Research says it helps with bonding.'

Then she got on with her tidying-up, willing him to go. It was infuriating how the sight of him made her feel things. It was a domino run of emotion starting with the instinctive tumble of attraction and love, which knocked into disappointment at herself, then battered into the mental turmoil of his betrayal. But at least now, she told herself, she had a new ending: bitterness may be in the place of hope, but she was working on going forward to build a life for her and the baby. If only he would let her get on with it and stop texting.

'Aren't you going to congratulate me?' he almost sang. 'I've got the job.'

Em felt herself plummet as if she was in a broken lift going down, down, down: there was no pleasure in knowing she'd been right about him. She shut her eyes and counted to ten. The email from head office about the manager's post must've landed while she had been training. Why couldn't they have given her a heads-up? It was a sign of how little they thought of her. But worse than that was that she'd lost out to Simon Brown. No, not lost, been played by him. He'd taken what was hers: she wanted to crumple down onto her knees and cry. But he was the father of her child and her new boss.

Digging deep for dignity, Em swivelled round, straightened her neck vertebrae and met his excited eyes to give him a contained 'very well deserved'.

Surely he could find a shred of decency to accept her words and leave?

But no, his smug mouth was twitching with mirth. She wished she had never set her eyes on him. Then to her absolute disgust, Simon Brown burst out laughing. Grotesque convulsions made their way from his Joker face to his shaking shoulders, past his swinging tie, into his hands which slapped his legs and made him bend double. It ignited the rage that had been building ever since the interview.

'How dare you, Simon Brown,' she roared. 'How dare you befriend me then use me?'

Simon Brown quivered as if her words had tasered him.

'How dare you use our baby against me in the interview for your own benefit? How dare you even bring it up without consulting me?'

He was cowering now and she felt the satisfaction of getting everything off her chest.

'You have shown your true colours and I'm very sorry indeed that you are the father of this beautiful, innocent life growing inside me. How dare you, Simon Brown!'

The rush of release meant she didn't care that she'd broken her vow to keep things civil. A man like him needed to be told that she would not be pushed about.

'And I wish to inform you, *boss*,' she said with her nose held high in defiance, 'that I will be requesting a transfer. Now, if you will excuse me.' Em picked up her things then marched towards him.

'Em!' he said in a very unbecoming high-pitched voice.

'What?' Em hissed, coming to a halt inches from his panic.

'Haven't you seen the email?' he said, his eyes wide. 'I didn't mean I got THE job. I meant I've got YOUR job – I'm going to be deputy manager. You've got the actual JOB JOB, the manager's position.'

Panting from his gabble, his arched eyebrows pleaded for a sign she understood. He was crouching in such a manner that Em wondered if he was on the verge of wetting himself. And then it hit her.

One hand went to her open mouth, the other went to her bump. Her files scattered all over the floor and her legs felt as wobbly as a newborn giraffe's.

'You. Have. Got. The. Job. Do you read me?' he said, nodding fast and furiously at her.

'Nooo!' she whispered, feeling her nostrils stretch with her disbelief.

'Yes!' he said, staggering back to standing as the surge of fight or flight finally passed. They both took a second to recover. Then tears sprang to Em's eyes.

'I've done it!' she said. 'I'm crying. I don't normally cry.'

She buried her face in her hands and saw herself as the sixth-former on the check-outs, the student on the deli and the employee on the payroll. Walking all of those miles in store, getting up before the crack of dawn, getting home in the pitch-black – it had all paid off. She began to compose herself, after all, she was the gaffer now! But, oh dear, she remembered in ghastly surround sound what she had said to Simon Brown just minutes before.

If she had the job, then his plan had back-fired. And he didn't seem disappointed. Or was it possible that she had got the wrong end of the stick? It wouldn't be the first time. Please, no, she thought, what if I've read it incorrectly? What if Simon Brown isn't the menace she thought he was, and now she was going to have to see him day-in day-out and be reminded of her screeching idiocy, until he or she left. Or he might make a complaint to HR. She might be disciplined or, more likely, sacked. Quick, she thought, she had to find out right now what had happened in his interview.

'Why did you tell the panel about the baby?' she asked. She

didn't have time to beat around the bush.

'Because I wanted to notify them that whatever happened I'd be looking at taking extended paternity leave – I wanted to give them notice of my intention of being there for the baby.'

Simon Brown appeared to be telling the truth.

'And why would you have wanted to do that?' she said, narrowing her eyes. She needed to sort this out for once and for all.

'So that you could go back to work, after a few months off with the baby, if you wanted to. If you didn't want to have the entire responsibility. We'd talked about co-parenting, hadn't we?' He spoke slowly and clearly as if he knew he had one chance to explain.

'Yes, we had but you could have done me the courtesy of giving me notice that you'd bring it up instead of wading in like that.'

Could she trust him, she wondered? Hold tight, she told herself, not yet.

'I was trying to do the right thing. Honestly.'

'And why would you have wanted to do that?' she asked, again. Spell it out to me, she wanted to cry, daring to wonder if there was a greater reason.

'I only ever wanted the deputy job. I told them that. And that you were the best person for THE job.'

'And why would you have wanted to do that?'

Her heart was racing as she drew closer to the truth.

'Because… oh, Em…'

There was something about his flushed cheeks and shy eyes which made her wonder if he was about to say something momentous. She waited, willing him to throw off his reserve.

'Because… you're going to be a fantastic boss.'

'A fantastic boss,' she said, weakly, feeling her heart wither. Despite everything, she still had feelings for him and she'd hoped he'd felt the same. How could she have even thought he would say anything else?

He produced a hand to shake and she took it; this would have to do and once her hormones had settled, she would be able to cope.

This moment, at the very least, marked the outbreak of peace – and what more could she wish for for her baby? She had the job, he had hers, and their child would be blessed with security and love.

'And you are going to be a fantastic deputy, Simon Brown,' she said as if it was an olive branch. 'We'll make a great team.'

His lovely plain face, one that most people wouldn't be able to pick out of a crowd, lit up like a lighthouse. He would always be special to her, that was a fact and she just had to accept it. It would be a strange path to navigate as friends, colleagues and parents. But being realistic, knowing who she was, she couldn't expect anything else.

Then it all turned a bit weird.

His lovely plain face sort of melted as if he was a triangle of wilting Brie that had been left out for too long. And still he kept hold of her hand. Beads of sweat dotted his forehead and his pupils were the size of those cappuccino saucers they had in the homeware aisle.

'What is it?' she asked him, unnerved. 'Is there something wrong?'

She touched her nose to check for bogies but it was clear.

'Nothing,' he said, his eyes watering. 'Nothing's wrong at all.'

'Right,' she said. He'd gone a bit cross-eyed. Was it his allergies? It was dusty in here.

'If you need to get your inhaler, that's fine,' she said as her hand slipped from his sweaty palm.

'I do feel a bit…' he said, patting his chest.

'Well, I'm a trained first aider so—' She tried to manoeuvre him to sit down but he began to protest.

'Em! I'm fine! Look, for God's sake…' he said, making her start with this out of character display of emotion. 'I mean, what I'm trying to get at… is this… I can't hold it in anymore… I love you. I always have done, since the first day we met by the world cheese display.'

No, no, no, no. He was wrong, she thought. 'It was the Cheddar section. I remember distinctly we were beside the mature, medium and mild lines when we were introduced.'

'Right, yes. But did you hear what I said?'

'Details are important, Simon Brown.'

She was refusing to acknowledge the thing he'd mentioned before because it wasn't happening. No one could be that lucky. Especially not her.

'Yes. I know,' he said. 'But so is listening. I love you, Emerald, do you hear me?'

'No.' Em covered her ears because she couldn't let herself fall for either it or him yet again.

He stepped closer to her and gently took her hands. 'I couldn't say anything when I was shadowing you,' he said, looking at her doe-eyed as though she was actually beautiful. 'It'd have been so awkward if you hadn't felt the same. That night together, it was so right, but I'd promised myself that Megan would come first, always. It was like I was punishing myself for messing up.

'When I realized the baby was mine, I could hardly tell you then – you'd think I was just doing it out of duty like I did with Megan's mum. Then there was the interview and I was scared you'd lose your focus if I'd told you. I've been through this in my head so many times, how I mustn't love you and your funny ways, and your wonky fringe, and the way you look slightly cross when you don't understand something, like you're doing now...'

Em hated her frowny face and she tried to unfurl her brow. But then she thought, what the hell, he likes it.

'...but I do love you. I've tried not to and I can't help it.'

New information just in: Simon Brown says he loves me.

She grasped hold of him tightly because if she let go she feared she'd float off and the bubble would pop, and it would be just her style to squash the love of her life from on high with her big pregnant bottom. Em desperately wanted to believe his words and she was almost there. Almost. 'You never showed it,' she said, still holding her armour close.

'How could I? Would you show it if you felt it was unrequited?'

His Adam's apple bobbed, as if it was laying itself bare at her mercy. Locking it away, containing your love: hadn't she done exactly that?

'I've waited so long to tell you. If we could be a family... Meg loved you that day we met on the beach. That made me realize she would be a part of us not apart from us. If you felt the same... Because if you don't I won't take the job. I'll never mention it again and I'll be the best dad I can possibly be and —'

She shushed him because she'd heard enough to convince her he meant every word. And that he was the most wonderful creature in the universe. Apart from Doctor Who, she thought

255

in brackets, what with his regeneration skills. It was time to accept her fortune; she was afraid it would disappear if she didn't.

'I love you, Simon Brown,' she said, seeing in his brown eyes flecks of gold, which she imagined were in his very DNA, 'Times infinity.'

And then as she kissed him, the loop-the-loop she'd felt on the night they made their baby returned. Only now, she didn't have to instruct her mind to clock off because she felt whole rather than two halves: both her heart and head were in perfect symbiosis.

Meanwhile…

Letty

Ross breezed into the swanky hotel conference room and declared: 'Blue-sky-thinking time!'

Walking to his seat at the head of the walnut table, he high-fived the guys and squeezed the shoulders of the women in his path, luckily not including Letty, as if he was on his way to get a bloody Oscar.

Ha, well, if her surprise went to plan then he would be the centre of attention – just not in the way he thought.

'Hope you've all brought your swimmers,' he slimed in a crisp white shirt, unbuttoned halfway down his chest. Oh, the irony of all that hair bursting out when he had not one follicle on his head.

'I'm looking forward to getting into that jacuzzi, I can tell you!'

What was the betting that he was a budgie smugglers man, Letty wondered?

He gave a leer and then an exaggerated groan. 'That assault course has made me stiff.'

Letty felt a bit of sick come up into her mouth. Luckily there was a vase of lilies blocking her from his direct eyeline. She could hide here, down the end, next to Sal and Jools.

'A couple of housekeeping matters,' he said, taking a seat next to his deputy, Nick. 'Tonight's fundraiser is for Hope, the children's hospice in Cardiff that we support. On the tables will be envelopes for our silent auction, so please encourage the clients you'll be sat with to give generously. For those kiddies who are only with us for a short time.'

His sincerity was good, Letty would give him that: associating himself with such a wonderful charity made him look squeaky clean.

'I also have another favour to ask of you,' he said, flashing a smile to his twenty staff.

'Gittings PR will be going live on all social media formats at the dinner. It will be a co-ordinated cross-platform push to spread the news that we care about communication and reputation. To launch it, I will be doing a quick speech – our clients are our friends, blah-di-blah – when you have a nice evening with friends, what do you do, you take a photo. Our first post will be a mass selfie taken by yours truly from the stage, so please remember your best smiles.'

Letty held up a middle finger under the table in his direction.

'What I want from you today are ideas on how we can represent our clients on this new format. Before we do that though, there's a short video to watch setting out our social media objectives. Dylan,' at whom he nodded, 'has even come up with a slogan – "hashtag in good hands".'

Oh, you beauty, Letty thought. She'd suggested it to Dylan when he was looking for inspiration and he'd fallen for it. Little did Ross know it was going to make him look like a serial groper.

'Do the honours, will you, Dylan,' he said, as he twirled round his chair to face the projector screen.

Dylan fiddled with his laptop – Letty's heart was in her mouth. She swapped nervous glances with Jools and Sal. It had taken a while for Letty to persuade her colleagues to join her: they'd seen it as a big old risk. Yet even if they lost their jobs, they could pursue him through the legal system.

This was it. Please, technology, don't let me down, Letty prayed. She'd slipped in the room earlier to upload a 'new' version of the video which Dylan had made. In cahoots with Jools and Sal, she'd aped the start of the proper one – using the same music and the same logos – so that at first no one would know anything was wrong, and Ross would suspect nothing.

Feeling hot then cold with nerves, she held her breath: she wouldn't know if it had worked for thirty seconds. The time dragged as footage played of Ross holding court, fighting PR fires, looking every inch Cardiff's version of David Brent.

The temptation had been to sensationalize his harassment. To savage him with a damning soundtrack and a bold narrative of the way he'd made her, Sal and Jools feel. But Letty had understood that the facts, in black and white, would speak for themselves. To simply expose a man who thought he was untouchable, had the right to harass his employees because they were women, and who shut down their discomfort with accusations that they couldn't take a joke.

Here we go, Letty thought, as the first still appeared. The wording of one of Ross's sexts to Jools, with the expletives in asterisks.

> Great to have you sitting on the board... feel free to sit on my ****
> any time.

It took a few seconds before the room, including Ross, realized what they were reading. She'd imagined he'd be up out of his seat stabbing his fingers at buttons to stop it but he seemed frozen.

The next still, a written description of Sal's ordeal.

> I was in the store cupboard. He came in, shut the door and touched
> my breasts.

Gasps came from around the room. The vein on Ross's neck broke free from his paralysis.

Then Letty's own experience when he'd invited her to go down on him.

'Stop this!' Ross cried, jumping up, his eyes swinging wildly from the screen to his employees.

The final still asked a simple question.

> Still think you're hashtag 'in good hands'?

Then the video stopped and everyone was open-mouthed. Letty, Jools and Sal swapped terrified glances – this was it, their destiny was in the balance.

Ross banged the table, demanding to know who was responsible. 'Who did this? Come on, who?'

He rested on his knuckles, like a gorilla, preparing to pounce.

'It wasn't me boss,' Dylan said, looking around confused, unable to comprehend how this had happened.

'You!' Ross, shouted, his mouth contorted, pointing a trembling finger at Letty. 'You... witch.'

Letty noted how the colour of his sweaty bald scalp matched his awful red chinos.

Unafraid, she stood up, ready to stand her ground.

He went to come at her but, thank the Lord, Nick leapt from

his chair and stood in his way.

'It's all lies! She set me up!' Ross gurned over the top of Nick's arm. His deputy towered over him. But while Ross twitched and fumed, Nick was quite still, radiating professionalism and control from his solid clean-shaven chin right down to the very stitching in his navy blue suit.

The room was silent apart from Ross's heavy breathing.

'If I were you, Ross,' Nick said, moving towards him, shepherding him to the door, 'I'd get yourself out of here.'

'What? But this is my business.' His eyes were popping out of his head in disbelief.

'Think about it, Ross,' he said, coolly but with precision. 'This is a classic case of crisis management. Take a deep breath, understand the business impact of this, your seedy behaviour, getting out. Everyone will lose their jobs, including you. You will be ruined. Or you can resign. Compensate your employees. Who, incidentally, have produced a blinder of a campaign, which will be taken into consideration during my reshuffle. I buy you out. We'll say you've taken early retirement. No one will be any the wiser. You can crawl back into the hole you've come from. And we can all enjoy tonight's gala dinner.'

This man was a genius – an actual blinking legend of a genius.

Ross looked around in desperation for someone to defend him. But everyone, even the ones who had always laughed at his innuendo, avoided his stare. Their disgust was almost palpable.

Comprehending he was in a corner, he began to backtrack. 'Okay, maybe I went a little bit too far. I'm sorry.' He gave an insincere smile. 'There, you three, there's your apology. I've got witnesses to say I did it at the first available opportunity.'

'I'm afraid what you've actually done,' Nick said, folding his arms, 'is to admit guilt.'

Nick turned to the team. 'It's time to vote. Who would like Ross to stay at Gittings PR?'

Ross was blustering now. 'I'm in charge here! Me! Come on, people. You need me.'

No one put up their hands.

'And who would like to work for me instead?'

Actions spoke louder than words as nineteen palms shot up into the air.

With a whimper, Ross dropped his head in defeat. His

stubby fingers went to his eyebrows, a shaky breath escaped his lips and then he shuffled away.

Letty had done it! She went to Jools and Sal for an emotional group hug, as other members of staff came to them, saying they'd had no idea and well done.

Then she heard her name. Nick was beckoning her over for a word.

She went to him expecting that her afternoon would be spent contacting lawyers, briefing Nick on the order of play at tonight's event and taking down a statement on Ross's departure. It wouldn't matter that it would only say 'left by mutual agreement' – the point was he was gone.

'How would you feel about a promotion?' he said.

She could've kissed him. Not like that though. And she knew right away by the swell of her heart that this was what her self-worth would be measured on. Lance just wasn't enough.

A Bit Later...

Frankie

It needed a lick of paint, a stunning white would do it, and a cooler look, but this place had potential, Frankie thought, taking in the peach-coloured ghost of a salon.

There was plenty of natural light, the sinks were in good condition and, if she moved things round a bit, she could have a nail bar too. High-gloss white floor tiles instead of this faded chequered lino, and padded grey leather arm chairs rather than the knackered split-vinyl seats, which reminded her of scorched legs from childhood car journeys.

Her very own beauty salon! She'd already thought of a name even though she hadn't had her business loan interview yet. It would be called Beauty Therapy: she wanted her clients to relax, whether that meant they sat in silence or offloaded their troubles. Of the four available premises she'd seen, this was by far the best one.

Only ten minutes' walk from home, in a strip of shops nestled beside Victoria Park, she could see herself working here. Alone at first while she built it up, but perhaps she could take on a trainee in the future. She'd rent the building with a view to buying it outright if she made it a success. The idea had been bobbing around in her subconscious for ages but only yesterday, with Dad's advice to be true to yourself in her heart, had she found the courage to Google properties and arrange some viewings. She'd been happy to do her job on the road when she was younger – she'd had a house and a man to look after then. The freedom of driving here, there and everywhere had suited her, yet now she wanted to create her own little kingdom.

The small space could fit four chairs – she wanted floor-to-ceiling mirrors to make it appear larger; the loo at the back needed freshening up, as did the kitchen area. But Dad had already said if anything needed doing he and Gareth would help. It was like having two dads, she'd realized in the forty-eight hours that had passed since Dad had come out. They'd popped round to hers together for the first time yesterday to do some gardening for her, but she knew it had been their way of introducing themselves as a couple. Dad had been so nervous. She could tell by the way he kept falling over his words; how easy it would've been for Gareth to tease him. Instead he was patient and kind, filling in when Dad stuttered.

As she'd made them cups of tea, she'd watched them working away outside. There were no public displays of affection, they were both too traditional for that: if a stranger had seen them, they'd have assumed they were just two blokes in the shorts they reserved for mucky jobs. But whenever they went over to inspect each other's work, one would rest a hand on a shoulder and they would share a tender look or say something which made the other smile. Seeing her dad's happiness out in the open was the most beautiful thing. He was loved by a good man and he loved him back.

Over a brew, she'd asked him, them, what they thought of her having her own salon. Dad had immediately offered to invest some money but she wanted to do this herself. His DIY skills would be more than enough.

'Don't go calling it Scissor Sisters,' Gareth had said, making her laugh, 'or people might get the wrong idea!'

Frankie giggled now amongst the cobwebs, remembering how she'd had to explain to Dad it was lesbian slang.

Yes, this felt right: not just location, career or price-wise. This was about doing something for herself. Floyd sprang to mind: he'd approve, she thought. His physical touch had faded, but his words and positivity remained like a pair of wings, ready to lift her when she needed a boost.

Floyd and her had been a lovely thing but it was never destined to be A Thing: it wasn't as if she could ever compete with Sasha. Not that that was what it was about. Definitely not. She had Jason, or at least she might have him. And actually she was okay with that: she needed a break from all of that. It was enough now to do something for herself.

Just then, the door tinkled – she'd get that changed, she thought, it was a bit too ye olde village shoppe.

'Jase!' she said as he walked in with his overalls opened to his waist, revealing his ripe-as-a-plum chest. 'What are you doing here?'

'I've found you! I've been looking for you everywhere!' he said, giving her a kiss on the lips. It was the most natural thing in the world, Frankie thought, as she breathed in salt which hung in his curls.

'You're in your dirties. Are you back with the boys?'

'Yes,' he beamed. 'Happy days are here again!'

He looked just like the man she remembered before his doubts surfaced – happy, relaxed and buoyant. And, wow, she realized, it made her heady with the thought he could be hers again.

'Why didn't you ring?' she said, shaking her hair at him as she crossed her eyes. She held up her phone, which she'd been using to take photos and record measurements.

'I wanted to surprise you!' he said, his brown eyes as warm as hot chocolate. 'Your dad said you were here. Looking at this place to rent. Get you!'

'Yep, it might not look much now but when I've finished with it...' she sighed, holding out her arms as if this was her territory already.

'If you need any scaffolding for a paint job outside, then I might know someone...'

Frankie laughed, feeling twice the person in his presence because he looked as excited as she was. Not to mention hot and earthy and— But what was he doing here? They'd messaged since Saturday, keeping it light, knowing their common ground was no longer established and mature, but raked over and sown with seeds. Heavy footsteps would irrevocably damage any chance they had of making it together again.

'So...' she said, prompting him to throw some light on his visit.

'Yeah, so...' he coughed then span around leaving trails in the dusty floor. 'Well, I wanted to know how your diary was fixed?'

'Sorry?'

'Your diary. What you've got on.' His smile was wide and deep and so very inviting. And his tone was playful. Amused and curious, she went in for a paddle. He had understood how fragile this all was, and he was meandering around until it felt safe to ask her out.

'Let me think... busy tonight, washing my hair tomorrow, might be free at the weekend...' she said, coyly.

'How about next week?' he said.

'Might be okay,' she said, now up to her calves, getting closer to him, ready to say yes to dinner or the cinema or anything.

'Next month?' He was moving towards her too, blinking slowly, heavily, which always sucked her in.

'Possibly,' she said, wading up to her waist, wondering if he was going to suggest a holiday.

'How about six months' time? Then…' Jason's face was no longer flirtatious but serious and intense.

'Yes?' she asked, treading water, wanting to know what he had planned.

'Nine months after that?' He began nodding at her slowly and pulled her into his embrace, as if he was her life raft.

Waiting, with her heart galloping, she met his eyes with expectation.

'Frankie, I want you to marry me all over again,' he said, wrapping his arms around her waist. 'We can have a blessing. And we can start trying for a baby straight after.'

She laughed with a gasp; where on earth had this come from? She'd thought he was going to ask her out for dinner. But marriage? And a baby?

'We can plan this wedding together, properly, I'll be there with you all the way, whatever you want,' he said, irresistibly. 'I got it so wrong before – I wasn't there for you, I left all the organization to you. I was a dick. But now I want the world to know I'm sorry and I love you. It'll be the biggest, grandest day you've ever had. And then we can start again with a baby, our baby.'

Stunned, she gulped and felt first tearful then indecently delighted: she was being offered everything she'd wanted on a silver platter by her very own Prince Charming.

'What do you say?' he asked her, moving his chest and head backwards to check she had taken it in. Then his enormous smile was shining on her.

'I… oh, God… I can't believe…'

'We can get you another ring, a new dress, shoes, veil, anything. We can do it in a church, or at a hotel, or anywhere. I've been looking into it, there are lots of places to do it. We can go on honeymoon again, Greece if you like, or somewhere exotic, and if we get pregnant straight away we could be parents, not this Christmas, but next!'

'Is this really happening,' she said, feeling light-headed, 'because I'm just... blown away!'

'I was going to ask you in a few days, have a bit of food, go for a nice walk, get down on one knee but seeing you here, checking this place out, I needed to get in quick before you signed your life away.'

Frankie took a step backwards, away from his body. Her surroundings, which had been blinkered by Jason's aura, swooped back into view. Over his shoulder she saw an old hairy broom unemployed against the wall, and a clapped-out beauty trolley still littered with clips.

'What?' she asked, digging the fingernails of her thumbs into her forefingers to make herself concentrate.

'Well, this salon. Look at the state of it! It's a shithole! If you take it on then you'll be bogged down with it all, and we'll never get round to doing a blessing, and you'll be too busy to think about kids.'

A solid brush in a crusty mixing bowl sat useless on a filthy shelf.

'It'll haemorrhage money too at first, you've no guarantee that your old clients will follow you here, and it hasn't got great parking.'

Old magazines and latex gloves littered the floor. Wires hung from the ceiling too. He was right: it was in a dreadful mess. But still she wanted it to be hers.

'Hang on,' she said, holding up both palms, 'you're talking as though I have to choose between you, us, and the salon. It is possible to have both.'

'Yes, of course, but I thought you wanted a baby?'

'I do! One day. What if I want to wait a bit? What if I want to start my salon first?' She wasn't even sure what she wanted now: she'd been so sure about the salon but now he was confusing her. Was she in fact aiming too high? She couldn't sense her gut feeling at all; she even wondered if she was denying him because he'd denied her.

'You can do that anytime! But the stress of setting it up might harm our chances. It might take a while too to conceive...'

Frankie looked at herself in one of the cracked mirrors. Her bottom half, of slender legs and full skirt, was displaced from her stripy vested top. She couldn't even rely on her reflection anymore. 'I need to think,' she said, covering her face, hoping the solution would be there before her when she could see again.

'I'll look after you,' he said, smiling down at her. 'I'll always look after you.'

The effect of his words, so sweet yet so off target, jolted her to attention. 'I don't need looking after!' she said, throwing her hands in the air. Jason looked bewildered by her outburst.

'But I bring in a good wage, you can stick to your mobile job until the baby's here, then you can go part-time, the grandparents will do their bit. I was thinking you could work three days a week and then they can share the childcare. Come on, we've wasted so much time, we should just crack on and have a family. It'll be the best thing that's ever happened to us.'

'You've got it all worked out!' she said. 'How can you have it all worked out?'

'I understand you must be feeling like you can't trust me, and that's fine. I've had time to think and this is my way of making it up to you. I'll try my hardest to make you happy and keep you safe, Tink.'

'But I've eaten oysters, I've had my hair done and finally I'm good at sex.' Frankie was trying to understand herself again, find the person she had become.

'What's that got to do with it?' he laughed, scratching his head.

'I'm not who I was,' she said, grabbing hold of the skirt of the new her. 'And there's something I have to know, Jason...'

'Anything...' he said, resting his hands on her bare shoulders, grounding her.

Boldly and without embarrassment, she said: 'Why didn't you try to satisfy me in bed the other night? Why didn't you give me the chance to work things through with you before you walked out?'

He hung his head and exhaled. 'You can't keep punishing me for needing time out. I've said I'm sorry.'

He looked up, eyes pleading with her.

'The sex, Jason. Answer me.'

'Why are you so hung up on the sex? It's got nothing to do with all of this.' He began to search the ceiling for someone to throw light on it for him.

'It's got everything to do with it. I'm not who I was. I want more. Less. Oh God, what I mean is… before, I had no idea about my own needs. I was happy to just follow you around. Our marriage, our relationship, was all about you. I had no self-worth or self-awareness or self-confidence. I never even thought about it back then, to be honest. But when you left I was lost. It's taken me this long to find out who I am, what's in here,' she said, thumping her chest. 'I need you to see me as your equal.'

'I do! I get it!'

She reached out and smoothed his cheek with her fingertips. 'Perhaps we need some more time, to talk.'

'Why? Aren't I here now?' he said, kissing her hand. 'Communication, I've been reading about it, they say it's the most important thing in a relationship, and that's what I'm trying to do now. I know I've hurt you, let me show you I can be the husband I should've been all along. Look, Tink, we've got an opportunity here to get back together, to make a family, to grow old side by side. We can take our kids to our special beach and, who knows, maybe take our grandchildren to our special beach? Share a portion of chips, jump the waves, build sandcastles.'

Staring at him, Frankie could see the same images as Jason and it was truly beguiling. She could almost touch the baby hair of their children and feel the sand beneath her feet. There was the taste of hot vinegary chips, and the sound of squeals and the sea.

Frankie knew it was all there waiting for her: all she had to do was say yes.

Saturday

Em

'I'll tell you what love is,' Em said, spearing patatas bravas with her fork, before inspecting her feet beneath the table. 'Goodness, look at my ankles, they're both swollen.'

'Love is swollen ankles?' Letty laughed through a mouthful of frittata at Viva Tapas.

'First, Letitia, pregnant water retention is not amusing, and second, you know I didn't mean that. And yes, I get the hilarity about me telling you two about love.' Her face flushed – for the millionth time since Simon Brown and her had become an item.

'You go for it, babes,' Letty said, holding up her sherry to Em's tap water. 'I think it's lush.'

'Me too,' Frankie added, joining the clink of glasses. 'Tell us.'

'Love isn't flowers and symphonies. It's an actual physiological process.'

'You've lost me there, babes,' Letty said. Frankie just nodded sweetly, which Em knew meant that she thought she'd lost it.

'We're at the mercy of our biochemistry. Lust is testosterone and oestrogen. Attraction, that's all to do with a group of neurotransmitters called monoamines. There's the high of dopamine. Then norepinephrine, otherwise known as adrenalin, and the happy feeling is serotonin. Attachment, well, that's down to oxytocin.'

'That's romantic,' Letty laughed.

'But it is!' Em smiled. It was as if she could actually feel the chemicals fizzing away inside of her. In the forty-eight hours that she had been with Simon Brown, everything had changed. Floyd's mess didn't both her, she had to be reminded to eat, and when Simon Brown was sleeping, she would stare in wonder at his symmetrical top and bottom lips and his precise sandy sideburns which ended at the exact middle-point of each tragus. Their tender sex, well, it made her believe in heaven. And with

269

so much time to make up, they were already discussing baby names and living arrangements.

'Seriously though, I thought love was all to do with the physical,' Letty said. 'But it's not.'

'What?' Frankie said, looking alarmed. 'But you've always said that sex is the glue in a relationship.'

'Listen, babes, I've had sex on the beach, sex in the sea, sex in a library, tantric sex, tie-me-up sex, boob sex, armpit sex and ice cube sex. I thought it was the most important thing: finding a deep bodily connection because it signified a spiritual everlasting love.' Then Letty's face darkened with sadness. 'But great sex is only great if you're doing it with someone you think is great and thinks you're great too. And that could happen in the most boring position in the world. The fact is, ladies, I've finished with Lance because the sex was too… exciting.'

Em and Frankie both reached out to her.

'It wasn't enough. I need more. Up here,' she said, tapping her head.

'Oh, thank God,' Frankie cried, 'you won't be going to Australia.'

'It would've been awful, you being ten thousand and sixty-six miles away,' Em said.

'Anyway, I have some good news,' Letty said, perking up, 'I've been offered my dream job at work – I'm going to be in charge of social media!'

Another round of cheers began but Frankie was late to the party – she was miles away.

'Have you decided yet, then?' Em asked her. 'About Jason and the blessing.'

'No,' Frankie said, quietly, 'it's been a mad few months. Separation, sex education, finding out Dad's gay, getting to know my mum properly for the first time. It's blown my mind, to be honest. I'd rather just take it easy. Wait for the confusion to clear.'

'Well, that's odd because Floyd is the same,' Em divulged. 'Do you know something, he told me he doesn't want to marry Sasha! Says he doesn't love her.'

Frankie's knife clattered to the floor.

'I'm wondering if there's someone else,' Em continued.

Frankie's mouth fell open. Then she dashed under the table. Goodness, all she had to do was ask for a new knife, there was no need to over-react.

'He didn't come home last night, or the night before. I've no idea where he is. I thought he was with Sasha at her mum's but apparently not. Letty, you don't know anything do you? Did he tell you, that time at the party when you were in his room?'

Frankie emerged from the floor with her knife.

'Is it you?' she whispered, staring at Letty with the widest of eyes.

'Is it her, what?' Em asked, not following at all.

'The someone else! I saw you with him too, in a bar.' Her voice was all wobbly and breathy, which was strange.

Em gasped – Letty? With her brother? Not in her flat, please God, no. On her best guest-room four-hundred thread count sheets from John Lewis.

'Me?' Letty hooted. 'You've got to be joking!'

'Thank the Lord,' Em heaved. 'The thought of a friend sleeping with my brother... well, I can't even begin to describe how ill that would make me feel.'

Frankie gulped. Perhaps the octopus that she'd finally tasted – and savoured – was giving her indigestion. Or maybe she was coming down with something. She was a bit pale, come to think of it.

'What were you doing then, meeting up with him and being in his room?' Frankie asked, looking icy.

Letty exhaled loudly. 'Getting some advice. I went to him about the legal stuff with Ross, seeing as he works for a law firm. And... well, look, I think I've got a bit of a spending problem. All to do with filling a hole in my life.'

'Oh, Letty! Why didn't you say?' Em said, appalled that her friend had suffered alone. 'I could've helped with money.'

'I didn't want to admit it. I didn't want to worry you either. But it's okay. Floyd's been brilliant, he's referred me to a counsellor so finger's crossed...'

Letty cocked her head then and Em followed her gaze: Frankie was crying. Why would that be?

This was quite some lunch: Em had thought she was much better at reading people's emotions these days, but she wasn't getting the tears at all.

And then Letty took a massive intake of breath.

'You. Are. Joking!' she said to Frankie. 'Oh my God. All this time and I didn't work it out. Fuck!'

Em had had quite enough now of this. 'Will someone tell me what's going on?'

But Frankie and Letty were staring at each other, locked in some kind of secret understanding.

'Please?' she pleaded.

Frankie looked down at her plate and spoke in a barely audible voice.

'My sex teacher. It was... it was... Floyd.' A fat tear landed right on top of a chickpea with spinach.

Floyd? Oh my word, this was beyond. 'My brother?' she spat, feeling her stomach go washing-machine full spin. The shock, the lies, the going behind her back, the laughing at her ignorance.

'Look, it's not how it sounds. We didn't actually do it. Much.'

Frankie squeezed her eyes shut, cursing her turn of phrase.

'Spare me the details,' Em said, holding up a traffic cop palm. It was quite the most upsetting, hurtful thing that had ever happened. And to think she'd been the one who'd suggested that Frankie needed a project.

'It wasn't like that, honest,' Frankie said, puffy faced. 'He just helped me. I haven't told anyone. I knew it would be upsetting. I'm so, so sorry, Em. Really. I know you must be so cross and embarrassed. But it's all over. It's done.'

Em was really irritated now: her bursting bladder wasn't helping either. 'But that doesn't explain why you're crying.'

'What is it, babes?' Letty said softly, getting up to give her a *cwtch*.

Something in Em changed then at the sight of Letty's compassion. Frankie was so distressed she was inconsolable. She went to her bag and passed over some tissues; whatever had been going on, she was still her friend and she was hurting.

'Thank you,' Frankie squeaked, meeting Em's eyes. In that moment Em could see how awful Frankie was feeling. She needed empathy, not judgement.

Em put a hand on Frankie's forearm. 'It's okay,' she said.

'It's not, obviously. But I'll get over it. I never meant to hurt anyone.'

'I know.' Em felt a stillness fall upon her. But Frankie's howling continued.

'Come on, babes, what is it?'

'I didn't expect to... I never wanted to... I think I've fallen in love with Floyd,' Frankie said through shuddering breaths, setting herself off harder.

Em didn't think anything could've topped Frankie's earlier revelation. But she was wrong. This was insane. And, for once, she seemed to have got her reaction right because Letty had looked up at her over Frankie's dipped head and was mouthing 'shit'.

'But what about Jason?'

'I don't know, Letty,' Frankie said, finally not leaking anymore. 'I mean, I was desperate to get him back and I do love him, but now I'm not sure. I've changed and he hasn't, well, hardly.'

The release of talking spurred her on.

'If I went back to him could we go forward? And I don't know if what I feel for Floyd is real or a projection of my uncertainty. Oh God, I've been holding this in for so long. These feelings for Floyd have been building and I've been denying them. It's just as Phyllis, one of my clients, said. She said, "sit on your feelings and they'll out".'

Then a resigned look settled on her face.

'But it doesn't matter because Floyd will never want me. How could he? When you said there was someone else, I thought, I hoped, it might have been me, but it can't be. He wasn't with me the last two nights... so that's that.'

'You need to tell Floyd,' Letty said.

'You think so?' she said. Then she looked at Em. As did Letty.

They were actually asking her for advice. On affairs of the heart. What a turn-up!

'You want to know what I think?' she said, flustered at the flattery.

Both of them nodded.

'Yes, you, Em. You know Floyd best of all, and you're the only one who seems to have worked out how to have a relationship. Not us two numpties,' Letty said.

This was true, Em thought. Wow.

'Well, I...' she began, just as the baby jabbed her. 'I'll have to tell you in a minute. I've got to go to the loo.'

Frankie managed a thin smile as Letty broke out into laughter.

Em got up and waddled to the top of the small flight of stairs which led to the ladies. She turned to tell them: 'I'll be as quick as I can.'

But as she did, she felt her ankle turn. The floor disappeared from beneath her. She saw the girls' faces falling diagonally as she went down at an angle. Then wallop, she landed once, twice, three times on her lower back as she slid down the steps. A wave of pain reverberated from her coccyx through her back and across her stomach. She heard herself cry out, and immediately Letty and Frankie were there.

'I'm not in agony,' Em said, trying to downplay her fall.

'We'll go to the maternity unit just to make sure,' Letty said, taking control as she supported Em's weight. 'We can ring on the way. Frankie, you settle up and we'll go.'

Had she not been pregnant, Em would've refused. She could live with a bruised bum and ego. But this wasn't about her. It was about their baby.

Frankie

'Almost there, Em,' Frankie said, hoping she had camouflaged her concern with confidence, into the rear-view mirror of her Mini, as they crawled through town. 'Be about five minutes, I reckon.'

A nod shook the curtain of red hair which was bowed over Em's bump.

'There's no bleeding, the midwife said that was a good sign, didn't she, Em? So that's good,' Letty said from the back ,where she had insisted on sitting to keep her company.

Em was distracted, rubbing her tummy in swooping circles.

'It's just a precaution, they said,' Letty reassured her. 'They want to give you the once over.'

'It was a small fall, an accident. Will you two stop fussing?' Em snapped, lifting her face to eyeball each of them before she looked pointedly out of the window. The green of her eyes which usually shone had become as dull as pond water – it was a sure sign Em was frightened. At the start of the journey, she'd rung Simon and played it down. She'd insisted he didn't need to come, but he'd just turned off the motorway on his way back from picking up some clothes in Bristol, so he'd be there ASAP. Em's mum had picked up her mobile on the third attempt – wasn't it lucky they were in Cardiff, at a TED talk on how to be self-sufficient because their home phone was playing up, otherwise they'd never have known. Em had relayed the conversation, smacking her forehead in frustration.

Now the car was silent, bar the sound of crunching gear changes and loud revs as every light that could turned red. Frankie felt an arm on her shoulder. Letty was telling her to take it easy. She took a deep breath and focused all of her energy into praying everything would be fine: Em had said it wasn't serious but you never knew with her.

In the quiet, Frankie ran through the twists and turns of lunch.

Letty ending her relationship with Lance, battling a spending problem but getting a brilliant job. Em's loved-up face turning to disgust at Floyd being her sex teacher.

Her own guilt at keeping it from her friends and her wild hopes dashed that maybe she was the 'someone else'. As hard as it all was, she thought, swinging the car onto the A road which would take them to Cardiff's University Hospital of Wales, she felt relieved it was all now out in the open.

Even though she had only gone and shocked herself by confessing she had loved Floyd ever since he had let her be herself, he was actually irrelevant because it wasn't reciprocated. Her feelings for him were a reaction to her circumstances. Not to mention his someone else. How silly she'd been over the whole thing: the surge of emotions she'd had from the relief of hearing he wasn't marrying Sasha, to the doom of her dashed hopes and getting carried away by seeing him with Letty.

She gripped the steering wheel hard at the memory of his lips on hers, his muscular chest and lean waist up above her, their union which had given her the most intense moment of her life. Then she felt her fingers flop because it was all in the past. And as a stab of anger reminded her, he hadn't come home for two nights: yes, she could think around it and come up with elaborate reasons for his absence but the most likely scenario was he'd gone to another woman for comfort. Had it been a two-night stand? Or was there more to it? She cast her mind back to their Thursdays and yes, there were definitely moments when he'd seemed distracted and miserable. Frankie had assumed it was because he was missing Sasha but perhaps it wasn't her at all: perhaps he had fallen for this other woman.

There was a stone in her belly as she realized that maybe she hadn't known him at all. She'd seen what she'd wanted to see, just as she'd done in her marriage. Had she learned nothing at all? Feeling foolish, the stone had become a rock at the thought Floyd might have broken their agreement to be exclusive. It would mean their arrangement was tainted.

A sour taste crept up her throat at the contamination, the pollution of something that had been so special to her. Frankie thought of Sasha then: she felt no pity because she'd bounce back, no problem. There'd never be a shortage of takers for someone like her.

But me? That was a different story. Frankie felt burned – she'd had her flight of fantasy and now it was time to accept her fate. She deserved nothing more.

A small downward turn of her lips and gritted teeth sealed the compartment in her mind labelled Floyd.

All that was important now was Em and the baby, she thought taking the last turning which led to the hospital grounds.

Suddenly, Em whooped and punched the air. Automatically, Frankie's feet went down towards the pedals and Letty flinched, raising her hands towards her head. But a punch in the air from Em told them in a split second it was a cry of delight not terror.

'The baby! It just kicked!' Em cried. 'The baby is fine! It's all going to be okay.'

'Thank God!' Letty said, holding her chest.

Only when Frankie had reversed into a parking space could she rest her head on her hands in relief.

They got themselves out of the car and began walking to the maternity unit.

'So you and Floyd,' Em said, in between them, 'I never did get round to saying what I thought.'

Frankie held up a hand. She'd sorted it in her head and there was no need. 'It's okay, I'm fine now and—'

Em ignored her. 'At first, I thought it was disgusting. But now I can sort of see you two together. Little and large, him up there, you down there. It'd be a meeting in the middle.'

'Yeah, I know what you mean,' Letty said.

'Whatever. It's not going to happen,' Frankie said, both touched by her friends, but sore from them pouring salt in her wounds. 'Because I've decided. I'm going back to Jason.'

'You what, babes? But you said you loved Floyd.'

'Floyd was in my life for a reason. To help. That's all. It was a crush. A reflection of my uncertainty. That's not grounds enough to throw away my marriage. Jason and I can make it work.'

Reaching the grey storeyed tower of the unit, Frankie opened the door for Em.

'It's time to be thankful for what I have and not to wish for anything else. Acceptance of who I am and what I want. I've proved I can be a sex kitten. Now I need to move on.'

She shut the door behind them firmly to show this conversation was over.

Looking around, she saw a couple fussing at a car seat in

which there was a bundle of newborn. She found she could just about imagine herself in this position too. The salon she could make a start on, she would insist on that to Jason, but then once it was up and running, they could begin a family.

At reception, Em announced her name and informed them there really was no need to go to any trouble because the baby was kicking. A nurse, who was called over, was having none of it.

'We'd still like to check you out. We'll give you a scan as you're almost twenty-one weeks anyway, so we might as well do it now,' she said, leading the three of them to an empty waiting area.

Just as they sat down, a wholesome-looking man skidded to their feet.

'Simon Brown!' Em said, her voice cracking as tears came to her.

So this was him! He was Em's equal in every way apart from her tummy: the same height, their lips met with neither of them needing to look up or down. Frankie watched with a lump in her throat as they hugged, embraced in their own little world. In low voices, they exchanged updates on what had happened and where she was hurting: it was beautiful but peculiar to see Em in a relationship. Clearly, he adored her, just as she did him.

Then, being the gent Em had said he was, he turned to Frankie and Letty with an apologetic face. 'I'm so sorry, that was so rude of me,' he said, putting out a hand to shake, 'I was just so worried. I'm Simon. Thanks so much for bringing Em here. Anything I can do for you, anything…'

'Emerald Good-Fellow, please.'

She was being called for her scan. Frankie and Letty watched Simon take Em's hand.

'Made for each other, those two,' Letty said dreamily. Then she came to and elbowed Frankie. 'Look who's here.'

It was Floyd, hovering beside his parents at reception. Em hadn't said he was in tow.

In spite of everything she now thought of him, her heart unfurled like a rose on fast-forward. Her mouth burned at the memory of his kiss, while her fingers tingled to touch his smooth skin.

Then he turned and, across the uncrowded room, he saw her. She saw it all in slow-motion: first his eyes widened, then his thick lashes batted downwards, his lips parted and his cheeks began to rise as the corners of his mouth went up into a crescent. He was walking towards her, the tongues of his Converse flapping like a dog's ears, his chest rising.

Frankie felt it all so acutely because it had to mean nothing. She forced herself to think of how he had two-timed her to protect herself from the attraction. She sat on her hands and looked at her lap, focusing on Em.

'All right, Letty? Frankie?' Floyd said. 'Where's Em?'

Letty explained she was in with the sonographer, and all they could do now was wait. Frankie lifted her chin coolly and his eyes became confused. But this wasn't the time nor the place to have it out with him. When his parents came over, everyone exchanged subdued hellos. The minutes ticked agonizingly by. Frankie couldn't bear to look at Floyd. Jason, she had to think of him now.

'What's a TED talk then?' Letty asked, making chit-chat.

'A lecture. At the university. On going self-sufficient. Mum and dad are into it. Recycling stuff, generators, composting your own poo, that sort of thing.'

'Floyd! Why do you always have to take it too far?' his mum said, tutting.

Frankie heard him protest. Then she sensed he was moving towards her. Please, no, she thought, as he plonked himself next to her.

'Everything gravy?' he said, leaning forward on his knees to talk to her.

'Yep,' she said, ripping a quick off her finger to drown out her excruciating discomfort.

'Good, good,' he said, rubbing his thighs. 'Um, I don't suppose you've got time for a quick chatteroon, have you? After this?'

She looked up at him then, wanting to tell him how inappropriate he was, but then the door was opening and Em and Simon reappeared.

Everyone got to their feet in a surge of concern.

Em's face was tracked with tears. Simon's eyes were wet.

Letty threaded her arm through Frankie's as fear raced through their veins.

'Oh God, what is it, love?' Em's mum said, rushing to her daughter with Floyd and their dad.

'It's… it's…' Em said, struggling to speak. 'Simon Brown, you tell them.'

'It's…' he sniffed. 'It's a girl! It's all okay!'

A chorus of happiness engulfed them, and it was only after a great deal of 'thank goodness' and 'we were so worried' that Simon realized he hadn't introduced himself.

'Simon. Simon Brown,' he said, offering his hand to Em's parents.

'Brown, is it?' Floyd said. 'Because Em never mentioned your surname.'

Even Frankie had to laugh.

Then once Em had instructed her parents to fix their bloody phone, she showed off some grainy photos. 'That's the head, that's an arm. Her measurements are all normal. Which is perfect. Normal is all I've wanted.'

Simon cleared his throat. 'We'd like you all to come back to Em's. Have a little celebration. A thank you for looking after us.'

'Who's going with who then?' Letty said.

'I've got room for Em and three more so…' Simon pointed at Em's mum and dad plus Letty.

Which left Floyd with Frankie. Letty gave her a look, to ask if she was okay with it. Frankie nodded stiffly – she could hardly make a fuss. She might as well get this 'chatteroon' out of the way too.

With dread, she asked Floyd where she was dropping him as the others drifted off.

'Er, Em's. Obviously.' He looked shifty, as if he was trying to work out what she was getting at. But she wanted him to spell it out.

'Oh because she said you hadn't been staying there… and that you weren't with Sasha… so…'

He shut his eyes briefly – she'd hit the target.

'Right, yep, I've had a couple of nights away,' he said. 'The lovebirds were a bit, you know, soppy and pukey, so I thought I'd give them a bit of space.'

'I see.' He was resisting the truth. How disappointing, how devastating.

'Are you okay?' he said, all innocent.

'You wanted a "chatteroon", so come on, let's do it.'

'Oo-er,' he said then he winced at his own stupidity.

She shook her head – he couldn't play this card with her anymore. The emotional freedom between them no longer existed.

'So, I wanted to let you know I've been feeling things,' he said, pushing his specs up his nose. 'Em clearly told you about me and Sasha. That's over. My call.' He nodded at her as he spoke.

'Right.' Frankie sounded terse, she knew that, but she was getting fed up with this drawn-out explanation: she wanted him to get it over with. Begin to move on from him.

'The thing is,' he said, scratching his nose, 'there's, er, there's another person involved. Has been for a while.'

Her heart cracked. Em had been right. And Frankie's worst fears were proven: their pledge of exclusivity had been a sham. That was how little he had respected her.

'It's complicated though. I've known her for ages. We've been sort of seeing one another. Not that I've ended it for her, because she's got her own stuff going on.'

'Listen, I don't really want to know,' she said, walking towards the exit. She felt dirty and stupid. She just wanted to get away from him. Distance herself from her own stupidity at falling for him.

'I'm fed up of wondering what if,' he said to her back. Then he caught her up. 'I want to be a grown-up. This woman, she's... beautiful and genuine and honest and I'd do anything to be with her.'

'Please, Floyd,' she said, the horrendousness of it making the car keys in her hand jangle. How it hurt to hear him talk about another woman like this.

She upped the pace and took in deep gulps of summer air to try to calm herself. But he matched her march through the car park.

'Are you going back to Jason?' he said, urgently.

'Yes. We're having a wedding blessing in six months.' Saying it out loud convinced her that that was what she was going to do.

'And are you happy with that?' he said, grabbing her arm and pulling her round to face him.

'I don't think it's any of your business,' she said, shaking him off.

Floyd murmured something and sneered.

'What did you say?' she asked, confronting him.

'I just said good luck with that.'

'You know what? You can make your own way to Em's. I'm done with this.'

She needed to get away: the pain was too much. Frankie could see the cars and began to run.

But Floyd's footsteps were in hot pursuit and a screech of tyres meant he'd crossed the road without looking.

'Are you mad?' she said as he landed next to her by the pay station. 'Why don't you just leave me alone?'

'How are you feeling about your dad?' he asked, desperately, as if he wanted to keep the conversation going.

'Why do you care? I'm happy that he's happy now. He said he'd been living a lie.' She found some coins and fed them into the machine, as her temper rose.

'Right. Good. There we are. That's it, Frankie!' He was looking at her with expectation. 'Because I really don't think you should go back to Jason. You're too good for him. Don't waste your life with him.'

'And what's that got to do with you?' she roared, drawing breath as she unleashed the emotions that she had been sitting on. She was so fierce, Floyd actually took a step back. 'You broke your promise!' she cried, waving her hands about. 'You met someone else when we agreed to be exclusive. All the time when you were my teacher you fell for this other woman, and you didn't say a word. I thought we were friends. And yes, you're right about Jason. I shouldn't go back to him. I should be alone. But what if I never meet anyone again? What if this is my one and only chance to be with someone? To have a family, to create a story that I can reread when I'm old and stuck in one of those sheltered places where no one comes to visit apart from your hairdresser?'

The euphoria of the release rained down on Frankie as she paused for breath. But there was one thing left to say. And what the hell, she was going to say it.

'You, Floyd Good-Fellow, are a liar and I can never trust you again. How could you do it to me? When I feel the way I do about you?'

Trembling, Frankie stomped off to find her car, unable to remember where she'd parked it, stalking up and down as she craned her neck to spy its crooked radio aerial.

Her body and mind were ablaze but the tangles had been straightened: the truth had been told. She didn't care she'd all but confessed her love – it was over, and now she could begin to think properly about Jason. No rash moves, she pledged, no sudden decisions. She had a clean slate now.

Finally, she came to her Mini and threw open the door but the handle whacked Floyd straight in the peanuts.

'Ouch,' he cried, doubling over in agony. 'Fuck, shit, Jesus Christ, Frankie! Now we'll never have kids.'

'I didn't know you were there, did I?' Then she rewound what she'd heard. Kids? She turned around, her mouth wide open. He was looking up at her from the crouch position, grimacing, with his glasses at an angle.

'I beg your pardon?' She tilted her head so the ear closest to Floyd was like a radar, ready to catch his words.

'I've been staying at Mum and Dad's,' he said, coughing from the pain. 'There's no one else. Well, there is...' he said, breathing hard. 'It's you, you silly bloody sausage. I love you.'

Then he whimpered and, still cupping his privates, collapsed on the floor.

Six Months Later... April

Frankie

'We've had quite a journey, haven't we, love?' Dad says, his voice echoing off the room's circular hug of stone.

'We sure have, Dad,' Frankie says, straightening the knot of his purple silk tie, which shines in the rectangle of warm spring sunshine flooding through a little window.

His smile launches a library of wrinkles, each one telling the tale of his life. From the strain of hiding who he was and the breakdown of his marriage to Mum, to the liberation of coming out and finding love with Gareth.

Frankie brushes the lapels of his cream linen jacket, picking off a strand of grey hair from his shoulder.

'Keep that for me, love,' he says, 'I can stick it back on my bald patch later.'

'You know something, Dad, this is only the second time I've seen you in a suit,' she says, remembering how he'd started off squirming in top hat and tails when she'd married Jason, but ended up refusing to take it off all night.

'Not much call for them in the plumbing trade. But I must say, I quite like the novelty.'

Then it's her turn. 'How do I look?' she asks, twirling around, her tea-length dress exploding over a full petticoat in a foam of ivory lace from her waist to her knees. The demure neckline gives way to teetering silver heels. It's a contradiction which reflects her two sides. There in her modest top half, the sensible and unassuming Frankie she's always known, but from her waist down, her blossoming sensual audacity. She's realized it's possible to be both. And this is who she is, who she's been all along, but in the last year has only got to know.

'Beautiful,' he says, clearing his throat. 'Absolutely beautiful, love. I'm glad you chose short and sweet. And your hair, well! You should think about becoming a hairdresser,' he winks, just in case anyone thought he was a bit of a softy.

She pats her half up-do, which begins pouffed and pinned

on her crown then sweeps down in waves to just below her chin. Smoky kohled eyes, heavy lashes and glossed lips make her feel like a film star. Not that film stars ever spend the morning at work in their own salons doing wedding hair. Dad had had a trim while Mum had gone for a French twist dotted with sequins. They'd had such a laugh together, sharing breakfast rolls over pints of tea – it wasn't like old times because Frankie couldn't ever remember it being so relaxed. They were making up for it now though. When Frankie had locked up, leaving a sign on the door which read 'closed early for wedding!', she was grateful she'd used waterproof mascara. She's got a feeling she'll be thinking that all day.

Frankie admires Dad's purple tulip buttonhole that is fresh from his garden. 'Lucky you had enough of these to go round,' she says, inhaling her bouquet which smells of hope and beginnings.

'Planning, you see,' he says, tapping his nose.

'Well, I never imagined I'd be here, did you?' Despite everything, she wouldn't change any of it. She didn't want to be anywhere else.

'What is it they say about "once bitten, twice shy"?' Dad laughs. 'Some people are just fools. They never learn!'

A tap comes at the wooden door and it creaks open. The registrar. It's time.

They both take a deep breath and then Dad presents the crook of his arm. Frankie slides hers through, but when they reach the foot of the winding stone stairs, it's only wide enough for single file. Looking up, Frankie sees a pretty runway of fairy lights wrapped over and under the handrail of the metal balustrade which will take them to the rest of their lives.

'I really should've got myself a pair of flats for this. There must be a million steps!'

'Don't worry, love, I'll catch you if you get altitude sickness.'

'I suppose that's the risk if you choose to do it in a lighthouse!' she says, starting her climb.

'Nash Point lighthouse, the only operational lighthouse in the UK, no less. A grade-two listed building still keeping mariners safe after hundreds of years, perched on a clifftop with views across the Bristol Channel...' Dad recites from the details.

'Don't forget the foghorn when you've done the deed!' she says, pausing to take in the messy waves swallowing rocks on the pebbly beach.

'It can be heard up to twenty miles away. So much for an intimate ceremony,' Dad says, catching his breath.

How apt it is that this declaration of love will sound far and wide, when it had caught them all so unaware.

By the time they reach the third floor, Frankie's thighs are burning. 'Just imagine how our legs are going to feel when we have to go up to the seventh floor for the photos in the lantern!'

'That's why this is the last time, right, love?' Dad whispers as they stop just short of the entrance to the wedding room. Their nerves exploding, they hear the opening bars of Frank Sinatra's 'Fly Me To The Moon' and they walk the soothing path of his voice.

Around the stone gallery strewn with traditional wooden Welsh love-spoons stand friends and family, their faces lit up as Dad and Frankie walk towards the registrar.

There's Letty, blowing kisses, her loose raven hair, topped by a crown woven from willow, tumbling over her bare shoulders. Her red lipstick gone, all that's left of the old her is a huge grin. In a flowing white empire-line gown that covers her toes, she resembles an angel, albeit one with a mega-tan from her solo holiday in Colombia, where she studied Spanish. A wad of compensation means she's now debt-free. With Lance a distant memory, she's soaring at work, qualified too, and has taken a vow of chastity – for now.

Beside her is Em, looking tranquil in an asparagus wrap dress, breastfeeding her strawberry blonde eight-week-old baby. Every inch the devoted dad with a changing bag strapped across his chest, Simon blows his nose. He's just as emotional as Em says he is: he was the same at their wedding just before Christmas in the Doctor Who Experience in Cardiff Bay.

Their daughter didn't come on Valentine's Day: she was five days early, a fact of which Em is immensely proud. Simon had only gone and delivered her in an unintended home birth, and then they'd named her Cariad, Welsh for darling. With their triple-barrelled name Good-Fellow-Brown, it turns out Em isn't quite so different from her mum after all. Em plans to go back to work soon so Simon can share her leave – she loves motherhood but she misses managing the supermarket. Oh, and she managed to get her parents to update their phone.

Then there's Mum, waving at them as if she is one of

hundreds wanting to be picked out of the crowd instead of a handful of guests. Frankie gives her an extra-special smile because they've become closer, more open, little by little, even if Mum still insists on staying super-blonde. She'd taken her role as matron of honour very seriously, only to be disappointed by the lack of a hen do. Instead she poured her excitement into the wedding cake, a six-layer rainbow sponge, which is bound to be as colourful as her purple fascinator and orange trouser suit. Colin, who's beside her in a matching tangerine cravat, has provided the car, a lovely old Morris Minor.

Even Judy has made it; her brown eyes look up from her bed at the front. She had to be carried up the stairs because of her arthritis but the wag of her tail shows she's feeling the love.

As they reach the registrar, Frankie meets the eyes of the man waiting, who is blinking back tears. She looks at Dad, who's just as watery-eyed.

'I think I'll be okay, now, love,' he says, hugging his daughter, then stepping forward.

'Gareth,' he says, his chin wobbling, 'Fancy seeing you here.'

'Clifford.' Gareth's voice is breaking. 'If we get this done quick, we can be in the pub within the hour.'

'Damn right, Gar,' Dad coughs, wiping his cheek.

While their backs are ram-rod straight, their fingers are entwined like ivy. All that time she'd spent worrying about Dad, and their love had been growing right under her nose. And Gareth is so involved in her life, helping her out with DIY and decorating, he's like a second father to her.

Frankie feels a hand pull her slowly to the left and she allows it to guide her into an embrace. She fits into his body as if she is meant to be there. They share a smile which is both comfortable from years of familiarity, yet also dances at the prospect of a future they'll compose together.

It hasn't been long but it seems like forever.

Frankie's mind leaps back to the hospital car park where she'd told Floyd she would neither jump into his arms nor Jason's: the person she would choose, she'd declared, was Frankie. She didn't want either man to save her – she was going to do it herself.

Confused and claustrophobic, she'd nurtured her own rescue package, starting with her salon Beauty Therapy. She'd rented out her house and moved into the flat above the premises. It was musty and full of cobwebs, but once it had been aired and cleaned, she'd loved its blank canvas. Leonardo settled in very nicely: at night, he goes in and out via a sash window to trot the rooftops, by day he curls up on a towel next to the washbasins, where he's tempted out by her adoring customers with treats.

It was only when her hands were raw from scrubbing the salon's floor, when she'd opened for business, when her client cards began to stack up, when her back was aching from twelve-hour days, when she was sure she was surviving, when she'd created a narrative of her own, that she acknowledged the feelings she had put into storage.

One winter night, Frankie had been finally ready to unwrap them. Carefully and cautiously, she'd peeled back the layers, frightened she might disturb a healing scar. But it was as if her heart had only been in hibernation: small pulses at first had awakened into booming beats which filled her head. Still, she had to know if it had all been circumstance, so she'd arranged to meet him on a wet Thursday in a deserted spit and sawdust pub down the road from her flat. There would be no fanfare, no dressing up, no pretence and no props. If it was going to work, it would do so on its own.

Nerves eating away at her stomach, she'd sipped a bottle of lager in the corner of the Duke of Clarence and watched the clock.

Five, ten minutes went by with just her, a middle-aged man staring at the wall and the barmaid, who had occasionally looked up from her book to give her pity eyes. Five more minutes she'd promised herself, feeling deflated, and she'd go. Then she would accept he had moved on too.

Suddenly, he'd burst through the once-grand but now tired wooden door in a tornado of soggy leaves and whirling crisp bags. All legs, knees, arms and elbows, he'd resembled a drunk on roller skates. In a bike helmet.

Drying his steaming wet glasses on his Parka sleeve, he'd rambled on apologetically. 'So sorry, I was held up at work, today of all days, then one of my nipples broke,' he'd said, tutting and shaking his head at the injustice of it all.

When she'd looked at him in horror, he'd explained with an awkward smile that he'd taken up cycling. 'Nipples are the flanged nuts which hold spokes in place at the, er, rim.'

He took a glug of Guinness and confessed he hadn't intended on drinking that night.

'In case you said something stupid?' she'd laughed.

'I might as well have a pint of tequila. Just to make sure I don't embarrass myself any further.'

Frankie couldn't hold it in any longer.

'It turns out I've missed your stupidity.' It was the understatement of her life: despite her efforts to keep him at bay, she had ached for his company, his laughter, his everything.

'Have you?' he'd said, moving his head backwards in surprise. His face had searched every inch of hers to see if she'd meant it.

'Honestly,' she'd said, feeling self-conscious even though she knew it was a bit late for that when they'd done the things they'd done.

Floyd's tummy had rumbled noisily – he'd not had time to eat. Funnily enough, neither had she, although nerves had been to blame.

'Do you fancy getting a takeaway?' she'd asked.

Floyd had shut his eyes and groaned. 'That. Would be amazing.'

And it had been. Their shy walk back to hers as they made small talk about the rain clearing and the starlit sky. Her key quivering in the lock, her hands trembling as she laid out forks and bowls. But once they'd tucked in – by candlelight because of a power cut – they had recovered their easy familiarity. He had intuitively known not to contact her but Em had let Frankie in on his casual, but completely obvious, questions about how she was doing. She'd learned too that Floyd had no interest in the dating scene anymore.

She had wanted to hug him as he oohed and ahhed at her salon, praising her for her hard work as he'd tried out each chair. Then they'd talked long into the night, as Leonardo sprawled across both of their laps, purring like a motorbike. Finally, at 3 a.m. when they'd been able to tear themselves apart, they'd shared a goodbye kiss, which had gone on and on, bringing back deep waves which quaked to her skin's surface in shivers. Neither of them had had to say a word about taking it slow. They'd known it would have to start from a new beginning, not from where they'd left off.

And Em would be informed.

'I don't want to do that whole Romeo and Juliet sneaking around, then dying thing,' he'd said, kissing her again before he stumbled off, his hot breath forming clouds into the night.

As she'd lay in bed too wired to sleep, she'd known it would work. And it did, effortlessly. Two quirky dates had followed; she'd held him up all the way round the ice rink at Winter Wonderland as snowflakes had fallen onto their noses. Then he'd taken her for a delicious but strange dinner at The Clink, a restaurant staffed by Cardiff Prison inmates. 'I didn't know we'd get patted down on the way in or that there'd be no booze,' he'd said, dragging her laughing into a bar for a nightcap.

On the third, he'd cooked for her at his place, a Victorian maisonette in need of renovation located in a tiny crescent backing onto the city's Bute Park. As a fire blazed in the hearth, they'd slowly undressed each other and discovered their bodies anew on his weathered leather sofa, where they made love as if it was the first time. There'd been no separate acts of prowess, just one long liquid scene of natural movement which ended in ecstasy for both of them. It had been perfect, instinctive.

'It's chemistry, isn't it, Floyd?' she'd said into his chest afterwards, realizing that that was what had been missing from her relationship with Jason. 'That's what we've got.'

'Yep,' he'd whispered into her hair, 'I'm just glad everything's working, by the way, thanks for asking, after you assaulted me in the hospital car park.'

Ever since, they've been a full-on couple, which Em is still coming to terms with. 'It's lovely, my brother and my best friend being together, but it's quite gross when you two hold hands,' she said last week when the gang had all met in the pub for a long and lazy Sunday roast.

Even though Frankie feels as if she's inside a big bubble of love, she's never been so free. Floyd doesn't try to hold her back or impose his ideas on her.

Sometimes, when she's sweeping up, she thinks about her past, but it all feels like a dream. She's divorced now and back to her maiden name Rogers. Floyd thinks it's very funny that when you say their names in a sequence – Frankie Rogers Floyd Good-Fellow – it sounds a bit 'oo-er'.

If she sees Jason, which isn't often but he's helped with some scaffolding so she could handpaint her sign, she gets a sense of déjà vu, as if a moth's wings are dusting her arm. She simply can't imagine how they ever lived side by side.

When she told Jase she couldn't 'marry' him, a week after Floyd's confession in the car park, she'd said they were too much like friends. He'd been a mess for a while and then bang, one night, he'd met a girl and they were already engaged. Whether or not it proved that he was one of those people who needed someone, she hadn't dwelled on it. She wants him as happy as she is.

Sasha, surprise, surprise, had landed herself a photographer's job on a billionaire's Caribbean island, where she parties with the rich and famous. The last they heard, she was having a 'spiritual connection' with the resort's water sports instructor.

Frankie's thinking about Floyd's offer that she should move in with him. She can imagine Leonardo stalking through the park, chasing butterflies and bees.

Before that though she wants to take on a Saturday girl at work, join a choir with Letty, spend time with Em and the baby and go glamping.

As far as sex goes, they're very happy indeed. But her bag of tricks was chucked out long ago. Who needs that stuff when you've got bags of chemistry?

'Here it comes,' Floyd whispers, as the grooms exchange vows and rings. 'Brace yourself! They're going to sound the horn. The dirty devils.'

She shivers from the tickle of his beard, which is back in all its glory. As the registrar announces them husband and husband, Frankie throws up her bouquet in delight. Everyone watches as it somersaults across the room – and lands in Letty's hands.

'You're having a laugh, aren't you?' she says.

Confetti flies through the air as an ear-shattering siren blasts across the land and sea.

And Frankie kisses Floyd with her mind, body and soul.

She thinks of Phyllis, her very first client at the salon, who comes in every Tuesday for a shampoo and set.

'What did I tell you?' she always says when she settles into the chair and unwraps some Welsh cakes for them to share. 'If you sit on your feelings, in the end they'll out.'

Phyll was right. Everything did change.

It's Frankie and Floyd forever.

We hope you enjoyed this book!

Laura Kemp's next book is coming in 2017

More addictive fiction from Aria:

 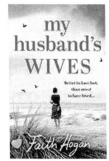 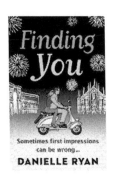

Find out More
http://headofzeus.com/books/isbn/9781784975883

Find out More
http://headofzeus.com/books/isbn/9781784977153

Find out More
http://headofzeus.com/books/isbn/9781784977481

Acknowledgments

Believe it or not, this is the hardest bit to write of any book.

How to tell those you love, those who put their faith in you and those who have to put up with mad starey editing eyes that they are entirely wonderful and without them you'd be nothing?

I'll try but these words are nothing compared to the thump of my heart.

Lizzy Kremer, my agent, who is Agent of the Year Every Year for her belief, support and swearing plus her unswerving rational thing which is my safety net when I'm bouncing up or down. For teaching me there is no such thing as an ordinary woman. Harriet Moore, at David Higham, too because she is very cool.

Caroline Ridding, my publisher at Aria, who is fist-pumpingly On It, whom I wave at across the sea on my mum runs.

Nia Beynon and Blake Brooks for saying 'yes, we can'. You get all the custard creams.

Jade Craddock, thank goodness for your eagle-eyed editing, you made it all much sparklier.

Debbie Clement, the cover is beautiful – thank you for bringing Frankie to life.

The authors I bow down to, generally on Twitter but also in bed (where I read your amazing books) – Milly Johnson, Lucy Diamond, Rowan Coleman, Clare Mackintosh, Rachel Abbott, CL Taylor, Amanda Jennings.

Book bloggers and readers, you are gorgeous the lot of you and the point of why we do what we do. Twitter pals and Facebookers and Instagrammers, you entertain me at all hours.

My friends for making life rich and hilarious and meaningful.

My mum, who passed down her love of words (stop beating me in Words With Friends), and dad, for running and sitcoms.

Finally, to my husband, son, dog and cat – I bloody slubs yousies.

About Laura Kemp

LAURA KEMP lives in Penarth, Cardiff with her supportive husband, gorgeous son, playful dog and ancient cat. Writing to Laura is compulsive. With 15 years journalistic experience and several successful books to her name, writing is her escape and her love.

Find me on Twitter
https://twitter.com/Laurajanekemp?lang=en-gb

Find me on Facebook
https://www.facebook.com/Laura-Kemp-374265565994740/

Become an Aria Addict

Aria is the new digital-first fiction imprint from Head of Zeus.

It's Aria's ambition to discover and publish tomorrow's superstars, targeting fiction addicts and readers keen to discover new and exciting authors.

Aria will publish a variety of genres under the commercial fiction umbrella such as women's fiction, crime, thrillers, historical fiction, saga and erotica.

So, whether you're a budding writer looking for a publisher or an avid reader looking for something to escape with – Aria will have something for you.

Get in touch: aria@headofzeus.com

Become an Aria Addict
http://www.ariafiction.com

Find us on Twitter
https://twitter.com/Aria_Fiction

Find us on Facebook
http://www.facebook.com/ariafiction

Find us on BookGrail
http://www.bookgrail.com/store/aria/

Addictive Fiction

First published in the UK in 2016 by Aria, an imprint of Head
of Zeus Ltd

Copyright © Laura Kemp, 2016

9 7 5 3 1 2 4 6 8

A CIP catalogue record for this book is available from the
British Library.

ISBN (E) 9781784976996

Jacket Design © debbieclementdesign.com

Aria
Clerkenwell House
45-47 Clerkenwell Green
London EC1R 0HT

www.ariafiction.com

19036878R00167

Printed in Great Britain
by Amazon